Praise for *The Plot to Kill Putin*

"Max Karpov has produced a cleverly conceived thriller that tracks reality. He captures perfectly the mentality of Vladimir Putin's Russia—its deep sense of insecurity that followed the collapse of the Soviet Union and the malign behavior that flows from it. And, on top of it, the book is near impossible to put down. A must read."

—Michael Morell, Former Acting Director and Deputy Director, CIA

"*The Plot to Kill Putin* is a well-written, thought-provoking thriller that is extremely timely in light of the allegations of Russian meddling in the 2016 Presidential election."

—Phillip Margolin, *New York Times* bestselling author of *The Third Victim*

"*The Plot to Kill Putin* is uncanny in its timeliness and brilliant in its portrayal of disinformation as the most dangerous weapon of the new Cold War. Max Karpov has written a masterful thriller that is genuinely alarming in its plausibility. A must-read for 2018."

—Joseph Finder, *New York Times* bestselling author of *Paranoia* and *The Switch*

"Max Karpov's *The Plot to Kill Putin* is just about the timeliest novel I've read this year. But this is no mere ripped-from-the-headlines knockoff. This is a fast-paced, vivid, surprising thriller, featuring a great new hero for our troubled times, former CIA agent Christopher Niles. Don't miss this one. I can't wait to read more."

—David Bell, author of *Bring Her Home*

"*The Plot to Kill Putin* is a cerebral, ground-breaking, all-too-plausible thriller made all the more prescient by the current state of U.S.-Russian relations. Max Karpov peers into his crystal ball in crafting a tale that's so cutting edge, flipping the pages may result in bloodied fingertips. Karpov proves himself every bit the equal of Daniel Silva in crafting the best book of its kind since Nelson DeMille's classic *The Charm School*. Searingly sumptuous storytelling sure to please fans of Brad Thor, Brad Taylor and th̶

—Jon Land, *USA Today* bestselling

"Compelling, authoritative, and extraordinarily timely, *The Plot to Kill Putin* is a cleverly plotted and disturbingly plausible journey into the dangerous realm of cyberwarfare. Max Karpov is a Kremlin-watcher whose extensive knowledge shines on every page. He's a fresh voice in the genre, and his insightful novel takes the underworld of espionage in unexpected and startling new directions."

—Carla Norton, *New York Times* bestselling author of *Perfect Victim*

"A tense tale of international intrigue, *The Plot to Kill Putin* is absorbing, thrilling, and frighteningly relevant."

—Laura McHugh, author of the International Thriller Writers Award–winning *The Weight of Blood*

"Gripping and powerful . . . a brilliant story written for our generation. *The Plot to Kill Putin* is a must read for any serious spy fan."

—Michael Brady, author of the *Into The Shadows* spy series

"A razor-sharp, bow-string-taut, brilliantly plotted example of the thriller-writer's art. For me the prose is up there with le Carre and Forsyth."

—E.M. Davey, former BBC investigative journalist, author of *Foretold by Thunder* and *The Napoleon Complex*

"Timely, plausible, and captivating, *The Plot to Kill Putin* is as prophetic as it is thrilling."

—Alan Jacobson, *USA Today* bestselling author of *Dark Side of the Moon*

"A tight, gripping tale of the men and women who face death in the hidden conflicts of superpower politics. Startlingly believable."

—Ben Bova, six-time Hugo Award–winning author of *Mars* and the Grand Tour series

"If you believe the Cold War ended with the fall of the Berlin Wall, think again! Max Karpov's explosive novel shows how Russia's sophisticated troll factories and bot armies could topple Western democracies as effectively as their T72 battle tanks and nuclear warheads. Karpov's knowledge of the

American intelligence community and Russian politics puts him on a par with John le Carré and Frederick Forsyth at their very best. But it is Karpov's analysis of the shocking power of a targeted post-truth and fake news attack that gives the book a contemporary and chilling atmosphere. A new master thriller writer has emerged, and I am looking forward to reading many more of Max Karpov's novels."

—Christopher Hepworth, author of *The Sleepwalker Legacy* and *The Last Oracle*

"Espionage, thrills, chills and, perhaps, a little too close to home, this is one book that you should not miss. Writer Max Karpov's ultimate talent stems from being able to explain all the intricacies of cyberwarfare while making sure to always keep the pace fast and the action nonstop."

—*Suspense Magazine*

"A well-written, fast-paced, and timely thriller . . . What is especially relevant and chillingly plausible is the whole concept of using a cyberattack to spread misinformation and fake news. Hello . . . "

—*She Treads Softly*

"The book may be a wake-up call, but first and foremost it is a brilliant plot showcasing a major literary talent."

—*stacyalesi.com*

"I was hooked from the moment I started reading."

—*Reading on a Budget*

THE PLOT TO KILL PUTIN

A Thriller

MAX KARPOV

ARCADE
CrimeWise

An Arcade CrimeWise book

For Janet and Mandy

Arcade Publishing books may be purchased in bulk at special discounts
for sales promotion, corporate gifts, fund-raising, or educational purposes.
Special editions can also be created to specifications. For details, contact the
Special Sales Department, Arcade Publishing, 307 West 36th Street, 11th
Floor, New York, NY 10018 or arcade@skyhorsepublishing.com.

Arcade Publishing® and CrimeWise® are registered trademarks of Skyhorse
Publishing, Inc.®, a Delaware corporation.

Visit our website at www.arcadepub.com.

10 9 8 7 6 5 4 3 2 1

Library of Congress Cataloging-in-Publication Data is available on file.

Cover design by Erin Seaward-Hiatt
Cover photo: iStockphoto

Print ISBN: 978-1-950691-15-9
Ebook ISBN: 978-1-5107-3482-1

Printed in the United States of America

"The person who yells 'Thief!' the loudest is the thief himself."

—Old Russian saying

PROLOGUE

A fter the long winter, it was spring again in Moscow. The last crusts of sooty snow had melted from the curbs and the city parks were bright with the colors of tulips and lilacs. At the Kremlin gardens, the apple and cherry trees were in bloom, filling the air with a familiar scent of anticipation.

On nearby Boulevard Ring Road, an unmarked white cargo van was moving through afternoon traffic, away from the great onion domes of the Cathedral of Christ the Savior, where ten days earlier President Putin and five thousand worshippers had gathered for Easter Mass.

The van's passenger, Ivan Delkoff, could hear the swish of the wet roadway and the bleats of car horns as the van moved through central Moscow traffic. But he could not see where they were going; he could only imagine. A large man with an aversion to enclosed spaces, Delkoff was seated in the windowless rear cabin of the van, facing backward, dressed in the sun-faded fatigues and combat boots he wore every day, as a familiar-sounding Russian music played faintly through the speakers. The only personal possession he carried besides his ID was a small photograph of his son, staring at the camera with his dark, innocent eyes, dressed in the military uniform he'd been wearing on the afternoon he was killed.

The drive alternated between the stop-and-go of city traffic and the full-on of the freeway, so that eventually Ivan Delkoff stopped guessing where they were and thought instead of the odd chain of events that had brought him here. And of the meeting he would soon be having with a man once known as Russia's "dark angel."

Delkoff was in his late forties now, a colonel in the GRU, Russia's military intelligence service, although he still thought of himself as a foot soldier in his country's larger war. He woke most days knowing that he had a role to play in Russian history, without knowing exactly what it was. Delkoff's stark appearance—the long, serious face and wide mouth that flattened like a piece of string—often caused people to underestimate him, to miss the tenacity and intelligence that had made him an accomplished military leader. In the Donbas, Delkoff's special forces units had routed the Ukrainian army and various ad hoc battalions, setting the de facto borders for a new "people's republic." For a time, some of the Russian separatists there had taken to calling Delkoff the region's "defense minister," a distinction he privately enjoyed. There were others who called him "the crazy colonel," which he didn't enjoy so much.

Like many in Russia's military intelligence branch, Delkoff had married young and divorced young. The death of Pavel, his only son, last summer in the Donbas had only deepened his commitment to the motherland. But it had also made him less tolerant of the Kremlin's political management of eastern Ukraine. Delkoff understood that the undeclared war in the Donbas had become the front line in a larger conflict, a moral and cultural war for Russia's future. But eastern Ukraine was also where that war had stalled. And Delkoff, like many Russian patriots, had come to resent the Kremlin because of it, especially its policy of sending men to fight without uniforms, to be buried in unmarked graves. There was a dangerous hubris now in Moscow, troubling signs that the average Russian did not see.

He'd spoken of it briefly over the winter with a Ukrainian journalist, who promised not to quote him. But then he'd done so anyway, a little more accurately than Delkoff would have liked, attributing his comments to "a Russian colonel on the ground in the Donbas."

Three weeks later, Delkoff had been called back to Moscow, on the pretense of a special assignment from the Kremlin. He was given a small office in the city and a generous weekly salary to do nothing but show up each day and read reports. A "case officer" was assigned: a short, broad-faced man who sat with him in afternoon "debriefings," asking questions and taking notes. Based on what the officer asked about Ukraine, Delkoff began to suspect that he was being set up for treason. He'd decided to vanish before that happened, to travel to Belarus where a small network of friends and family would take him in.

But then Ivan Delkoff learned that his "assignment" wasn't from the Kremlin after all. Two days before he planned to disappear, Delkoff found out that it was actually Andrei Turov who had summoned him to Moscow. And knowing that changed everything.

Turov had once been part of the president's inner circle, the Leningrad coterie that formed Putin's unofficial private politburo. He'd worked briefly for the FSB, successor organization to the KGB, and then as secretary of security services, early in Putin's presidency. But for the past fifteen years, Turov had run his own private security business, based in Moscow. His clients included the Kremlin, for whom Turov occasionally did "black ledger" work, benefiting the president but never tied to him directly. In the mid-2000s Putin had supposedly called Turov Russia's "dark angel."

But that was then. More recently, there had been stories of a rift between the president and Andrei Turov. Last fall, several of Turov's branch offices had been seized by the government, and there was talk now that he was under pressure to leave Russia. The stories echoed those of other powerful men who had shown too much ambition or independence in Putin's Russia. Men such as Mikhail Khodorkovsky, once the richest man in the country, who'd spent ten years in a Siberian prison camp after crossing the Russian president. Or Boris Nemtsov, the former first deputy prime minister, a prominent Putin critic who was gunned down in front of the Kremlin in 2015. Or Alexander Litvinenko, the former KGB officer who accused Putin of corruption, then died an agonizing public death over twenty-three days from a dose of radioactive polonium.

The idea that Turov had crossed over to the president's less-than-forgiving side was what made this April summons particularly interesting to Ivan Delkoff. It was the only reason he was in the back of this van today and not in Belarus.

An hour passed, and another ten minutes. Finally the traffic sounds began to fade. Delkoff pictured the neighborhood they were in: breezy lawns, shade trees, new flowers. One of Russia's new gated developments outside Moscow. Delkoff had heard that Turov liked to do business in rented houses, rather than in Moscow offices or in the mansions favored by the oligarchs. He listened as the cargo van slowed, backed up, and came to a stop; he heard the mechanical whirring of a garage door.

The man who opened the doors of the van looked familiar: small and thickset, with a stubbled face and shaved head. This was Anton Konkin, Turov's loyal gatekeeper, like himself a former FSB officer. Delkoff followed the smaller man down a hallway to a dark-paneled library, where Konkin gestured him in and closed the door.

The room was unlit, with a floor-to-ceiling bookcase, dark-wood tables and chairs, a leather sofa. Like the rest of the house, it felt new, as if no one actually lived here. But then, scanning the furnishings, Delkoff saw that Andrei Turov was in the room, too, seated behind a desk in the corner.

"*Zdravstvuyte,*" he said, greeting Delkoff with the formal geniality of an innkeeper. He offered a firm handshake and motioned for him to sit on the leather chair in front of the desk. "It's an honor to see you again. It took us a while to get you here."

Turov's eyes stayed with Delkoff as they sat. They'd met once before, seven or eight years ago. Turov conveyed much the impression he had then—an ordinary-looking man, middle-aged, with short-cropped gray hair and firm lips that lent a sensible expression to his face. But there was an otherworldly quality to his pale blue eyes that was a little unsettling, like the eyes of a wild dog. "We are indebted to you," Turov said. "You have made important strides in the Donbas. Even though I know that you are not pleased with how the war is going. None of us are."

Delkoff nodded, being careful. His first instinct was to distrust men he didn't know. And Turov, despite his unassuming demeanor, had a reputation as a magician, a man who could deceive people in ways they didn't see or even imagine.

"Russia's passions were awakened in March of 2014, as you know," Turov went on, meaning the annexation of Crimea. "But you understand better than anyone the problem we have faced since then."

Turov's eyes stayed with him. This issue—"the problem"—had come up several times in his debriefings. Delkoff had taken it as a test of loyalty then; now, he saw it was something else.

"We have an assignment that you are uniquely qualified to carry out," Turov said, with his even temperament. "That will help us to at last end this war. To win it."

Delkoff sat up a little straighter. He knew that Turov was talking about the larger war now. The war for a greater Russian society, anchored in tradition, discipline, morality—all those things the West had lost or was losing.

"It's important that we speak openly here," Turov said. "I would like to hear what concerns you most about Ukraine."

"The same things that concern you," Delkoff said, glancing at the closed file on Turov's desk, and the printout of notes beside it. Turov had vetted him for weeks, he knew, since long before he'd been summoned to Moscow. His team had talked with Delkoff's estranged daughter in Belarus, his friends and his ex-wife. "The same things that concern the men fighting there, and their families," he said. "That we don't finish what we started. Otherwise, what was it for?"

Turov nodded for him to go on.

"I'm concerned, as many Russians are," Delkoff said, "that our weakness will leave us vulnerable. That it will open us up to riots and xiv | MAX KARPOV

a Western-led fascist revolution—like what the Americans did in Kiev, and in the Middle East. The hypocrites."

Turov's eyes brightened for a moment, giving affirmation to his words—"riots" being the preferred term to "protests"; "fascist" preferable to "democratic."

"And, of course, we fight the complicity at home every day, don't we?" Turov said. "We are concerned about what you call"—he glanced at his notes—"the 'politicized management of the war.' As you know, his approval ratings top eighty percent now," he continued, "but what are those polls really measuring? People do not realize how isolated, and paranoid, he has become."

Delkoff nodded but said nothing, knowing that they had just crossed a line. He saw in Turov's reasonable face now what this "assignment" really was. Not a proxy op for the Kremlin, as he'd been led to believe when called back to Moscow. It was the opposite: he was being recruited by the right-wing elites within the government, a small cadre of interior ministers and military generals who understood that the current leadership, which had brought Russia to the brink of greatness again, had grown too reckless and unpredictable—too closely bound to the ego of one man—to survive.

"Already he has put us in a dangerous game of brinksmanship, as you know," Turov said. "There is no strategic plan anymore, except what is in his head."

"And that changes," Delkoff said.

"Yes, exactly. The developments in America, of course, have only emboldened him. But he is still the same man. A little man, puffed up with power. Too afraid of showing weakness to be a real leader."

Delkoff waited, stirred by Turov's words. He did not know the finer details of history as Turov did, but he understood its basic lessons: oppression does not last, hubris does not win, popularity is a transitory business; men who lead repressive regimes leave terrible legacies.

"The problem is, he will never step down on his own," Turov said, speaking more softly, and Delkoff saw a flicker of regret in his face that he understood; it was possible to love the president's intentions but disapprove of his methods. Delkoff thought of his son's mother wailing in her theatrical voice, after learning their boy had been killed: *"Putin did this. Putin killed my son."* Delkoff had scolded her to be quiet, although he had secretly shared some of that same feeling. "We find ourselves at a regrettable impasse," Turov went on, showing the palm of his right hand. "We have no choice now but to open a new front."

Delkoff said nothing. *Open a new front.* It was a phrase that he himself had used, many times.

In the span of seven minutes, Andrei Turov explained the operation that Delkoff had been chosen to carry out. The framework was already established. Delkoff's role would be to recruit and train a small group of soldiers, and then to oversee the plan's execution. The ordinary qualities of Turov's manner seemed to fall away as he detailed the operation; Delkoff saw a hard inner shrewdness in him, an aptitude that he hadn't imagined when he'd walked in the room.

"We believe you are the only one who can do this successfully," Turov said. Delkoff felt the hairs on his arms prickle. *Of course,* he could do it. It was the assignment he'd been preparing for all of his life. But at the same time, Delkoff understood that he wasn't being *asked.* He was fairly certain that if he said no, he would not leave this house alive.

But Delkoff had no intention of saying no.

He listened to the terms and logistics. There was one connection he would have to make—a Ukrainian oligarch named Dmitro Hordiyenko, who would supply the arms and equipment. The rest would be up to him. Delkoff's remuneration would be so substantial that there was no need to negotiate.

"And what about afterward?"

"For Russia?" Turov answered indirectly, assuring Delkoff that the motherland would be in capable hands. "I can't give you names. But I can tell you that you would not have been chosen if we thought you would disapprove of the outcome in any way." He nodded at the leather folder on his desk.

"And what about me?" Delkoff said.

"We'll work with you. You won't have to return to Russia if you'd prefer to start a new life elsewhere. That will be your choice." And Turov explained this, too.

By then, Delkoff was already beginning to think of the men he would hire: an eager Russian soldier named Alexander Zelenko, who'd fought with him in Luhansk and reminded Delkoff of his late son; Mikhail Kolchak, a corrupt Ukrainian missile commander, who would bring strong personal motives to the mission; and his own cousin, Dmitri, who would help him once it was over. "And the blame?" he said.

"The blame will fall on the SBU," Turov answered, meaning Ukraine's security and intelligence agency. "But, ultimately, on the Americans. It's their hypocrisy, as you call it, that has pushed us to this. As the Russian soul has awakened, the American soul—what passes for one—has been asleep. For too long, the Americans have been allowed to invade sovereign nations, indiscriminately killing tens of thousands of civilians in the name of 'democracy.' Then they condemn us for sim-ply defending the ethnic Russian people of Ukraine against oppres-sion, a matter that has nothing to do with them. We need to turn that around. And we will. This is something they will not see coming."

Delkoff nodded, careful not to show enthusiasm. "And how do I know I'm not being set up?"

"You don't," Turov said. "But you know that I pursued you. You know that we have common concerns and can help each other. You'll have to trust me."

Delkoff was silent. He *did* trust him, that was the strange part of this: there was something reassuring in Turov's face, in his steady manner and physical ordinariness. It made you stop noticing what he looked like and enter into the realm of his thoughts and ideas. When they shook hands, Delkoff noticed that Turov was wearing a cheap off-the-rack jacket, the sleeves slightly long, and that assured him, too—as if, in a sense, they were wearing the same uniform.

As the cargo van returned Delkoff to central Moscow, he felt as if some of Russia's divinely inspired historical mission had just been handed to him. The same music played tinnily from the van's speakers but it sounded different now: a triumphant Russian melody, which caused Delkoff's eyes to sting with emotion. *Betrayal out of loyalty to a higher cause is no longer betrayal,* he thought, a line he knew from school days, although he couldn't recall who'd said it. Gogol, perhaps. Or Tolstoy. Like many of his generation, Delkoff had been raised believing in Soviet greatness without ever actually having seen it. His father had made it seem tangible, like a place that he would visit someday, and he'd felt its proximity all of his life: in the country's patriotic songs and ceremonies, in the monuments and brick ramparts of Red Square, in his own son's decision to join the military; sometimes he heard it early in the morning now, just in the way the poplar trees rattled outside his apartment windows, a haunted sound that he thought of as the whispers of dead soldiers.

Delkoff believed in Russia's destiny as a great power, which would one day span East and West—a dream that still burned in many Russians. But there was a street-level battle under way now that had made his country's greatness harder to see, particularly in Moscow, where new skyscrapers and construction cranes had stolen the skyline, and vulgar Western billboards overpowered the historical monuments. Perhaps this was what Turov meant by "complicity."

Still, Delkoff did not know for certain that this assignment was not some elaborate setup. He considered that as he rode the crowded Metro train back to his apartment in Troparevo. It was still possible that someone would surprise him in the hallway of his apartment house as he stepped from the elevator, as other Kremlin critics had been silenced on other Moscow evenings.

Nothing happened to Ivan Delkoff that night, though. And nothing happened over the next fifteen weeks, as he discreetly implemented Turov's plan, meeting with the arms supplier Hordiyenko in Kiev and hiring and training the five men who would carry out the mission.

Nothing happened until that afternoon in August, when the world's eyes suddenly turned again to Russia and history changed.

August 13.

By then, it wasn't Turov's operation anymore. By then, it was Ivan Delkoff's operation.

PART I

THE
CATALYST

PART 1

THE
CATALYST

ONE

Tuesday, August 10. Cyclades Islands, Greece.

Christopher Niles stepped out of the sea into a perfect late-morning breeze. Crossing the narrow beach, he smelled flatbread cooking at the taverna next door. He saw Anna Carpenter sitting on a towel drying in the sun, her wet hair pulled back, and felt a tug of gratitude. The first two days of their vacation had been largely rained out, but Tuesday had dawned clear and balmy and there was no rain forecast again until the weekend. It would be a perfect day for their "conversation."

They had traveled to Greece at Anna's insistence in order to disappear. To escape the demands of Washington and talk about their future. Disappearing was easier for Christopher now than for Anna, who was a public figure again, the recently elected US Senator from Maryland. In Greece, though, privacy hadn't been an issue. She'd been recognized on the flight and once at Athens International Airport. But since arriving on the island, they'd been just what they wanted to be: two anonymous American tourists on summer holiday.

Next month, they returned to their respective careers in D.C. Chris would begin a yearlong visiting lecture post at George Washington University, leading a seminar entitled "Russian Spy Craft in the 21st Century." The class was spun off from a talk he'd given in the spring on the FSB and SVR, Russia's domestic and overseas intelligence agencies. Next semester, he'd teach "War and Society," exploring the impact of American politics and public opinion on warfare since World War II. Both drew nominally on his two-decade career as a government analyst and intelligence officer.

If someone had told Christopher Niles three years ago, when he first met Anna, that he'd be teaching and lecturing now, he would have laughed. It wasn't a life he had imagined for himself. But Christopher's growing frustrations with his employer—the US government—and Anna's gentle but persistent prodding had finally conspired to change his mind. What surprised him wasn't just how easily he'd adapted to academia but also how little he missed intelligence work. All his life he'd harbored a tendency toward obsession, a need to fix big, sometimes unfixable problems. It was a trait passed on to him by his father, which had served him well in his work but often came at a personal cost. Anna had helped with that. Even his physical appearance had adapted, as she liked to say. Christopher still had the rangy build of a college athlete, which he'd been, but his blond hair was turning to gray and he'd taken to wearing glasses, which gave him a studious look more in line with his new job.

They had been together now for two and a half years. But Chris and Anna's careers, and their independent natures, had so far kept them from making a commitment. Greece was supposed to be about changing that. The plan was to spend six days at the beach, away from electronic distractions, and decide what to do with their life. But they still hadn't had "the conversation," deciding to wait until the weather turned. This morning, they no longer had that excuse.

As Chris approached from the water, Anna sat up and watched, smiling faintly. The sand was bright and a little startling this morning after all the rain. Her skin felt warm as they kissed.

"Something to drink?" he asked, drying off, knowing she'd want a strawberry Ouzito from the taverna next door. Anna looked good in the sun, her skin smooth, a small spray of freckles on her nose and cheeks.

Chris walked across the warm sand to the taverna. Inside, two fans stirred the air. Greek folk music played from speakers, all violin and guitars. Waiting in line, he glanced across the screened terrace at Anna, reading her book in a circle of umbrella shade, and something closer caught his eye. On the other side of the screen: a small, slightly disheveled-looking man was pacing the concrete walkway, hands clasped behind him, scanning the beach like a military inspector; a tourist, perhaps, who'd become separated from his wife. But there was something familiar about him—the measured step and breezy wisps of white hair, the short-sleeved shirt, slacks and hard-soled shoes. Not the attire of a man on vacation. In fact, it almost looked like Chris's old boss, Marty Lindgren.

"Sir?"

"Sorry," Chris said. He stepped to the bar and ordered two Ouzito cocktails, watching the bartender as she nimbly sliced strawberries and squeezed in lime juice. When he glanced back toward the water, Christopher noticed the man outside looking in through the screen; he recalled a story children used to tell growing up: how everyone has a double somewhere in the world. It wasn't really true, of course, although he'd often met people who shared the mannerisms of someone he knew.

Chris paid for the drinks and carried them down the concrete passageway to the beach, invigorated by the sea air and the anticipation of his talk with Anna. When he looked up again, he saw the white-haired man coming his way, stepping with a familiar urgency.

"Christopher? There you are. I almost didn't recognize you with the glasses."

"Martin? What the hell?" Their first confused impulse was to shake hands, but Chris's were full and there was no place to set the drinks. "I hope you're not going to say you came here looking for me."

Martin flashed his old smile: thin-lipped and slightly reluctant, more pronounced on one side than the other.

"Let me deliver this, I'll be right back," Christopher said, handing Martin his drink and walking onto the sand with Anna's.

Anna was sitting under the striped umbrella, reading the last pages of *Eleni,* the Greek novel she'd started two weeks ago to get in the mood for their trip.

"You'll never guess who I just ran into," Chris said.

"Should I?"

"Probably not." She took the drink and gazed up at him, her dark blond hair beginning to dry in the heat. Anna had classical features—"standard," she'd called them—but a slightly mischievous tilt of the head that wasn't standard at all. "In the interest of time," he said, "I'll tell you: Martin Lindgren."

"Oh." Anna waited a moment before turning. She smiled at him and waved. Martin, on the edge of the sand, hesitated; then, as if on seven-second delay, his smile appeared and he waved back. "What in the world is Martin Lindgren doing here?"

"He hasn't explained that yet. I have a feeling it's not to see the archeological sites."

Chris felt a tightening in his chest as he returned to the taverna. Martin's appearance on this idyllic morning could only be a bad sign. Why would he have flown eight hours to see him without even calling first?

"I like her," Martin said, nodding toward Anna as he handed over the drink. He led Chris onto the terrace, where he already had a table and a cup of coffee. There was a travel bag on one of the chairs, a Greek newspaper and rumpled copy of the *Financial Times* sticking out. "Sorry to do this unannounced," he said as they sat.

"I'm surprised you found me. We were trying to stay under the radar. I guess you couldn't phone or email first," Chris added diplomatically.

Martin ducked his head to the side in that good-natured way he had, which always reminded him a little of Ronald Reagan. Martin had a handsome, angular face, dark blue eyes, and the elegant gestures of an earlier time.

"I could have, I suppose. But I needed to do this face to face. You're not scheduled to return until the end of the week. This, unfortunately, can't wait."

"Okay," Chris said. During his time as a CIA officer, he had worked several times for Martin, who ran a small independent branch of the Central Intelligence Agency known as the AS Division. His office gathered human intelligence, prepared analyses, and carried out small-scale black ops, mostly using private contractors. Where there was consensus on an issue in the intelligence community, Martin's branch looked for alternate scenarios; hence its initials. AS Division was born out of the new emphasis at Langley on so-called "anticipatory intelligence," although the weight the division carried these days wasn't great. Chris, who'd left the government two and a half years ago, still moonlighted occasionally for AS.

"Something's going on and I need to enlist your help," Martin said. "Something with Russia. Very time sensitive. If you'll hear me out." He paused as the waitress came over to top off his coffee. Martin thanked her in Greek. Chris observed the clean, square cut of Martin's fingernails as he reached for the cup.

"Something involving—?"

"We don't know. That's the problem." Martin set down his cup. "All sorts of stories are circulating. Some you've no doubt heard."

"I've heard the saber-rattling."

"Well, yes. But more than that." Martin drew in a long breath, his version of sighing. Since leaving Moscow three years ago, Chris had followed the same stories as everyone else: Russia's announcements of new weapons programs, exercises with nuclear-capable Iskander missiles in the Baltics, violations of US airspace off the coasts of California and Alaska; behavior calculated to test the limits of NATO and the US. "They're running exercises right now—today—in the Baltics with forty thousand troops," Martin said. "But there's also chatter about something less orthodox. Including sponsorship of terror strikes within our borders."

"Russia wouldn't be involved in anything like that," Chris said.

"No. Probably not." Martin had an odd habit of periodically closing his eyes and nodding as if to a private conversation, revealing reptilian-like eyelids. "Actually, I think they're planning something else entirely," he said, "something that we're not even considering."

"Why do you think that?"

Martin leaned forward and made a quick scan of the terrace. "Two reasons," he said. "We've had some intel about a movement of dark money from St. Petersburg through a BVI company. Not a lot, nothing particularly out of the ordinary by Russian standards. Except that one of the accounts involved the Alkaev Group."

"Oh." Chris felt the outside world close in momentarily: the Greek music, the voices and silverware from the kitchen became muted, as if he'd gone underwater. "That's different."

"Yes." And at last he understood why Martin had come all this way. The Alkaev Group wasn't just Russia, it was Andrei Turov. Alkaev was one of the offshore companies Turov had set up to support illegal activities benefiting the Kremlin; more specifically, activities meant to infiltrate and undermine the United States. Turov was a master of perception warfare, who'd engineered high-production-value disinformation campaigns that the US couldn't match. And often couldn't see.

Chris had learned of Alkaev four years ago, while stationed at the American embassy in Moscow; he'd written an analysis warning of Turov's plans to broaden Russia's sphere of influence by weakening other nations. But because he'd never determined the group's specific long-term strategy, Washington had taken no action—or seemed particularly interested. It was not in step with the US intelligence agenda at the time. The consensus then was that Russia had become so diminished economically that it no longer posed a threat, and that Putin, despite his much-publicized bravado, was largely irrelevant as a player on the world stage. This was before Crimea. Before Iran. Before the proxy war in Syria. Before Russia's political influence campaigns in Hungary, Germany, France, and the United States. In fact, Russia's diminished economy was exactly why the US *should* be concerned, Chris believed. Declining nations are sometimes the most dangerous kind.

"What does Langley think? And the White House?"

"They're still no more keen on Turov than before. He's so far off the radar he managed to avoid the sanctions list," Martin said. "That's why I need your help. The IC knows how to deal with Russia. But not Turov. They never have."

Christopher gazed at the sea, recalling the unfortunate outcome of his last tour of Moscow. He sipped his drink, reminding himself that this was Andrei Turov's genius: his ability to make himself a man no one—least of all, it seemed, the CIA—took very seriously. He'd structured his projects so they used a handful of operatives who kept their dealings nearly impossible to track. Chris's report had quoted a former Russian parliament member calling Turov "probably the most devious and dangerous man in Russia." He might've just said "in the world."

But that was four years ago. Turov's status within Russia had changed since then.

"Andrei Turov's semi-retired now, isn't he?" Chris said. "I heard he sold his businesses and was living in the country. There were even rumblings of some big falling-out with Putin."

"That's the story, yes." Martin's lip quivered involuntarily. "You know how some men fake their own deaths? I think he may have faked this falling-out with Putin. We have intel that they met in February and March. And have had several phone conversations since." The vertical lines returned to Martin's brow. "I can't go into all of it right here, except to say we've got one high-level asset in Russia, and signals intercepts supporting what she tells us."

"And so, what—you're saying there's something I could do that America's sixty-billion-dollar intelligence community can't?"

Martin kept down a brief, conspiratorial smile. Chris's former boss held an old-school belief in the power of the individual over the organization. He had issues with the restructuring of the intelligence community, which had tripled in size since 9/11 but continued to "miss" key events, as the media liked to point out, the rise of ISIS being one of the best known. "You remember you once told me, there's weakness in numbers?"

"Did I?" Christopher liked the sound of that, though he didn't remember saying it.

"That in certain cases, a team of four or five people, focused on a single objective, could do more than all seventeen IC agencies?" His eyebrows rose for emphasis. "Well, this is one of them. Although I'm not talking about a team of four or five at this point. Just you."

"I see," Chris said, not missing the qualifier *at this point.*

"We have a second source on this, in London. It's someone you know. We think he may have something actionable on Turov. But he insists on giving it to you directly. That's why I'm here."

"Okay. You're not talking about Max Petrenko, by any chance?"

"Yes, as a matter of fact."

Now Chris smiled. Maxim Petrenko was a security "consultant" who'd made and lost a fortune during Russia's Wild West era, the Yeltsin years; later, he'd managed one of Turov's security firms. But he'd fled the country in 2011 or 2012 under a cloud of corruption charges after giving an indiscreet newspaper interview. Now he ran a small spy shop in London. His work mostly involved peddling information, Chris had heard, paying anonymous sources—drivers, security men, prostitutes—and selling what he learned to third parties, often Russian intelligence. He reminded Chris a little of a dirty drug dealer, who cut good information with bad. "Petrenko's not entirely reliable, though, is he?"

"This is different," Martin said. "Someone connected with Turov has given him something we think is credible. You could probably complete the deal in ten minutes."

Christopher let his eyes drift to the beach, finding Anna, holding her book on her lap and gazing at the ocean. *Ten minutes in London, maybe. But first I'd have to get there. And who knows where those ten minutes might lead?* The late-morning breeze carried a breath of sea mist through the terrace screens. As Martin explained, Chris thought of the possible directions this day might have taken. But he also felt a gathering interest. Martin had known that just mentioning Turov's name would produce this response.

"He's agreed to meet with you in London tomorrow afternoon. It's set up, actually." Martin reached for his bag. "I've got your travel documents here."

"Ah. You know how to spoil a man's vacation."

This time, Martin didn't smile. He looked at Chris with anticipation, until it was clear to both of them that he would accept. Anna would be disappointed; but she wouldn't object. Anna was a veteran diplomat, whose rivers of patience ran deeper than his. It was one of her talents to absorb setbacks without showing it. Also, Anna believed, as he did, in serving when called.

"What do you expect he's going to tell us?"

"A name. Someone Turov's dealing with. Hopefully a date. Whatever's going to happen, it's going to be soon, possibly within a week. He's agreed to answer two questions. After that, it's up to you."

Christopher sighed, imagining how much Petrenko had billed Martin. But that wasn't the point: if this really was Turov, the threat transcended cost, or any personal reservations he might have. Anna, he saw, was putting on her shirt and sandals, looking their way. "What do you *think* it's about?"

Martin wrinkled his nose. "I go back to what you wrote in your report—Turov has this idea about a new, sophisticated kind of warfare. Something we won't anticipate. It's about a story: Russia's going to tell a story. They're going to make the world believe it, and repeat it. We have indications it will probably begin with a single event. Some sort of an attack."

"An attack on us."

"In some fashion. But not the kind of attack anyone in the administration will be looking for." Anna had slung her bag over her shoulder and was walking in a steady, graceful rhythm over the sand.

"And what about this other thing—?" Chris said. "The signals intercepts?"

"There's a phrase NSA has picked up. Something called 'the children's game.' We know Turov also used it in a phone conversation with the president this spring."

"Maybe just a reference to his grandchildren?"

"Probably not. We think it's the event. That could be your second question. The payment transfer is done. Surveillance arranged. All you need to do is show up in London."

"Well, I'd prefer to pass on the surveillance," Christopher said, more concerned that it would draw attention to Petrenko than to him.

Lindgren suddenly smiled broadly, and Christopher misunderstood, thinking he was smiling at what he'd just said. But then he saw: he was looking at Anna, who was standing in the arched entryway, letting her eyes adjust.

Martin leaned over to Christopher. "I hope she won't be too angry with me," he whispered.

TWO

The meeting with Max Petrenko was scheduled for twenty past four in Holland Park. Petrenko ran his business now from a rented two-room office in upscale Mayfair. He was having trouble paying rent, the London case officer told Christopher, and might have to relocate at the end of the year. If Petrenko really knew something about Turov, as Martin believed, it was probably a fluke.

Christopher took a cab to Abbotsbury Road and walked into the park, stopping at a bench near the Japanese garden as instructed. For nine minutes he sat, glancing at the passersby. He was beginning to wonder if he'd chosen the wrong bench when he saw Petrenko marching up the path, dressed in an ill-fitting seersucker suit. For a moment Chris didn't recognize him: the Russian had put on weight and his forehead appeared taller than he remembered. Petrenko seemed to miss him at first, walking past with swinging arms, then turning and pretending to do an elaborate double take. "Christopher Niles?"

Chris raised his eyebrows and stood. The pretense was two old acquaintances bumping into one another in the park. "Max."

"My goodness. How long has it been?" They exchanged greetings over a lengthy handshake, and began to walk, Petrenko talking in his deep-throated broken English, gesturing with a familiar Russianness:

balling his fingers and opening them dramatically. Telling Chris about the changes in Moscow since the late nineties when Petrenko had made his fleeting fortune there—his voice tensing up when he mentioned the current president, becoming more relaxed when the topic was Yeltsin. "I knew him, of course, years ago," he said, meaning Putin. "In Leningrad. He was nothing then. A bureaucrat. But fiercely loyal. Later, he wanted me to travel with him. You can imagine how that would have ended." Petrenko was talking almost like a ventriloquist now, his lips clenched and barely moving.

"I knew Yeltsin, too, a much more gracious man," he said, speaking robustly again. "He could have been great. History gave him that. But the alcohol . . ."

"I'm curious, though. You asked specifically to see me."

"I did."

"You've heard something about our friend, I'm told," Chris said, prompting him as they strolled past the formal gardens. "I understand you have a name."

"I do." Another half-minute passed before he spoke again. Finally, he turned to Christopher and, with his ventriloquist's lips, gave him the name—first, patronymic, and last: "Ivan Mikhailovitch Delkoff."

Ivan Delkoff. It was a name Christopher knew. Delkoff was one of the rogue separatist leaders in eastern Ukraine, a fanatic right-wing Russian commander. "The crazy colonel," some in the Russian media had labeled him.

"They met in the spring, I'm told," Petrenko said. "In Moscow. It followed Turov's visit to the dacha in April. I will give you the dates."

By *dacha* Chris assumed he meant the Russian president's home, outside Moscow.

"I'm told Delkoff was followed by FSB for several weeks early in the summer. He's made at least two trips into Ukraine since then, supposedly to plan strategy with Russian separatists. But I understand he also met with a deputy director from SBU on at least one of them," he added, naming Ukraine's secret service agency.

Christopher said nothing at first, not quite believing him. "Why would he meet with the SBU? They should be enemies. Of the worst kind."

"Yes, I know." He stopped talking briefly, as a pair of joggers ran past. "Should be. Enemies with a common enemy. And purpose, perhaps."

Christopher processed what he was saying: the implication being that their "common enemy" was Russia's president, Vladimir Putin. Could Turov be working for a fifth column within the Kremlin now? Could the target be Putin himself? That would make it a far different operation than Martin Lindgren had suggested. Did Martin *know* this? Did the White House?

"You have a second question," Petrenko said.

"Yes." Chris allowed a smile. "I was told our friend may be planning something called the children's game. Does that mean anything to you?"

"Yes. It does." Petrenko pointed to a new path, and didn't speak again until they had come to a green lawn with a giant chessboard and two-foot-tall chess pieces, set up as if mid-game. Christopher sensed that this was where he'd been headed all along. "Sit?"

They settled on a wooden bench facing the chess board. Petrenko nodded at it. "Children's mate," he said. "You call it beginner's mate, I believe."

"Beginner's mate in chess. *That's* the children's game?"

"Yes. Would you like me to show you?"

Christopher wondered at first if he was going to get up and move the game pieces. But he was searching for a pen, patting his shirt and trousers pockets as if doing a Columbo impression.

"Beginner's mate is defeating your opponent in four moves," Chris said.

"Correct."

Russia, of course, tends to underestimate the West, he thought. *And overestimate itself.*

Petrenko showed his smile—which resembled a forced grimace—as if he could hear what Chris was thinking. "Of course, they say that America plays a different game," he said. "America's game is Pigeon Chess: you knock over the pieces, shit all over the board, and then strut around as if you've won." His head thrust back and he snorted twice, revealing a lopsided alignment of teeth. This was a joke that Putin himself told, Chris had heard. Anti-Americanism was still rampant in Russia, a country where nearly all television news was state-controlled. Many Russians attributed the country's economic woes to the US. It was a classic diversion: invent a villain, then blame the villain for your troubles. "If you have one more question, go ahead," Petrenko said, a sudden tension in his voice, "because I have to go."

"What's it about?" Chris said. "What are the four moves?" Petrenko flicked the fingers of his right hand dismissively. "An attack in the Baltics? A Crimea-style forced annexation?"

Petrenko's head tilted to one side and his lower lip jutted out: *perhaps*. "Candidly? My impression is it will be something much closer to home. Your home. But I can't tell you what."

"How soon?"

"Soon." Petrenko smiled evasively. "Days, perhaps. I don't know, exactly."

"Who's he doing this for? Who's Turov working for if not the Kremlin?"

Petrenko made a face, as if he hadn't considered that, and checked his watch. "I could find out more, of course. But it would involve some risk."

"How much?"

"Eighty-five?" *Eighty-five thousand.* Christopher Niles lifted his chin neutrally to show he had heard. He wondered what the sea breeze felt like right now on their Greek island. They rose and began to walk again, through the blue afternoon shadows to the park entrance, Chris beginning to sift what Petrenko had given him: the unlikely tip that Ukraine's secret services were involved in Turov's op, the threat of "something much closer to home." He thought of a soldier he knew who'd worked with Delkoff once, a former Navy SEAL named Jake Briggs. If this was about Ivan Delkoff, then Christopher wasn't the right man for the job. But maybe Briggs was.

Stopping at the road, Petrenko forced a smile and clasped his arm, bringing the pretense to a close: two old acquaintances bumping into each other in the park. Petrenko moved closer, peculiarly closer, to shake his hand; he could smell the onion he'd had for lunch. When he pulled his hand away, Chris felt a USB drive in his palm.

"One other thing you might consider," Petrenko said. "Assuming the game is four moves? You might consider that at least one of them has already been played. Some time ago. And no one in your country noticed." He smiled, adding, "Let me know about the offer."

Turning, Max Petrenko was nearly run over by a speeding bicyclist.

THREE

Ivan Delkoff sat on a wooden ammo case in the abandoned barn, looking out at fields of yellow sunflowers as he smoked a Russian cigarette. He was dressed in his usual attire—faded camo fatigues and combat boots, the boots so worn in places they resembled reptile skin.

Alexander Zelenko, his lieutenant, was just outside talking with Pletner, the driver, telling him war stories in his nasally voice, unaware that Delkoff could hear him.

When Delkoff had first hired Zelenko, the Russian soldier reminded him of his own son, with that resolute mouth, the prominent Adam's apple, and dark, liquid eyes that seemed eager for anything. This talkativeness, though, was something new. Something Delkoff hadn't seen during their weeks of training.

The operation was two days off now and Zelenko was worrying him.

They had stopped at this farm near Donetsk to switch vehicles and eat a quick lunch before the final leg of the journey. Zelenko had cooked the three of them chicken cutlets on a propane stove and they were having a smoke now before moving on. They were inside the checkpoints again, in Russian separatist-controlled territory, part of the self-proclaimed Republic of Donetsk, what Delkoff considered

Novorossiya. New Russia. Or *Malorissiya*. Little Russia. But they were moving toward disputed territory, where the Ukrainian army still held positions.

Delkoff finished his cigarette and listened to Zelenko telling Pletner about the tank battalion he'd belonged to shortly after the war began, in 2014. How one of their tanks had been hit through the turret, but they'd gone on, routing the Ukrainian guards, liberating a village from the *khokhols*—the derogatory term some soldiers used for Ukrainians. "Sometimes, the enemy are men just like you," Zelenko told Pletner. "But if you think that way for long, you're dead. In war, killing is just a survival tactic."

He was showing off. Using the kind of langauge he'd heard Ivan Delkoff use. He could get away with it because he was talking to Pletner, who was twenty-one and didn't know war. Delkoff had always encouraged Zelenko—too much, he now realized; he'd probably helped give him the sort of confidence that would only get him in trouble. A prideful confidence.

But this wasn't just pride. Zelenko was also nervous, more than he should've been. Nervous about something besides the mission. *A man talks when he's no longer at peace with his thoughts.* Something he had read once.

Delkoff flicked away the last of his cigarette onto the barn floor and crushed the embers with his boot before going out. He squinted into the sun, feeling the afternoon heat on his face, smelling the odor of his own body.

Zelenko stiffened, seeing him, but Delkoff smiled and they all turned to the fields, waiting for a breeze to rustle the sunflower stalks.

"We ready?" Delkoff asked Pletner.

Pletner was a tall man with broad, blunt features—but the acquiescent eyes and bright teeth of an innocent, largely indistinguishable from other young men of the same age.

They set out again in silence, Pletner driving the camouflage Tigr reconnaissance truck along the unpaved farm road, more comfortable behind the wheel than anywhere else, as dust boiled up behind them in the heat. They rode past untended corn and onion farms, two-room wooden cottages, an unexploded missile jutting from a front yard, a combine, a schoolhouse with a Swiss-cheese pattern of artillery holes in one wall. Interrupted lives. Ukraine was the world's largest producer of sunflower oil, but many of the farms and seed-crushing plants in Donetsk territory had been abandoned this summer. The barn where they'd stopped for lunch now stored Grad rockets and mortar shells.

Delkoff sat in back, thinking of his family and the war, as he always did, and of those places where the two had intersected. But at the same time he watched Zelenko, giving him a hard smile each time he turned around.

For Ivan Delkoff, the war was more than a quarter century old now. It had begun the night the Soviet flag was lowered for the last time outside the Kremlin. December 26, 1991. On Friday afternoon, it would move to a new front, in the farmland north of here. The Americans, naturally, didn't know this. The Americans' war had ended just as Russia's was beginning. They'd been so busy high-fiving each other they failed to understand Russia was never going to roll over and become "Westernized." They'd wanted a simple outcome to the so-called Cold War, something resembling one of their action films— the good guys win, the Russians lose—and arrogantly assumed that American "democracy" could be exported around the world like a fast-food franchise. But Russia was a great and complex country, with traditions that most Americans, with their truncated attention spans, did not understand. When no one bothered to correct them, they assumed they'd won, having no idea how resilient and unusual the Russian spirit could be. The Americans had been asleep all these years—as Andrei Turov had told him in the spring—inviting retaliation.

Delkoff thought of his father—bureaucrat, soldier, patriot—who had ingrained these nationalist ideas in him, holding court with Delkoff and his brother in the living room of their tiny south Moscow apartment, drinking vodka from a fruit jar and talking of the Soviet victory over Hitler in the Great Patriotic War. A man Delkoff would never resemble, except in that fundamental belief in Russian greatness. Delkoff thought of the battles in his own life that had led him here, beginning with Transnistria in 1992, the two wars in Chechnya, and the failed secret operation in Estonia five years ago. He remembered the battles his son had fought in the Donbas, and his thoughts returned, inevitably, to the one that had killed him on that rainy afternoon near Lugansk last summer—the stupid ambush—and he felt angry all over again.

It was nearly dusk when they reached the farm property that would serve as the command post for Friday's operation. Delkoff undid the padlocks on the warehouse doors and they pulled the truck inside, parking it next to the TAR—a target acquisition radar, the tank-like vehicle Delkoff had transported here two weeks ago.

In the back of the warehouse was Delkoff's makeshift office. He'd moved in a cot, a desk, and several folding chairs, along with a small refrigerator and steamer trunk. In the trunk was a ten-liter jerry can filled with gasoline, an automatic rifle, a Makarov handgun, a scout combat knife, and a bag containing his change of clothes, money— both euros and Ukrainian hryvnias—as well as three passports and a simple disguise Delkoff had purchased from a Moscow costume shop.

In six and a half hours, the unmarked trucks from the north would arrive, after passing through Ukrainian-controlled territory, with the missile launcher and the mobile command post. The equipment and transports would be stored here beside the TAR until Friday afternoon, when history would change. When Delkoff's battalion would at last open a "new front."

The three men sat on folding chairs in the farm road that night as the air cooled, stars glistening above the sunflower fields. Delkoff went through the operation details again and talked about battles he'd fought, in Transnistria and Chechnya, while Zelenko and Pletner listened, reserved and attentive.

But Zelenko was looking at Delkoff a little strangely tonight.

Lowering his eyes just a moment too soon several times. And that told Delkoff what he needed to know.

No, Zelenko wasn't like his son, after all. It wasn't even close.

By the time the other two men retired to the basement of the farm-house for a few hours of sleep, Delkoff had made up his mind. It was all there in Zelenko's eyes: the reason he was acting so nervous today wasn't because of their mission; it was because of what he planned to do afterward.

Delkoff had dissected Turov's plans enough by then to know that at some point they would involve a secret assassin. Delkoff knew too much to be allowed to survive, despite the magician's assurances. And Zelenko, by appearances the most unlikely man for the job—small, timid, sneaky in a transparent way—must have been his choice, for that very reason. *Zelenko was Turov's assassin.*

"Get a few hours of sleep," he said, patting Zelenko on the shoulder. "I'll wake you when they arrive."

FOUR

Wednesday evening, August 11. Northern Virginia.

Walking alone from customs into the main terminal building at Dulles International Airport, Anna Carpenter felt a vague uneasiness, a sense that something was coming, something people weren't ready for. Maybe it was just the contrast between Martin Lindgren's urgency and the sleepy city that she was returning to. Washington officially closed for business at the end of July for a five-week summer "recess." Members of both houses of Congress returned to their home states for the month or went on vacation. No legislation was passed, there were no committee meetings. The Supreme Court was on hiatus. Even the president was in the midst of a two-week holiday. If someone wanted to catch America asleep at the switch, August would be a pretty good time to do it.

Mixed with these uneasy feelings were more personal concerns, which Anna had been fighting ever since leaving Christopher in Greece. It still bothered her how quickly the Turov assignment had gotten into his bloodstream. Martin had given him a taste again, and she'd seen the transformation. A reminder of how his work could turn Christopher into someone she barely recognized: compulsive, single-minded, emotionally detached. His father had given him that. Chris and his half brother were the products of a brilliant but demanding man who'd set unrealistic standards for his sons. Carroll Niles had been an influential figure in the counterintelligence community for three decades, recipient of a Distinguished Intelligence Medal. People now routinely referred to him as a "gentleman" spy; but he'd also been a taskmaster, a remote figure who rarely praised his sons, who'd waged his own war with the Washington bureaucracy. In the weeks after Anna met Chris, she sometimes felt that he was still fighting his father's unfinished battles.

The interruption of their trip stirred other memories, as well, of the sudden breakup of Anna's marriage six years ago. She still faulted herself at times for that: for being too career-minded and not making enough room for family, for failing to anticipate that her husband couldn't deal with her becoming a public figure, or that he'd ever be unfaithful.

Greece had been Anna's idea. A chance to shut out the noise in their lives for a few days. She never imagined she would be returning to Washington alone, with this sort of apphrension in her head.

"*Mom!*" David Carpenter, Anna's twenty-four-year-old son, reached out and squeezed her arm, breaking her reverie. She'd almost walked right past him. "I was waving for, like, five minutes. Didn't you see me?"

"No, I guess I didn't." Anna smiled, feeling a rush of affection for her tall, earnest son. He looked sharp in jeans and a crisp blue dress shirt, watching her with his dark, inquisitive eyes. "Sorry, honey." She rose on her tiptoes to kiss his cheek. "Guess I'm a little jet-lagged."

David took her carry-on and began to walk, staying a step ahead of his mother, deftly dodging the pedestrian traffic as if it were important to be first to baggage claim. Anna's son was six two and a half—six inches taller than she was, and still something of a "string bean," as people used to call him (her staff had labeled him "Jonah" once, thinking he resembled the character on *Veep*). But he carried himself with a professional assurance now, which seemed to have grown in proportion to his career. After floundering for a year or so during the divorce, David had found his calling in computers, without a lot of guidance from his mother—and none from his father, who'd run off to California with his much-younger girlfriend. Success had given her son ambition, rather than the other way around, and he'd risen quickly from an IT tech to a "bug hunter" to a "cybersecurity analyst." He worked now for one of D.C.'s largest threat-intel firms, monitoring the dark web for terrorist and cybercrime activity, with clients that included defense contractors and the federal government. David's career had given him an anchor and a sense of purpose he'd never known growing up. And it had made his mother proud.

As they approached baggage claim, Anna noticed a two-man TSA VIPR team in body armor walking their way carrying semiautomatic rifles. Something was different at Dulles tonight, she could see. She waited until David hoisted her bag from the carousel before placing a call to Ming Hsu, her chief of staff. "I'm back," Anna said, following her son to the garage.

"Welcome," Ming said, in her factual manner.

"What's going on at the airport? I'm at Dulles."

"Nothing specific. Heightened chatter. I'll have something for you in the morning." Anna had known Ming for more than ten years, and understood what she was saying: *Go home, get a good night's sleep. If you're going to worry, save it for morning.* She clicked off and hurried to catch up to David. For the past several weeks, signals intelligence had suggested that Russia was preparing some sort of military move in the Baltics. At the same time, there'd been increased chatter among known Russian agents within the States. As a member of the Senate Select Committee on Intelligence, Anna had been briefed on both issues before leaving for vacation. But tonight was the first she'd heard anything about US airports.

David, she saw, had stopped in the parking garage, setting her bags down behind a smart car. "This is your *car*?" she said. "When did you get *this*?"

"It's Malika's." He pointed a key fob and the hatch popped open. "Don't worry, it's safe."

Anna's concern was less about safety than about how David, she, and the luggage were all going to fit. But her bags went right in. He shut the hatch as if he'd done this many times. Malika was David's first serious girlfriend, a woman about half his size and far more outgoing, but for mysterious reasons, they were a good match. He'd met her at work last year, and they'd recently moved into a house together out in the Maryland suburbs.

"Careful," Anna said as he lurched into the aisle lane. It was the first time she'd been in a smart car and it didn't feel safe at all. It felt as if two-thirds of the car were missing.

"We get a lot of clown car jokes," David said. An SUV going much too fast swerved around them, horn blaring, as he pulled into the traffic lane. "Jerk," he muttered, glancing in his side mirror to see if anything else was coming.

They rode in silence out onto I-66, David driving a little fast. Anna finally relaxed enough to check her phone for messages and news. Besides the ongoing political wars between Democrats and Republicans, there were more tensions with Russia: in the Baltic Sea, a Russian Su-24 fighter jet had flown within sixty feet of a British Navy ship. There was also a vague report about a plan to attack American universities in the fall, with a "possible Russia link." But once she got past the headline, Anna saw that the "plan" amounted to nothing more than an email exchange between two college students in North Dakota, one of them born in Russia.

"So?" David said, as if they'd arrived in a safety zone. "What's going on, Mom?"

"How do you mean?"

"You're back three days early. Chris isn't with you. There were VIPR teams at the airport. There's been a spike in troll activity and some strange cyber hacks over the past two days—"

Anna turned off her phone. "I told you, Chris was called away on business." They rode in silence for another mile, Anna watching the mirrored office buildings, the gauzy afterglows of sunset. "But tell me about that," she said. "A 'spike in troll activity'?"

"Yeah." David glanced at his mother. "Just—some weird stuff coming across."

"Okay. And could you be a tad more specific?"

David smiled. He cleared his throat unnecessarily, a habit from his teenage years. Sometimes, Anna learned things by comparing notes with her son. But it usually took a little prodding. "The intel is that Russia is planning something against NATO, right? Or against us?" Anna allowed a small "mmm-hmm," to keep him going. "Isn't that why there were VIPR teams at the airport?"

"Maybe," she said. "What's the 'weird' part?"

"The weird part is there's tons of online activity all of a sudden saying the opposite."

"Really. The opposite being what—that *we're* planning something against *Russia?*"

"Yeah." He gave her an appraising glance. "You don't *know* about that?"

"No, I guess I don't." Anna wondered if this was why David had seemed so anxious to pick her up at the airport tonight. "What sites are we talking about?"

"Military websites at first. But it's all over Twitter now."

"Think you could show me?"

"Sure. If you want."

Anna knew that Russia's so-called troll factories churned out thousands of phony Internet posts each day, flooding Western news sites with pro-Russia and anti-Western opinions, along with fabricated stories promoting Moscow's agendas. The government also sponsored automated bot programs that repackaged pro-Russia opinions and had managed to plant malware on systems throughout the United States. The Kremlin actively recruited freelancers—some of them students, some from the cybercrime underworld—for this work, for what were euphemistically called "science squads." Washington didn't have an equivalent program or effective countermeasures, and there were moral and ethical questions about how far the US should go in devel-oping them. For years—as a congresswoman and as an intelligence analyst at the State Department—Anna had pushed for a stronger legal framework for cyberwarfare, without much success.

"Did you say cyber *attacks,* too? Against us?"

"No, cyber *hacks,*" David said. "Against us, NATO, European gov-ernments. You know what Russia's motto is, right, Mom? Do unto oth-ers as you think they're going to do unto you."

Anna laughed. That sounded right. She was reminded of Putin's famous remark about ISIS in Syria: "As I learned on the streets of Leningrad, if a fight is inevitable, then you strike first."

"So what do *you* think?" she said. "What are you hearing?"

"Something in the Baltics?" He exhaled dramatically. "I mean. Russia could move on Latvia or Belarus in three or four days and we couldn't do much to stop them, right?"

"Maybe," Anna said. "But not without creating international outrage."

He seemed to hesitate before agreeing with her. "Unless they were able to convince people that they had a legitimate *reason* for it."

"Is *that* what you're hearing?"

"Not really," he said. "I'm just saying it's possible."

"Okay." Anna thought about that, and the scenario in the Baltics that had been talked about for years: Russia creates a pretext for striking a NATO neighbor. NATO is then forced under Article 5 to respond. If it doesn't, Russia has, among other things, rendered NATO obsolete.

David glanced at his mother expectantly now, as if she were going to tell him more. But she wasn't; she was thinking. They settled into a long silence, coming at last to the rolling, leafy suburban neighbor-hood where Anna lived. Her house was a split-level, built in the early sixties; it had come with an acre of property and a creek, which created the illusion of being in the country even though she lived just ten min-utes from the Capital Beltway.

Anna's nearly identical dachshunds, Zoey and Mr. Smith, skittered maniacally to greet her as she came in, their toenails scratching on the hardwood floor. It was Wednesday, so Carlotta, her housekeeper, was off until morning. It felt good to see the familiar furnishings, the antique chairs and tables Anna had inherited from her grandparents, the art pieces she'd collected in her travels, the pile of *New Yorker*s, the photos of family and of people she'd known during her career in public service.

Anna knelt to give the dogs some attention and they quickly rolled onto their backs in surrender mode. "How's Mr. Smith?" she said, rubbing his belly. "How's Zoey?" The dogs had been named as pups eight years ago. David had suggested "Joey" and "Zoey." David's father—Anna's ex—thought that Mr. and Mrs. Smith would be funny names, for some reason. So, in the way that family decisions were made back then, they compromised, ending up with Zoey and Mr. Smith. It struck Anna as a very Washington kind of solution.

"Malika made you some crabbies," Kevin said, hesitant, it seemed, to come inside. "They're in the refrigerator."

"Okay, good." With both dogs satisfied, Anna stood. Kevin often brought over Malika's famous "crabbies"—crab meat mixed with cheese-and-horseradish spread, heated on baked bread rounds—knowing that Anna loved them.

"Want to come in and have one with me?"

"No, I can't stay. Early meeting tomorrow," he said, summoning his deeper, more declarative voice.

"All right, then." After seeing him off, Anna poured an inch of scotch with a splash of water and sampled one of Malika's crabbies. Delicious, as always. She went into Christopher's study with her drink and checked messages for a while. The room was immaculate, as he'd left it; same as the small apartment Chris still kept downtown. She imagined where he was right now—a hotel room in London, asleep probably—and wondered what he had learned today about Andrei Turov.

She skimmed several of the sites David had given her, and

discovered a few on her own, browsing through posts claiming that the US was planning "covert action" or a "BIG MOVE" against Russia. Several posts contained similar misspellings and grammatical errors, suggesting they came from the same source.

She found two emails in her in-box from Harland Strickland, the administration's senior director for counterterrorism, and a friend. Strickland had left the same message twice: "Call ASAP when you return. We need to talk." Anna decided it could wait until morning. Strickland was a presidential adviser with an inside track on upper-tier intelligence issues. But he was also something of a character. His "ASAP" was rarely as urgent as it sounded.

Before preparing for bed Anna studied the framed photo of Christopher on the bookshelf. It was one of her favorites, a candid moment caught last spring on a hiking trail in the Blue Ridge Mountains: Chris turned, half-smiling at her over his shoulder. Seeing the clarity and peace in his blue-gray eyes, she wondered what their life would've been like if they had discovered each other twenty years earlier. If he had become an academic instead of a spy.

She took a hot shower, pulled on pajamas, flossed and brushed, then crawled into bed. She lay awake for a while in the darkness, listening to a light rain in the trees through her open window. Thinking about Christopher and Greece, about how the sunlight had sparkled on the Aegean so promisingly Tuesday morning. About Russia. And the strange apprehension she'd carried home to Dulles. What had that been about?

Anna knew she couldn't talk to anyone about Christopher's assignment, but what David had told her tonight was a different business. Over the past two decades, she had built up a network of good contacts in the intelligence and military communities. Anna was looking forward to calling on some of them in the morning.

FIVE

By late morning, though, it was no clearer to Anna Carpenter what was going on with Russia than it had been the night before. She'd gone in early to her tiny "hideaway" office in the basement of the US Capitol, savoring the quiet and the chance to spend an hour by herself working the phone. But no one had told her anything she didn't already know.

She was back in her office on the fifth floor of the Hart Senate Office Building at lunchtime, finishing a phone call, when Anna heard a familiar voice in her outer office. She looked up, surprised to see Harland Strickland, the counterterrorism adviser to the president, chatting with Ming. Anna recalled the messages he'd left her the day before: *Call ASAP when you return. We need to talk.*

"Greetings!" he announced, strolling in with his easy, loose-jointed stride as soon as she set her phone down. "Heard you came back early. Sorry to surprise you. Bad time?"

"No, good time. I tried to reach you earlier."

"I saw your call." She gestured for him to sit but Harland was already helping himself, pulling at the creases of his pants, stretching out his long legs. Harland Strickland was in his mid-sixties but looked ten years younger, his once-boyish face grown more authoritative with age and with the rakish salt-pepper goatee he'd added last year. "So—how was the trip?"

"While it lasted: perfect," Anna said.

"Good, good." He set the dark green file folder he was carrying on her desk, and gave Anna his customary once-over, as if she were wearing a low-cut blouse. Anna dressed conservatively; there wasn't much to see. Strickland was a charmer, with a self-confidence that was set a notch too high, Anna sometimes thought. When she was in the midst of her divorce, they'd gone out for drinks a few times. Sometimes now he acted as if their relationship were more personal than it really was. "Talk in private?" he said, glancing at the door.

"If you'd like."

"Have you heard about this?" He pushed the folder across her desk.

Anna opened it. Inside was a two-page printout, a news story, dateline Washington. Anna began to read, with growing surprise. After two paragraphs, she looked up. "What is this?"

"It's the story the *Post* wants to run tomorrow. The *Weekly American* has the same thing. It was alluded to in Jon Niles's blog this morning. As you may know." He gave her a sober look and let it linger, implying that she had some sub-rosa connection to Christopher's little brother. Anna continued reading.

The story he'd brought her alleged that a small group of "senior US military intelligence officials" had met "secretly" on at least three occasions to discuss allegations that the Kremlin was planning an extensive disinformation operation to damage US credibility. The discussions had included "an option for Russian regime change," the story claimed, citing "sources speaking on condition of anonymity."

"They sent it over for an official response," Strickland said. "We're not giving them one. The DNI is urging them not to run it, naturally," he said, meaning Julia Greystone, who oversaw all seventeen US intelligence agencies. "Everyone can smell the shit-storm this would cause."

"You're not saying it's true?"

"Of course it isn't. There were no secret meetings."

"So? Where's it coming from? Why are they taking it seriously?"

"We don't know. I was thinking maybe you could tell *me*." The glint in his dark eyes reminded her for a moment of a drawn sword.

"Sorry," Anna said, closing the folder, understanding now why he was here. "I just got back in town last night. I don't know anything about it."

He nodded, but didn't believe her. "This isn't something that's come up in your committee, is it?"

Anna felt a bristle of anger, but summoned a smile. He was talking about the ongoing political tension between a group of analysts in the Defense Intelligence Agency, the external intelligence service affiliated with the defense department, and the White House. Several analysts felt that their recommendations for a harder line on Russia were being routinely discarded by a White House that often acted without the input of experts; two had asked to meet with members of the Senate Select Committee on Intelligence to air their grievances. It was garden-variety partisan politics, Anna thought, more about hurt feelings than anything else. Strickland was suggesting the analysts had leaked—or invented—this story to undermine the administration, and that Anna was somehow complicit.

"This is bullshit, Harland. You know that. Don't tie the analysts' beefs to me. We met with them once, at their request. This never came up. This is the first I've heard of it."

She pushed the folder toward him; he pretended not to notice. Strickland was one of the craftier people Anna knew in the intelligence community, although his moral anchor sometimes dragged a little, she'd found. He personified what was wrong with Washington: the maze of secrets, the insiders who treated intelligence as high-stakes poker, the bloated government that fed on itself and allowed the game to go on. Harland enjoyed being a player, talking with reporters off the record, then seeing how their stories shook out in the morning papers. It might have been largely harmless if not for the influence he seemed to have in this current administration, which far exceeded his job description.

"The trouble is," he said, showing a practiced smile, "this makes it sound like it's risen to the NSC level. Which is roughly the same as saying it's risen to the White House—"

"But you said it's not true."

"Right, it's not. Those socks have no elastic. Even though there are some in the Pentagon who would like to *see* us take a tougher stand on Russia. But no, there's never been any talk about preemptive action or 'regime change.' Believe me."

"So, why are you concerned?"

"Well, because. You know how the media twists things." Strickland's real concern wasn't the story, in other words; it was what the media would do with it. His nonverbals were still implying she had some knowledge of where this story came from. "And also, we obviously have disloyalty somewhere in the administration. Which, yes, concerns me." He tried a smile. "I'm just saying, we need to be together on this. Better having them inside the tent pissing out than outside pissing in. To quote somebody."

"LBJ."

"Right. Anyway," he said, taking the hint. "I didn't know if you'd heard."

"Sorry I can't help you on this, Harland."

He winked, to show that he didn't take things too seriously; although, of course, he did. "Anyhow," he said, patting his knees before standing, his way of closing the conversation. He took the folder back and tucked it under his arm, conceding this round. "Welcome home, Anna. You're looking good. Really. Vacation suited you. We'll talk soon."

When he was gone, Anna swiveled her chair to face the computer. She wished that she could discuss this with her father, the way they used to talk at length about Russia when she'd worked at the State Department. But that was no longer possible. Anna's parents lived in North Carolina now, and her father suffered from advanced Alzheimer's. Although they still spoke once or twice a week, he was never lucid for more than a few seconds at a time. Like all US Senators, Anna Carpenter had her pet issues, among them cybersecurity and climate change. But her father's disease had also made her a champion for funding Alzheimer's research, treatment, and prevention.

Anna found Jonathan Niles's blog and clicked today's entry. "There's a strange mood in Washington this week . . ." it began,

> . . . particularly in the intelligence community, where officials are comparing notes about a so-called "Russia threat." This on the heels of an outrageous story circulating over the weekend that Russia may be "sponsoring" a series of terror attacks this fall on American universities. A few of Washington's "Russia hawks" have grabbed hold of this unsubstantiated story, calling it further evidence of US weakness against the escalating threat of Russian aggression.
>
> At the same time, a more legitimate concern has emerged: that Russia's ongoing military escalation may be the prelude to a move on Latvia, Estonia, or Belarus. There has even been talk among some in the IC about a US "preemptive" move to head off such an attack. One intel official—while strongly denying the claim—expressed concern that the allegation might leak to the media and be used for "political purposes."

Anna smiled. *Okay.* Now Harland's comments made more sense. She looked out the window at the massive Calder sculpture *Mountains and Clouds* in the atrium and made a mental note to call Jon Niles. She had only met Christopher's half brother three or four times and still had trouble squaring his reporting with his demeanor—which struck her as aloof, scruffy, and a little fragile; he was Christopher's opposite in some ways. He reminded her a little of her son at times, someone who lived his life in a minor key. Chris had alluded several times to the sibling "rivalry" between them, although it often seemed more like a sibling cold war.

Six hours, she thought, glancing at her desk clock. *Six hours and Christopher will be home.*

SIX

As the Continental flight began its descent to Dulles International Airport, Christopher Niles closed his MacBook and gazed out the window, thinking how fortunate he was to have Anna Carpenter waiting for him. Anna had awakened in Chris thoughts and feelings that had been dormant for much of his life. She had encouraged him to live differently, to cultivate a healthy poverty in his thinking, so that finding simple things could be exciting again. He was more than ready now to pick up where they'd left off.

Christopher had given Martin Lindgren his "ten minutes." In the morning, he would hand over his report on Max Petrenko and put Andrei Turov in the rearview mirror for good. He'd decided all that in London: he was going to stay retired from the Turov business this time, regardless of what Martin had in mind. He cared too much about Anna to allow Turov into his head again.

Besides, Chris didn't think that he was the best man for the job anymore. Not since Petrenko had identified Ivan Delkoff as the organizer of the so-called "children's game."

He gazed down at the Virginia countryside, recalling another late-summer afternoon at Dulles. September 14, 2001, a Friday. Chris had flown on one of the first D.C.-bound commercial flights from Europe after 9/11. He'd been on assignment in Paris then, scheduled to return on the twelfth. But no planes flew to Washington on September 12 that year. He remembered how the passengers had spontaneously broken out in applause as the plane touched down safely on that afternoon. Many people of Christopher's generation had never before experienced the raw, gut-level patriotism they felt in the hours and days after 9/11. Many had never imagined that just the *idea* of America could be so threatening to anyone.

Every time he'd returned to Dulles since then, Chris felt the ghosts of that day, and recalled the audacity of what nineteen Middle Eastern men had pulled off, to the surprise of the entire American intelligence community. Using US commercial airliners as their weapons, they'd bombed the military and financial power centers of the United States, after months of training for their operation right here at US flight schools. *There's weakness in numbers.* Martin was right about that.

This time, the plane landed without applause. Seatbelts clicked, cell phones chimed. The sounds of life going on. There was a new generation coming along that was learning about 9/11 as a history lesson. That worried Chris a little.

He walked out toward the concourse with his carry-on, feeling that small lift he got every time he entered an American airport: the sail of his imagination filling with something that felt like American ingenuity, mixed with the mundane sights and sounds of the airport, the smells of Cinnabon and Dunkin' Donuts. Christopher had visited seventy-nine countries in his life; he was happy every time he returned to this one.

Seeing Anna, wearing a white skirt and black sleeveless blouse, made it better: the smart smile, the slightly wild quality in her green eyes.

"Welcome home, stranger," she said.

"Do I know you?"

"If not, we better to get to know each other. My name's Anna."

"Chris," he said.

They hugged for a long time, and walked to the baggage claim holding hands. Christopher knew then that they were okay, even if there was ground to make up.

As they walked through the concourse, he began to notice that something was different at Dulles tonight: there were armed tactical units in the corridors and an increased presence of uniformed police.

"So?" she said. "How was the ten minutes?"

"Good. I did what I was supposed to do."

"And . . . what comes next?"

"Nothing comes next," he said. "I meet Martin in the morning. He may want me to do something else, he may not. But if he asks, I'm going to tell him no. That was it."

"Really."

"Really." He felt her hand tighten in his, always a good sign.

While they waited for his luggage, Chris told Anna in general terms about the Petrenko meeting. "I don't know that there's much I could do, anyway," he said. "I'm going to recommend he bring in someone else, who knows more about this than I do."

"Someone in particular?"

"Jake Briggs."

"Oh, okay." Anna was not a fan of Jacob Briggs, who was rough-edged and unpredictable, kind of a military cowboy. But that wasn't going to be their concern.

"We left some unfinished business back in Greece, didn't we?" he said, as they walked to the exit. "I wonder if we could make up for it now?"

"I think we ought to."

Chris heard a hollow echo in the silence that followed, though, and he felt angry at himself that he'd been so easily drawn back into Andrei Turov's world. A canine enforcement team passed them going the other way; as they reached the exit doors, a TSA officer, leaning against a railing, gave him the once-over.

"Wonder what that's all about."

"Unspecified chatter," Anna said. "I noticed the same last night."

The exit doors slid open. It was warm outside. His glasses fogged with humidity as they came into the night air of Virginia. A black Chevy Suburban pulled forward and stopped. The driver came around to open the back door for them.

Anna relayed the news from Washington while they rode away from Dulles, down I-66 toward the D.C. Beltway: all of the vague allegations flying around about Russia, and the online claims that the US was considering a "preemptive" move. Chris said nothing, absorbing it all.

"I was reading your brother's blog this afternoon," she said. "He seems to know more about this than I do. It makes me wonder who's talking to him."

"Jon's always had his sources," Chris said. "It's a strange talent he has. People talk to him. He's pretty good at what he does, actually. For a liberal, he's not such a bad guy."

Anna laughed quietly in the dark. "*You* haven't talked to him in a while."

"No, I guess I haven't. I think Jon may be in one of his phases, actually, where he waits a week or two before returning my calls."

"Wonder why."

Chris sighed. Beyond politics, it was a complicated relationship and he didn't feel like going into it now. Jon and Chris had the same father but different mothers, and Jon had always been fiercely private toward his older brother; there were rooms of his personality he had never let Chris see, and probably never would. "I sort of understand it," he said. "When I worked for the Agency, I'd do the same thing sometimes. I'd avoid his calls because I knew he was going to ask about my work. Now he probably thinks I want information from him."

"You each want something the other has," she said.

"I guess."

"That's classic sibling rivalry," Anna said. "Going back to Genesis."

"Is it? Okay. Unfortunately, I don't think there's much I can do to change it." They dropped into a brief silence. Anna had a knack for drawing Chris out on subjects he wouldn't discuss with anyone else. Especially this one. Sometimes he felt an anxious pang when he thought of his quirky brother. Knowing that what was in Jon was also in him: a restless quality looking for a place to land. Sometimes it felt healthy to talk about it; sometimes not.

"I remember when Jon first decided he was going to be a journalist," he said, recalling a conversation he hadn't thought about in months. "Our father said, 'If you're going to pursue this, then you have to do it right. Tell stories that mean something, that can help your country. Write a story someday that'll change the world.'"

"That's setting the bar a little high," Anna said.

"Yeah. It's not the standard advice they give out in journalism school," he said. "It ignores the realities of having to get up each day and go to work, interact with people, and earn a living. His mother always understood the more practical side of life better than our father."

In truth, their parents had instilled in them both a sense of curiosity. But they were curious in different ways. Chris, who was four years older, looked at the world and tried to figure it out on his own. His brother asked questions, which had made journalism the natural career choice. Asking questions had also become Jon's style of social interaction. One of Chris's football coaches used to call him "the man with the questions."

"Would you mind if I called him?" Anna asked.

"Jon?"

"I wanted to ask about his column. Maybe we could even help each other," she said.

"Sure, if you'd like." Chris felt a moment's resentment, and waited for it to pass. It was fine. Right now, Jon was one of hundreds of journalists in D.C. chasing the same story. Maybe Anna could help him find what other reporters were missing; maybe she could put the story in a context he hadn't considered.

"Sure," he said again. "But let me try him first."

SEVEN

Thursday evening, August 12. Suburban Maryland.

Jon Niles eased up on the gas pedal, reminding himself that he wasn't really going anywhere tonight. He was killing time, driving his old Mustang down an unlit two-lane rural road in a part of the county that hadn't changed much since he was a kid. He'd told his girlfriend Carole Katz that he'd be working late again, which was technically true. Some of his work involved thinking and some involved waiting. He was doing both tonight.

For as long as he'd been a reporter, Jon liked to go out driving after work, to take stock and give the day some perspective, occasionally blasting out of his thoughts with music—the Stones from the late sixties, or Springsteen from the late seventies. Or something newer, like Lana Del Rey. When he was younger, he'd often have a tall can of Budweiser between his legs. These days, he waited until he got home.

But there was a more specific reason he was on the road tonight: Jon was hoping to hear from the anonymous caller he had come to think of as his "9:15" source. 9:15 was a woman who seemed to read his blog and Twitter feed faithfully, and who'd twice called to share insider information about US military strategy. Both times she'd called within a minute of 9:15. Jon had no idea who she was. Over the years, he had cultivated sources this way: he took blind phone calls, anyone who rang his number. Occasionally, it paid off.

9:15 had put him on to a potentially big story: what she claimed were high-level discussions within the US intel community about a "preemptive strike" on Russia. Some of what she told him checked out, but there were still big holes in the story, and allegations that had been met with denials or awkward silence by his sources in intelligence and national security. He'd twice alluded to it in his blog, thinking someone might come forward. But no one had; not yet. Jon hoped to find more tonight, as he'd hoped each night since 9:15 first called. But that would be up to her, not him.

His eyes went to the dash clock: 9:07. One minute since he'd last looked. Jon still had faith in his chosen profession, even if there were lots of reasons he shouldn't. People didn't read newspapers much anymore, and they didn't have a lot of patience for lengthy, in-depth reporting. They were "getting their news," as pundits liked to say, from social media now; except it wasn't really news they were "getting." The information they absorbed was increasingly filtered and customized, telling them what they already knew, confirming views they already held. When the media uncovered ethical wrongdoing these days, the wrongdoers could dismiss the reporting as "biased" and were sometimes given a pass. On cable "news," the prosaic tradition of objective reporting had been replaced with the highly competitive game of peddling opinions to create consensus. When it was done well, viewers became convinced that they cared about things that didn't really interest them at all. All of which was creating what Jon thought of as a bigotry of indifference toward those things that really mattered.

And yet . . . he maintained an abiding faith in his profession, partly because journalism was the only job he was any good at. When he was focused, Jon had sometimes been able to break stories that no one else in Washington was reporting. There was no secret to it, other than persistence and patience, and the fact that he tended not to run out of questions. But Jon sometimes had trouble with the focus part—going back to J-School, when he used to load up on courses that had nothing to do with his major just because they interested him. He'd been an "experience junkie" for years, traveling for the sake of traveling and entering into several ill-advised romantic relationships. Only in recent months did he realize that he was becoming too old for that; collecting experiences was starting to seem like a substitute for living a life. It was something he was going to have to deal with, an appointment he'd have to make with himself.

9:09. The road turned slowly toward familiar reference points: the ominous oak that could've been scenery from a horror flick, the sagging barn that had stood since before he was born, before redevelopment churned through the D.C. suburbs, linking everything to the city. There were still rural pockets like this, two-lanes that felt like secret roadways into the past.

9:10.

The road straightened and Jon reflexively hit the music button and pressed the accelerator: *Lights out tonight, trouble in the heartland, Got a head-on collision, smashin' in my guts, man, I'm caught in a crossfire, that I don't understand . . .*

He let up on the gas where the road turned. *How did we become such a nostalgic country, anyway?* he wondered, although he already knew the answer: failure. It was one of Jon's theories; everything had turned to crap for America in the mid-seventies: the presidency, the economy, Vietnam, the dream of an expanding middle class. The gasoline supply. A stunning series of failures had engulfed the country, leaving people distrustful of government and skeptical of the post–World War II notion of the US as a beacon for the free world. Then, as if to make up for it, when the decade ended we hired a president who told feel-good stories and made people nostalgic for an earlier version of itself, a president whose style alone became a form of leadership. And now the country was nostalgic for *him*.

Jon pressed twice on his brakes. Distantly, in the rearview mirror, he saw headlights; ahead, as the road turned, the red glow of taillights.

For the past week—since he'd been writing about Russia—his life had felt a little like that.

He slowed again and jammed the brakes: his cell phone was ringing on the passenger seat. "Damn!" he said, punching off the music and skidding to a stop on the shoulder. It was 9:16.

"Hello?"

"Jon?"

"Yes. Go ahead."

"I don't have more than a minute," the woman said. "Can you talk?"

"I'm listening."

"You didn't print what I gave you. You left out most of the details. It was good information." Perfectly enunciated words, syrupy voice, heavy breathing during the pauses; Jon pictured his caller, for some reason, as dark and statuesque, late forties or early fifties.

"I know. Thing is, I'm having trouble confirming some of it, okay?" He was out of the car, walking into the field as if the outdoors might add some clarity to her words. The car behind slowed, double-flashing its lights at him as it passed. "Could we go over a couple of things you said? Real quickly?" When she didn't respond, he went on: "You said at the last meeting of this group, there was talk of a preemptive strike, right? That was the word—"

"Which would leave no US fingerprints."

"Which—wait, *what?*"

"That's a direct quote," she said. "From someone in the room. Maybe that's your story." There was a light, spooky insistence in her voice, different from the other times.

"A preemptive strike on Russia. Which would leave no US fingerprints."

"Right."

"Okay. Go on," he said, feeling a rush of adrenaline. "Tell me what that means. And which room are we talking about? Can you give me the names—?"

"And here's something else," she said. "I understand there was also a meeting about this in Kiev. Last month, okay? And that someone from CIA was there, in the room."

"A meeting about this preemptive strike on Russia, you mean. In Ukraine?"

"Mmm-hmm. Some of this is starting to leak on military websites, by the way," she added. "I'm told the *Post* has some of it now, too."

"Okay," Jon said, "but don't do that."

"Do what?"

"Play news organizations off of one another. Can you give me a name? Or a time frame? I want to do this, but I need specific details to confirm—"

"I'm sure you can find more from your sources," she said. "Gregory Dial may have been there, from CIA. And one of the generals. I'd guess there aren't a lot of people in that circle, are there?"

"'Circle' meaning—?"

"Meaning it's a small group. As I told you. Probably just five." She paused, breathing heavily. "Most people aren't paying attention, anyway. Eighty-five percent of national security meetings are on the Middle East. People don't know what's really happening with Russia. What the US is planning. Someone needs to report that. Quickly."

"Okay," Jon said, concentrating for a moment on breathing normally. *What the US is planning.* "That's where—Tell me about this 'no US fingerprints' thing. Where does that—?"

"And I asked you not to record these calls, didn't I?"

Jon said nothing. Which was probably a mistake. Because a moment later, she said "Buh-bye" and was gone.

He walked across the field to his car, his shoes sticking lightly to the earth. Jon *had* recorded her this time, actually, and was thinking about who he might go to now for a voice ID. He stopped and listened to the silence, turning in the stillness. He used to come out to these same summer fields with his ex-girlfriend Liz Foster, four or five years ago, parking among the cornfields like they were high schoolers, dousing the lights to make out.

Jon pushed the play button on his recorder app and waited. Nothing. He checked the list of phone recordings. *Nada.* It wasn't there. "No! Damn it! Shit!" he shouted.

He tried again, several times, but nothing had recorded. The app hadn't worked. He sat on the trunk of his car, fuming, breathing the warm air and craving a beer. Letting his heart rate return to normal as he began to recreate the conversation in his head. *Someone needs to report that. Quickly.* There was an urgency in her voice this time that hadn't been there before. What was that about?

Jon finally called Roger Yorke, his editor at the *Weekly American.* Yorke had been Jon's mentor since he first went to work at the magazine eight years ago. He lived on a leafy suburban street in Chevy Chase, where he was probably in his second-story study right now, reading history, sipping an iced bourbon. Yorke was a tall, introspective man with a mop of gray-white hair, a Brit who'd lived in the States for the past twenty-odd years editing the left-leaning *Weekly American.* Some journalists called him "the philosopher," always respectfully, because of his deliberative manner and his tendency to put the news of the day into historical context. In his earlier career, Roger had been a foreign reporter, writing from war zones and on intelligence issues. He was still a reporter at heart, Jon thought, stuck in an editor's job, with good sources in the intel community and at the Pentagon.

"So obviously she has an agenda," he said, after Jon reconstructed the conversation. "I wonder, in fact, if her agenda may be the real story here. Rather than what she told you."

"Possibly." Jon batted gnats from the air. It was a typical Roger Yorke thought puzzle. But Jon was more interested in what she'd said about Kiev, and about "no US fingerprints."

"So, then, to recap," Roger said, "we know that this committee— was it a strategic advisory committee, she called it?"

"Right, Russia advisory group," Jon said. "Five members, representing the Pentagon, NSC, State Department, and the IC."

"We know that they met and discussed some sort of covert action. And the only name she's given you is Gregory Dial at CIA—who categorically won't talk with us."

"Or with anyone in the media."

"And she mentioned one of the generals again, whom she won't—or can't—name. But you think it might be General Rickenbach." Roger's mostly Americanized accent became British again when he pronounced "can't" as "cawnt."

"That's who it sounds like."

"And now she's saying there was also a meeting last month in Kiev. Same subject: covert action on Russia. And that we had a CIA man there—was that Greg Dial again, or did she say?"

"Didn't say."

Jon waited, as Roger thought it out. "It sounds as if she doesn't really know the whole thing, then, doesn't it? Like she's overhearing it in dribs and drabs." Jon listened to the discreet sound of ice clinking as Roger swallowed a sip of bourbon. "Anyway, we're not going to solve this tonight, are we? Let me make a call," he said, which was one of Roger's standard exit lines. "Go home. We'll revisit this tomorrow."

"All right, I will." Jon took a long breath of the night air and returned to his car. He sat for a while and checked messages, noticing a missed call and text from Christopher. Jon's older brother had been calling recently, sometimes leaving a message that he "just wanted to see how you're doing." The sort of thing Jon used to do, years ago. Strange.

Instead of heading home, he decided to drive out to see Carole Katz, his girlfriend, at her modest wood frame house among the cornfields. Carole was up past midnight most days, and urged Jon to come by anytime. Their relationship had become increasingly casual, which bothered him a little. He stopped on the way at the Gas 'N Go for a six-pack of Budweiser. The familiar white-haired clerk looked up and smiled when he came in, as if she'd been expecting him.

On his way to Carole's, though, Jon changed his mind. He was too wrapped up in this story now to sit under the stars with Carole and listen to music, which was usually what they did at night. He needed to get home and write out everything he could remember from his conversation with 9:15.

Jon lay awake until well past 2:00 a.m., thinking about the phone call. Hearing the insistence in her voice: *Someone needs to report that. Quickly.* He thought of his father's admonition to tell a story "that can help your country," whatever that meant, and the way he used to pit Jon against his brother, as if trying to force a bond between them that never really formed. Jon attributed some of that to Chris's unwillingness to accept another woman in the house after his mother's death from cancer. He thought of his own mother, a quiet, gentle woman who'd returned to her native Switzerland after their father died. "Do something great today," she used to tell him, although her definition of "great" was different from most people's, certainly Christopher's. What she really meant was, "Do something unexpected, selfless, generous."

Maybe that's your story, 9:15 said. Jon replayed the conversation over and over, sensing that somewhere in their brief exchange she had given him an important clue—not only about Russia but about who she was. Maybe Roger was right. Maybe that *was* the main thing: to figure out 9:15's motivation. Maybe everything else flowed from there.

EIGHT

Thursday, August 12. Eastern Ukraine.

As distant headlights swung through the mist, Ivan Delkoff stood on the narrow gravel road, a Kalashnikov AK-103 strapped to his shoulder, a Makarov handgun and an NR-40 combat knife at his waist. It was twenty minutes past two, meaning the Ukrainians were arriving early.

The air was cool, thick with moisture. Delkoff had spent most of the past two and a half hours sitting on a wooden folding chair on the dirt road, chain-smoking Sobranies, occasionally eating a stick of beef jerky. Thinking about Zelenko and the little Makarov pistol he'd found hidden in his travel bag.

Delkoff had suffered from insomnia most of his life. It had grown worse since he'd quit drinking fourteen months ago. When he fell asleep too early, he often woke at night from battlefield dreams: dead soldiers coming to life in the farmlands, or his son searching for him in pitch-dark fields among the casualties. So Delkoff had developed a habit of staying awake as long as he could. There were times when he found solace in the deep silence of early morning, as if he'd wandered into some undiscovered country. But other times the stillness felt suffocating, reminding him of what he had lost and what he had squandered.

This morning was mostly that, so he was pleased when he finally saw headlights winding through the sunflower fields from the north: two long, unmarked diesel trucks; a lowrider transport towing the Buk antiaircraft missile launcher; and a midsized cargo truck, bearing the mobile command center radar unit.

Delkoff walked down to the farmhouse to wake his men. "*Vstavay.* Let's go!" he called, shining a flashlight in their faces, holding the beam for an extra moment on Zelenko's eyes.

Delkoff walked back to the road. An hour earlier, primed with suspicion, he'd gone downstairs and taken Zelenko's travel bag. Digging through it as the men slept, he'd found the pistol stuffed inside a sock with his change of clothes and something else that seemed to be an electronic transmitter. He removed the bullets and returned the gun to his bag. Delkoff gave the soldier credit; he'd searched their packs before setting off and found nothing. There was only one reason Zelenko would have smuggled a gun into this operation. Finding it confirmed what Delkoff had suspected earlier: Zelenko was Turov's assassin. The bullets were intended for him.

The ground rumbled now as the trucks came closer, their headlights diffused in the mist. In a war without insignias or uniforms, these two vehicles had passed as a Russian Volkov artillery unit at the checkpoint eighteen kilometers northwest of here. Delkoff himself had arranged the passage, to make sure no one examined their cargo or noticed the men's Ukrainian accents.

Delkoff and Pletner walked out to meet them—"the Ukrainians," he called the other team, although one of the three was actually Estonian—while Zelenko opened the warehouse.

The five men exchanged cursory greetings in Russian, all of them dressed in military fatigues, none quite the same design, color, or fabric. They'd been through more than a dozen drills together now, but it still felt like an unholy alliance to Delkoff: soldiers from different armies fighting for the same outcome and no one really at peace with it. Friday night, after the operation, they would all go back to being enemies again. That was the idea, anyway.

Mikhail Kolchak was a missile regiment commander from the Ukrainian army, a compact man almost Ivan's age, with four grown children, all married and living in Kiev. He had intense, military eyes offset by a soft, splotchy face, with tiny red and green veins on his nose and cheeks. The two missile operators were closer to Zelenko's age, one a muscular bodybuilder type from Kolchak's SBU regiment, the other a lean man with sinewy arms, an engineer and former intelligence officer from KaPo, Estonia's intelligence service. Good soldiers.

They stored the vehicles in the warehouse, where they would stay until Friday afternoon, safe from Russian satellite surveillance. Afterward, the men went in the farmhouse to sleep, the Ukrainian team upstairs, the Russians downstairs. In the morning, they all gathered back in the warehouse for breakfast as Delkoff reviewed the mission. They took turns, then, running simulations, Delkoff watching the men closely, keeping them busy all day.

Delkoff sat out alone again Thursday night in the Ukrainian farmland, waiting for daylight the way he had waited for headlights the night before. It was quiet again, the strangest part of the night, when even the breeze seemed tired, whispering in the sunflower stalks. Occasionally, he recited part of "The Sacred War," the song Delkoff's father used to sing to his sons: *Arise, vast country, Arise for a fight to the death . . . Fly over the Motherland . . . This is the people's war, a Sacred war!*

Delkoff fingered the wooden cross around his neck, the cross his son had worn. This morning, with the old Russian melody in his head, he felt more certain about his assignment than ever before. If God existed, this was what He had put him on earth to do. He'd never felt that as strongly as he did tonight.

It was close to four in the morning when he decided at last to go inside, locking himself in the room at the rear of the warehouse. He stretched out on the cot in his fatigues and army boots, closed his eyes, and was asleep almost instantly. When he woke, ninety-five minutes had passed. Delkoff walked outside and urinated into the corn field.

He walked down the unpaved road, his boots crunching the gravel. There was no music in his head anymore.

His thoughts kept returning to Zelenko, whose eyes had reminded him of his own boy . . . dark, recessed, seeing life from a distance, but eager if you called on him, eager for anything. Pavel's life had ended in an instant, exploded by Azov battalion fire two hours from here, on a little farm road like this. He'd been killed by contract soldiers from Ukraine's National Guard, days before one of many "cease-fires" went into effect. Killed by men like Kolchak and this missile operator, who'd probably celebrated their strikes with high fives and cries of *Slava Ukrayini!* "Glory to Ukraine!"

By the time Delkoff returned to the warehouse, the air had lightened, and the corn and sunflower stalks glinted with dew. He could see the impressions his boots had made in the dirt going the other direction. Zelenko and Kolchak were standing together again, in the cleared field beside the warehouse, Zelenko talking and gesturing. But when he saw Delkoff, Zelenko turned away and lowered his arms.

"This is the day," Delkoff said. *August 13*. It seemed, already, a historic date.

Late that morning, they ran a full launch simulation from inside the warehouse, Delkoff sitting with Kolchak in the tight quarters of the command vehicle. Afterward, they relaxed in the shade, watching sunlight strengthen above the fields in a cloudless sky.

Zelenko heated up canned chicken stew for lunch, which they washed down with warm tea drunk from canteen cups, the men gathered around a wooden table Delkoff had pulled from the farmhouse. They kept their eyes on their plates, each in the channel of his own thoughts. The lunch gave Delkoff a chance to recall why he'd selected these men, each of whom brought his own skill and motivation to the operation: four of them, including Zelenko, had lost a friend or family member to the war, and they blamed Russia's president for that. Even Tamm, the Estonian, had motive: his brother, who'd worked for KaPo, the Estonian security forces, had been jailed in Russia for a month on phony espionage charges. Kolchak, on the other hand, came from a family of Ukrainian businessmen; he believed that what happened today would create new economic opportunities in his country. He was fighting for that.

This afternoon, all of them would get what they wanted. Together they would produce an outcome that would break the impasse over Ukraine and allow the motherland to rise again. And even if these five men were not able to enjoy the fruits of that victory personally, their families would be taken care of.

At 2:00 p.m., and again at 3:00, Delkoff put the team through launch simulations in the warehouse to keep everyone alert and motivated. Especially Zelenko. If Zelenko knew that Delkoff was on to him, he did a good job concealing it.

The first signal from Moscow came at 3:47, a coded text on Delkoff's phone: the president's plane had just lifted off from Moscow's Vnukovo International Airport, bound for his vacation palace on the Black Sea, 885 miles to the south. A two-hour-and-twenty-five-minute flight. It would take about half that time for the plane to come into range.

Delkoff and Kolchak stood watching as the vehicles growled out of the warehouse, their Caterpillar tracks rolling across the road and into the cleared field. Pletner moved the radar module first. Then Tamm lowered the ramps from the transport truck and drove out the mobile command unit. Finally, Kolchak guided the missile launcher over the ramp of the lowrider truck, parking it between the other two so the three vehicles were lined up in the field side by side, ready to go. The rumble of the monstrous vehicles stirred something in Delkoff as powerful as any patriotic music, bringing tears to his eyes several times.

Zelenko climbed into the radar module to turn on the optical tracking systems while the "Ukrainians" began activating the command unit. Delkoff waited outside, keeping lookout. He recalled how dark the clouds had been over his son's rainy final battlefield last summer. Today, the skies were perfectly clear.

His thoughts were interrupted by the familiar grinding sound of the missile unit rising on the transloader: the giant four-missile carrier tilting up from its flat position, as if waking from a great sleep, then beginning to rotate, the four eighteen-foot missiles pointed into the sky at a seventy-degree angle.

Delkoff could hear the music again in his head as he walked back, feeling the Russian winds blowing across these Ukrainian fields. He knew the histories that bound the two countries: how Russia had begun as a settlement on the Dnieper River, in Kiev, back in the ninth century. How many years later, in 1922, it was Ukraine that had helped create the Soviet Union, and also Ukraine that had caused the empire to break apart, with its declaration of independence in 1991. Now, again, Ukraine would play a historic role, in establishing Russia's return to greatness.

He watched the radar receiver groan to life, rising up on the turret and swiveling in slow circles as if sweeping the sky for its target.

Delkoff finally went inside the TAR to observe Zelenko, although he did not like being inside. Claustrophobia was one of Delkoff's weaknesses; very few people knew that.

He crouched closer and watched Zelenko's screen, seeing what had just happened—the plane was beginning to turn slightly to the west from its normal path south, meaning it was heading toward Ukrainian airspace. Zelenko's face was damp, but his hands were steady and his eyes remained fixed on the controls in front of him as the hypnotic pattern blinked on the circular radar screen. He barely seemed to notice that Delkoff was there.

The radars were operating on automatic now, and Delkoff controlled the authorization codes for the missile launcher. Even if Zelenko had some sort of a meltdown, there was nothing he could do to sabotage this mission—although sabotage probably hadn't entered his thoughts. He was here to complete his job successfully, and then kill Delkoff. Nothing else. He'd been paid well for that.

Before going back out, Delkoff patted Zelenko on the shoulder, feeling a flicker of compassion for his "son." He had no intention of ever going in the radar unit again.

Outside, he breathed deeply the Ukrainian air and turned toward Moscow, to the northeast. Toward where the president's plane would appear in the sky, at 33,000 feet. He smoked a cigarette, touching the cross around his neck several times. He talked to his son, telling him again what they were doing, his eyes moistening with emotion in the warm air.

When he finished, Delkoff crushed the cigarette under his boot and walked to the command vehicle. It was time.

Kolchak and his two men were seated in front of the guidance and radar screens. The horizontal blink on Kolchak's screen was the plane. Delkoff knew this from dozens of simulations; he'd seen the same signal in real time, as well, from tracking Ukrainian military transports over the past three years. This, of course, would be a very different target.

He stood directly behind Kolchak as the radar shifted from SEARCH mode to TRACK. And then, at 5:12, Kolchak began a litany of verbal operational checks: "Optical system check. TRACK mode check. Lock target . . ." Finally, the last, "IFF override," removing the Identification-as-Friend-or-Foe lock that prevented the launch. There were no barriers left. "Ready," Kolchak said. He stood, yielding his seat at the center module to Ivan Delkoff.

Delkoff heard the grinding of the launch rails elevating and locking in position. He typed in the ten-digit activation code, which he and Kolchak had built into the system weeks ago, and which he'd carried only in his head. *The combination to Russia's future,* he thought, smiling to himself, as he had done many times over the summer.

Then he nodded at the controls and stood, returning the seat to Kolchak. The missile launch was now operational. It would take less than five minutes to activate.

Delkoff observed the rest of it from over Kolchak's shoulder. He didn't understand all of the signals they were monitoring, but he knew what was happening: the radar data had been transferred to the "seeker" controls in the heads of the missiles—data containing the plane's location; its height and trajectory; all the information necessary to find, attack, and take down the president's plane.

"Ready for launch," Kolchak said.

The last phase was to unlock the command-fire control. All it took, then, was to press two buttons. They'd practiced this, too, many times. The Estonian, Tamm, pushed the first launch release. The Ukrainian, Kolchak, the second. There was good reason for that.

"Launch," Kolchak said. Moments later, the ground began to tremble and then the command center shook violently, as if it were being consumed by a massive earthquake. Delkoff felt the first of the eighteen-foot missiles burst from its launch chute, then the second.

Then he heard the explosions, like sonic booms, coming seconds apart: a sound they hadn't heard in any of the simulations. And, at last, silence. The men kept their eyes down at first, before cautiously trading glances. Twelve seconds was all it had taken for the missile to reach the plane, for the fragmentation warhead to take out the cockpit and front fuselage, blowing up the fuel tanks. *It was done.*

Delkoff was the first to look. The launch site was smothered in smoke, the air acrid with the stench of burning rocket fuel; a ribbon of sunflower stalks was on fire. Delkoff pushed open the hatch and stepped out, hearing a sound he recognized from other, smaller operations: debris still falling from the sky, a faint sound like broken glass in the distance. And Delkoff knew: *the president's plane was gone.* Turov had been right: America was about to be shaken from its sleep. But so, too, was the motherland. He turned and watched the other men emerging in the smoke, as if they'd just materialized on another planet. Which, in a sense, they had. The "Ukrainians." Like three statues in the smoke. Then "his" team came out of the radar vehicle.

"The new front has opened," Delkoff said aloud, coughing as he tried to outpace the smoke. He said it louder, calling to his son, to his father, to his country, tears stinging his eyes, some of it caused by the smoke, some by his patriotism: *"Arise, vast country."*

NINE

Friday, August 13. Washington.

Christopher Niles shaped his hands into parentheses and peered through the window blinds into his brother's living room. Jon had lived in this unpretentious apartment just over the D.C. line for three years now and Chris still hadn't been invited in.

He tried knocking first. Now he wondered if Jon still lived here. He saw a dozen cardboard boxes inside, piles of books and magazines, a few pieces of mismatched furniture, two framed paintings leaning against a wall, a dress shirt on a hanger hooked over the knob on a chest of drawers. He pushed his face against the glass, looking closer, and saw the familiar old writing desk in a corner, with scraps of notes tacked to a cork board. His brother's work station.

Chris had decided to swing by Jon's place before his "debriefing" on Petrenko, which was scheduled for 10:00 at Martin's office. Sometimes, the best way to catch his little brother was to just show up. After talking with Anna last night, Chris had decided to try reaching out to him again. He'd even decided to offer help with the story. Maybe tell him about Andrei Turov. If Chris wasn't going to pursue Turov, maybe Jon could.

Talking, though, had never been their strong suit, and he knew it wouldn't be easy to begin now.

"Help you find anyone?"

Chris looked down at a young woman walking her Yorkie. "Jon Niles," he said.

She arched her eyebrows and smiled. "Good luck. He keeps strange hours."

They walked into the parking lot together. She was an American U student, she told him, who seemed just as interested in Jon's where-abouts as Chris was. Jon deliberately set himself up as a man of mystery sometimes, he knew. Women were intrigued by it, though seldom for long. Jon seemed to have a different girlfriend every eighteen months or so. Chris sometimes wondered if he was still searching for the sort of woman he'd imagined as a teenager, listening to his rock albums on headphones; the kind who didn't actually exist in real life.

By the time he reached the main gate to the 258-acre CIA campus off GW Parkway, Christopher was thinking again about Anna. About getting their life back and making plans.

He was ready to hand off his "ten-minute" project to Martin. It felt like his last official act for the US government.

"Turov's operation—whatever it is," Martin Lindgren said, as he slowly poured tea into his nineteenth-century-style English cup, "has been in the works for at least two years, we believe."

Chris nodded, although he suspected the op had been in the works much longer than two years. Certainly in Turov's mind, it had.

"What Max Petrenko knows is limited, probably to what he told you," Martin added. "We're not interested, frankly, in paying him another $85 K."

"I didn't think so," Chris said, watching the steam rise from Martin's cup. Petrenko's USB drive had contained a single file, which was largely worthless—a rambling seven-page report on "the children's game," with a few names and dates, and a lot of wordy and improb-able speculations; parts of it read to Chris like a seventh-grade term paper. "Although I have to say, I'm a little concerned about Petrenko. Knowing what he does."

"Yes, well." Martin set his teacup down gingerly, the handle gripped between his thumb and forefinger. It was one of Martin's many incongruities: the proper demeanor, the slightly disheveled appearance. "So, what are we missing?"

"Why Turov would hire Ivan Delkoff, for starters."

"Is there an answer here?" He reached for Chris's report, then seemed to change his mind.

"The obvious one would be his connections in the region. On both the Russian and Ukrainian sides," Chris said. "On the other hand, Delkoff's been critical of the Kremlin's stops and starts in Ukraine. He lost his son there. Because of that, I wouldn't put him together with Turov or the Kremlin. So he must've brought something to the table we're not looking at."

Delkoff and Turov were—by temperament, experience, and physical appearance—opposites, Chris knew: Delkoff, a big, brashly nationalistic military commander; Turov, a canny, close-to-the-vest oligarch with strong ties to the Kremlin. Russia's "crazy colonel" and its "dark angel." Both men had served in the FSB years ago and held their own grandiose ideas about Russia. But as far as he could tell, their paths had never crossed before. Why now?

Chris was also trying to make sense of the detail Petrenko had told him about Delkoff meeting with the Ukrainian secret service. *Had he gotten that wrong?*

"What about this idea of a fifth column?" Martin said, seeming to read his mind. "A coup within the Russian military?"

"Possible. Except I don't see Turov being part of any plot to kill the Russian president. Unless there *has* been a dramatic split between them. But I don't see any reason to think that."

"Nor do I," Martin said. Chris's phone vibrated; he let it go. "And what about this chess game business? Petrenko said the first move may've already been played? What does that mean?"

"I don't know. Some sort of infiltration that we don't know about, I imagine." Martin frowned as his desk phone rang. Chris's sounded again, too. "Or," he added, "it might just be a bluff on Petrenko's part. A way of upping his salary, so to speak."

"Is that what you think?"

"Not really."

"What I'm getting is that it's more serious than a penetration. The goal is to break us apart in some manner, tilt the—"

The office door burst open and Julie Patton, Martin's normally staid, middle-aged assistant gave them each a wide-eyed look.

"I'm sorry, sir," she said. "We've just gotten word that the Russian pres—"—her breath failed her mid-word—"president's plane has crashed. Or been shot down. In Ukraine."

"What?"

Martin followed Julie out to her office, Christopher in tow. They all stood in front of her computer, watching the news report coming across in real time on CNN.

It took Christopher about a minute to understand what had happened. *What Turov had managed to pull off.*

That much he knew right away: this was Andrei Turov's doing. It had to be. The IC had been on edge for weeks, fielding nonspecific intelligence that *something* was coming. Some sort of "hybrid" or unorthodox attack against the West.

And that, he sensed, was exactly what had happened, although it would be hours—maybe much longer—before the intelligence community or anyone else in the US government figured that out. He only regretted that he hadn't done so earlier.

So this is how it starts.

"I have to deal with things now," Martin said to him. "Can we regroup at 4:00? Julie!" he called.

"I'm right here," she answered. "Mr. Niles at 4:00."

Christopher knew that the best thing to do was get out of the way. He'd never seen Martin so flustered.

But he also knew, as he walked down the corridor away from Martin's office, that he was no longer retired from the Andrei Turov business. It wasn't even an option anymore.

TEN

Somewhere in Belarus.

Ivan Delkoff stared out the train's window at the flat, sliding darkness of the countryside. He imagined the hours and days that lay ahead, traveling from Minsk to Riga, and from there on to northern France, to Germany, to God knew where else. Delkoff had long ago stopped celebrating victories. If you felt the urge to celebrate, and you possessed a heart and a soul, you did it privately, or not at all. War wasn't like sports. Or, as a fellow soldier had once told him, sports was war for cowards. War was business, the most serious business in the world.

For the soldiers who had brought down the Russian president's plane, however, those considerations didn't pertain. *Let the men celebrate. But let them celebrate quickly.*

He had broken out a bottle of vodka and five plastic glasses and allowed his makeshift regiment to toast what they'd done. *To Novorossiya.* He even managed to share in their mood of revelry, but skipped the alcohol, knowing what still lay ahead. An hour later, after most of the smoke had cleared, there was still a cloying smell of rocket fuel in the air. But it was remarkable how quickly the calm of that great summer day had reclaimed the countryside, the only sound again becoming the sunflower stalks creaking with the breeze.

Victory was a complicated business, Delkoff knew. How you processed it mattered at least as much as the victory itself. Delkoff had loved the Russian president, and what he had done for the motherland. The whole idea of *Russia Mir,* a Russia without borders, a moral example for the rest of the world: all of that was a fine dream. But Delkoff had also loved the contract soldiers and volunteer fighters who'd given their lives for it in the fields of eastern Ukraine: Pavel and thousands of other Pavels, some of them buried in mass graves, or laid to rest in secret ceremonies because the Kremlin didn't want to admit that it had inserted real soldiers into this war. You didn't celebrate knowing that. You moved on. He heard the voice of Pavel's mother again in his head—the hysterical wail after she'd learned what had happened: *Putin killed him, Putin killed my son!*

Kolchak had set up a crude camera outside of the radar station and they replayed the sequence several times on a computer monitor—the men crowding in and cheering as the trail of smoke from the heat-seeking missile tagged the target and the plane exploded. Later, he would upload this video to YouTube, so the world could see their work.

He shut the celebration down as soon as the bottle was empty, and ordered the men to their vehicles. Turov had created two escape plans: the "Ukrainian" battalion would travel the same roads that had brought them here, hauling their missile launchers back into Ukrainian-controlled territory. After passing through the first checkpoint, they would detour to an abandoned coal processing plant, where they'd be met by two SBU agents. Ukrainian security would ferry them to a safe house and, ultimately, home. The missile launcher and radar command would stay behind, locked in the processing plant.

That was the story they'd been told. It was the story they would carry in their heads as they traveled to the checkpoint. Once there, their trucks would be stopped by Russian Spetsnaz officers, already tipped off that they were coming, and they'd be killed. This was the necessary outcome; the story they *hadn't* been told.

Turov's plan, after all, wasn't just to kill the president. It was equally important to establish responsibility. In another day or two, the Kremlin would announce that two Ukrainians and an Estonian, all former intelligence officers, had been killed after opening fire on Russian soldiers at a checkpoint in Ukraine. They would also announce that the SA-11 missile system they'd been transporting had been recovered—minus two rockets—conclusively linking the assassination of the president to Ukrainian intelligence, and ultimately the United States.

Delkoff would follow the second escape route: he would journey east with Zelenko and Pletner through an hour and twenty minutes of farmland to the Russian border. On the way, they'd switch vehicles at the same sunflower farm where they had stopped for lunch two days before; from there, they would continue southeast, from the border crossing at Shramko to Rostov-on-Don, where Turov had made arrangements to deliver the three of them to a safe house. And then on to new lives.

This was the story they'd been told. No one had explained that they, too, would most likely drive into an ambush at the first checkpoint. And that they, too, would be killed.

The teams traded quick goodbyes. Hands were shaken, backs patted. Because of what they had just done, and the short celebration they had shared, there was real emotion in the men's voices. All except Zelenko, Delkoff saw, whose emotion appeared self-conscious.

When the Ukrainian team's vehicles finally rumbled away down the dusty farm road, Delkoff summoned Zelenko alone into the warehouse.

"I just want us to go over the route one more time," he said. Delkoff spread the map on the rickety wooden table where they had all eaten lunch. He stepped back. "Show me again."

Zelenko's hands were unsteady as he smoothed the map, moving his fingers to find their location in the Donbas countryside. There was still a smell of chicken stew in the room.

Delkoff gripped the combat knife in his left hand. He stood slightly to the side but still behind Zelenko. Watching the sad, alert tilt of Zelenko's head, the mole on his neck, the garden of little hairs in his left ear. "What are you going to do to me?" Zelenko whimpered. Not at all like his son now.

Delkoff said nothing. As Zelenko began to straighten, Delkoff stepped toward him. He raised his left hand and plunged the knife into the side of Zelenko's head, just above the ear.

Zelenko made a gasping sound. He fell back into the table and crashed to the floor, the knife still in him. In seconds, he was dead.

Delkoff walked to the barn entrance. He squinted out at the brown fields in the glare of late sunlight. Now there was only Pletner, who was waiting for him beside the transport vehicle, with his thick, erect posture, his eyes wide and vacant. Delkoff waved him over.

"I need your help for a moment," he called. Delkoff could see the young man's fear as he walked to the warehouse. He almost felt what Pletner felt, the blood thumping in his temples. Pletner was young and malleable, and he would do whatever Delkoff asked. It was best to get this over with as quickly as possible.

Delkoff waited until he was standing in front of him. He raised Zelenko's pistol to Pletner's chin and fired. Pletner's eyes widened and then closed before he went down.

Delkoff dragged Pletner's body into the center of the barn. He removed the jerry can from the steamer trunk in the back room and spilled gasoline in zig-zags across the floor, leaving his phone and the flame-retardant pouch with his own identification beside Pletner's body. Then he pulled the knife out of Zelenko's head and removed Pletner's wallet and keys.

From the doorway, Delkoff turned back to the dead soldiers, thinking about Zelenko's eager eyes, the resolute way he'd looked at him when they'd first met, in Donetsk, all those months ago. "You did a good job, comrades," he said, and felt his eyes tear up. Ivan Delkoff did not feel good about this part, but knew it was necessary. Zelenko had said it himself: *In war, you think differently. You have to or you don't survive. In war, killing is just a survival tactic.*

He lit a wooden match and watched the trail of fire leap across the warehouse toward the radar truck, consuming the furniture, the hay bales, Zelenko, and then Pletner.

"Forgive me," he said as he walked away to the transport vehicle, feeling his son's cross.

Delkoff began to drive, not east toward the checkpoint, as he was supposed to, but west, a long detour to another abandoned farmhouse. He had stored a travel vehicle there, a Hyundai Solaris with Ukrainian registration, along with a work shirt and dungarees. Delkoff had planned this escape as carefully as he'd planned Turov's mission. The two had been parallel operations.

By evening, Delkoff was driving alone on the M03 highway north toward Kharkiv. Delkoff knew how to reverse engineer an "escape." Knew where to drop breadcrumbs, how to set up a credit card trail, how to use CCTV surveillance to his advantage, how to slip information to the SVR and FSB. He knew how to lure Russia's security services to Belarus, instead of northern France, where he would actually be. People always underestimated Delkoff, and they'd probably do so again.

Those weren't deceptions that would hold for long, though. Delkoff knew that. If he was lucky, they might give him four or five days to make more permanent arrangements with his cousin, Dmitri Porchak. Delkoff sat in his window seat now as the train rolled through the countryside, the lights of distant towns skimming past. Breathing the taste of rocket fuel still in his lungs. He was on the 1:32 a.m. train from Kharkiv to Minsk tonight. In Minsk, he would board a car to Riga, where on Monday he would fly to Paris. No one would expect Delkoff to catch a train in Kharkiv, nor would they be looking for him in Riga, let alone France. He was trying to keep his mind clear of voices now, but his father's patriotic music kept stealing his thoughts: *We shall repulse the repressors Of all ardent ideas . . . Arise, vast country! Arise, vast country!*

In the train station, Delkoff had avoided looking at televisions, or overhearing conversations. He didn't want to know about it yet. Deferred gratification was part of his plan. For Delkoff, it was a necessity: not to look until he had arrived safely in France on Monday. Because Delkoff didn't entirely trust himself. If he looked, he was afraid he would lose his center; he would be tempted to have a drink, to talk with a strange woman, to give himself away.

Also, he was trying not to draw attention to himself. Delkoff was a big, beat-up-looking man, who tended to draw curious glances anyway. Now he was wearing a paste-on beard and a knit cap, which probably made him even more of a curiosity.

He stared out the window from his private darkness as the train rumbled north. The lights in the countryside were like fires of freedom tonight, he thought, beckoning him to a new life. In another day or two, the Kremlin would announce that they had killed the perpetrators and recovered the missile battery. But they'd be too humiliated to mention Delkoff. He was sure of that. Delkoff had now successfully extricated himself from Turov's plan. What happened next was up to him. Not Turov. Not Russia. Just him.

ELEVEN

Capitol Hill, Washington.

The news from Ukraine quickly blanketed Washington in a fog of confusion and misinformation. Everyone in town, it seemed, was asking some version of the same question: "What've you heard?"

"At this stage," Anna Carpenter told her son David, who called at lunchtime expecting an inside scoop, "all explanations seem plausible and any explanation seems premature."

"Mom."

"What."

"Remember that conversation we had coming back from the airport?"

"Of course. What are you hearing?"

"I'm hearing the worst, same as you." He exhaled. "I'm hearing *we* did this."

"What are you talking about?"

"It's all over Russian social media. It's starting to get out now on English-speaking sites."

"That *we* did this? But not seriously."

"Seriously," he said. "They're tying it back to CIA, saying we met with a Ukrainian arms dealer in Kiev over the summer. They've even put out a name."

Anna was speechless, hearing the conviction in her son's voice. "Well, that's absurd."

"You're sure?"

"Let me call you back." Anna clicked off and swiveled to face her computer. *Was* she sure? No; if she was, she wouldn't have been so abrupt with David. It took less than two minutes for her to find what he had been talking about: several websites out of Russia and eastern Europe were giving surprisingly detailed accounts of the attack: the "assassination," they called it, had been planned by an anti-Russian Ukrainian oligarch, Dmitro Hordiyenko, and carried out "with the backing" of America's CIA. There were no named sources, and no one in Washington or the mainstream media seemed to be taking it seriously. But something about the story bothered Anna. There was an unusual authority to it. A sober tone not typical of Russian propaganda.

She sat in her office searching through Twitter traffic, switching channels on television, anxious to learn more. An hour and a half earlier, when the news broke, interns and Senate aides had rushed into the hallways, shouting that Putin's plane had been shot down. Now what felt like a stunned silence filled the floor. Everyone was quietly soaking in the news, hunkered down on phone calls or staring at televisions or computer screens. Christopher had phoned just once, while she was talking with David. She hadn't been able to reach him since.

Because of Anna's seat on the Senate Select Intelligence Committee, she was one of the go-to people reporters called for security and intelligence stories. But she wasn't returning media calls on this one. This was a story no one could adequately explain yet.

And something else bothered her: whatever had happened to the Russian president's plane—sabotage, coup, a Ukrainian military attack—the US intel community had missed it. Completely. No one had seen this coming. Not even Christopher.

There was no official confirmation yet that Russia's president had been on board the plane. But just before noon, mainstream news agencies began quoting "high-level Russian sources" verifying it. "REPORT: PUTIN DEAD" flashed up as a news banner, first on MSNBC, followed quickly by the identical words on CNN and Fox and as cut-ins on the networks. Moments later, she heard one of her entry-level office interns shouting: "Putin's dead! CNN reporting: Putin's dead!"

Anna stared numbly at the words on her television. The idea of nuclear Russia with no one in charge was chilling. The lack of a viable succession plan had always struck her as one of the most disturbing aspects of Putin's Russia—even if, technically, there *was* a plan: under the Russian constitution, the prime minister became acting president, with elections required within three months. But given the covert nature of Russian politics, the succession wouldn't be so neat. Everyone knew that. Russia analysts were already beginning to predict a prolonged behind-the-scenes power struggle, and a period of dangerous insecurity for Russia and the world.

The danger was exacerbated by the flurry of recent personnel changes in Moscow, Putin appointing former bodyguards to key security posts and as governors in three regions. In a political environment that valued loyalty over expertise and competence, the president's men—the devils we didn't know—were even more concerning than the president.

Anna stared at her TV as new details came across: military experts saying that the president's plane had probably been brought down by a surface-to-air missile, similar to what took down Malaysia Airlines Flight 17 in July 2014, over a nearby region of Ukraine, killing all 298 onboard. Then, just after 12:30, a fuzzy photo appeared almost simultaneously on dozens of Russian websites, supposedly showing Dmitro Hordiyenko, the Ukrainian businessman and alleged arms trader, sitting in "a Kiev restaurant" with "an unidentified American CIA officer."

Minutes later, Anna found a clip of the provocative speaker of Russia's state Duma, telling a Moscow journalist, "We're getting reliable reports now that the assassination was planned and carried out by

American CIA, with help of Ukrainian SBU. You can be assured there will be serious repercussions if true."

As she watched the news, Anna kept flashing back to one thing: the story that Harland Strickland had brought to her office and laid on her desk yesterday morning, alleging that the US was secretly discussing a preemptive attack against Russia.

What was going to happen to that story now? Was it possible that was what had just occurred? Had Harland somehow *known* this was coming? Was that why he was so nervous about it leaking?

The vice president's chief of staff called Anna's office just before 1:00. Could Anna attend a special National Security Council briefing at the White House?

She had been hoping to meet Christopher for lunch. But the vice president's urgent request superseded that. Instead, she asked her chief of staff to call her a car for the 1.2-mile drive down Pennsylvania Avenue to the White House.

TWELVE

Situation Room, the White House.

The meeting was already under way when Anna arrived, tucked into her seat, and made a quick survey of the men and women around the table: intelligence officials; NSC staff; and reps from the White House, State Department, and Pentagon. An odd group, pulled together by the vice president from among those still in town. On the bank of wall monitors were fuzzy but dramatic still images of the white-red-and-blue presidential plane beginning to come apart in midair.

The accounts of what had happened resembled by then a giant, ungainly ship, Anna thought, which was beginning to turn in a clear direction. The stories officials had "heard" were becoming the same story, in some cases word for word: the downing of Putin's plane had probably been a "military coup," planned and carried out by two or three Russian generals and a former head of Russian security services. Several TV reporters whose tweets were known to be in sync with White House messaging had already begun spreading this story in 280-character doses, attributing it to "senior White House sources" or just "sources."

Anna had no idea where the coup story started, but it filled obvious gaps. How else could the president's plane, armored with advanced antimissile technology, have been so vulnerable?

General Jared Coffman, the head of the US European Command base in Stuttgart, Germany, was giving a summary of what was then known, his face filling one of the screens: ". . . the missile, which appears to have been a Buk SA-11, Russian-made. Ground-to-air, which would have exploded within ten feet of the cockpit, puncturing the plane with shrapnel. It was the shrapnel rather than the missile itself that brought it down."

"Which is exactly what happened with the Malaysia airliner attack in 2014," said General Harold Rickenbach, seated three seats to Anna's left.

"There are similarities, yes," Coffman replied, then paused before elaborating. "Initial indications are the crash site was probably fifty to sixty kilometers from where MH17 went down. And we do have surveillance assets in the area reporting a Ukrainian missile battery was seen in the vicinity on Friday.

"President Putin had been traveling from Moscow to the presidential palace at Cape Idokopas near Sochi when the attack occurred. The plane was just about halfway there."

"This is still contested territory?" asked General Rickenbach.

"The crash site appears to be in separatist-controlled territory. But the launch point may be contested. Too early to say."

Anna noticed, as she had before, the striking contrast, in temperament and presence, between the two generals. Rickenbach was a thickset, intense man with a large, bald head, flushed skin, and dented nose. Coffman, a light-skinned African-American with dark hair, had a long, sage-like face, drooping eyes, and earlobes the size of teaspoons.

"These new images seem to confirm that there were most likely two explosions," Coffman said. "Meaning the first missile may have been destroyed and the second got through."

"Would the Ukrainians have access to that sort of weapon?" asked the vice president.

"Both the Russian and Ukrainian militaries have SA-11 missiles and launchers, yes," Rickenbach said. "The Ukrainian arsenal has a somewhat older model than the Russian army."

Anna knew Rickenbach, and detected from the slightly elevated pitch of his voice that he was privately ecstatic about what had happened in the skies above Ukraine. And he wasn't the only one. For the Russia "hawks," a lot of America's intelligence headaches, and imagined future headaches, might have just been cured.

"This *shouldn't* have been possible, though," said Julia Greystone, Director of National Intelligence, with her even, commanding tone, addressing Coffman rather than Rickenbach. "I mean, how would they have gotten through missile defenses? I'd hate to think Air Force One could be that vulnerable. There must've been some sort of internal sabotage."

She watched the screen, waiting for Coffman to respond. It was no secret that Rickenbach and Greystone didn't care for each other. Rickenbach did not like the fact that a woman had the top intelligence post in the country, working for a president he only grudgingly respected.

"Also, the plane obviously shouldn't have been flying that route," added the vice president. "It shouldn't have been anywhere near Ukrainian air space."

"That's correct," Coffman said. He called up a map on the adjoining screen, with a simulation of the plane's flight path. "The route to Sochi should have been well clear of this," he said, pointing to where the plane had veered west over Ukraine. "To answer the director's question, the Ilyushin is equipped with infrared SAM missile defense systems and radar jamming. Safeguards, of course, aren't foolproof."

General Rickenbach's assistant was crouched beside his chair whispering to him, Anna noticed, interrupting the presentation. "Okay," the general said, as the assistant stood and began to walk away. "I'm told these are just coming in now—" New, clearer images filled the monitors: a sequence of four still photos showing the presidential plane coming apart in sequence. "These were taken by a sunflower farmer, supposedly, in the Donbas."

Anna glanced at Harland Strickland down the table, who wouldn't look at her, remembering again the allegations he'd brought to her office. She saw him exchange a glance with Craig Kettles, the second-term congressman from Mississippi, perhaps the most ardent anti-Russia voice in town.

"If I may," the vice president said. "Recognizing this is all preliminary: What are the possible/probable scenarios? What are we looking at?"

The general yielded to Dan Borrell, the NSC's senior director for Russia, a small, gaunt man who'd led the Russia studies program at Harvard for several years.

"Motivationally," he began, clearing his throat, "I would suggest five possible scenarios. With the obvious caveat that this is still very early," he said, sounding like the nervous academic he was. "First, we can't rule out the possibility that this was a terror attack. Chechen rebels, or jihadist groups from Chechnya associated with ISIS, would have had the motivation certainly, although it's unlikely they could've carried out something with this level of sophistication. Second, there are right-wing, pro-nationalist factions within Ukraine, and within the Ukrainian military, in particular, who may have had access to these weapons. There are also forces outside the military—Ukrainian oligarchs who run private militias in eastern Ukraine, for example—who could have acquired the equipment through back channels. The problem with those scenarios, of course, is that they don't explain why the plane was in Ukrainian airspace.

"A fourth possibility," Borrell continued, "which would address that, is what Director Greystone suggested, that the plane was brought down by forces within Russia, either the military or the security services. Given the complexity of the attack, this would be the more likely scenario, in my view. There is a small faction—which includes at least a couple of cabinet members and several of the generals—that regards the president's policies as dangerously destabilizing; that privately favors—favored—regime change."

"A coup, in other words?" the vice president said.

"Yes," Borrell said. After a pause, he added, "And then, finally, there is the possibility of a lone wolf internal sabotage, although that would seem less likely."

"Explain, please?" Julia Greystone, the intelligence director, raised her eyebrows and gave him her steely look.

"Meaning: the possibility that this was a solo suicide mission. That a crew member, a pilot, or a passenger was able to smuggle some sort of explosive device on board. Although this looks more like a missile than a bomb."

"So in your estimation, the most likely scenario—"

"—is that this was a coup, an internal operation, carried out by forces within the Russian military. But tailored to look like something else."

There was a long silence as everyone stared at the sequence of the plane blowing apart.

"Unfortunately," said the vice president, "I don't know how many of you are picking up on this yet, but there's another story that was starting to circulate as we came in here. And that's that *we* did this. There are even specific details, or allegations, linking *us*—CIA or the NSC—to a Ukrainian oligarch—"

"Dmitro Hordiyenko," Anna said. "He's been an outspoken critic of Putin for years. He helped fund opposition movements in 2011 and 2012, during Putin's reelection campaign."

"Okay, yes, thank you," the vice president said, showing a surprised smile. "I don't know how much traction that's going to have. But it's out there. The idea being that we had information Russia was planning something big against us and preempted it with this."

Anna listened to the humming silence in the room. *There's one other possibility,* she thought. And Anna was a little surprised it hadn't come up yet.

She glanced again at Harland Strickland, who was leaning now toward Maya Coles, one of his allies, an assistant secretary of defense and one of the administration's "Russia hawks."

"And we *do* have confirmation that the president was on board now, is that correct?" Director Greystone asked.

Suzy Carson, the special assistant to the president for Homeland Security, responded in her incongruously high voice, which always surprised people who didn't know her. "Not *officially*. Although there are photos now of him arriving at the airport in the afternoon. And there is an unconfirmed report of Putin boarding the plane. So. Still waiting on that."

"What's the mood inside Russia?" the vice president asked.

"We're getting reports that officials have been taken to secure sites," Carson said. "They're claiming new intelligence is warning about additional attacks . . . and there have been some spontaneous demonstrations, supposedly, in Moscow. People holding up Russian flags and pictures of the president." She looked down at her phone, processing several things at once. "They're not playing *Swan Lake* yet," she added, referring to the old Soviet practice of televising a loop of the Russian ballet when a leader died. "But it's getting to that."

The official silence from Moscow felt ominous, Anna thought, a sign that the president probably *was* dead. On one of the wall screens, Coffman, the Eurasian commander, said, "What I can add, from here, is that the president was flying with staff and a small group of businessmen. And we have the list of names now. Unofficially." He began to read them. Some Anna recognized, most she didn't.

Coffman was on the tenth or eleventh name when Suzy Carson interrupted, waving her hand frantically like a middle school student in class. "Okay, sorry," she said. "Here we go: a source in the Russian foreign minister's office is now confirming it: President Putin is dead. We have a source confirming. The president *was* on board the plane."

Anna glanced around the table as a stunned silence filled the room. The vice president was the first to speak, a lilt of emotion in his voice:

"I would just say, to everyone, that we obviously need to be very dili-
gent about making any comment—or responding at all—until we have
this confirmed officially."

His eyes settled surprisingly on Anna. There had always been a
slightly distant bond between her and the vice president. Long before
they were in their current jobs, Anna used to see him at church on
Sundays in Bethesda and they'd often exchange a few words. "Anna,
were you going to say something?"

Anna sat up straighter and cleared her throat. She *wasn't* going to
say anything, but would if he wanted her to. "I'd agree with the vice
president," she began. "And I might add, in light of the allegations of
Ukrainian involvement: we should at least be aware of the possibility
that Moscow may use this as justification for a retaliation in the region.
Whether the story's true or not. But I agree, at this stage, our response
needs to be very measured."

She quickly scanned the faces around the table. General Rickenbach
worked his mouth as if there was an unpleasant taste on his tongue.
Emotions were raw; Russia was a topic that elicited strong opinions.
Anna glanced at her phone: *Where's Christopher?*

"I won't disagree with the senator," Rickenbach said, without looking at her, "but I do think we need to be prepared to respond forcefully if Russia is going to make accusations that we did this. Let's not
forget that we're dealing with a severely wounded animal right now
in Russia, regardless of who's in charge. They're a country that sees
military power—hard power—as their best means of buying political
advantage. Underestimating that would be a huge mistake."

Anna noted the half dozen or so subtle head-nods around the
table. But some of the reactions struck her as odd: the similar blank
faces of Congressman Kettles, Maya Coles, and Harland Strickland.
Along with Rickenbach, the Russia "hawks" in the room. As if concealing some shared knowledge. Was it possible that the US *was* involved
in some way?

"Anna?" the vice president said, nodding to her again. "Anything to add?"

Anna shook her head, thinking again of the explanation that no one had mentioned. And seeing a more complicated problem ahead: a problem that didn't involve Russia at all, that was much closer at hand, right here in this room.

"No," she said. "Not yet."

THIRTEEN

Southwest of Moscow.

Andrei Turov received the news at his country home thirty kilometers from Moscow. He was seated behind the old mahogany desk in his office, a converted nineteenth-century dacha, talking with Olga Sheversky about her trip tomorrow to Switzerland, when he noticed Anton Konkin coming up the trail beside the lake, the early evening sun gleaming through the leaves off the top of his bald head.

Normally, Anton came to his office twice a day, arriving with the precision of a train, at 10:00 in the morning and 5:00 in the afternoon, laptop tucked under his right arm. Anton was Turov's buffer, and his liaison to the offices in Moscow and St. Petersburg. He was also the most loyal man that Turov had ever known. Possibly the most loyal man alive.

This unscheduled appearance took both Turov and Olga by surprise, although Olga's surprise was more genuine than his.

Turov had quietly been laying the groundwork for his retirement for several months, shipping selected valuables to his vacation home in Switzerland, where Turov's daughter and grandchildren had relocated nine days ago. "August 13" would be his last operation based in Russia. The Kremlin understood that, although they hadn't yet given permission for him to leave the country. He expected that by week's end.

Turov's spread in the country comprised more than seventy-nine acres. He also owned four office buildings in Moscow and three in St. Petersburg, as well as properties in Switzerland and France. He held stock in several of Russia's largest natural gas and oil companies. His network of security businesses had been valued at close to a billion US dollars. Turov enjoyed the game of Russian business and he played it well. But he also understood that all he owned could be stripped away in an instant. These days, his greatest concern was ensuring that his family was provided for when he was gone. His own possessions had become less and less interesting the older he got, for the obvious reasons. He often took refuge these days in a quote from Solzhenitsyn, which he kept in a small picture frame on the top shelf of his bookcase here: "Own only what you can always carry with you: know languages, know countries, know people. Let your memory be your travel bag."

Turov's greatest loyalty was to his family, which now included Olga and Anton. A family did not have to be blood, but it had to be for life, he believed. He had told his daughter Svetlana that he was retiring here to the country on doctor's orders; that he'd been warned he might suffer a stroke if he didn't. In part, this was true. But the greater threat to his health had become political. There were men in Putin's circle now who did not particularly want Turov to survive, who did not trust him.

For years, Turov's life had been so entwined with that of Russia's president, and the greater good of their country, that he had suppressed many of his own personal desires. He wished sometimes now that he had made these moves years earlier. But, as Olga liked to say, "We get old too soon and smart too late." It was the condition of being human.

In addition to serving as caretaker of his country property, Olga was Turov's personal assistant and occasional lover, a simple, sensible woman he'd come to rely on and care for. When he had first met her, Olga reminded him of one of those darting sea birds he'd watched as a boy by the Black Sea, bobbing their heads as they competed for breadcrumbs. Turov used to pick out the smaller, less confident birds; Olga had been one of those. But she could be tenacious when given a chance, and he'd done that for her. In exchange, she had taught him many things about life that his upbringing had neglected.

Anton stood in the doorway of the office, looking past Olga to Turov, waiting to be acknowledged. "I am sorry, boss," he said, stepping in the room as soon as Turov spoke his name. "There's been some news. I thought you should know as soon as possible."

His presence caused Olga to lower her eyes and dutifully withdraw. Anton could be an imposing figure, not because of his size or appearance but because of his abrupt manner. Both Anton and Olga played key roles in Turov's life but they remained strangers to each other, like two animals who competed for an owner's affection. If they'd had fur on their backs, it would've stood up when they crossed paths.

"The president's plane," Anton said, once they were alone.

"Yes?"

Anton waited until he saw Olga walking on the sun-dappled path back to the main house before giving him the details of what had happened in eastern Ukraine.

"It's done, then," Turov said.

"Yes."

"You've been monitoring the reaction."

"The reports tying the attack to the United States are widespread and gaining credibility," Anton said. "The Americans are responding predictably. I spoke to our man in Washington. Ketchler. I'll have a report for you in the morning."

"Very good." For Turov, the news meant that the second move in "the children's game" had been played successfully, and the third was now under way. The game still depended on a fourth move, though; but that would be up to the Kremlin. "Thank you, Anton," he said. "You are important to me. I will see you at ten o'clock, then?"

"Yes."

They shared a formal smile before Anton turned to go. And then

Turov called Olga back to his office to tell her the news, summoning the appropriate emotion in his voice.

Olga glanced several times at Putin's portrait on the wall behind his desk as Turov spoke. It was the same picture that hung on the walls of thousands of Russian offices throughout the country, in the Kremlin and in every town hall and municipal tax office: the steady blue eyes, the firm set of his mouth. She glanced, too, at the photo on his desk, of Turov and Putin, a decade earlier, sharing an intimate laugh.

Tears filled Olga's eyes, and Turov stood to hold her, feeling the warmth of her face against his neck, the gentle heaving of her chest. He thought of his old friend, the president, knowing that what had happened a thousand miles away—what Turov thought of as "The Catalyst"—would forever change the way that people thought of Putin. Turov had first met Vladimir Vladimirovitch when they were students together at Leningrad University. He knew him to be a prin-icipled and moral man who understood the unique responsibilities of the "Russian soul," as the political philosopher Ivan Ilyin had called it. The real purpose of Turov's operation—despite the elaborate fiction he had told Ivan Delkoff—was to win for Putin the respect that the West had denied him. The West's propaganda machine found malicious intent in nearly everything Putin did. Every action, however benign— the simple act of going to church, as Volodya had done on Sunday in Moscow—became the calculated machinations of a madman, in their view. The annexation of Crimea, rightfully seen by Russians as the reclaiming of a sacred land, the baptismal site of Saint Vladimir, who brought Christianity to Russia, was portrayed as an "illegal" land grab. The president's motives in the Middle East, which reflected a deep concern for the persecuted Christian population there, were seen as geopolitical strong-arming.

The Western media refused to even acknowledge the great reforms the president had brought to Russia or the remaking and reawakening of Moscow he had helped orchestrate. They had deni-grated the spectacular Sochi Olympics before the Games even began and spread false rumors in 2016 about state-sponsored blood-doping in an effort to destroy Russia's athletics programs. To many in the West, the president was unstable, a militaristic dictator, a twenty-first-century Stalin, whose ambition was to reconstitute the Soviet Union at any cost. This was the dirty game the West—and its arrogant leader, the so-called "United" States—played, against anyone who threatened them.

"We'll be okay," he said, as Olga dabbed the tears from her face. She was looking out at the green meadow. Turov looked, too. Until ten days ago, his twin grandchildren had raced through the wild grasses here each evening, playing a made-up game, a hybrid of hide-and-seek and tag. Turov missed them enormously now.

"Was it the Americans?" Olga asked, her wet brown eyes flashing anger.

"Yes. We think so," Turov said. "But, of course, it's going to be hard to prove."

Olga crossed herself privately. "The West has removed God from their culture," she said. "And this is the result."

"Yes, that is true. You have said that for many months." Turov sighed, anxious to log on to his computer to observe the reaction himself. "I'll see you later this evening, then. Let me finish my work now."

Breeze rustled the oak leaves as she walked away, carrying a subtle perfume of wild strawberries through the screen. It was ironic: Turov's assignments for the Kremlin often involved uncovering information about other people's weaknesses. *Kompromat.* But since meeting Olga, he had come to see weakness in a different light than the Kremlin did. Weaknesses were what made people such as Olga appealing.

Turov had moved here full-time in the spring, after hiring Delkoff, so that he could monitor the operation from a safe distance. His younger daughter Svetlana jokingly called this room his "space capsule," because of the row of computer monitors on his work table, which seemed to her incongruous with the country setting. On her last night here, before leaving for Switzerland, Svetlana had looked at

Turov like a little girl and asked, in her needy voice, "Do we *really* have to go away *again?* Aren't you coming with us?"

"I *am* coming," he said. "Of course, I am. But I have meetings first."

Svetlana, watching him with her stark, still-innocent eyes, had suddenly broken into a sob, as if the unknown were too much for her to bear. At times like that, he sensed, she just wanted to be hugged by her father. Svetlana's fear of abandonment had grown worse over the past three years, particularly since her older sister Sonya had moved away. What a strange, clinging companion memory was. The set of Svetlana's mouth retained traces of her childhood pucker, a look that most little girls lost as they became teenagers. It still reminded Turov of a particular moment: an afternoon in the country, high summer, cottonwood seeds swimming in the air, when as a still-young man Turov had looked into his infant daughter's eyes and they'd had a stare-off, Turov with an adult's sense of wonder, recognizing that this little creature possessed her own consciousness, that she would grow into a woman with political opinions, prejudices, and a sense of morality. And he'd felt a great responsibility at that moment to keep her from the world's corruptions. It was a responsibility he still felt today. Svetlana did not remember that, of course. The memory was only his.

Both of Turov's daughters had been enticed by the West's empty promises, for no other reason than that they were young and controlled by their passions, by adrenaline and pheromones. But Svetlana had come back to him and Sonya had left. Putin was right, of course: American culture *was* poisoning the world with its *poshlost,* its action movie values and immoral youth culture. The decadence of Moscow was very much an imported Western decadence, shamelessly preying on human vulnerability. Svetlana's older sister had been spoiled by it, embarrassing him as a teenager before going off to live in England with her mother, whose life had ended tragically. Svetlana had been spoiled, too, but not permanently. She'd become pregnant, out of wedlock, but she'd been responsible enough to acknowledge her mistakes and come back to her father. And he had taken care of her, and the twins, as he always would.

Alone now, Turov allowed himself to savor a private glow of victory, watching the sky darkening through the trees. He took half an hour to monitor the reaction online, seeing that Anton was right: the news was all good, better even than he'd expected.

He sipped a glass of Russian red wine, as he did each evening before closing his office; and he felt even better, preparing for the pleasant walk back by the lake to the main house, where Olga would come to visit him later.

But as he shut down his computers, Turov was startled to see a figure walking along the trail through the mist, moving like a figment from a ghost story. The man's small, sturdy stature made him think for a moment that it was Putin himself, or his ghost, coming here for a reckoning. Then he realized that it was only Anton, returning for another unscheduled meeting.

Anton waited silently outside as Turov finished shutting down and locking up his office. Then they walked together toward the lake through the night shadows.

"There's been a problem, boss," Anton said. "A problem at the checkpoints. Everything did not go to plan."

"A problem with the Ukrainians, you mean?"

"No. The Ukrainians were fine. Everything with the Ukrainians went smoothly. The problem was the other side," Anton said. "The other team missed the checkpoints. The men are unaccounted for."

"Zelenko?"

"Unaccounted for."

Andrei Turov stopped walking. *How was this even possible?* They'd spent weeks training Zelenko and Pletner, and hired backup security at the checkpoints as insurance. He studied Anton's whiskered face, and looked past him, to the dark houses, the familiar wooden roofs, the moon seemingly perched in the pine branches.

"Delkoff?"

"Unaccounted for. I have men on the way there now. I assure you we'll get him."

Turov had no doubt about that; but would they get him in time?

So, Turov thought, *my instinct about Delkoff was correct after all.* Although he hadn't expected such an elaborate betrayal. Turov had taken a chance with Ivan Delkoff, a man he didn't really know, despite their extensive vetting. Delkoff had connections in the murky Donbas. He knew the officers and soldiers who could be bought and sold and trusted not to talk. He had the skills to mobilize a small group of men to take Russia's war to a "new front." But Delkoff was also primitive, hungry, and impulsive. Who knew what he'd do if allowed to survive?

"We need to stop him, Anton, wherever he is."

"I know. Apparently, there was a fire at the launch site. One or two men were killed there. He may already be dead. I'm waiting on details." He said this as if it were somehow reassuring. But it only made Andrei Turov more concerned.

"Wake me with news, Anton," he said, trying to remain calm. "Wake me any time of the night. We need to put everything we can into this."

"We will. We are."

But Anton did not return to him with any more news. And Turov endured a long, very difficult night, listening to the tree frogs and the wind scraping branches on the side of the house. At daybreak, Olga's goodbye was tender but weighted down by his own uncertainty.

And, then, later that morning, Anton made another unscheduled visit to Turov's office. It was not to deliver the news Turov hoped to hear. It was again something unexpected: Andrei Turov was being summoned by the Kremlin, for a meeting at noon on Tuesday.

FOURTEEN

Capitol Hill, Washington.

When Anna Carpenter returned to her office at the Hart Senate building, she found five printouts spread across her desk. Ming Hsu, her chief of staff, was good at keeping Anna apprised of whatever was trending in official Washington. The reports from the Russian media sites were now trumpeting a new allegation: not only had a "secret CIA committee" met to discuss a possible strike on Russia, but they had devised a plan that would leave "no US fingerprints," according to "sources."

"Where did this start?" Anna asked.

"The German newspaper *SZ* had it just as you were going in to the meeting," Ming said, looking on with her knowing eyes. "It's gone whirly in the last hour. It's just starting to get into the mainstream media. The *Post* has it with a breaking news banner."

She pushed one of the stories closer, from USAToday.com. Anna read: "In the weeks before today's attack on the Russian president's plane, US intelligence and military officials met secretly to discuss plans for a 'preemptive' strike against Russia, according to a German newspaper report. The talks included high-level negotiations between US military intelligence officials and an anti-Putin Ukrainian oligarch named Dmitro Hordiyenko, a supporter of right-wing paramilitary forces, according to unnamed sources."

"Geez," Anna said. "This can't be happening."

"I know," Ming said. "But it is. People are repeating it. They're saying you can't make this stuff up."

Yes you can, Anna thought. *Of course you can.* She turned her eyes to the atrium. *This is coming too fast. Way too fast.* Even assuming none of it was true, it would take a major PR counteroffensive to refute these claims. "Can you get Harland Strickland on the phone?"

Her mind kept flashing to Harland's visit to her office the day before, and their brief conversation. But Harland was not available. Anna sat at her desk and tried several other colleagues without success. Even her son was suddenly out of reach. She tried Christopher again, feeling the same uneasiness she had coming off the plane on Wednesday evening. But his phone went to voice mail.

"Turn on CNN!" Ming shouted from the outer office. Something new was coming across—a video clip posted to YouTube showing the moment of impact: the missile's trail of smoke, the Russian president's plane exploding, the image freezing just as the debris began to rain down.

Anna watched the footage loop, spellbound and horrified, reminded of the 9/11 video of the airliners crashing into the World Trade Center towers; that, too, had played repeatedly on cable news before the networks finally realized it was in bad taste to keep showing it.

She took an elevator to the ground floor and slipped out of the building onto Constitution Avenue. She wanted to breathe some real air for a few minutes, to get out among the trees and people and clear her head. Others seemed to be doing the same. A lot of them. She walked toward the National Mall, thinking of times she'd come out here to marvel at the man-made grandeur, the symmetry of the monuments and neoclassical buildings, the remarkable stories they told about her country.

She stood on a corner and looked through the trees at the Capitol dome, remembering that she was two blocks from what had most likely been the fourth target of the September 11 attacks. She thought about her father and the "divided nature" he used to tell her we all carry around in us—a capacity for greatness and a capacity for destruction. Anna wondered, as everyone had back in September of 2001, what else was coming.

When Christopher finally called, it surprised her how relieved she was just to hear his voice. "Where are you?"

"GW Parkway. I'm headed back over to see Martin," he said. "I wonder if you could join me. I'm taking an idea in to him. Can you get away?"

"If you want me, sure. I just sat in on an NSC meeting," she said. "What's going on?"

"I'm not entirely certain. But I think things are only going to get worse."

"Yes, I'm sure they are," Anna said. "This is coming too quickly."

She listened to the outline of his idea, impressed that he'd already fit so much together. There was an edge of certainty in Chris's voice, and an urgency. Anna understood that. She didn't know exactly what had happened. But she knew enough to know that her country was under attack. "Thoughts?" Christopher finished.

"My thought is that they may actually be giving us an opportunity," Anna said. "I'd like to be involved if I can."

"Good. I was hoping you'd say that," Christopher said. "See you there."

FIFTEEN

Western Virginia.

Jake Briggs had been running hills that afternoon. Briggs was between jobs, trying to enjoy some quality downtime with his wife and children. But he was starting to "grow rust," as an old CO used to call it, feeling a restlessness in everything he did. He'd woken that morning knowing that he had too much time on his hands, and his thoughts kept getting stuck in the same places—regrets, anger, guilt, all the negative garbage that comes with not having a driving purpose to your day.

He'd finally gone out running, knowing that if he pushed himself hard enough, or long enough, he might be able to sweat away some of those thoughts. For a while, running intervals in the foothills, pumped up on Metallica and AC/DC, it had worked. And now, earbuds out, soaking with sweat in the warm, insect-filled air, Briggs felt revived.

There was a bright fog over the Blue Ridge Mountains to the west as he came through the thick brush back to their house, feeling grateful again for what he had. Jake Briggs's children were always the yank at the end of the line, wherever he went, whatever he did. Freedom was an idea with many meanings, like the national flag, but Briggs always defined it in terms of his kids, and what he was leaving for them. No one should be denied the security to raise a family safely, but in many countries, particularly in the Middle East, where Briggs had spent three years of his career, that security didn't always exist. It was something that bothered him every day.

He walked in the house dripping sweat. Grabbed a bottle of water from the kitchen, and a towel from the linen closet. He passed the kids watching a video in the living room and stood in the doorway to his wife's office, sponging his face with the towel. Today was payroll, Donna's busiest day. But the TV was on in her office. Which was strange: Donna never watched television during the day.

She didn't greet him. Didn't say anything. Then he saw why.

"What the fuck—?"

Briggs moved closer, seeing the footage of the Russian president's plane exploding midair. The Fox Breaking News banner across the bottom of the screen ran: *PUTIN DEAD.*

Donna muted the sound and spoke low, so the kids wouldn't hear. "They were just saying it's ninety-nine percent certain that he was on board."

"Jesus, what happened?"

"Terrorism, I guess. They don't know yet." She handed him his phone. Briggs took it, keeping his eyes on the TV. When he finally looked down, he saw a missed call notification, and a name from his past: Christopher Niles. Briggs knew immediately that the events had to be related; Chris was calling because of the attack on Russia's president. He had to be.

Briggs walked down the hall to his own office and returned the call, but got Niles's voice mail. He began to click through television channels. Watching as the commentators struggled to explain what had no explanation yet.

When he stopped sweating, Briggs took a quick shower. Then he went into the living room to be with his kids Jamie and Jessie. Wanting to feel normal again for a few minutes, he tried watching the video with them—some animated caveman movie called *The Croods.* But Briggs couldn't sit still. He went back outside, walking down the gravel drive to the main road, checking news updates on his phone.

Briggs was a retired officer with the Navy's Special Warfare Development Group—known as SEAL Team Six—who now operated a small military contracting business from his home in rural western Virginia. Years earlier, he had run night rescue missions in Afghanistan and Pakistan and helped train his military counterparts in both countries. During his seven-year stint as a SEAL, Briggs had occasionally displayed an independence and defensiveness that had gotten him in trouble. "His idle is set too high," one commanding officer had written. The word among his superiors became that Briggs had issues with authority, which had been particularly evident during a joint ops with the CIA in Estonia, a job he probably shouldn't have taken.

Pushed out of the SEALS a few months later, Briggs returned to Virginia to start his life over. It had been a rough transition. He'd failed in his first contracting venture and went through several months of depression, beating himself up over it. After another false start, Briggs had lowered his expectations and managed to build a small security business from scratch. He now recruited former SEALS and men from its army counterpart, Delta Force, along with other ex-military. He'd even managed to sell his services back to the government a few times, although most of his work these days was far more mundane than hostage rescues. His biggest contract now was providing onboard security for container ships off the coast of Somalia.

Briggs had met Christopher Niles five years ago on a special op to force Russian-sponsored aggressors out of Estonia, a mission that was never publicized. Niles, the CIA liaison for the SEAL team, was the most focused man Briggs had ever known in the IC, and also among the smartest. Although, to Briggs, that wasn't saying a lot. Chris Niles had a disciplined, inborne intelligence, a way of cutting through the bullshit, the hypocrisy and bureaucracy. He also knew, as Briggs did, that some rules needed to be broken. And that sometimes it was okay to forget the finer gradations and see a problem in its most basic terms. Terrorism was his favorite example. Briggs had gotten close enough, often enough, to know that terrorists, while technically human beings, were a more primitive species; that their chemical makeup contained the instincts of a barbaric medievalism; and that if those instincts were allowed to survive and flourish, they had the capacity to destroy civilization. Not by ingenuity or force of numbers or any of that, just by sheer dumb tenacity; if they were able to get control of a nuclear weapon, which wasn't as far-fetched as people thought, then they could win. Terrorism was in a fight with civilization, a war it shouldn't by rights even be allowed to enter. But Washington didn't understand that; it didn't know how to defend itself effectively.

The assassination in Ukraine was clearly terrorism, although Briggs couldn't say yet what kind. He knew a little about the Russian president; knew that he'd stolen the equivalent of millions of dollars while in St. Petersburg in the 1990s and gotten away with it; that he'd later steered much more than that—billions—into personal accounts while serving as Russia's president (and earning an annual salary of about $187,000). But in a culture that rewarded corruption, Briggs didn't especially fault him for that. He was more bothered by the people who'd died because of his oppressive policies, and in the wars that Russia had fought since 1999, some known by the public, some not.

"What's going on?"

Jake's son Jamie was in the doorway. He'd wandered away from *The Croods,* sensing something was up. Briggs felt an impulse to shield his son. Then he thought better of it. Instead, Briggs punched up the sound. "It's the president of Russia," he said. Jamie stared, shuffling into the room, his light brown eyes wide, his hair mussed from lying against the sofa pillows. "That was his plane. They blew it up."

"Is he dead?"

"Not officially. But, yeah. He's dead."

His boy stared at the screen. It hurt Briggs, seeing him like that, as the cable channel replayed the explosion over and over and over.

He thought of something Donna had said, when they'd first started dating, back when she still talked about such things: *When we truly love someone, we give them the power to break our hearts.* "Who killed him?" Jamie asked.

"Terrorists."

"Why?"

"We don't know. They didn't want him alive any longer, I guess. Come here," he said. Briggs grabbed his son and swung him onto his knee, lowering the volume again. He watched his son's face as he stared at the television, Jamie's eyes riveted by the replay. Briggs realized: Jamie would remember this afternoon for the rest of his life. He'd remember sitting on his old man's knee on the day that Vladimir Putin was blown out of the skies over Ukraine. He'd remember the moment. *This moment.* Right now. Long after Briggs was gone, his son would think back to this warm summer afternoon in Virginia. He would tell people about it. *This moment. Right now.*

"Why didn't they want him to live?"

"There's no good way to explain it, Jamie," Briggs said. "Except some people think he's a bad man. And I guess they thought he'd become too powerful."

"So they killed him?"

"That's what it looks like."

"Who are they?" he asked. "The tear-iss?"

"We don't know who they are," Briggs said, his eyes suddenly tearing up with emotion. Briggs had seen men blown up in battle several times; he'd exchanged last looks with dying soldiers. Those things never went away. But the look on Jamie's face right now went deeper because it was his own flesh and blood.

In fact, Briggs had been wondering the same thing as Jamie: Who *were* these terrorists? Ukrainian rebels? Chechen extremists? It could even be the right wing within Russia, the generals. Or an organized crime group working a contract; or one of Putin's enemies who'd somehow managed to get a bomb inside the plane. In a country where nearly half of the economy was based on corruption, anything was possible and the truth was hard to know. It was like having *The Godfather* as a national model.

"He doesn't need to see that," Donna snapped, her voice startling them both. Their heads turned simultaneously to the doorway. Jake muted the sound.

"He's all right," he said lamely.

"Jacob!"

Briggs turned it off to make peace. Jamie pouted for a while, storming around the way he did, thrusting his arms out, until Briggs escorted him back to the living room and Jessie and the movie. But none of that interested Jamie anymore, and he kept looking up at his dad as if trying to glean information from his eyes.

Briggs wondered if Donna would've let Jamie watch the planes going into the Trade Towers in 2001. *He* would have; of course he would. Kids should know what evil looks like. Why not? It was one of his country's character flaws, he thought, although Donna disagreed. Briggs had never been big on the idea of sheltering kids. Or the everyone-gets-a-trophy mentality. What passed for fairness and equality these days was eroding America's best qualities, Briggs thought, basic stuff like individualism and the pursuit of excellence. The whole concept of guaranteed "equality" made him nauseous, although Donna didn't agree with that, either.

Briggs took the return call from Christopher Niles on the deck, picturing his old colleague: tall, intense, with silver-blue eyes, dark blond hair, an athlete's build. It struck him as funny—hard to imagine, really—that this former intel officer was a university teacher now, standing in front of spoiled rich kids in a D.C. classroom talking about Russia.

"You've seen the news," Chris said.

"Watching it now. What's up?"

The sun was low over the trees, a jagged line in the mist. Soft breezes blew across the yard. It felt like a storm coming. "I need your help," Christopher said. "It has to do with Ivan Delkoff." The name sent a jolt through Briggs. Chris didn't repeat it, or offer a lot by way of explanation. But he didn't have to. The name was enough. "Can you meet me in the morning?"

"Yeah. Of course," Jake said. His thoughts had already shifted away from this Virginia countryside to a street in Estonia, and to Delkoff, a huge man, cursed with perhaps the most serious-looking face Briggs had ever seen: long, nearly lipless, with a shaved pate, large nose, and small concentrated eyes. At first, for a few seconds anyway, Delkoff's size had unnerved him. But they'd ended friendly, even though working for different sides, spending more than an hour together at a restaurant in Narva drinking Estonian beers. Delkoff knew no English, Briggs little Russian or Estonian, but they'd talked in French, Delkoff bragging on his son. He had big hopes for his boy, who was going to become an intelligence officer one day, he said.

Briggs walked back inside the house and told his wife that Christopher Niles had just offered him a job. Her arms remained crossed. "What'd you tell him?"

"He wants to meet me tomorrow. I told him I'd be there." *In a heartbeat.* He didn't say that. He didn't say that he was going to get to work right away, either, digging into his old files on Ivan Delkoff before catching three or four hours' sleep.

They stared at the silent TV together, the loop of the explosion still playing behind the pundits' commentary. "Is it about that?" she said.

"I don't know." Christopher hadn't said. Not technically. When she looked at him again, he searched for something in his wife's eyes that resembled approval. He didn't find it. But this was his family, so that was all right.

"I guess I'll find out tomorrow," he said.

SIXTEEN

CIA headquarters. Langley, Virginia.

Martin Lindgren looked up at Christopher from behind his desk, his eyes flat, his graceful features drained of their vitality. The concerns that had caused Martin to travel all the way to the Cyclades Islands to find him made a lot more sense now.

"You understand this," Martin said.

"Some of it."

"Have a seat."

The two men eyed each other as Christopher settled. In retrospect, there'd been at least two warning signs that he should've picked up on. But what most concerned Chris now, if his assumptions were correct, was that Turov's operation had an enormous—maybe insurmountable—head start, and the intelligence community probably wasn't even aware of it. He wondered if he'd be able to sell Martin on his idea, and how tightly the White House was going to keep its reins on this.

"Anna's coming to join us, by the way."

"Good." Martin's face momentarily brightened, as he had expected. Martin appreciated the depth of Anna's experience and know-how. Plus, he liked her personally.

"How were your briefings?" Chris began. Martin's mouth twisted and he shrugged. "You talked about how unlikely this was, I imagine.

You talked about all the ways it was wrong." Martin nodded slightly. "Wrong that the Russian president's plane didn't have working missile defenses. Wrong that it was flying over a corner of Ukrainian air space. Wrong that a president obsessed with being in control would have allowed his plane to become that vulnerable."

"Okay," Martin Lindgren said. "And that's significant because—?"

"It's significant because it means Putin wasn't on board that plane," Christopher said. "He couldn't have been."

Chris's old boss looked at him steadily, as if it were taking a while for his words to cross the room. "Except," Martin said, "all of the reports we're getting say he was. There's footage of him arriving on the tarmac. We have good Russian sources saying he was on board." Their eyes turned simultaneously to the TV across the room, then back to their conversation.

"Which might end up being the best evidence we'll get that the president was complicit in this," Christopher said.

"You don't actually know that. You're speculating."

"I'm speculating." He took a breath, willing himself to sound less certain. Of *course* he was speculating, but he was angry, because the reports implicating the United States *were* coming too quickly, as Anna said. And the US's initial response felt weak, and wrong, as if there were some internal roadblocks he didn't yet understand. "But I know Andrei Turov. I probably should have suspected this as soon as we had Delkoff's name. I blame myself for that."

"What are you talking about?" Lindgren frowned, the vertical crease lines emerging between his heavy eyebrows. "How could we have known?"

"Delkoff was a Russian GRU commander in the Ukrainian war for the past four years," Christopher said. "He was responsible for shooting down dozens of Ukrainian military transport planes and helicopters. He may have even been involved in blowing up the Malaysia airliner in 2014. MH17. Maybe that's what got Turov's attention."

Martin shut his eyes for a second, revealing his reptilian eyelids.

"My guess," Chris said, "is that they're going to float this idea that Putin's dead for another few hours at least, as the general chaos of the story unfolds. Let it generate some international sympathy and outrage. Sometime tomorrow, then, the Kremlin will announce that the president's alive. They'll say they plan to vigorously track down whoever did this. Even if they have to chase them into the toilet," he added.

Martin allowed a small smile, acknowledging Christopher's reference to Putin's famous warning after the Moscow apartment bombings in 1999. "And then—?"

"By then, the story of US involvement will have gone viral, as it's already starting to do. Worst-case: We're talking protests worldwide, flag burnings. Diplomatic freeze-outs. Talk of Russian retaliation."

Martin winced in that strange way he had, opening his mouth as if he'd crunched on a piece of sour fruit. "The Russian president wouldn't have been involved in something like *that*," he said.

"No. I don't think he was," Chris said. "I think this is what Turov calls a parallel game. He advances the Kremlin's agenda by doing things the Kremlin can't do itself, for obvious reasons. My theory is, Turov took this plan to the president. The president listened. He *wasn't* involved. Except he allowed it to happen."

"By not boarding that plane."

"That's what I think. Maybe they'll say his security services intercepted a last-minute warning that the US, or Ukraine, was planning an attack. Or some emergency caused Putin to miss the flight. I don't know. Obviously, it will be difficult to prove. They've got plausible deniability. And in the meantime, we get blamed, our credibility takes a huge hit. Russia wants us to be perceived as what they actually *are:* a country not constrained at its highest levels by the law or by a sense of morality."

"Someone else had to be involved, though," Martin said. "The pilot or air traffic control, someone who would have put the flight on that route."

"That's what we'll need to find out."

The desk phone buzzed, interrupting them. Anna Carpenter had arrived.

Martin Lindgren stood to greet Anna, putting on his charming face, kissing both cheeks and holding her hands before sitting down again.

"The victims of the crash included a Chinese human rights advocate, I just heard," Anna told them. "And an interior minister who'd been quietly critical of the president for some time."

"Convenient," Chris said.

Martin reached for his tea, his eyes staying with Anna. "What else do we have?"

"I just sat in on an NSC meeting," she said. "There's clearly a division within the administration over how to respond. And how we respond, needless to say, is a big part of their calculation."

Martin nodded, still watching her.

"In the plus column," Chris said, "which is a very small column at this point: I think Delkoff's involvement may give us an opening. If there's a weak link in this, it's probably him."

"Why?"

"Because of who he is. I'm going to make some assumptions here," Chris said. "Ivan Delkoff may be the only person who could have made this happen. Delkoff knows eastern Ukraine, the checkpoints, the duplicitous players, the weapons traders. He's probably dealt with this Hordiyenko and knows the anti-Putin forces there. Supposedly, he's even become sympathetic to some of them lately, turning against the president."

"But then Delkoff wouldn't have become involved unless he really thought he was killing the president," Anna said.

"Exactly," Chris said. "Which is why Turov would have made sure Delkoff was killed, either during the operation or immediately after. That's my second assumption."

"How many assumptions are you making?" Martin asked.

"Four."

"Okay."

"Third assumption: Delkoff's going to anticipate that and plan an escape. He's resourceful, stubborn, and egotistical. He's going to think that he can outplay Turov and the Kremlin's intelligence services. Which maybe he can, for a while. But—assuming he's still alive—he's going to find out soon that Turov has used him and double-crossed him. And he's probably going to want some sort of revenge.

"That's my fourth assumption. And that's where we may be able to capitalize on a weakness in Delkoff: his fanatic brand of patriotism."

"Go on."

"Delkoff once told a Russian journalist that he admired Gavrilo Princip, the Bosnian Serb whose assassination of Franz Ferdinand in 1914 set off World War I. He wants to be known for playing a role in Russian history. He doesn't want to be a footnote. And I think that will work to our advantage. Either way—whether he's alive or dead—I suspect Delkoff may leave behind evidence implicating Turov. And—if we're lucky—the Kremlin."

Lindgren sighed through his nose, not quite with him. "I should tell you," he said, glancing at Anna, who was attentively taking in their conversation, "I sat with the president and the national security adviser for a few minutes this afternoon, and they've already got good intel on this. And their explanation isn't what *you're* telling me. Not at all."

Chris raised his eyebrows, pretending to show concern. *Good,* he thought.

"They have intelligence tying this back to a missile commander from the Ukrainian security services," Martin said. "A man named Kolchak. But they think the order probably came from the Russian military. There are reports that at least two of the men involved have already been killed and ID'd at a checkpoint in Ukraine."

"Okay."

"I brought up Turov's name and the response was underwhelming," Martin added. "The Russian Ops Desk doesn't believe it. The national security adviser doesn't think he's involved. There are even some stories, evidently, that Turov is gravely ill or dead."

Chris frowned so that he wouldn't smile. "Turov's not dead. But it doesn't surprise me he'd put that story out. They never took Turov seriously enough, as you know. The White House seems to be playing this exactly as he wants."

"And so—what are you suggesting?"

Chris took a long breath, and thought of downtown Moscow: the lights and traffic along Tverskaya Street, the ripe scent of the Moskva River, the spicy-doughy aromas from the Georgian restaurant near his old office. "Does your offer still stand?"

"I don't know. Did I make one?"

"In Greece you said, quote, I'm not talking about a team of four or five *at this point,*" Chris said. "I took that to mean an offer might be coming at some future point."

"To do—?"

"I want to go over and track down Turov," he said. "And have someone else go after Delkoff. Either to find him or, if he's not alive, to find what he left behind."

"Okay," Martin said, tentatively. "And what will you do if you find Turov?"

Chris said nothing at first. He was still working through the details. "I think I can get Turov to talk with me," he said. "Maybe to deal. Turov's an extraordinary strategist, as we know. An extraordinary man, in some ways. But it's the ordinary parts of him that interest me."

"Go on."

"His operation has been a success so far," Chris said. "But he's going to have to share that success with the president. And eventually that will become a problem, given their personalities. I can maybe hasten the process along." He glanced at Anna, knowing that Martin still wasn't with him. "Maybe I'm wrong," he continued. "Maybe I won't be able to get anything. But even if I don't, we're only talking about a two-man op. And this is what your division does. Right?"

Martin smiled mysteriously, glancing at Anna again. "And here I thought you wanted nothing more to do with Turov," he said. "I thought you wanted to put him behind you."

"I did. Then the plane happened. I see what this is now."

Martin's assent was all in his eyes. Chris wasn't ready to lay out all the specifics of what he was thinking. He wasn't ready to tell him about what he considered his "secret weapon" in Moscow. But he knew Martin wasn't expecting that. Instead, he explained his idea in general terms. Martin listened, pretending to be slightly more skeptical than he was. And when he finished, he could see that Martin would go for it—some permutation of it, anyway—as long as he kept it small, and it didn't interfere with what the White House was doing. "I already have someone to help with Delkoff," he said.

"'Someone'?"

"Jake Briggs." Martin showed his sour-fruit grimace. "I know. But the thing is, Briggs has a bead on Ivan Delkoff. I just spoke with him. He worked with him before, an operation in Estonia five years ago. Believe me, the HUMINT on Delkoff will be worth more than anything we're going to get out of Fort Meade."

Briggs is also a wilder breed of soldier, unpredictable and a little crazy, and we may need that to get to Delkoff, Chris thought.

"Just you two."

"There's weakness in numbers," Chris said. "Right?"

Martin allowed a brief smile. "And what would you need?"

"Transportation, cover, a weapon for Briggs. A G-5 to bring us home would be nice. That's all. Five, six days tops. Frankly, I don't think we'll have the luxury to go that long. You see what's happened in just the past four hours."

"You want to run it black, independent of the IC," Martin said.

"I think we'd have to." It was what Martin wanted, too, of course; it was what AS Division did. Alternate Scenarios. But Martin was playing this a little coy, seeing how revved up Chris was.

"So," he said, "you're suggesting we do an end run around the entire intelligence community?"

"Someone has to," Chris said. Martin broke into a rare full smile. "Give me six days. If I'm wrong, you don't lose much. If we wait until the administration figures this out and builds consensus, it may be too late."

"And what does Anna do?" It was clear to Chris that he wanted Anna involved. They'd worked together once before, he knew, during her years at the State Department, although Anna had never really talked about it. Chris averted his eyes now, letting her tell him.

"We were talking in Greece, after you left," she said, "about Russia waging a non-linear, non-military war. A war of perception."

"The Gerasimov Doctrine," Martin said.

"Yes." They shared a quick, knowing look. The Gerasimov Doctrine was Russia's vision of twenty-first-century warfare, a form of combat that relied primarily on the tools of emerging technologies rather than traditional military weapons. "That war's already started, I think," Anna said. "They've just created the narrative for it. We need to create a better one. I've got a few ideas how to do that."

Martin gave Anna a long look, as if this were a conversation to be continued later. Despite his somewhat jaded demeanor, Martin Lindgren was an optimist, who believed what Anna did: that the US was fundamentally a good nation, with deep reserves of decency, but sometimes, because of that decency, it was a country that didn't anticipate evil very well. It didn't foresee the extent of dishonesty and deceit driving its enemies or know how best to respond. Its dishonesty was less sophisticated than Russia's. "When do you start?" he said.

"Now," Anna said.

Chris nodded. "Russia's going to shut down to Americans very quickly, I suspect. I'd like to fly over tomorrow. That would get me there on the afternoon of the fifteenth."

"And what if we're already ahead of you?" Lindgren's blue eyes seemed to momentarily sparkle.

"I don't know. Are you?"

Now it was Martin's turn to surprise. "You're going to Moscow to research a story," he said. "You're a college instructor researching a piece you're writing for an online think tank. About the changing role of the Russian Orthodox Church. We've lined up two interviews in Moscow. A historian at the Carnegie Moscow Center and an Orthodox priest. Beyond that, you'll be on your own."

Christopher said nothing at first. They had already prepared a cover for him, not expecting it would be needed so soon. Knowing the Orthodox church was a subject that interested him. "They're not going to buy that, of course," he said.

"Probably not. But we can't have you going over as a CIA contractor, can we?"

Martin shared a smile with Anna.

"And what made you think I'd be doing this?" Christopher said.

"Hope springs eternal."

"I guess it does."

So. It wasn't only Russia that was good at deception, Chris thought.

Anna and Christopher walked across the parking lot to their cars without speaking. The warmth and humidity had seeped from the air in the last hour of daylight; the leaves seemed to synchronize in a long, slow rustle. When they reached her car, Anna turned and touched his face tenderly. Christopher looked toward the city, and he recognized the act of faith they were all sharing by doing this: they were rejecting almost categorically the possibility that the United States *had* been involved in an assassination attempt on the president of Russia.

"Race you home," he said.

SEVENTEEN

The Weekly American offices. Foggy Bottom, Washington.

I guess I'd like to know more about your mystery source," Roger Yorke said to Jon Niles. The longtime editor sat on a corner of his desk with his long legs crossed and patted absently at his mop of gray hair. "We all would," he added.

"Right," Jon said, feeling three sets of eyes on him: those of Roger and staff writers Elizabeth Foster and KC Walls. KC was the magazine's new political reporter, a talented, ambitious twenty-seven-year-old with unruly red hair and freckles, who had ninety-seven thousand Twitter followers and appeared occasionally as a guest commentator on MSNBC. Jon sensed that she was angling for a way in to the Russia story, even though it wasn't her turf.

"Last night, you told me about this 'no fingerprints' business," Roger said. "Now the same words are all over the Internet, and our country's credibility is being challenged."

"I know."

"That's kind of, like, a big deal, isn't it?" Elizabeth said, her eyes shifting from Jon to Roger. Jon felt an inexplicable clutch in his chest. Liz had been his girlfriend for two years, and she still got to him: just that habitual widening of her eyes, the way her voice quivered slightly on *isn't it?* "It's almost starting to remind me of Iran–Contra," she added, looking to Jon for a nod of approval.

"From what KC was just telling me," Roger said, ignoring Liz's comment, "someone at the NSC level is confirming what your source said—that there *was* a discussion of preemptive action, which would leave no US fingerprints, quote unquote. We need to find who that was."

Jon sighed. KC, he suspected, was fudging a little.

"Actually, I probably shouldn't say this," KC said, scooting forward, her eyes staying with Roger. "Because it was said in confidence. But, for the sake of the story: I heard that the *Post* may also have an anonymous source on it. A woman. So it's possible the same source has been calling multiple media outlets."

"A telephone source?" Jon said.

"I think so," she said. Speaking to Roger.

"And maybe they're having the same conversation we're having?" Liz added, irrelevantly.

"Can you find out any more on that, then?" Roger said, his eyes gesturing to KC. "If you're comfortable with it."

"Sure."

Jon huffed, almost involuntarily. Roger, he suspected, had invited KC to this meeting as a way of kicking his ass a little, shaking off some of his cynicism about journalism. Occasionally, these *Weekly American* staff meetings felt almost like interventions. But he didn't need that today. After his conversation with 9:15, Jon was fully engaged.

"It's interesting," Roger said, looking distractedly out the picture window. "The academics talk about Russia as a country in search of an idea. But I think they have one. Two, really, which go hand in hand. The first is to position themselves as a moral leader for the rest of the world, an alternative to what they call the decadence of the West. Us. And the second is to create a Eurasian alliance that diminishes the importance of *our* alliances. That's what's behind BRICS and the Shanghai Cooperation Organization, which they see as alternatives to

NATO and the IMF. And now they're talking about creating a new international apparatus to fight terrorism, which would bypass military blocs such as NATO."

"But—so what else are you hearing about the preemptive strike thing?" KC asked, scooting forward. Roger's tangents made KC uneasy.

"What I'm hearing," he said, "is that preemptive action was *discussed,* as Jon said, but probably not as a real option." He glanced at Jon. "Although what really concerns me right now is something else; it's the story the administration is starting to tell internally, that the attack was a coup. That it was the Russian military that shot down the president's plane."

KC frowned.

"What concerns you about it?" Liz said.

"What concerns me is that no one seems to know exactly where it's coming from. There's a feeling I'm getting—from a good source now—that it may be based on very weak intelligence," he said. "Or worse."

"Oh," KC said, getting it.

"In other words, some senior officials are worried that we may be about to push a story forward just to slow down Russia's story about us," Roger said. "Generally, fighting disinformation with disinformation is not a good idea. Especially on this scale." He peered at his bookshelf, which was stuffed with history and philosophy texts. "The concern is, if we rush out a story that doesn't hold, then we look like we're covering something up."

"Which would only strengthen the Russian version," Jon said, noticing how KC's eyes widened at the words "covering something up."

"It's not possible we *are* covering something up, is it?" Liz asked.

"Well. I would hope not." Roger gave her what Jon thought of as his paternal look. "There *is* a group within the administration, of course—and Jon has written about this—that's been saying Russia is an underrated threat. And there's also been the suggestion, online, that this might have been carried out by some sort of star-chamber group within the administration, independent of the White House." Jon saw Liz mouth the word *Wow*. "But I would place that in the category of unfounded conspiracy theories at this point."

KC watched Roger Yorke attentively. But Roger's thoughts had moved on. "It's funny, I've always thought Russia's need for autocratic control was a result of its unwieldy size," he said, glancing out the window again. "It gives them a perpetual inferiority complex. Eleven time zones, two hundred nationalities. Eleven percent of the world's landmass."

"But a population less than half the size of ours," Jon offered.

"Yes." Roger let his eyes rest on Jon's for a moment. "And so: let's go at this full throttle and see what happens." He nodded to Elizabeth and KC, in turn, which was his way of thanking them but also dismissing them. "If you don't mind, I'd like to talk with Jon for a minute."

KC wasn't pleased by this. Jon could see it in the flippancy of her body language as she rose and strode stiff-legged from the room. Her mood shifts could be abrupt, and not always synced properly with her personality. Liz, following behind, turned in the doorway to trade a smile with him. Jon got up to close the door.

"I do want to keep you on this," Roger said, playing with the knot on his loosened tie. "Assuming you're interested."

"Of course I am."

Roger's face crinkled in a preparatory way, which meant he was about to reveal something candid. "Just so you know, KC's a fine reporter, on congressional politics and the environment, but this isn't her bailiwick. I know who her source is. So don't worry. This is your story. But I do think we need to shift to a higher gear now.

"It's complicated by the fact that there are competing accounts out there. Noise at the expense of comprehension, as you like to say." He fixed Jon with his most direct look, which was always a little disconcerting. "What can you tell me about your sources on these Russia meetings? You've heard it now from three people?"

"Including my 9:15 caller, yes, three and a half," Jon said. Roger nodded for him to explain. "9:15 was the first. Then Craig Kettles, the congressman, talking off the record, who told me there'd been discussion of preemptive action, although he claims he wasn't in these meetings. Then 9:15 called a second time and used the word 'strike.'" Roger nodded almost imperceptibly. "I then went to two people in the IC who confirmed the meetings happened, but wouldn't discuss details. Then one of them walked it back when I brought it up again on Tuesday."

"When you say walked it back—"

"Denied it," Jon said.

"Denied preemptive action was discussed? Or denied the meetings happened?"

"Both. Said I misunderstood his answer. Now he won't return my calls."

"Mmm." Roger nodded as if all of this were making sense to him. "Okay, so—three and a half, I see." He looked toward the Mall, his eyes receding slightly in the light. "The one who walked it back—would that be Harland Strickland, possibly?"

Jon frowned. "How—?"

"He did the same with someone else. Strickland's the main driver, I'm told, behind this coup narrative," Roger said, his eyes back with Jon.

"I need to talk with Strickland again, then."

"Yes. Good." He studied Jon. "How much help are you going to need on this?"

"Help? None," Jon said. "Let me pursue my sources for a couple days, see what I can find."

"Good." Roger Yorke seemed to like that. Jon wondered if this was the real purpose of today's meeting. "All right, then," he said, smiling faintly. "Just keep in touch."

"I will." Jon walked out of Roger's corner office fired up, ready to exorcise the Jon Niles who drank beer every night and wasted his evenings. Roger was nudging him to something better. Nudging him awake . . . *Maybe that's your story,* 9:15 had told him. *No, maybe* you're *the story,* Jon thought.

He glanced over at Liz Foster's cubicle as he passed and nodded hello. Liz gave him a double thumbs-up. "Big stakes," she said.

"Yep."

"Call me later, if you want to talk about it or anything, okay?"

"Oh? Okay." Jon hesitated for a moment, wondering what she meant by that. It was still hard to read Liz Foster sometimes. Normally, he would have stopped and tried to feel her out. But this time, he didn't. This time he kept going.

EIGHTEEN

Western Virginia.

Growing up, Jake Briggs had always been aware of the shadowy corners of American life, look-the-other-way places where illicit deals went down: the edges of parking lots, back rooms, clearings in the woods; places where drugs and weapons were sold, where trysts were carried out, fights fought; city blocks that became floating red-light districts or open-air drug markets after dark. Places every city and community had, which managed to survive by a kind of unnatural selection, staying a few steps ahead of the law.

Ivan Delkoff was like one of those places, Briggs thought. A law unto himself, inventing his own rules as he went along. A man who probably thought that by carrying out the August 13 attack, he'd been a defender of Russia. But then again, Russia itself was like one of those places.

Briggs set out driving to Dulles that morning with Ivan Delkoff in his head. He'd gone through data searches for more than four hours and reviewed his files from the mission in Estonia, where he met Delkoff. He'd learned all he could about Delkoff's past, his family, his temperament, his bad habits, his singular skills, his failures and successes.

Thinking like the enemy had become a cliché in intelligence circles.

But for the most part, it was more a theory than a practice, an idea the bureaucracy of the IC wasn't really built to sustain. Thinking like the enemy—really thinking like the enemy—meant allowing a demon into your head and letting it live there for a while. It wasn't a nine-to-five job. To really think like the enemy, you also had to feel what the enemy felt; and once you'd given those feelings a space in your psyche, it could be hard to get them out. That was the part of his work Briggs didn't like so much. Christopher Niles had that problem, too, he knew; when he worked a case, he was all in, there were no half measures. Washington didn't always respect that. But it was okay. You could love the country without having any love for the government.

Briggs would have preferred doing this op more convention-ally: going after Delkoff with a team, using a helicopter rescue unit to extract him from wherever he was hiding. But Chris had made it clear this wasn't that kind of job. The op for Briggs was simple. He needed to find Ivan Delkoff, make contact, and give him an incentive to come in. That's what Lindgren's division did: small, off-the-books operations. Drug deals, Briggs called them.

It was two and a half hours from Briggs's home in western Virginia to Dulles International Airport, where he was supposed to meet Niles and Lindgren in a conference room at ten o'clock. Donna had gotten up early to fix him a breakfast of scrambled eggs and sausage. "This really isn't much," he'd tried telling her. "I'm being hired to find some-one and talk with him, that's all." It wasn't hostage rescue. It probably wouldn't even involve weapons.

He watched the lines on the road now, the spooky early morning light rising from the fields. Missing his children already. How would this week fit in their lives; where would the events in Ukraine settle in their memories? Would he ever be able to tell Jamie what he'd done in the days after the Russian president was blown out of the sky? How he'd tried to help fix things?

The countryside brightened as he approached Dulles, and his thoughts were all with Ivan Delkoff again. Briggs had a pretty good idea now where Delkoff was: he'd already mapped the escape route he'd likely taken out of Ukraine. It was not a route that CIA or anyone else would be looking at. Not right away. Lindgren, he was pretty sure, would place Delkoff in Belarus or on the outskirts of Moscow. But those locations, Briggs knew, were too obvious.

He chugged the last of his Red Bull, seeing the airport signs, feeling energized. When Briggs was working, caffeine became one of the essential food groups.

The way to get to Delkoff—assuming he was alive—was to offer him something he wanted. And Briggs knew that he could do that. He understood Ivan Delkoff. He even saw some of himself in him, although he didn't like thinking that. Delkoff was a stoic man who had put himself on the front lines of a people's war, a *narod,* fighting for an idea rather than for land or politics. Ukraine was one battle in that war. He'd also fought in Chechnya, where he'd suffered a shrapnel wound, and in Georgia and Transnistria. And Crimea, where he helped force the referendum that enabled Russia to annex the peninsula, much to the chagrin of the West. He'd given his life to the war, and lost his only son last summer to the fighting in eastern Ukraine.

But there was something less tangible, too, about Delkoff's war. Briggs understood that human beings were by nature among the most aggressive creatures on the planet. Most people channeled those impulses into careers or sports or hobbies; some, who weren't so fortunate, fought with them all their lives, or deadened them with drugs and alcohol. Delkoff accepted his human nature head on and tried to give it a larger purpose. Briggs liked that about him. Above everything, Delkoff wanted to believe that the sacrifices he'd made for his country, including his son and family, had not been in vain. That was what Ivan Delkoff most wanted, he sensed: to play some role in Russia's destiny. And that's where Briggs could help. That's exactly what he could give him. Briggs did not even know, yet, that Christopher Niles was thinking the same thing.

NINETEEN

Washington.

The announcement came just after 7:30 a.m., 2:30 in the afternoon, Moscow time. Anna held out her phone to Chris over a plate of half-eaten scrambled eggs, hash browns, buttered toast. They were at a window booth in the Pancake House on Wisconsin Avenue, the windows fogged from air conditioning. The Breaking News banner reduced it to two words: *PUTIN ALIVE*.

The story began about as he had expected—"Russian President Vladimir Putin was not on board the presidential plane that was shot down Friday over Ukraine . . . The Kremlin is now calling the attack 'a brazen but failed assassination attempt carried out by the West.'"

"'Brazen' being the code word for United States?" Anna said.

"Evidently," Chris said, scrolling through the article. "The Kremlin has confirmed that twenty-six people died in the attack . . ." Chris skimmed through the official condolences, looking for the next part, the part he hadn't expected so quickly: "Russian military intelligence officers have captured a missile launcher that they say was used in the attack and have detained three soldiers in eastern Ukraine near Donetsk. Two of the men are believed to be Ukrainian nationals and a third is Estonian. The Estonian was a former member of KaPo, Estonia's Internal Security Service.

"One of the three men has been identified as Mikhail Kolchak, an official of the SBU, Ukraine's intelligence service."

Too fast, Chris thought. Just what Anna had said. *This is coming too fast.*

"You see what they've done," she said, taking her phone back. "They've just indirectly blamed Ukraine and Estonia."

"Not so indirectly."

"They've established justification for retaliatory strikes on those countries."

Chris said nothing. This was unfolding like the programmed moves in a game whose outcome had already been determined. A deception that no one in Washington had seen coming. Not because it was too big, but because it was too small. It was what Martin had warned of on Tuesday in Greece: *I think they're planning something else entirely. Something we're not even considering.*

"This is what Turov does," he said. "It wasn't an attack on Putin, it was an attack on the United States."

"Disguised as an attack on Russia."

"Yes. And yesterday was just the opening salvo. The real attack is what's happening now. This story they're telling that the media's unwittingly repeating." Christopher glanced around the restaurant, thinking of his conversation with Martin yesterday. Diplomatically, Washington was going through the motions, saying the right things—offering "thoughts and prayers" for the victims, reacting almost as if Russia were a brother nation, not the country it had been punishing with sanctions for years. But at the same time, the stories that the US *caused* the attack were spreading faster than Washington could keep up with, making the administration's efforts at statesmanship seem like a grand hypocrisy. This would become the official line now from Moscow, he knew: *two Ukrainians and an Estonian* had carried out the August 13 attack. With support from the Ukrainian military, and the US.

If the attack on the president's plane was the second move in a four-move game, then maybe this, the disinformation campaign, is the third. But what was the first move?

"What are you thinking?" Anna said, reaching for his hand. "You're a mile away."

"At least."

"I was being conservative."

"I have that effect on people." He waited for her smile, which took slightly longer than expected. "Sorry," he said.

"Tell me."

"I'm just thinking: if someone from our side *was* involved in this, did they think the president was on board the plane? Or did they know he wasn't?"

"That's a strange thought," Anna said. "Why would you think someone from our side is involved?"

"I don't. I'm just speculating. Something Max Petrenko said. I'm just worried there may be another part to this I'm not seeing. Which would make our job harder."

"Someone from our side—meaning inside the government?"

Christopher shrugged. "Or someone with access to the government. A spy in the house—it's a phrase Turov uses. I'm just considering all options. And probably getting ahead of myself."

"More coffee?" the waitress asked.

Chris turned and smiled. "Please," he said.

Anna went back to her phone as the waitress topped off his cup.

"Look at this," Anna said, after she'd walked away. It was a clip of Russia's assistant foreign minister, saying, in English: "America has finally crossed the line. These are very desperate people. They've been trying to destroy Russia for twenty-five years. Remember, Hitler wanted to destroy Russia. Napoleon: the same. We shouldn't forget what happened to them."

"I recognize the Hitler line," Anna said.

Yes. They were the words Putin had used in his War Day speech several years ago, comparing the West to Nazi Germany. Tough words, but considered irrelevant bluster at the time.

"What are *you* thinking?" he asked, handing back her phone.

"I'm thinking what I told you yesterday," Anna said. "That despite everything, they've given us an opportunity. It's up to us what we do about it."

Chris liked that, as he did the intensity and openness in Anna's face. Before she could explain, though, his phone buzzed. It was Jake Briggs.

He took the call as he walked outside. It was warm on the sidewalk, a scent of auto exhaust in the air, sharp glares of sunlight among the buildings and windshields. He had a tender feeling turning and seeing Anna through the glass, looking down at her phone attentively as Briggs talked; Briggs so pumped up about Putin and Delkoff that it didn't seem to matter if anyone was on the other end.

Anna had eaten maybe a quarter piece of toast while he was gone. "Briggs," he said. "He's at the airport already, an hour and a half early. He wants to see me ASAP."

"Why?"

"He just heard the news. He wouldn't say anything else. Just that he needs to talk before Martin Lindgren arrives. You want to drive me?"

"Let's go."

TWENTY

Dulles International Airport. Northern Virginia.

Jake Briggs was pacing the conference room in that stiff, slightly
side-to-side way he had, as if his legs were wooden poles. He wore
a black T-shirt, cargo pants, and work boots, and held a Starbucks cup
in his left hand. Briggs had been a wrestling champ in school and still
carried himself like one. A muscled five foot six, he'd been state high
school champion at 170 pounds and wrestled 174 in college. Before
he'd found wrestling, he once told Chris, people used to pick on him.
It was hard to imagine.

His dark eyes turned as Chris entered the room and his faintly
pockmarked face creased into a familiar smile. His skin had a natural
dirty tint, as if he'd been working in a field.

"Professor."

"Jacob."

Briggs gave him a hard handshake and quick man-hug. "Like the
specs," he said.

"Thanks." They sat at one end of the conference table. Martin
Lindgren had rented the room for their ten o'clock, but Briggs was
already at work, his laptop opened, papers spread out. Meeting Briggs
could be like encountering an old obsession, Chris thought: realizing
that he hadn't really gotten past the obsession, he'd just set it aside.

Anna, who'd come to see him off, went for coffee while they talked. Briggs didn't particularly like Anna, and she was okay with that. It wasn't just the obvious differences—Briggs was a soldier, Anna a politician and diplomat; Anna had been raised Catholic, Briggs was an atheist. There was also something that caught in their personalities— his, mostly—that prevented them from meeting halfway.

Briggs nodded at his PC: the video clip of the Russian minister making his Hitler comparison. "They're hammering us, aren't they?" he said. "War bait."

"Maybe."

"I see they're reporting an Estonian and two Ukrainians. No mention of Delkoff, though."

"Not yet."

"It means he's still alive."

Christopher nodded. He'd been thinking the same: Delkoff could only be a part of the story Russia was circulating if he was dead.

Briggs was looking at him pointedly, as if Chris knew what he was thinking.

"What."

"You knew, didn't you? When you called me yesterday, you already knew. You knew Putin wasn't on that plane."

Christopher shrugged and nodded. "Speculation."

"How?"

"Because. I know who did this," Chris said. "I don't know all the specifics yet or where it's going exactly. But I know who did this."

"Okay."

"And I need you to help me get to him. I think we can do that through Ivan Delkoff. He's going to be our point of entry. That's why I need you."

Briggs rubbed his hands together, watching Chris appraisingly. "Okay, professor," he said. "And so why aren't you in the Oval Office right now, telling the president all this?"

"Because the White House has their own idea about who did it.

Russia Ops has three names now and a theory, tying it to Ukrainian intelligence. They've already made up their minds. They're not particularly interested in contradictory facts. And, besides," he added, "even if I told them, and they believed me, I suspect they'd handle it wrong."

This drew Briggs's second smile of the morning, a huge one.

Christopher gave him a cursory biography of Andrei Turov as they waited for Martin: how he'd come up through the FSB and earned a prominent place early in the president's inner circle, then built a private security business in Moscow while continuing to work in the shadows for the Kremlin.

Briggs watched him intently, drawing it all in, saving his questions. When Christopher finished, Briggs shared what he'd learned about Delkoff. Like Anna's son, Briggs worked with offline and dark-web databases, sources Christopher couldn't access. He also had a unique ability to hack into the thought processes of the people he was pursuing. Chris was amazed by how much he'd already learned about Delkoff in a few hours. But then Briggs was one of those people who would wrestle with an assignment if you gave him two months, but transform into a superhero if he only had a couple days.

"So, assuming Delkoff's alive," Chris said. "Where is he?"

"Lindgren is going to tell us Belarus. I'm fairly certain of that. Gomel, Belarus, is where his trail will lead. He has family there, an ex-girlfriend. Maybe an estranged daughter. He knows some ex-military there. Russian patriots, who'd hide him if he asked."

"But Belarus isn't where he is."

"No," Briggs said with that certainty of tone that rubbed some people wrong. He moved several papers on the table. "He also has a cousin who used to live in Gomel. Dmitri Porchak. Former Belarus state security. Retired now, living in northern France. He may be—or may have been—involved in drug trafficking. Little Dmitri, he was called. He was fairly close with Delkoff at one time. Dmitri's ex-wife's family has relatives scattered along the French coast. It's a region Delkoff has probably visited a few times, too. That's where he's going to be."

"France."

"Yes."

Chris studied him. "Has there been some recent contact, then, between Delkoff and this cousin?"

"No," Briggs said. "None that I can find."

"Okay."

"That's why I think his cousin's helping him. I think they set this up some months ago, and he's deliberately distancing himself so no one will look at that. He probably left a false trail back to Gomel."

"All right." Briggs liked to place his chips on a single number, Chris knew, and he wasn't always correct; but he gambled with such certainty that people tended not to question him. He had a good feeling about Briggs on this one, though. And he also liked the fact that Briggs spoke French. "So, northern France?"

Briggs opened a folder and pulled out a black-and-white map. "In here is where Dmitri's wife's family lives. The Opal Coast. They have several properties here. I kind of have it narrowed down to three or four spots—probabilities. I'm still working it."

"You don't think the Kremlin will know this?"

"They might. But first they're going to look at Gomel and the Moscow suburbs. Of course, the sooner we get started, the better chance we have of beating them."

"And what if we're wrong?"

Briggs shifted his eyes to the corridor. He didn't look at Christopher again right away. "Then we keep monitoring the intel," he said. "I'm just saying, that's where I'd go. We're doing this as a drug deal, right?" Chris nodded, recalling Briggs's term for a small-scale black op. "I mean, I'd *like* to do it as an extraction, as I told you. But you're not going there."

"*We're* not, no," Chris said. An extraction would mean approvals and knowledge up the chain of command, involving NSC, DNI, and the White House. It wasn't that type of operation.

"The sixty billion boys won't go for that, I know," Briggs said, an edge in his voice; sixty billion being an approximation of what the government spent each year on intelligence.

"No, and Martin won't, either. It's got to be cleaner than that," Chris said.

"Okay, gotcha." Briggs kept his eyes down, trying to show some humility, which came across as slightly comical. In fact, Chris wanted to bypass the IC as much as possible. He'd been handed a budget and an objective, but beyond that, the details were up to him. Both he and Briggs were independent contractors. Meaning that if they went to France, they wouldn't bring in the French intelligence service, the DGSE. It wasn't that kind of mission.

"And if you do find him, you think Delkoff will talk with you?" Chris said.

"Sure. Because he has a motive now. Yesterday, Delkoff thought he'd killed the president of Russia and gotten away with it, right? Today he realizes the president is alive and he's been set up. There's a lot of motivation in that picture, I'd say." Briggs scratched his shoulder and nodded at something in the corridor. "Is that him?"

Chris saw where he was looking: Martin Lindgren's clipped, urgent walk, a thin leather briefcase flapping off his leg.

"Just don't say anything that's going to get under his skin," Christopher said.

Briggs showed a pained look that contained a trace of amusement. "Me?"

TWENTY-ONE

Martin Lindgren's assessment was much as Briggs had predicted: Ivan Delkoff had probably gone to ground in Gomel or Minsk, Belarus, where he had family and friends. "The intel shows that's where he is, although we don't know precisely where."

It was more than informed speculation. There were also surveillance images: grainy printouts of a man standing on a train platform with a duffel bag. "That's Delkoff," Martin said. "ID'd by facial recog at the Minsk railway station."

Martin spoke mostly to Christopher as he described the intel findings, glancing several times at Briggs. Briggs sat expressionless, listening, palms flat on the table. Chris handed him the photos and he examined them quickly and gave them back.

"We need to check face recog through de Gaulle, as well," Briggs said to Chris when Martin had finished. "That would be a tremendous help."

Martin looked to Christopher for clarification.

"We don't think he's in Belarus any longer," Chris said.

"Although this would seem to be pretty good evidence that he was."

"Right. *Was*," Briggs said.

"We think he's probably in France," Chris said. "Although naturally we wouldn't want that to leave this room."

Chris nodded to Briggs and Briggs began to explain his theory to Martin, keeping his eyes on the table. He repeated the scenario he'd given Chris, except his tone was a little different, a mix of detachment and irritability. It wasn't because of Martin, it was because of what Martin represented; it was as if he were talking to the Agency itself.

He'll go along with this, Chris sensed as Briggs wrapped up. He could feel his former boss warming slowly to the former Navy SEAL.

"It all turns on motivation," Briggs said. "Delkoff wouldn't have done this for money or recognition. He did it for history. His dislike of the United States was never personal. But his vendetta against Turov now probably is."

"Still, we're going to have to offer him something," Chris said.

Martin glanced at Briggs. "Figure out what he wants. We'll build a supplementary budget."

"And arrange for a flight to bring him in?" Briggs said.

Martin closed and opened his eyes. They'd already budgeted for it, Chris could see. "But how exactly does this relate to what *you're* doing?" he asked Chris.

"Ideally, the parts fit together. What Delkoff gives us I then take to Turov and use as leverage. It creates incentive for us to deal. That's our Plan A, anyway."

"What's B?"

"We don't have one yet."

Briggs lifted his chin in assent, about an inch too high. Lindgren cleared his throat. Christopher knew he shouldn't have let the conversation go this way. "And if he doesn't cooperate," Briggs said, "if he refuses to talk, we take him out."

Martin glanced at Christopher, the frown deepening.

"He's just messing with us," Chris said and smiled, figuring the "us" might soften Briggs's offense. He didn't want them to seem like a pair of cowboys, although that was probably how they appeared. "Anyway," he added, "it won't come to that."

"And in the meantime," Briggs said, this time to Martin, "it would help if we *could* seem interested in Belarus. Make contact with some of the people he knows there, in Gomel and Minsk. His girlfriend, his ex-wife. And it would be helpful if none of what we're talking about is ever discussed at National Security level."

"It won't be," Martin said.

They spent another ten minutes going over details of the op. Then they closed their respective folders and briefcases. Christopher had left out one key detail: a woman he knew in Moscow named Amira Niyzov, who would serve as his "secret weapon." Amira would plug right in to his cover as an academic researching the Russian Orthodox Church. But it wasn't something he could talk about yet, not even with Martin Lindgren.

Anna Carpenter read Jon Niles's blog as she sat in the waiting lounge at a vacant gate:

> Random observations: Supposedly it took the Civil War to change the "United States" from a plural to a singular—as in "The United States is" instead of "The United States are." As much as we think of our country as a single entity now—with shared values, laws, and favorite television shows—the August 13 attack is showing us how divided that entity can be. With a growing number of people convinced the US did have a hand in last Friday's assassination attempt, look for secession movements to rise up in two or three states, beginning with Texas and California. . . . Meanwhile, there are strong divisions within the administration over how to respond to the allegations, with some pushing the story that Friday's attack was a Russian coup attempt. The conflicting stories seem straight out of the Russian playbook. Noise at the expense of comprehension. Or what the Russians call *maskirova*—little masquerade . . .

Anna looked up from her tablet. Briggs, Martin, and Christopher were at last coming out of the conference room: Briggs first with that thick-legged wrestler's walk, checking his phone; then Martin and Christopher. She watched as they said their goodbyes, a study in contrasts: Briggs compact and tense, even his laugh had attitude; Martin and Chris more at ease, Martin with his thin, graceful gestures, Chris in the moment, operating on a higher plane than when he went in, in the service of big ideas again. She had fallen in love with him in part because of that look, and the promise that came with it—a life that combined passion with the pursuit of emotional and intellectual growth. And for the most part, that's what they were living—or had been, until Martin came for him in Greece. Anna was drawn to independence, to people who competed with themselves more than with others, a tendency that had made it difficult at times for her to form binding ties. She'd been attracted to the independence in her husband, too, although he was a very different sort of man: a Foreign Service officer who became a local politician and then, late in their marriage, decided he wanted to open a restaurant. Anna had supported him through all that, and they'd made the marriage work. She had been teaching law when they met, expecting a career in academia. But she found herself pulled increasingly toward public service. Daniel had trouble adjusting to that. He was never comfortable accompanying Anna to events where she was known and he wasn't. She'd thought it was just another problem for them to solve. But they never did. In the end, Dan had tunneled out of the marriage, carrying on with a young woman he'd promoted from waitress to manager at his restaurant. Anna had recently learned from David that they'd finally broken up, and that he was solo again.

"Grab a cup of coffee?" Chris said, as they walked away down the corridor.

"I think I'm getting tired of airports," Anna said. "How did it go?"

"Martin's on board with Briggs. More than I expected. Of course, he's not risking a lot. Just two of us," he added, trying to make a joke. Anna didn't smile.

"Sorry." They walked in unison for a few steps, but otherwise felt out of sync. He wasn't going to tell her a lot, Anna knew. His thoughts had gone somewhere else.

"I have an idea how to do this," she said. "I figure we've only got a window of a few days to respond. After that, our lack of response *becomes* our response."

Anna wanted to discuss his brother's blog, and the media's role in all this. She wanted to tell him that Jon and his magazine were part of the plan she was starting to formulate. But she could see that Christopher didn't want to talk about that now. He had his own agenda. And that was okay, too.

They ordered coffees and sat at a tall round table by the corridor. Chris was catching a United flight to Paris that afternoon, connecting on to Moscow. Anna watched him gazing down the concourse, distracted with his mission. She waited for his eyes to return to hers. When they did, he reached across the table and took her hands. Anna squeezed.

"When I get back, how about we get married?" he said.

. Anna smiled, and felt her eyes moisten. Chris was still able to surprise her. "You know, I've always hoped you would propose to me in an airport fast-food restaurant," she said.

"Only the most romantic spot will do."

She leaned over to kiss him.

TWENTY-TWO

Southwest of Moscow.

The message from the Kremlin was brief and unambiguous: the president wanted Andrei Turov to travel to Novo-Ogaryovo, the presidential residence outside of Moscow, to help him prepare the speech that he'd deliver to parliament—and the world—on Friday.

This was welcome news, even if it meant delaying Turov's trip to Switzerland and the start of his "retirement." Friday's speech would be a turning point for Russia. It would be the president's chance to explain how the US's idea of globalism had failed, creating a culture of dissension and terrorism around the world. The president would then introduce his plan for an international anti-terror security network, to prevent future August 13s from ever happening, and render obsolete politically based military blocs such as NATO. It would be a giant step toward the eventual eradication of Americanism—with its unbounded greed, reckless militarism, and cheap sentimentality. The world was ready for something better.

The meeting would also give Turov a chance to shore up his own relationship with the president, which Anton had confirmed was strained because of the whispering campaign by some of Putin's advisers. Turov would remind his friend of the importance of the "fourth move" and reassure him of his loyalty.

The request from Moscow also eased some of the loneliness that had come with the departure of Svetlana and the twins. And now Olga. Turov was relieved to have the president's speech to focus on for a few days. He rehearsed lines in his head as he walked the grounds and swam laps in his indoor pool, knowing that the president, too, did his best thinking on his morning swims. And all weekend Turov played videos of Putin's greatest speeches, jotting ideas, stimulated by the conviction and power of Volodya's words.

Four times he watched the groundbreaking Munich speech from 2007—when the president had surprised the world with his sharp warnings about the US's global ambitions, in the midst of their Iraq debacle. "The United States has overstepped its national borders in almost all spheres," he'd said. "Who could be pleased with that?"

Turov's favorite, though, was still the president's address to the Valdai International Discussion Club, on October 24, 2014, which he watched over and over again Saturday afternoon. This was the speech where Putin made the case for a new Eurasian power base to replace the Western model, an alliance that would join Russia with China and India, keeping Moscow at its center. In the same speech, he had rebuked the US's clumsy efforts to "reshape the world to suit their own needs and interests. Pardon the analogy, but this is the way nouveaux riches behave when they suddenly end up with a great fortune, in this case in the shape of world leadership and domination."

He'd gone on to describe—forcefully and eloquently, Turov thought—how, through its ill-advised interference in the Middle East, America had inadvertently created Al Qaeda in the 1980s and ISIS in the 2010s. "I never cease to be amazed by the way the Americans just keep stepping on the same rake, as we say here in Russia," Putin said.

Turov marveled at how persuasive his friend sounded. After Brezhnev's slurred diction and the nodding manner of his successors, after Yeltsin's pitiful, clownish behavior and Medvedev's bumbling efforts to mimic Putin, the Russian people had a real leader, a strongman. A man destined for greatness if he wanted it. The Americans had missed the transformation Putin had undergone in 2008 when he'd trained for months with speech coaches to prepare for what was coming. The Americans, with their comic-book culture, missed a great deal.

Fortunately, the stories about the US's role in August 13 were more convincing than even Turov had anticipated. And the Americans were causing some of the damage now themselves, with their internal confusion over what to do.

As he worked, Turov occasionally glanced out at the grounds, expecting to see the grandchildren, or his daughter, or even his little friend Boris, Svetlana's cat, who used to perch on the windowsill and look in at Turov with his symmetrical black-and-white face. But all of that was gone. There was a funny new dynamic in its place: a feeling of sadness seemed to linger like a stubborn melody over his time alone.

At two minutes before five o'clock on Sunday, Turov put aside the speech as Anton approached for his afternoon meeting. Turov was expecting an update on Ivan Delkoff.

He waited as Anton set up his computer. First, Anton showed him the latest charts compiled by the Moscow office, ranking dozens of US media organizations on their coverage of Russia. The rankings ranged from "1" for "Very Unfriendly" to "10" for "Very Friendly." The median continued to climb slightly above the "Friendly" line, Anton pointed out, even though many of those companies would probably dispute their rankings if given the chance.

Anton then called up the most recent footage that his men had sent from the Donbas, showing the launch site and the charred aftermath of a warehouse fire.

"The command base was established adjacent to the launch site," Anton told him. "It was set on fire after the operation. We have confirmation that two men died inside. One of them, we believe, was Delkoff."

"So he's dead."

"We think so. My man believes that Pletner may have set the fire. I will have a more complete report for you tomorrow."

Turov frowned. This did not sound right. "Pletner?"

"Yes." The two men locked eyes, but Turov was silent. "Do you think the president will ask about it when you meet with him?" Anton asked.

"No," Turov said, studying the steady eyes of his loyal assistant. "He's made it clear he's not concerned about details. Thank God. So long as there were no problems. No, he's more concerned about his speech on Friday. As I am. But I'm glad you've brought me this, Anton. At least we can assure him that Delkoff is dead."

TWENTY-THREE

Northwest France.

But Ivan Delkoff was not dead. Wearing a skull cap and paste-on goatee, oversized dungarees and a dark jacket, he had arrived in Riga on Sunday afternoon, carrying his fatigues and personal effects in a duffel bag. His cousin Dmitri arranged a room for him there overnight. Delkoff had passed the time reading an adventure novel by Fyodor Berezin, the writer who was being heralded as "the Russian Tom Clancy," a reference Delkoff did not get. He also read his old university history book, which Delkoff preferred to the more current, Westernized-propaganda histories.

On Monday, using a forged passport, Delkoff had boarded an afternoon airBaltic flight to Paris. It was onboard that he took a small sip of vodka, the first drink he'd allowed himself in fourteen and a half months. Immediately a door opened in Delkoff's head, to a place that he'd nearly forgotten. When Delkoff was a young man, alcohol had been his "fuel for adventure," he used to call it. But eventually the adventures came to interfere with his life, as they did with anyone who grew to enjoy alcohol too much. Now he was feeling the good part and wondering why he'd ever stopped. He ordered a second drink as he pondered the question, deciding to take this one more slowly than the first. His thoughts were clearly on an elevated level by then—he'd begun to imagine new routes of escape that he hadn't considered before.

What had happened was incredible. They'd shot the Russian president out of the sky. And yet life went on. People were reading books on the airplane and watching movies, as if nothing had happened. Quietly tapping their phones or sleeping. The muted nature of the response even made him laugh at one point, which caused a tall man several rows in front of him to swivel his head and look. The alcohol had taken Delkoff to a refuge, where he could rest with his thoughts for a few hours. Before starting over in a different country, under a different name. Someday, Turov's men might stop hunting for him. And maybe—a year from now, perhaps longer—it was even possible that he could return to Russia and be welcomed as a hero.

Delkoff blocked out the noise around him as he walked into the concourse at de Gaulle. He averted his eyes from the people gathered below a television set. Fighting the stimuli, the sounds and smells, the knowledge of what city he was in: all of it conspiring to stir his appetites—for conversation, for a large meal, for female companionship. Delkoff had to rely on his own internal disciplines now.

He bought a liter of vodka at the duty-free shop, careful not to engage with the clerk, and then carried his purchase and his duffel bag to the open-air car park to meet his cousin. If he could keep his vices to vodka tonight, he would be fine.

Little Dmitri looked the same as always, small and stout, wearing baggy old blue jeans, an open gray jacket, and an untucked flannel shirt, his brush-like mustache slightly lopsided, and walking in that determined straight-ahead way he had, the way he went through life. Delkoff loved him.

"Well," Delkoff said, trying to slow him down. "We did it."

But Dmitri didn't want to discuss it now. "We'll talk when we get there," he said. He had a worried look on his face. But then, Dmitri always wore that look. "We can't say anything in front of Artem, all right?"

"Of course." Artem was Little Dmitri's driver and bodyguard, a former Russian soldier from the North Caucasus region who was nearly as big as Delkoff. Delkoff had been around him a few times before, but they'd never had a real conversation. Artem wasn't much for small talk.

Delkoff settled in the back seat of the SUV, feeling insulated as they pulled away from the terminal. Watching the airport parking lots and runways skim past, the lights of the Paris suburbs beginning, and then seeing the darker points of the countryside, Delkoff sipped from his vodka. The drive to the coast would take two and a half hours, Dmitri said. Delkoff was looking forward to seeing the ocean again, breathing the night sea air. It had been too many months.

A CD of Russian folk music played quietly through the speakers, and no one spoke. It was not the sort of music Delkoff would ever play. But he began to hear familiar melodies and they reminded him of his parents, and the cooking smells from his old childhood kitchen in Kapotnya. Hearing the well-worn rhythms of "Kalinka," Delkoff instructed Dmitri to turn it up. He began to tap along with his hand on the top of his thigh.

"Play it again," Delkoff said when it finished. Four more times they listened to the Russian folk song, Delkoff sipping his vodka and nodding his head in time.

But even as he enjoyed the music, Delkoff wondered why they weren't listening to news. Didn't they want to know what was happening in Russia? Even if they weren't able to talk about his operation, didn't they want to know? Or was Dmitri overcompensating, as he often did?

"Kalinka" ended for the fifth time and Delkoff asked Dmitri to turn it off. He wanted to think for a while. They rode for several kilometers in silence, Delkoff knowing by then that something was wrong. He should have asked Dmitri for an explanation straightaway, while they were still at the airport. He should have stopped him outside the terminal building and demanded that he tell him what he'd heard.

He waited until they were on the westbound A13, a dozen or so kilometers outside the city. Then Delkoff leaned forward and tugged his cousin's jacket collar.

"Pull over," he said. "Tell him to pull over. I need to piss."

Artem put on his flashers and pulled off to the hard shoulder of the highway. They sat there for a long moment as traffic whooshed by. Then Delkoff got out and stood waiting for his cousin. Dmitri came out with his jacket flapping in the wind.

"Well?" he said. Delkoff turned away from the traffic, leading his cousin off the pavement. "What is it? What's wrong? Has someone found out about me?"

Little Dmitri just looked at his cousin, his eyes glistening in the night air. Delkoff breathing the exhaust from the SUV. "You don't know?"

"What are you talking about?"

Dmitri glanced at the dark countryside. He seemed to be summoning the courage to tell him. "The president," he said. "You don't know what happened?"

"Of course, I know," Delkoff said. "We shot his fucking plane out of the sky."

Dmitri's eyes seemed to turn in on themselves. "The president," he said. Then he began the sentence again: "The president wasn't on board. He never boarded the plane. You don't know that?"

Ivan Delkoff stared at his little cousin as the traffic rushed past. He asked him to repeat what he had just said, because it didn't make sense. Hearing it a second time, Delkoff grabbed Dmitri by the front of his jacket and lifted him off the ground. He felt so angry that he was tempted to carry his cousin to the highway and toss him into traffic. "What are you talking about? You're lying!"

"No, why would I be lying?" Dmitri said. "He's still alive. They say he was given some warning at the last minute, telling him not to board."

Delkoff let go of his little cousin. This wasn't the place to discuss it, but Dmitri tried anyway, his quavering voice drowned out by a passing truck. Delkoff turned away, letting out several profanities. He looked at the faraway glints: farms, houses; rooms where people were watching news of the Russian president on their televisions. He turned in place, looking several directions for somewhere to go. His life suddenly seemed like a cage.

Returning to the back seat of the SUV, Delkoff felt enormously foolish. Too foolish to speak. He thought of his son's charred face and felt himself beginning to cry. Artem raced the SUV into traffic, driving too fast to compensate for whatever was wrong.

The magnitude of the betrayal was unfathomable. Andrei Turov had deceived him in a way that Delkoff had not even considered possible. And the worst part was the question that kept repeating in his head as he stared numbly at the passing French towns: *Had Delkoff actually been working for the man he thought he was going to kill, then? Had the August 13 attack been set up by the president himself?*

If so—if Delkoff's mission *hadn't* been for Russia, and the greater good—then Delkoff was no better than a hired killer. They sped in silence through the darkening night, the fastest vehicle on the freeway, Delkoff drinking again, his window opened an inch for the cool air.

Somehow, we'll get through this, he began to tell himself as they drew nearer to the coast. Somehow, he'd endure this betrayal the way he had endured physical and emotional challenges all his life; he'd endure it the way any soldier did. Delkoff had seen most of the ways that men were diminished by war; he'd seen tough, wounded soldiers crying for their mothers on the battlefields of Chechnya and Ukraine; he'd seen separatist fighters in the Donbas raping a dead Ukrainian woman in a farmhouse once, laughing because there were others to share the experience; and he'd seen his son's face, like a mask from some American horror movie, the features all burned off. Whether war finally ruined you or made you stronger, it always changed you. If you were lucky and brave enough, in time the bad made you good. It maybe even made you immune to the smiling dishonesty of the world, and made you think that nothing could get to you anymore. Delkoff had thought that on occasion.

But here was something that had: Andrei Turov, Russia's "dark angel," had completely outplayed him with his dark magic. August 13 had been the opposite of what Turov told him it was. It had been an operation to *strengthen* the president, not kill him.

Delkoff had never believed that Andrei Turov would simply let him go. That's why he'd planned an elaborate escape. But he didn't think Turov was lying to him, either, when he'd said, in his candid voice, "You are the only one who can do this successfully."

On the two-lane coast road they passed sand-dune beaches and rock pools. Half a dozen seaside towns whipped by, the air windy and smelling of sea brine. But Delkoff barely noticed. Not until Artem pulled off onto a rough gravel-dirt road, stopping by a tiny restaurant on a hill. The terrace was lit with a string of colored Christmas lights.

Dmitri turned to face his cousin. "I'm just going in to buy a bottle of wine. I'll be right out." Artem left the engine running.

Delkoff lowered the window, beginning to feel a little better. He gazed at the old couples sitting at small tables on the terrace and it felt very inviting to him, a warm, civilized slice of the world. Artem, he saw, was watching him in the rearview mirror.

Dmitri returned with his bottle of red wine and they continued into the darkness away from the coast. Delkoff saw where they were headed: a porchlight in the rolling country, a two-story restored stone farmhouse on a property owned by Dmitri's ex-wife's family. He saw the shapes of a barn and a smaller stone house behind it as Artem parked. "Here we are," Dmitri said. "This will be your home now for a day or two."

Delkoff was silent. He followed Dmitri inside. There was an old-wood, slightly moldy smell in the house. Delkoff took his duffel bag and vodka upstairs to a small corner bedroom with a beamed ceiling. He closed the door and opened the windows, tuned to the silence and to his own thoughts.

By that point, Delkoff was beginning to formulate a plan: Turov was the enemy now, and Delkoff's most effective move would be a direct strike on Turov's vulnerability, an attack that Turov would not anticipate. Delkoff knew how to do that.

Once he'd decided on the basic details, Delkoff went downstairs to tell his cousin. Dmitri and Artem were in the living room, watching the news on RT Français.

"Come outside with me for a minute," Delkoff said to Dmitri.

They walked together across the scrubby field, Delkoff breathing the grassy freedom of country in the freshening night air, savoring what he had now in his head.

Artem stepped out too, watching them from the doorway.

"We can't stay here. You know that," Delkoff said. Stopping, he tried to pass his cousin the vodka; Dmitri wouldn't take it.

"That was never the plan," Dmitri said. "We can still travel to Germany tomorrrow."

Delkoff shook his head. He looked up, and pointed at the sky.

"You know what those are, Dmitri?"

"What do you mean—the stars?"

"No. Some of them are stars. Some of them aren't stars."

Dmitri's wide forehead creased as he gazed up. "What are you talking about?"

Delkoff took a drink of vodka. He screwed the lid back on. "Some of them are stars and some of them are satellites. It wouldn't surprise me if some were watching us right now." They both looked at the canopy of stars. "But you know what? I have something more valuable than anything they have now, Dmitri. Right here."

He tapped the side of his head. His cousin didn't understand at first.

"There's enough right here to bring down the president of Russia, if I wanted to, Dmitri, you know that? And I do want to. I've decided. I need to borrow a computer. Do you have one I can use?"

"Of course."

He told him the rest as they walked back to the house, their boots crunching across the dirt and gravel.

"I'm going upstairs and I'm going to write for a while. When I finish, we can make a decision about tomorrow."

Delkoff set up his cousin's computer on a small wooden table against the wall. Then he began to write, pecking at the keys of the Cyrillic keyboard with his index fingers, like an accountant punching numbers on an adding machine. What he was creating would be Delkoff's official account of what had happened on August 13 and what had led up to it. A confession, in effect, although he preferred to call it his "Declaration." That was the word he typed at the top of the first page. A "Declaration" that would implicate not only Andrei Turov, but also Vladimir Putin, in the attack on the presidential plane. Which was really an attack on the West. He understood that now.

His feelings of anger and humiliation were outweighed by a compulsion to do right. Delkoff felt a surge of excitement every time he recognized what he was doing: creating the historic record of August 13. It was even possible that he could sell this document to the Americans.

As he wrote, Delkoff began to understand a deeper truth, and it humbled him: the assignment that Andrei Turov had handed him back in April *wasn't* his destiny, as he'd thought at the time. But *this* was. The air cooled and moistened as he worked, the smells of hay and sea water thickening as the window curtains puffed out with the breeze, an eerie, gentle sensation that reminded Delkoff for some reason of coming to the Black Sea as a boy, and watching the great Russian Navy ships from the docks. Delkoff didn't sleep much at night anyway, so he was pleased to have this new mission before him.

But at 9:50, he saw that he was about to run out of vodka, and the vodka was helping him write. Delkoff walked downstairs to ask his cousin if there was any more in the house. Dmitri and Artem were still watching the news.

"We don't keep vodka here," Dmitri told him.

"Then we'll have to go out and get some." He held up the nearly empty bottle.

"We can't. Not this late."

Delkoff looked at the clock on the mantel. "What about your friend at the restaurant?" he said. "Won't he sell us a bottle?"

"He might." Dmitri looked at him disapprovingly.

"Then let's go."

"*You* can't leave."

But Delkoff didn't want to stay. Not tonight. Dmitri pulled on his old jacket and the three of them went out again: Artem driving the SUV back up the gravel road toward the coast. Delkoff in the back seat again, breathing the sea breeze, the taste of alcohol a desperate but delicious craving. It wasn't smart being out like this, he knew, but Delkoff didn't care. The world's horizons seemed enormous again.

He agreed to stay with Artem in the car as Dmitri went in the little restaurant. Delkoff let the window down. He listened to the ocean. Artem's eyes were watching him again in the mirror.

"You smell that?" he said to Artem.

"Smell what?"

"French air," he said. "Not like the air in Russia."

Artem lifted his nose and turned his head slightly. Delkoff was amused by the way his giant nostrils quivered. "Smells the same to me," he said.

Watching stars over the Channel, Delkoff imagined what was coming. Imagined his enemy, Turov, the Russian coward, the president's lapdog. What he really wanted now was to contact the Americans. That was his future now: across the ocean.

It was a great surprise, then, when Dmitri came out of the restaurant carrying—along with a liter of vodka and a bottle of red wine—an envelope with a message for Delkoff.

Somehow, despite Delkoff's months of planning, and his carefully worked-out exit from Ukraine, the Americans were already a step ahead of him.

The Americans, ingenious as they occasionally were, had already been here and managed to leave Ivan Delkoff a message.

PART II

THE FOURTH MOVE

TWENTY-FOUR

Washington.

Two days after the attack on the Russian president's plane, anti-US protests flared up in Moscow and St. Petersburg, a reaction to the suddenly widespread belief that the CIA had supported or planned the attack on Russia's president. Fueled by aggressive social media campaigns and unsubstantiated news stories, the protests also seemed to stir long-simmering hatreds of the United States around the world.

Russian journalists paraded out stories about America's past bungled attempts to kill world leaders—Cuba's Fidel Castro, the Congo's Patrice Lumumba, Rafael Trujillo of the Dominican Republic, Muammar Gaddafi of Libya, and many others—and the US's record of killing civilians during brutal military campaigns, from Japan to Vietnam to Iraq.

"History," one Russian commentator noted, "is finally catching up with America's conception of itself. It should come as no surprise that a country founded on the genocide of its Native American population wouldn't think twice about ordering the assassination of the president of Russia if they felt threatened enough by him. Fortunately, for Russia and the world, America has finally been caught—and will at last be punished for its legacy of crimes."

Reports from Russia continued to warn that "additional US

attacks" might be imminent, possibly "against civilians," both in Russia and in "countries with Russian interests."

The evidence of US involvement in the downing of the presidential plane appeared to gain legitimacy on Sunday with a splashy, but sketchy, story online about a trail of emails between Dmitro Hordiyenko, the Ukrainian arms supplier, and a senior CIA officer named Gregory Dial. "The Hordiyenko Connection," tweeters called it. The report also alleged a transfer of five million dollars to Hordiyenko from an offshore account controlled by a CIA front company.

"The American Fall," read the headline of a *Wall Street Journal* op-ed on Monday, playing off "Arab Spring," a forecast some Russian academics had been predicting for years: American democracy was in trouble, the story claimed, the United States in danger of breaking into separate pieces under the ordeal of political, racial, and economic conflicts.

The virulence of the anti-Americanism took many at home by surprise, although others seemed to welcome it. Protests tapped a current of distrust some Americans felt toward their own government. Early Monday morning, the words "USA Kills" were spray-painted on the front wall of the Lincoln Memorial. The site was closed for hours, covered behind tarps while the graffiti was blasted off. But a photo of it went viral, and the image, with the seated figure of Abraham Lincoln in the background, became a symbol for the new anti-America movement. A large, seemingly spontaneous protest errupted later that day on the National Mall.

The stories linking the US to August 13 felt like calculated fabrications to Anna Carpenter. But she was angered by the White House's official silence about them, and by the political infighting—among elected officials and, even more rabidly, media pundits—over what had actually happened and what to do about it. On Sunday evening, the White House chief of staff called Anna to ask if she would go on television Monday to talk about the attack. By this point, the protests seemed like early volleys in a war against the United States, fought with stories instead of weapons. Anna was glad to help.

On the *Today* show Monday, Savannah Guthrie asked her: "Senator, let me begin by posing the question Americans are asking this morning: Did we do this?"

"Absolutely not," Anna Carpenter said. "The United States does not assassinate world leaders—"

"Although you can't deny that there have been government-sponsored assassination attempts in the past—Fidel Castro, as just one example. These have been well-documented—"

Anna winced privately, having walked into that one. "If you're asking me to defend something that happened more than fifty years ago," she said, "I can't. But if you're asking me did we have anything to do with the attack on Friday, I *will*. This goes against who we are as a nation. And I would point out that there is no credible evidence—"

"But at the same time, people do *believe* this, don't they, Senator? I mean, you've seen the reports: we hear that there was talk within the CIA and at the Pentagon for *weeks* of a quote preemptive strike on Russia. And a plan that would leave 'no US fingerprints.' And now, there are new reports of leaked emails, linking the CIA with this Ukrainian oligarch—"

"Savannah, it's important to understand that most of these so-called 'reports' originate with the Russian media. They have in Russia a sophisticated propaganda apparatus, including troll factories and bot generators. Troll factories are, basically, opinion factories. They fabricate pro-Russia opinions and circulate them over the Internet. I think it's possible we're underestimating what effect some of that is having—"

"So, just to be clear: You're saying these allegations are fabrications? That the CIA never even *talked* about a preemptive strike against Russia?"

"I don't believe it was ever discussed seriously, no. Frankly, I think we've been caught off guard and we're spending time now talking about the wrong things."

"So let me ask you, Senator: who *was* responsible for the attack, if not the United States?"

"That's what the investigation is for, Savannah," Anna said. "I don't think speculating at this point is useful." She was tempted to tell her what she *did* believe: that Russia itself was behind the attack on the president's plane, that it had been devised to have the very effect it was having. But not now. Anna didn't have the foundation to make that claim publicly. And it would have been insensitive to the families of the twenty-six people who were killed. Telling the truth about what had happened wasn't her business. Not yet.

On Tuesday, the story changed again, with an op-ed in the *Washington Post* by a former US ambassador to the United Nations. Titled "1991, American-style," it compared the United States to the Soviet Union more than a quarter century earlier. The op-ed, released Monday evening, became Topic A on Twitter and the cable news shows Tuesday morning. And suddenly, the media were teeming with stories about secession—as Jon Niles had predicted in his blog—suggesting that the secession movement in Texas could spark a national trend, catching fire in the manner of same-sex marriage and marijuana decriminalization. "If it ever comes to that," Texas's governor told Norah O'Donnell on *CBS This Morning,* "Texas's energy resources and independent electrical grid make us uniquely situated to operate as a stand-alone entity." He cited surveys showing that most eighteen- to twenty-five-year-olds in the state identified themselves as "Texans first, Americans second."

In her first interview of the day, on *Morning Joe,* Anna was asked to respond to the secession story, which struck her as an irrelevant distraction. "Leaving aside the question of whether secession is legal or not," she replied, "which, based on the Supreme Court's ruling, it is not—I don't think it's realistic. I think it's just more premeditated hysteria in the wake of last Friday's tragedy—"

"But that's not what I'm asking," Joe Scarborough said. "Just stay with the editorial, Senator: do you think it's *possible* secession will gain a foothold in this country?"

"I don't believe so, no," Anna replied. "Although the fact that you're asking me, and we're having this conversation—"

"So you dismiss the comparisons to 1991, when the Soviet Union broke apart into sixteen separate nations."

"I don't see a comparison, no," Anna said. "We're held together in this country by ideas that didn't exist in the Soviet Union then, Joe, and don't exist in Russia today. We're an open, competitive society; they were a closed society and are increasingly becoming that way again.

"We're not a perfect union, by any means, but when we do make mistakes we have a system that shines a light on them and holds people accountable. There are other countries—and to a disturbing degree Russia is chief among them—where that light has been snuffed out. But there's a more general accountability that comes with that. It's up to all of us to pay attention. If our democracy is being threatened, the first thing we need to do is recognize that threat. Being silent is often the same as being complicit."

Anna realized as she walked off the set that she probably sounded more strident than she intended. But she felt good, buoyed by her belief that the US's system—the world's oldest democracy—still worked better than any other, despite its flaws. Coming through the midday D.C. traffic back to Capitol Hill, Anna scrolled down her messages and saw that the early response was mostly positive. Some tweeters thought she was setting the stage for a presidential run, which was the last thing on her mind.

"The president loved it," Chief of Staff Corey Fishman called to tell her. "He wants to know why you're not doing more."

"I guess because I have this job as a US Senator," Anna said.

"He also wants to know if you'll meet with him for five minutes this afternoon. At 2:45. Can you manage that?"

"Yes, certainly." There was something slightly ominous about the request, but Anna was able to put that feeling away. She hadn't been to the Oval Office in months, and she recognized that this could be her chance to find out why the administration's response to the August 13 attack still seemed so tepid. And, maybe, even to learn what was really going on with the US and Russia.

TWENTY-FIVE

Surfing the newscasts and talk-radio shows in his old Mustang, Jon Niles began to feel as if he were driving through an unfamiliar country, where people really believed this: that some secret group within the intelligence community had hatched a plot to assassinate Russia's president, and then—in the manner of recent American blunders abroad—failed spectacularly in carrying it out.

Jon's attempts to get closer to the truth over the past three days had mostly fizzled. He'd talked with more than a dozen people, but the sources he most wanted to reach—those who'd spoken about the "secret" Russia meetings—were no longer taking his calls. Finally, he decided to track them down where they lived. Literally. Beginning with Congressman Craig Kettles, who'd been the first to confirm to him what 9:15 had said about the "preemptive" strike talks. Kettles was also known as one of the strongest Russia "hawks" in Congress.

Something about the story of US involvement still felt inherently wrong to Jon, but as new details came out—and pundits argued over them, always along partisan lines—the story also became more confusing. Russia blogs had introduced the phrase "assassination committee" over the weekend and the American media were making it part of the national dialogue.

Driving the Beltway through the Maryland suburbs, Jon punched on the Rolling Stones to give his thoughts a break. He turned it up: the drum intro to "Honky Tonk Women" carried him into the fast lane, and he stayed there through "Paint It Black" and "Gimme Shelter," speeding by the slower rush-hour traffic for miles before his thoughts about August 13 began to steer him back into the middle lane. He finally slowed down, realizing that he ought to be looking for his exit.

Kettles owned a townhouse in a tony section of Potomac. Jon had found him through a county property records search. Kettles was an ambitious, canny second-term Democrat from Mississippi, who had managed to build surprisingly strong alliances in the defense and intel communities during his four years in Washington. He was an educated man, with two master's degrees, but could talk like a country bumpkin when he wanted.

Jon parked in front of his house and turned off the engine. The front door of the townhouse was open and Jon saw what he thought at first was a child peering out through the storm door glass. Then he realized it was Kettles.

Kettles stepped onto the porch, his arms wide like a gunslinger's. Jon got out and went to meet him. "Mr. Kettles? Jonathan Niles. Sorry, I've been trying to—"

"This is not convenient, okay?" The congressman's tie and collar buttons were undone; he must've been dressing. "If you want an interview, you have to go through my office."

"I did, actually," Jon said. "I've been trying to reach you for several days. Since Saturday. I'll make this quick. I just have a follow-up question on something you told me about this Russia committee . . ."

Kettles held up a hand to stop him. He had the manner of a large man although he was actually quite short, five foot three or four. Many who'd only seen him on television didn't know that. "Come on around," he said and turned abruptly, leading Jon into a tiny walled yard beside the townhouse. He closed the wrought-iron gate. The lawn furniture was wet with dew, so they stood. Kettles crossed his arms as Jon began to explain why he was there.

"When we first talked about this," he said, "you told me—off the record, of course—that you'd heard there was a group within the administration, a committee—" Kettles was making a low "mmm mmm" sound to hurry him along. He had dark, intense eyes but otherwise the face of a poker player. "—and you confirmed that they'd discussed, among other things, a proposal to take some sort of covert action against Russia in response—"

"No." Kettles raised a hand to stop him. "First of all: I'd never've used the word *proposal*. Okay?" Kettles's Mississippi accent curled around the word *proposal*.

"Okay." Jon glanced at his notes. "But it was discussed—?"

"No."

"Okay, let me see . . ." Jon flipped back several pages, found the word *proposal* underlined. "Here we go . . . you confirmed to me that there was a small group within the administration that met several times to discuss Russia. Five people—"

"I *heard*."

"You heard, right. And you also heard that this group may have opened channels with anti-Putin interests in Ukraine?" Jon took a breath. "Would that be Hordiyenko, the arms dealer?"

Kettles flashed a smile. "No, look. Let me tell you what's going on. Or what I *hear* is going on. Jonathan. Off the record, okay? I'm sure you know that one of the generals was forced to resign the other week for telling the president things he didn't want to hear. Right?"

"No. I'm not sure I do."

"Okay? Now. You didn't get that from me, by the way." He blinked twice and continued, his assertiveness still several times larger than he was, it seemed. "But here's a question: Is it possible there are forces within this administration that have a Russia policy we don't know about? That are more concerned about Russia than we think?"

"Is that what you're saying?"

"No, it's what I'm *asking*." He tilted his head, smiling momentarily. "It is sort of funny, isn't it, that we haven't heard an official denial yet from the White House. Why is that, do you think?"

"I don't know. Respect for the loss of life, maybe?" Jon said. "What do you think?"

"No idea. But I will say this—and I'm not the only one, as I'm sure you know, who's saying it. But it wouldn't surprise me if someone in the administration knew about this. Or was involved."

"In shooting down the plane?"

"I didn't say that. But, I mean, there's a kind of logic to it, isn't there? Considering what's been going on. All the talk about Russia. If we could somehow eliminate all that in a single afternoon, replace their leader with someone more stable. If there was some *guarantee* that it'd never be tied back to us—'no fingerprints'? I mean, sure, there are some people who'd want to at least take a *look* at that. Don't you think?" Jon wasn't so sure, but he said nothing. "I'm not saying they *did*. But, I mean, bottom line, Geopolitics 101: when we show weakness, our enemies grow stronger. And over the past decade, we've in effect helped create a monster. Right?"

"The United States has."

"The West has, sure. We let Russia get away with Chechnya. Let them get away with Georgia. Crimea. Ukraine. We let them go into Syria, Afghanistan. We let them develop cyber capabilities that are a threat to democracies around the world. And what's happened? They've only become a bigger threat. Now, I know some people in power don't like to see it that way."

"But some do."

"They should."

"But not to the point of plotting to assassinate the Russian president?"

"Well. You tell me." He smiled and turned, nodding toward the gate. Kettles was good at talking elliptically, making his points indirectly. Jon closed his notepad. "I'll tell you one thing, though," Kettles said, walking to the gate. "As background. And then I need to go in and finish my Cheerios. I'm told this meeting in Kiev *did* happen. Okay? With the CIA man? And that could prove very damaging to the administration. If the details are ever known."

"The meeting between Hordiyenko, the Ukrainian arms dealer, and the CIA?"

"Very damaging. That's where the deal was made, I'm told. If there *was* a deal. I don't know if there was. But if there was. So I'm *told*. You'd have to source that elsewhere."

"Any suggestions?"

"Well. Have you tried to contact any of the five people who were supposedly in those meetings?"

"I've tried Gregory Dial, who won't talk to the media," Jon said. "You indicated one or more of the generals was in the room. Rickenbach? Of course, he doesn't talk either."

Kettles waited until they were standing outside the gate, surveying his street. He squinted at the sky, as if thinking very hard, and then said, in a softer voice, "You might ask Maya Coles if she was there. Okay? I'm told she may've been."

"Really."

"Mmm. I'm *told*. She might've been in Kiev, too." He suddenly began to blink. "But. Of course, that can't ever be tied back to me."

Coles, the undersecretary of defense for national security, had been one of Jon's sources. But she'd told him she *wasn't* involved in discussions about Russia and didn't know anything about a "Russia committee." Jon wondered if she was hiding behind semantics, as she often did.

"This whole thing is drawing denials from the NSC, of course," Jon said. "And DNI Julia Greystone says the preemptive strike talk is fiction."

"Well. Of course." He squinted irritably. "It's her *job* to say that." He disliked Greystone, as did many in the military, for being too close to the president and at odds with the Pentagon. There was also the fact that *she* disliked *him,* or didn't take him seriously. Kettles kept political scorecards; he had his own standings of dozens, maybe hundreds, of people in Washington.

"I know you reporters are all tripping over one another right now to find out what happened." Kettles suddenly flashed a warm, surprising smile, and extended his hand. "Let me finish my breakfast. And I'd appreciate it if you don't ever come to my home again."

"Sorry," Jon said. *Here's hoping I won't need to,* he thought. "Appreciate your time," he said. Jon sat in his car for several minutes, scribbling notes about what Kettles had just told him. The sun was bright now, flaring above the townhouse roofs, burning moisture from the air. Craig Kettles was cunning, pushing an agenda, and at the same time looking out for his own political fortunes. Jon could picture him one day testifying against the president in some special-committee ethics investigation or FBI criminal probe.

On talk radio, a longtime Republican senator was chastising the Democrats for the "conditions" that had led to the August 13 attack. Internationally, the story didn't carry such distinctions. This was the United States again, a single entity. It angered Jon that the media had reduced the attack story to politics when the real issue ought to be national security.

While he'd been talking with Kettles, Jon saw, he'd received a call from US Senator Anna Carpenter, of all people. Christopher's girlfriend. *That* was sort of interesting.

Something about his brother's attitude in recent weeks bothered Jon a little. He hadn't returned Christopher's last couple of phone calls. It wasn't anything specific, just that his brother seemed a little above-it-all lately, ever since he'd taken the job as a university lecturer. It made Jon sad. But Anna Carpenter he liked. She had a pluck and an intensity that he admired. Not to mention an interesting smile. Before he set off back to the Beltway—and wherever this story took him next— Jon returned Anna's call.

TWENTY-SIX

Southwest of Moscow.

Andrei Turov had spent much of Monday refining the draft of the president's speech that he would present to him at the dacha outside of Moscow. But the enthusiasm that Turov felt all weekend had been dampened by the news Anton had brought him that morning.

The dispatch he expected confirming Ivan Delkoff's death had instead confirmed the opposite: Delkoff was alive. There were surveillance images of him at the train station in Minsk over the weekend, wearing what looked like a paste-on beard and a stocking cap, and also at the airport in Riga Monday afternoon, without the hat. Anton had begun piecing together Delkoff's route of escape, a slow trail that seemed to lead to northern France.

Fortunately, the president trusted Turov, and did not want to be bothered by the details of August 13. He would not be aware of Delkoff's flight. Not yet. But the escape seemed like a bad sign, and it gnawed away at Turov's concentration as he polished the speech.

The afternoon turned unseasonably warm. Heat pooled in the meadows, and the leaves outside his office window stood perfectly still. Turov felt the vacuum of what was missing—Svetlana, the grandchildren, Olga, Svetlana's cat Boris. With Olga and his family here, these last four months had been the happiest time of Turov's adult life. There were mornings when he had looked back at the long valley of his working days and seen clearly what he could never see then: how cluttered and unrewarding his life had been. The consolation was that Turov could try now to make up for those years. The shame was that it had taken this long to get the right desires into his head.

But today he worried about something else: the unexpectedly terse replies from the Kremlin over his planned travel to Switzerland. He'd have to take that up with the president tomorrow.

With sunset approaching, he forced himself to think like the president and train his thoughts on the speech again. The attack on the president's plane showed Russian vulnerability, something Putin normally did not like to acknowledge. But Turov saw in this weakness a strength. The president would go before the Duma on Friday and the world would see a face of Putin it didn't know, and they would feel empathy. And some would feel anger. He would talk about the families of the twenty-six men and women who had been murdered aboard the plane. He would talk about the forces working clandestinely to undermine Russia. And he would cite the words of the great Russian general Anton Denikin, who had said, more than a hundred years ago, that his country was "one and indivisible."

He would talk of the "war" on terror—a war the United States had bungled colossally after 9/11, even to the point of invading the wrong country. He would talk of Russia's moral leadership in a new world order, describing the essential human values that separated Russia from the West. Those in the West no longer even took their lives seriously anymore, creating false excitements about inconsequential events, celebrities, and awards shows to fill their time. The president would talk about the dangerous waters of the West, whose surface glittered like rare jewels but which no longer contained any depth of purpose or moral responsibility.

It was a speech that would change Russia. And for that, his old friend would give him a reprieve to spend some time with his family. All the same, it was good practice in Russia to be in more than one game at a time. And if the president was not receptive to Turov's ideas and tried to outmaneuver him, Turov would have to outplay the president. He could still do that. The president's weakness was that he was a tactician, not a strategist. Turov could be both.

As the late sun narrowed to sword-like shards of red and gold in the trees, Anton finally arrived with an update. He opened his computer on Turov's desk and showed him the latest: a new surveillance video from de Gaulle airport. A satellite image of two men walking to a car park. "That's him," Anton said. "The other man is his cousin."

"You're sure."

"Yes, no question. Dmitri Porchak is the cousin. Little Dmitri. I have a team headed to Paris right now. They will be at his house by morning."

"This won't just be another trick by Delkoff?"

"No. He was lucky before, he won't be this time." It was hard to tell much from the images, but Turov could hear the conviction in Anton's voice. "He will be dead before noon."

"You are sure."

"I am certain."

TWENTY-SEVEN

Suburban Maryland.

"Work from my place if you want," Carole Katz said. It was a standing invitation, which Jon Niles made use of too often. He associated Carole's little wooden house in the country with his own bad habits: drinking beer, tweeting, watching the "news," or staring at the cornfields. And she had made it easy, telling him early on to "keep the key," their version of commitment.

Jon had awakened that day with the crazy idea that he might even have a chance again with his old girlfriend Liz Foster. He got that occasionally, usually for no discernible reason. Part of it was just the Niles stubbornness, a desire to get right what had gone wrong the first time. It still felt strange sitting with her in staff meetings, this beautiful, knotty woman he'd put on a pedestal for months, now just an agreeable coworker.

Jon drove down the country lanes for a while, listening to some middle-period Beatles, before finally circling back to Carole's house. He needed to pick up a few clothes there anyway. Plus, it'd be quiet. Sitting in the kitchen, he placed calls to Gregory Dial and Maya Coles. He knew that Dial, the CIA officer named in the online "preemptive strike" stories, would never call him back. But he was pretty sure Coles, one of the president's national security advisers, would. Particularly if he left a slightly provocative message, which he did.

He watched the news for a few minutes as he waited, becoming angry at how the newcasters all repeated the buzz-phrases "assassination committee," "no fingerprints," and "preemptive strike," which only seemed to reinforce Russia's version of what happened.

It took eight minutes for Maya Coles to call back. "Where are you getting that I had something to do with this 'no fingerprints' thing?" she said, an edge in her voice. "I assume you were kidding."

"You know I don't kid about things like that," Jon said. It was Maya Coles's style to get right to business. "Actually, I'm told you *were* there when it was discussed. And also that you were at this meeting with Hordiyenko, the Ukrainian arms supplier, last month. In Kiev."

Her silence stretched out. Politically, Coles leaned to the right, like Kettles, but unlike Kettles she was also a staunch defender of the president and his policies.

"I take that as a yes?"

"Off the record?"

"Of course."

"Where'd you hear about Kiev?"

"So it's true—you were there?"

"No," she said, and made a startling throat-clearing sound. "Hey, Jon. Don't play into this conspiracy crap, okay? There *was* a meeting but it had nothing to do with assassinating the president of Russia. Don't be manipulated, honey."

Jon was scribbling *don't play into conspiracy crap . . . don't be manipulated, honey*. No matter how many times she used the word "honey," it always felt disconcerting.

"So why are we having this conversation?" he said. "Why *is* there a conspiracy theory? I mean, there's *something* out there that's scaring the administration. Tell me what it is."

She laughed loudly, one of her standard deflections. Jon waited.

"Okay, here's a question for you, Jon. And this is just conversation now."

"Okay."

"What if a handful of people *did* have intel about a planned assassination? From within the Russian military, I mean. I'm not saying *good* intel. But say we had something. And failed to bring it to Mr. Putin's attention. Is that the same as being complicit?"

I don't know, Jon thought. *But you're changing the subject.* "You didn't answer my question about the meeting in Kiev," he said. Maya Coles said nothing. "I understand you were in the meetings in Washington, too, that we talked about before." More silence. "When this 'no fingerprints' idea was first floated."

"When we put out the hit, you mean?" she said.

"Can I quote you on that?"

"No. Okay, look," she said. "For starters: I'd be very careful about how you handle that no fingerprints thing."

What sounded like a garbage truck went by on her end. "You're not denying it, then."

"I'm not denying the words ever came up in conversation. As table exercises; war games. But never for real. Maybe if you told me where you heard it, I could elaborate."

"I can't give you a name. But I've heard about these meetings from several sources."

"And therein lies the problem," she said, a muscle of anger again in her voice. "Since reporters are never in the room when these national security issues are discussed, and the information is classified, your stories are by definition based on leaks. And leaks aren't information. They're cherry-picked to reflect someone's agenda. By definition."

"So help me out, then," Jon said. "I know there were five people in the room when this 'no fingerprints' thing occurred. You were one, I'm told. General Rickenbach was one, Gregory Dial from CIA. Edward Sears from the State Department—?"

This last was a bluff to see how she'd respond. Maya Coles laughed loudly. "Nice try," she said. "Listen. Jon. Here's the deal. Since you're pushing it. I'm willing to tell you the real story, okay? As much as I can—if you agree to verify it elsewhere."

"Okay." When she began a statement with "Listen"—rather than her usual "Look"—it meant she was going to tell him something significant. "Listen" also carried a note of sincerity, although it was never clear how sincere her sincerity was.

"Off the record. There's a big story that's about to drop, okay? Maybe not the story you guys would like and I'm sorry about that. But a big story. The real story."

"Go ahead."

"There's intel, HUMINT, which you'll be hearing about very soon—they're just dotting the *i*'s right now—about one of the Russian generals. Okay? That's all I can say. But here's a prediction: within forty-eight hours, that's all you guys are going to be talking about. In the meantime, the responsible thing is wait until it's been vetted. What's the adage you guys use—better to get it right than get it first?"

"I don't use that one," Jon said. "Tell me about this general, though. This is someone within the Russian military who was working with Hordiyenko in some way?"

"That's what I understand. But you have to source that elsewhere. Okay? Hey, Jon: gotta go. Just remember: it's more than your own personal glory that's at stake here."

"I'll remember," he said. Maya Coles clicked off.

Jon opened his computer and typed in his notes from their conversation, pausing several times to watch the "Breaking News" on television—although "Breaking News" was the permanent banner now on all the cable networks, and "breaking news" seemed redundant to him anyway. *What did she mean about someone in the administration knowing?* Kettles had suggested the same thing. How far within the administration *did* this go?

When all three news networks were on commercials, Jon wandered into the living room, where he became distracted for a while with

Carole's matchbooks. Carole kept a couple hundred matchbooks in a large fish bowl, an inheritance from her father. Freddie Katz had been a salesman who traveled the US highways in the sixties and seventies, back when people still smoked openly in public. Jon picked through a few of them, imagining an older, more dimly lit version of the country, with cigarette machines and juke boxes, names like Starlite Lounge, Dew Drop Inn, Pine Cone Motel. They made him feel lonesome.

With Carole, he was a little pre-nostalgic now: they hadn't broken up yet but he was already missing her. He looked at the print of *House by the Railroad* above the table. Carole liked Hopper's old houses and window shades, the gleaming slants of sunlight. She loved gothic architecture. Jon preferred *Gas* and *Shakespeare at Dusk, 1935:* fading light, encroaching nature, the lack of people.

His cell phone startled him. It was Anna Carpenter calling back.

"Good afternoon," she said, a buoyant tone that felt contagious. "I read your blog today. I thought maybe we could meet. I suspect we may have some mutual interests."

"About—?"

"Russia. Noise at the expense of comprehension?"

"Okay."

"Tell me when you're free."

"Okay," Jon said. "How about now?"

To his surprise, Anna Carpenter accepted. If he could make it downtown, she'd meet him in an hour at the Starbucks on Capitol Hill.

As he drove away toward the city, Jon began to wonder about his brother again. The real reason Anna Carpenter was asking to meet him, he suspected, had to do with Christopher, not Russia, or truth, or noise at the expense of comprehension. It was even possible that Christopher would be there, he realized. But, then again, maybe not. He hoped not.

TWENTY-EIGHT

MOSCOW.

Christopher Niles knew, as he walked from the plane into Moscow's Sheremetyevo Airport Sunday afternoon, that he was under surveillance. He knew, from having worked in Moscow for eighteen months, that the FSB ran surveillance from the observation room in the control tower.

He was arriving as himself: a college teacher researching the Russian Orthodox Church, ahead of a class he was teaching and an op-ed he intended to write. It was his job over the next two or three days to do nothing that would make anyone think otherwise.

It wouldn't be easy. Russia had grown increasingly wary of Americans since economic sanctions were imposed in 2014 after Russia's annexation of Crimea. American embassy staff and their families were now routinely harassed, sometimes in bizarre ways. Diplomats reported Russian agents breaking into their homes at night, turning on lights, rearranging furniture. One diplomat returned home to find someone had defecated in his living room.

Chris's task in Moscow was to find and meet with Andrei Turov. He had left messages for him before leaving Washington and was confident that he would call him back. But until then, he'd have to wait and not arouse anyone's suspicions.

Russia's intelligence services knew who he was; they knew of his tenure in Moscow. If the FSB wanted, they could pull him in at any time on a pretense—to check his "paperwork," or for some other contrived reason. They could easily create enough interference to sidetrack the mission. But Chris didn't think they'd do that. They'd be more interested in following him, hoping his movements would give away the real reason he'd come to Moscow. It presented an interesting challenge.

He had two interviews scheduled for Monday morning, and expected to spend the afternoon at the Tretyakov Gallery, which was home to the finest collection of Russian art in the world. The Tretyakov would be a pleasant diversion. On Tuesday, he would meet Amira Niyzov at Christ the Savior cathedral and take her to lunch nearby. Amira was a prominent Russian online journalist who wrote about culture and religion. She was, he hoped, the "secret weapon" in Christopher's plan.

He checked in to the elegant Hotel National on Tverskaya Street Sunday evening and found two waiting messages. Both interviews Martin had arranged for Monday had canceled. Stanislov Ryzanov, the Russian Orthodox Church spokesman, left regrets that his schedule now "makes it impossible" to meet, this week or next. His other appointment, a scholar-in-residence at the Carnegie Moscow Center, said "circumstances" prevented him from rescheduling. "Circumstances" were August 13, of course.

Chris went for a walk that evening to Red Square, watching sunset wrap around the candy-colored domes of St. Basil's Cathedral. He tried to be just a tourist on his first night, enjoying the grandeur of Red Square, the cool night air and restaurant aromas, not thinking much of Turov. Later, he walked down Tverskaya Street, gazing in the shop windows, his memories stirred by the Cyrillic signs and the stream of traffic thick with SUVs and BMWs, by the grilled kebab aroma from a familiar Uzbek restaurant. Walking was Chris's favorite recreation, and Moscow had been a city he'd always enjoyed exploring, ever since his first visit in 1996, particularly the medieval streets off the main arteries. But he couldn't help notice the changes this time. There were many more construction cranes in Moscow than on his last visit, and most of the vendor stalls and kiosks were gone. It was again a city in transition.

There were also changes not visible from a street level. Vladimir Putin had continued to realign the country's power structure, he knew, giving the security services a stronger role, moving former bodyguards into governorships and top intelligence posts, taking policy-shaping powers away from the Foreign Ministry. In Moscow, the line between Kremlin-sponsored black operations and *mafiyas* activity had further blurred. And stringent new laws had been passed limiting public protest. Who would have imagined when the Soviet Union broke apart in 1991 that Russia would look like this a quarter century later?

As he walked the narrow backstreets, Christopher fell naturally into surveillance-detection mode—scanning for moving shadows, repeat vehicles, shapes in windows. Eventually—briefly—he got a clear look at the Russian agent who was tailing him: a stocky man with close-cropped gray hair and wide-set eyes.

Chris felt a familiar obsession as he returned to the hotel. When Martin had recruited him last week in Greece, he'd felt wary of returning to work for the US government, afraid he'd be jeopardizing the precious life that he was building with Anna—the sort of life he'd never had before. Tonight, walking through the heart of Moscow, with its enormous, largely hidden deception industry, he didn't feel that so strongly; tonight he felt as if he were answering a summons. He felt like an athlete, becoming sharper in anticipation of the main event.

Russia's war on the West had begun here almost invisibly, while the US was looking the other way, focused on Afghanistan and Iraq. Led by an unlikely new president with little political experience, and spurred on by a revitalized petro-economy, Russia had seized the chance to change its destiny. Each year under Putin, the country had increased military spending as it exerted political power in Europe and the Middle East and interfered with the aspirations of its immediate neighbors—particularly those with eyes for the West, such as Ukraine.

Russia's brutal incursion into Georgia in 2008—the scope of which took US intelligence by surprise, although the conflict had been building for months—should have been ample warning about how far Russia would go to keep its former republics in line. But the US underplayed the threat, despite the forecasts of several analysts, among them Christoper Niles.

Chris spoke with Anna before going to bed on Sunday, playing the role of a college teacher visiting Moscow on a research trip. He knew that the hotel room was fitted with cameras and listening devices. Hearing her voice, he regretted again how Martin's assignment had separated them, and he lay awake afterward, trying to will himself to sleep, consumed by an emptiness that he couldn't quite shake. He thought of all the years he'd given to the agency, the precious time he'd spent doing the wrong things. He could never get that time back, of course, but there was a value in understanding those mistakes, he told himself; a lesson for how to live the rest of his life.

In the morning, the bad feelings were all gone. Chris wandered through the medieval side streets near the hotel again. He joined a tour of the five-domed St. Clement's church, with its glittering Baroque interior, staying to chat afterward with the tour guide. He ate lunch at an outdoor café on Stoleshnikov Lane and then walked to Tretyakov Gallery, where he spent much of the afternoon observing the religious art. Art that Anna would have loved, particularly Rublev's great *Trinity* icon in the Hall of Old Russian Art.

Late in the afternoon, he took a cab past his former office, at the American embassy, where a crowd of weary-looking anti-American demonstrators were milling on the sidewalk. Someone had pelted the building with eggs earlier, and no one had gotten around to cleaning it. Upstairs, on the top floor, was where Chris had worked for eighteen months.

Seeing the building stirred contrary emotions, reminding him that he might still be working here if his last job hadn't gone bad. If he hadn't discovered details of a Russian disinformation plot against neighboring Estonia, and tried to pass it on to his government. The plot had involved the arrest of an Estonian border guard on charges of espionage and sexual misconduct—then using that arrest as propaganda to inflame anti-Estonia sentiment among the country's twenty-five-percent-Russian population.

Christopher's source was a Russian asset named Marina Vostrak, a diplomatic aide he'd begun to cultivate months earlier. Marina wanted to deal, she said, but was becoming nervous about their arrangement. Chris took her concerns to the chief of station, who asked him to wait. They couldn't risk compromising "a larger case," the COS said. Several days later, Marina Vostrak went missing. And three days after that, Chris watched the news from his embassy office as an Estonian guard was arrested and the campaign began. He was still waiting to hear about the "larger case."

Washington's failure to prevent the Estonia operation was disheartening but hardly surprising. What happened to Marina Vostrak, though, was. The day after the border guard's arrest, Marina was found strangled to death in a garbage bin in Tallinn. Chris felt worse than devastated; he also felt responsible.

He'd gone to war with the Agency briefly after that, as he had several times in the past. But it was shooting spitballs at a battleship. He'd ended up quitting the government soon afterward, to become an independent contractor. The whole business had cost him income and prestige. But he'd also met Anna, and that made it worthwhile.

The cab carried Christopher past Turov's headquarters, a kilometer from the US embassy, a nondescript office building where troll and bot factories operated on the sixth floor, he had heard. Turov lived in the country now with his daughter Svetlana and his grandchildren, supposedly. Turov's gatekeeper, Anton Konkin, lived there too, as did a girlfriend, Olga Sheversky.

He channel-surfed Russian state television that night, searching for an objective discussion about last Friday's attack. But there wasn't any. In the more than three years since Chris had last been in Moscow, several of Russia's best-known journalists had fled the country. Many prominent intellectuals had left as well.

Instead of discussion, he found "news": more US documents had been leaked, indicating that a Ukrainian SBU officer named Mikhail Kolchak, one of the August 13 "co-conspirators," had met with American CIA officer Gregory Dial in Kiev last month. Further "evidence," the news reader said, that the US had been behind Friday's attack.

The Russian foreign minister was being interviewed on another channel, calling this latest leak "an incredible development" and "a declaration of war."

"Our president's high approval ratings show one thing very clearly: that Russians are united," he said, gesturing like an orchestra conductor. "Americans, needless to say, are not."

This was Turov's credibility equation, Christopher knew: Russia gains by August 13, the US loses; they were the same story, two ends of a seesaw. A new, more effective means of warfare. Instead of taking lives and destroying property, which was the old way, you won by simply changing what people thought about the United States.

His cell phone rang. Christopher reached for it and checked the message screen. It was a pre-arranged, coded text from Martin Lindgren: Jake Briggs had just contacted Ivan Delkoff in France.

The first connection was made, then. The second would come tomorrow.

The last thing he did before going to bed on Monday was call Anna. They spoke a little longer this time, and a little less self-consciously. Christopher told her about seeing Rublev's *Trinity* icon, how he wished she could have been with him to see the Russian art. It was 2:30 in the afternoon in Washington. Anna was in her tiny unmarked "hideaway" office in the basement at the US Capitol, she told him. She missed him very much.

Chris lay awake afterward again, feeling a little better than he had after their talk on Sunday. But their life together felt faraway again, a boat against the current . . . He thought of Anna's steady eyes on the beach in Greece as he'd walked toward her from the sea, ready for their long-delayed "conversation"; the way she reached for his hand without hesitation as they strolled through the village in the afternoon, and how they had talked themselves to sleep that night, lying in the dark with the windows open . . . But eventually Chris's thoughts drifted back to Andrei Turov. If his instincts were wrong and he didn't hear back from Turov tomorrow, or the next day, then this job would be nothing more than an aborted two-man black ops mission. Chris would write a report, it would be filed away, and he would get on with his life at the university. It was SOP for Martin's division, anyway: consider scenarios no one else was looking at. Being wrong was built into its charter.

But there was another idea that Christopher began to entertain as he lay in this nineteenth-century-style Russian hotel room waiting for sleep. An idea that had first come to him in Greece, what seemed like the small voice of his wilder instincts: what if the meeting with Petrenko in London had been a *part* of Turov's deception? What if the real reason he was in Moscow tonight was that Turov had called him here?

There was no empirical evidence to support the idea—or even much logical rationale for it. Except that Christopher knew how Turov's mind worked. It would be interesting to see what happened tomorrow.

TWENTY-NINE

Tuesday, August 17. Moscow.

He ate a small, late breakfast in the elegant Moskovsky Hall dining room, with its panoramic views of Red Square. Afterward he crossed the Patriarchal footbridge to the magnificent Cathedral of Christ the Savior, stopping midway across the Moskva River to take in the view. It was stunning in the late-morning light: the Kremlin in one direction, the three-hundred-foot statue of Peter the Great in the other. Cathedral of Christ the Savior was the largest church in Russia and the tallest Orthodox Church in the world. It had, like much of Moscow, a strange and broken history: constructed originally in the nineteenth century, the cathedral was destroyed by Stalin in 1931 to make way for a grand Palace of the Soviets, which Stalin envisioned as an enduring monument to socialism. But, for various reasons, Stalin's palace was never built. In the fifties, Khrushchev turned the site into the world's largest outdoor swimming pool. In the late 1990s, with the Russian Orthodox Church in ascendance, the cathedral was rebuilt, resembling in nearly every detail the building Stalin dynamited in 1931.

Christopher spent half an hour marveling at the interior rooms of the Cathedral—the marble chapel, the frescos, the shrines of the Temple—making sure that by 11:20 he was in the gift shop. He selected two books about the church's history and a medallion to take home to Anna. As he was paying at the register he spotted Amira Niyzov lingering by the exit, wearing a long skirt and thin black sweater, which seemed to blend with her untamed black hair.

"Want to get lunch?" he said, his eyes adjusting as they came out onto the street alongside the river. The clouds were white and glowing with sunlight. "My treat," he said. "You choose the restaurant."

Amira Niyzov was a slight woman in her early forties with large brown eyes and hollow cheeks that gave a false sadness to her face. "So you are a history professor now," she said, as they walked the narrow stone street to the restaurant.

"Teacher, actually. Guest lecturer."

"Teacher, then. And we have a common interest again after all this time," she said, speaking with her precise diction and cultured English accent.

"Do we?"

"You're here writing about the Russian Orthodox Church."

"Ah, yes." Chris smiled. It was possible sometimes to miss the trace of humor in Amira's words. Outwardly, she was a waif, but there was a tough, unyielding quality at her core. Fifteen years ago Amira had been active in a now-defunct liberal political party—back when Russia still had real political parties—and she'd been friends with Anna Politkovskaya, the courageous—reckless, some said—opposition journalist who'd been shot dead in her apartment elevator in 2006. Amira had always been careful, in her way. Raised a modest, moderate Muslim, she had distanced herself as a teen from her parents' religion, using journalism to cultivate broader interests in religion, politics, and Russian culture. She'd been through a bad marriage and a divorce, but it was part of her life that she didn't talk about, as if it had never happened. Even when she was politically active, Amira always presented herself first as a culture and religion writer, an objective journalist.

Chris hadn't spoken to Amira in three years, but they'd remained connected by a bond of respect and occasional emails. And by something else: a shared understanding of who Andrei Turov really was and what he could do. In the late 2000s, Amira had briefly pursued Turov, intending to write a story on his donations to the Orthodox Church. Turov agreed to meet with her at his Moscow office. But then he'd insisted that she not write about him, claiming that he wasn't important enough. Amira accepted that, but didn't believe it. Her real interest in Turov was the same as Chris's: the secret work he did for Russia's president, not his donations to the church. Later, they would compare notes, although she had made the unusual request that they never use Turov's name in any of their conversations. He became "the crow," because "crows are an especially smart bird, and he is that," she'd said.

The fact that she had accepted Chris's invitation to meet today told him something, although he wasn't sure what. Amira was living under cover now, in a sense, abiding by the country's increasingly restrictive rule book.

He opened the door and they entered the small, familiar Georgian restaurant, taking a table in a private, parlor-like room by the front window. A waiter brought them a pot of tea.

"It's not such a good time to be an American in Moscow, is it?" Christopher said, after they ordered—*pelmeni,* dumplings filled with onions and mushrooms, borscht soup. "Both of my interviews canceled yesterday. You aren't worried about meeting me?"

"To talk about the church? No, of course not," she said, her eyes staying with his. "It's become an important topic in Russia. I'm happy your country has at last taken notice."

"It's interesting how things have changed, though," Chris said. "In the eighties, going to church was how you stood up to communism. Now, the church seems almost a branch of the state."

Amira looked away. "It's true," she said. "Ninety-five percent of the churches in Moscow were destroyed in the twenties and thirties. Communism left us an atheist country for seventy years. But over the last two decades, 23,000 new Orthodox churches have been built. And seventy percent of Russians now call themselves Orthodox Christians."

"Quite a role reversal," Christopher said.

"Yes."

Chris glanced out the window and recognized the same stocky man he'd seen following him on Tverskaya Sunday night. "The only reason we adopted 'In God We Trust' as our motto in the 1950s, you know, was to draw a line between our country and yours," he said.

"Yes, I think the line's still there, we've just sort of switched sides." Amira reached for her tea. There was an ambiguous, slightly off-kilter quality about her that he liked.

It felt safe sparring with Amira about the church, and they carried it on through the meal, discussing the United States's drift toward political correctness, its legalizing of same-sex marriage, and Russia's ambition to become a "traditional values society," the moral alternative to the West. Amira spoke with a professional detachment, causing Chris to wonder if maybe she had missed his email reference to the "crow" and really *was* here just to talk about the church.

They were finishing their meal when he pointed to a man holding an English language paper outside. In the headline, he saw the words "No Fingerprints" in quotes.

"The news is all about last Friday now, isn't it?" he said, in a quieter tone. "It's going to make your president more popular than ever, I'd imagine." Amira shrugged a *perhaps*. "And make things tougher for the opposition."

"Maybe yes, maybe no." They were testing each other, Chris sensed, circling the topic for a way in. But this was where he needed to go, if just briefly: there was a network of opposition forces that was still very much alive in Russia, waiting for something to join them together and light them up again. Amira was a link to that network. There was also a shadow society in Russia, sponsored by the exiled businessman and Putin critic Mikhail Khodorkovsky. His Open Russia foundation had for months been recruiting political and business leaders who—in

theory, at least—could take over when the current regime finally top-
pled, although no one expected that to happen soon.

"You planned to write about him. Several years ago," Christopher
said. "The crow."

Amira moved her hand dismissively on the table. "There wasn't
much to write. He convinced me he was like hundreds of others in
Russia. I never saw a story there."

In fact, *no one* had ever written a story on Turov, as far as Christopher
knew. "Supposedly, there's been some kind of falling out now with the
Kremlin?"

"Maybe," she said. "Or maybe he just wanted to retire. Actually,
what I hear is that he's concerned about his family. About *nevyezdniye*.
Do you know what that is?"

"It's the policy that prohibits people with access to state secrets
from traveling to countries that have extradition treaties with the US,
isn't it? Something like that?"

"Something like that," she said, a subtle smile briefly lighting her
face. "Four million Russians are on the list now. He's very much a family man. He's more concerned for them, I suspect, than for himself."
Chris could see that she was privately energized by this turn in the conversation. She leaned forward, adding, "You think he had something
to do with last Friday?"

"Don't you?"

"The story I'm told, and it's well-sourced, is that the missiles were
Ukrainian military. Purchased by Hordiyenko for a private militia. The
missile battery was seen in Ukrainian territory that day. Last Friday.
There are supposedly photos that match up."

"Yes, most of that's been reported," Chris said. "But where did the
backing come from? Who ordered it?"

"Well. From what I'm reading, it came from Washington." She gave
him a calculated look, not quite smiling. "Why? What do you think?"

"What I think," Chris said, "is that the crows always return to the
cornfield. Metaphorically speaking. I think the whole thing could've

been pulled off with a very small number of people—ten, maybe. Only three or four of whom knew what they were really doing."

"And one of those three or four—?"

"Had to be the top, yes," he said, meaning the Russian president.

Amira drank her tea and set the cup in the saucer. She took her time responding. "Even if that's true, it would be almost impossible to prove."

"I understand that," Christopher said. He glanced outside and then leaned closer. "But my question is: What if you had some evidence? Theoretically. Could you do anything with that?"

Her dark eyes gleamed with a new interest, but in the next moment she looked away. Chris knew that Amira blamed the Russian president for the loss of several good friends in the opposition movement. But she wasn't stupid. Everyone knew that the Russian president's loudest critics had short life expectancies. "Theoretically, I would be skeptical," she said, her voice a whisper. "Because, even if true, there'd be layers between the crow and those who carried it out. Just as he keeps layers from his business with the Kremlin. That's how he's survived."

"Until now, anyway," Chris said. "But what if one of those layers contained the details about what actually happened?" Her eyes narrowed slightly. "If you had those details, you would still have access to the network, right?"

Amira didn't answer right away. "What do you have?" she said finally.

"Right now, nothing. But it exists. If I were able to broker something, would you be interested? Or would it just put you in jeopardy?"

"That depends." She watched Chris more closely now. This was the crux of it, he knew; they had to trust each other to move this forward. "Why are you asking?"

"Because what I'm talking about would be enough to change things," Chris said. Her eyes quickly scanned the room and returned to his. "To accomplish what some of the people who aren't alive anymore *wanted* to accomplish." He thought of Marina Vostrak—the dour, worried face of his Russian asset, who'd been murdered in Tallinn. And then, for maybe fifteen or twenty seconds, Amira let him in, telling Christopher what he needed to know without saying a word. On the other side of those eyes was a world hidden and protected, still wild, angry and full of possibility; Chris saw what he needed in those twenty seconds. He completed the transaction he'd come here to make.

"How soon?"

"Less than forty-eight hours," he said, hopefully.

Amira reached for one of the books he'd purchased at the gift shop. She opened and began to page through it, talking to him about the history of Christ the Savior cathedral as Christopher's watcher walked past the window again. Amira told him how Tchaikovsky's *1812 Overture* had been written with the cathedral in mind and was first performed there in 1882. How part of the cathedral's first floor had originally been a memorial commemorating Russia's defeat of Napoleon. They became slightly more detached as she spoke, but he appreciated what she was doing; it was as if their orbits had brought them close enough to see each other's faces through the windows of their capsules, and now they were preparing for reentry to their own worlds. At one point, Amira wrote a number inside the book's back cover, and asked him to use it for future communications.

When they walked outside, there was a smell of rain in the breeze and a gray starkness to the neighborhood. They walked two blocks before saying goodbye, giving each other a warm hug. Chris felt lifted by the scents of baked bread and laundry—by the connection they'd just made—as he walked back to the National. The operation had depended on the meeting with Amira. And the meeting had gone as well as he had hoped. Better, even.

The first connection had been Delkoff. He had just made the second.

Chris returned to the hotel hoping to find a response from Andrei Turov. The third connection. Coming up the elevator he recalled the one time he had met Turov, across a chess table in Gorky Park: Turov ordinary, as he'd heard, only more so, down to the uneven cut of his fingernails, the lowered blue eyes, the modest smile, the stray nasal hairs; you wanted to look around and say, "Who're you? Where's Turov?" But Turov was an illusionist. Even his surname was an invention, Chris had learned, taken from a medieval principality in Belarus where, supposedly, his family descended from royal blood.

When he reached the room there was no response, though. Christopher turned on television, feeling anxious again, imagining where Anna was right now. Where Andrei Turov was. He lay on the bed and closed his eyes, surprised at how tired he felt. Thinking about Amira, the way she had let him into her world for fifteen or twenty seconds. How one person could change a country; how one country could change the world. *It's about waiting now,* he reminded himself. Managing time and expectations.

The trill of his phone startled him.

Christopher reached for it on the nightstand. Wondering if he would recognize Turov's voice after four years. *The third connection.*

The voice on the other end was familiar. But it was not Andrei Turov's. And the news it bore was not what Christopher expected. Or wanted to hear.

THIRTY

Northern France.

The Americans' first contact with Ivan Delkoff came on the evening of August 16: an envelope left in a small seafood restaurant off the coast road. The envelope had actually been left for Delkoff's cousin, Little Dmitri, who went to the restaurant in the evenings to drink a pint of ale with the owner and one of the local fishermen. Someone, evidently, had noticed that.

Dmitri's nightly habit would be discontinued now that Delkoff was here; he had assured his cousin of that. But on Monday night, he'd come to the restaurant for a different reason: to buy Delkoff a pint of vodka so he could return to the house and finish writing his "Declaration." It was funny: For months, Delkoff had considered himself a conspirator; now, he understood that he was something else, a witness. His plans were not about survival and concealment anymore; they were about making sure his country's deceptions became known. And that meant he had to rely on basic rules of combat. If your enemy is stronger than you are, evade him. If your enemy is temperamental, seek to irritate him. If your enemy is a clever coward—as Andrei Turov was—expose him. That was what he was going to do. Delkoff's initial strategy after August 13 had been escape and evade. He'd planned to use France as his base for two or three days, then he'd travel on to

Germany; from there, to South Africa. He had already arranged his accounts so that his family members would be taken care of for the rest of their lives. And so that Delkoff had enough ready cash to avoid leaving an electronic trail.

Dmitri came out looking sullen, as always, his open hunter's jacket flapping in the sea air. Delkoff heard the bottles clinking in an old paper sack. They rode inland, dipping into a shallow and coming to the turn with the upside-down rowboat. Dmitri touched Artem's shoulder, asking him to stop. He turned and signaled Delkoff.

The two men got out, much as they had on the drive from Paris. Artem stayed behind the wheel with the engine running, watching in the mirror.

They walked down the road behind the SUV. Then Dmitri stopped and handed him the envelope. "For you," he said. "Not me. You." His cousin watched like an angry police sergeant as Delkoff opened the envelope.

It was a brief note, handwritten in French. Delkoff read it in the moonlight: *Turov sait que vous êtes ici. Je voudrais vous aider. Appelez ce numéro. Jake Briggs, USA.* "Turov knows you're here. I want to help. Call this number. Jake Briggs, USA."

He read it again and passed the note to his cousin. Dmitri looked up at Delkoff when he finished, his mouth parted, as if someone had hit him in the stomach.

"Who the fuck knows you're here?" Dmitri said. "You know this person?"

"I've met him. Several years ago," he said. "I met him in Estonia."

Jake Briggs. He *did* know him. But Delkoff was still trying to form a clear picture. He studied the countryside, the dark wooden houses perched at odd intervals in the moonlight. Was Jake Briggs out there somewhere right now, watching him?

"It's a trick," Dmitri said. Delkoff saw the look of concern in his cousin's face. He understood: no one was supposed to know he was here.

"Call him," Delkoff said. "Go ahead and call him."

Dmitri pulled his phone. Artem was outside the SUV now, too, smoking a cigarette, watching. He wasn't supposed to know about any of this, he was just security. But Delkoff was sure he'd picked up most of it by now. Maybe all of it.

"Ask him a question," Delkoff said. He felt the fresh breeze from the Channel and became inspired. "If he gives the right answer, we'll meet him. If he doesn't, we don't." Dmitri remained silent. "All right?" Delkoff said. "Ask him the name of the restaurant, in Narva."

"What the fuck are you talking about?"

"Ask him the name of the restaurant. If he doesn't know, ask him what beer we drank."

Dmitri finally did what he requested. Delkoff heard his cousin pushing the buttons. Delkoff stepped away from the road and began to urinate. He watched the stars and the strange, iridescent light in the Channel. He felt the outlines of his son's medal in his shirt pocket, and thought of Pavel's willingness, his form of patriotism. He recalled the little crease of smile Pavel would reveal as a boy, glancing shyly up at his dad.

While he finished peeing, Delkoff turned and saw Dmitri walking toward him.

"Antalya Kebab," Dmitri said, holding the phone on his jacket. "You both had Põhjala."

Son of a bitch. Delkoff grinned. *Yes.* "Tell him we'll meet him in the morning, then. First thing."

"He doesn't want that. He wants to meet you tonight," Dmitri said.

"In the morning. Tell him I'll call him myself, first thing. Where's he staying?"

Dmitri relayed his words and then turned back to his cousin. "He says tonight. He wants to talk to you now."

"No." Delkoff began to walk back to the car, anxious to return to the document he was writing. It was an odd coincidence: he'd been thinking earlier that he'd do this as a "walk-in" at the American embassy in Paris. Instead, they'd come to him. They'd made it easy.

He looked over his shoulder and saw Dmitri still talking on the phone, facing south now. "Tell him I'm too tired tonight," he called to his cousin. "First thing in the morning. Eight o'clock. I'll have something to give him then. A document. Tell him that."

Delkoff got into the back seat of the SUV and waited, breaking open the liter of vodka. He watched the Channel, thinking that maybe his future lay over there now, across the ocean. He drew on his kaleidoscope of American images: Coca-Cola signs and fast-food restaurants, neon-lit interstates, the Grand Canyon, the Google logo, Marilyn Monroe, Mount Rushmore, the Abraham Lincoln monument, the Empire State Building, and—high up in the California mountains somewhere—the sign: HOLLYWOOD.

They rode back to the farmhouse without speaking, Delkov drinking vodka, the SUV bouncing on the gravel road. Dmitri's silence felt thick with anger; Delkoff's was a mist of hope. It might've been funny, except Delkoff cared very deeply about his little cousin. And he worried about him, as he always had.

He walked up the steps to his room with the bottle of vodka, feeling reenergized, and closed the door. He pulled off his combat boots, sat at the wooden table, and went to work, using both index fingers on the Cyrillic keyboard. Delkoff knew that he needed to keep his story simple. But he had to include all of the pertinent names and details. Because what he wrote tonight would very likely become the official record, an account that would stand up to anything Turov and the propagandists tried to pass off as the truth.

He paused from his work only to drink and, several times, to look at the picture of his son Pavel. When Pavel was a boy, he was often caught in photos looking to the side. Delkoff had tried for a while to startle him out of it. "Hey! Look straight ahead, boy!" he'd say, clapping his hands. But it only embarrassed Pavel and caused him to look down . . . And he recalled something else, a memory of Pavel he'd forgotten: tossing his boy into the lake from the end of a dock when he was five or six years old and Pavel paddling frantically in the steel-colored water, his face like a frightened dog, his eyes darting to his father's as Delkoff shouted encouragement. God, he loved that boy so much. Why had he let him go to war? Why hadn't he tried harder to save him?

When he finished his "Declaration," Delkoff read through it twice, making only a few small revisions and additions. He was very pleased. Then he began to write a more personal account, a record of his own thoughts and feelings as the operation had unfolded. This one was easier, and more dramatic. It might one day be the opening to a book or movie. *We felt the ground shaking like divine thunder,* he wrote, *the great Russian-made rockets bursting out of their launchers, the sensors locking in, chasing the elusive target. This was what we had been hired to do and we all felt enormous pride knowing we were fulfilling the secret destiny of our country. I thought of my son Pavel. He had given his life to this cause of Russia Mir months ago, but he was with us on that afternoon. He was there with his father in the sunflower fields. He was right there, as were all the men who had given their lives to this war. We were all together at last on that afternoon in the brown sunflower fields of the Donbas.*

Of course, I still believed at the time that I was working for Andrei Turov, and for the good of the Russian Federation. I did not yet imagine that the Kremlin itself had a hand in this. That they might even be paying my salary. Now, of course, I know. I know many things that I did not know on that clear afternoon.

Delkoff stopped, looking up at the motion of the blowing curtains, filled with a sense of purpose. He could do with words now what the missiles had failed to achieve; he could force the Russian president to face his crimes. Not only that: he could force Russians to see their leader's deceptions. This was Delkoff's mission now, to tell the real story about his country. Because if he didn't, the story would never be told. And then what? Ivan Delkoff would go down as the engineer of a failed attempt on the president's life, that was all. His role in history would be written by other men and, almost certainly, trivialized. Or, just as bad: he wouldn't be known at all.

Delkoff finished and decided to take a break, to give his eyes a rest. He lay down on the narrow bed against the wall, still dressed in his fatigues, and immediately fell asleep.

When he woke, the sun was a sharp glare through the glass. Delkoff sat up groggily. The room appeared dusty and unfamiliar. A breeze puffed out the curtains and he smelled sea brine and coffee. Slowly it came back to him: the trip to the restaurant, the note, his mission.

Then he heard what had awakened him: Little Dmitri was in the hallway calling out his name, banging on the door and trying the knob. Had he locked it? It was Tuesday morning, already past 7:30. "*Ebat'-kopat'*," he said to himself. *Oh, shit.* Delkoff unlocked the door and let his little cousin see that he was okay.

"Come down for breakfast. We need to call the American."

Delkoff nodded and closed the door. He *wasn't* okay, really, but he would be. He stuck his head out the window, breathing deeply the morning air. It was a beautiful day. He looked across the grain fields toward the Channel, blinking at the blue horizon.

He returned to the table and refreshed the screen on his computer. It was still there. His "Declaration." And the first-person account that accompanied it.

Delkoff began to read what he'd written, but began to have trouble focusing on the sentences. The house felt like it was moving, as if Delkoff were on a ship. He'd forgotten the way vodka could do that, take him on a wild ride through his memories and emotions. And then . . . you wake up, your head's thumping, and you can't put together the simplest thoughts. Like: which should come first, breakfast or shower? Delkoff couldn't decide. He walked to the bathroom first and violently threw up. Then he settled in for a long, hot shower. There was a time, years ago, when this had been his life—when he'd spent every morning just waiting to feel normal again; often, it wouldn't come back to him until afternoon, and then he was grateful just to be able to think clearly for a couple of hours. The war had pulled him out of that cycle; it was why he'd quit drinking, because you can't live that way in war and be any good. War turned some people into drunks; it'd done the opposite for Delkoff.

He made the shower run ice cold over his chest and face and stayed under it for several minutes. Then he dressed in his fatigues and army boots, feeling better, his skin tingling from the cold as he walked downstairs, his son's medal in his shirt pocket again, Pavel's cross around his neck.

"It's five till eight," Little Dmitri said as he sat at the breakfast table.

"What time did we say?"

"First thing. Eight o'clock." Dmitri wrinkled his nose. Delkoff watched him, trying to figure what else was wrong. The air from the meadow already felt warm through the kitchen windows. Something good was trying to bubble up in Delkoff's sore head. *We can delay this a few minutes,* he thought, reaching for the orange juice carton.

He poured a small glass of juice. Dmitri cooked him fried eggs and bacon. "I'll call him in ten minutes," he said.

The breakfast brought Delkoff back a little more; he could feel his mental energies recharging. He had always been able to adapt. People didn't know he could do that. Delkoff understood that he'd made a mistake when he took that first drink on the plane to Paris. But he could put that in a box now and bury it, as he could his earlier mistake. He could only afford to be fighting his enemies today, not himself.

"I've heard bad news," Dmitri told him. "I'm told they went to my sister's house in Gomel yesterday. We're going to have to move quickly."

"Is she all right?"

"They didn't harm her. But they interrogated her and threatened her. I'm sure they'll be coming for us soon."

Delkoff reached for a piece of buttered toast, feeling enormous affection for Dmitri again, for all that his cousin had done for him. Delkoff knew his options: He could hide and work his networks; if he was lucky, he might last another week or two. Or he could deal.

"Before I go," Delkoff said, "I want to review my accounts with you again, Dmitri. And then I want you to leave here. As soon as I do."

Delkoff would take what he needed in cash and leave the rest for Dmitri. He'd never been very interested in financial wealth, anyway. Most of his fortune—and that's what it was now, since signing on to Turov's project—would help his family and Dmitri's family.

"Now go ahead," he said. "Call the American. Deliver the message that I'll meet him at 10:30. Tell him I have something important to give him." He looked at his cousin's disapproving face and dabbed at the crumbs on the plate with his fingertips. "Make it 10:15."

Dmitri said nothing. Delkoff knew what he was thinking. He watched his little cousin as he began to clean the plates. "The trouble with our president is that he never was a real soldier, isn't it?" Delkoff said. "His training was to deceive foreigners, and he's good at it. But now this man controls all of the armed forces, and that is not good."

"No, it isn't," Dmitri said. They had talked of this before. Both were wary of powerful men who had never served as soldiers, particularly men as ambitious and devious as Russia's president.

"Can you trust them, though?" Dmitri asked, wiping his hands. Meaning the Americans.

"Look who I trusted before. And where it got me."

"That's not an answer."

"No," Delkoff said. Dmitri was right. "The answer is: yes, I can trust them." He could trust the Americans because the Americans were not as deceitful as the Russians. The Americans were all the things that Andrei Turov said they were: superficial, arrogant, wasteful, self-absorbed. But Americans were resourceful and they had a strong sense of right and wrong that many Russians didn't have. And when the Americans made up their minds about something, good luck.

There was something else, too: he kind of liked this Jacob Briggs, what he could remember of him. He was a tough, unrelenting little man, not given to easy loyalties. Built like an American mailbox. A wrestler or boxer, he'd said. A man who looked at you and made you think he wanted to hurt you. But you looked again and saw he didn't. Delkoff remembered that.

"All right?" he said. "Tell him I want to meet. 10:15. It'll give me time to finish."

"Where?"

"You decide."

Dmitri shrugged. He made a suggestion: there was an old caretaker's cottage behind an unoccupied residence twelve or thirteen kilometers north, a small inland tract. "Don't tell him where yet," he said. "Just have him drive in that direction. We'll give him directions as he gets closer."

"The important thing," Delkoff added, "is you need to get away from here, too, Dmitri. You hear me? You need to go on holiday for a couple of weeks. Because they'll be coming; within a day or two, they'll be here. You know that."

There was emotion in his cousin's face, too, a faint quivering of his lower lip. The money, Delkoff's departure. There was a lot of emotion between them that morning, and neither man was comfortable with emotion. The sun was sparkling on the English Channel as they set out twenty minutes later, as though heralding what was ahead. Delkoff carried his country's history in his shirt pocket now. That was a good feeling; a very good feeling.

The Russian clean-up team arrived in Paris just after 7:35 a.m. There were two men, sent to France by Anton Konkin. Both were former members of Directorate A, the special forces counterterrorism unit of the FSB. The men were now independent contractors, working for Andrei Turov's security firm.

They first caught sight of the old stone farmhouse at twenty-five past ten, and watched from a distance through binoculars for the next half hour. It appeared vacant then. There were no lights visible, no movement inside. No vehicles outside. But they knew from satellite surveillance that Delkoff was staying there.

The clean-up team pulled their rental car behind the barn adjacent to the house and parked, hidden from view on the only approach road. They broke a back-door window to get inside. The house still smelled of breakfast: eggs, bacon, coffee. There were three sets of clean dishes in the kitchen sink.

The two former FSB men walked through the house carefully, room by room, discovering suitcases in the downstairs bedrooms, clothes folded neatly in drawers and on a bed. Upstairs, they found Delkoff's duffel bag, a computer, an empty liter bottle of Stolichnaya on its side, an old photograph of a boy who might have been his dead son.

The men who were staying here had probably just gone into the village. They'd be back.

The clean-up team decided to wait. They had nothing else to do. Nowhere to go. They had all the time in the world. They pulled up chairs and watched the road from two upstairs windows, smoking Russian cigarettes. There was just one road in and one road out. They would be right here waiting when Ivan Delkoff returned.

THIRTY-ONE

First thing in the morning. Jake Briggs had already done his workout. A hundred push-ups and a hundred sit-ups, same as every morning, followed by a dozen wind sprints alongside the water. He had showered and eaten a light breakfast. Now, at eight o'clock, he was waiting by his rental car, bag packed, ready to go.

He'd slept for almost four hours in the rented room. Then he'd laid awake, waiting for sunrise, hearing the Channel through the open window, the seagulls, occasionally a dog barking or a car starting in the village. Thinking about holding Jamie on his knee last Friday, watching the news from Ukraine, the look in his boy's eyes. "Tear-iss," he'd called them.

It was Briggs's second night in France. There wasn't going to be a third.

Celeste, the woman who ran the boarding house, rose early to walk her dog. She'd brought Briggs criossants and coffee after seeing his door was open and they'd chatted for a few minutes. Celeste was a widow, a smart, attractive woman who ran the apartments with her forty-year-old son. Briggs had walked with her down to the beach and she'd shown him the flobarts, the old flat-bottomed fishing boats still used by the local men. Briggs told her he was on a business trip, driving to Paris after a sightseeing detour. He didn't give details. She didn't ask.

Patience, he told himself. *Turn anger into patience, weakness into strength.* Briggs sometimes wrote sayings like these on scraps of paper, like homemade fortune-cookie messages. Anger was Briggs's Achilles' heel. The military had done its best to knock some of that out of him, but they'd never quite gotten the job done. Nor had the process of growing older done it, as it did with most people. He'd felt a raw anger this morning, knowing that Ivan Delkoff was only a few miles away; that he could go after him if he wanted. He knew from satellite photos, and his own surveillance work, where Delkoff was, just down the road from the little restaurant where his cousin went for a drink each night. Briggs had memorized the surrounding roads and the terrain of the adjoining properties.

Delkoff's security at the house was an unknown, though, and Briggs couldn't risk failure. He wanted this op to be something that he could tell his son Jamie about one day. He reminded himself of the objective as he waited: get Delkoff in his car and drive him to the Paris airport. Nothing less, nothing more.

Patience. Already patience *had* served him well, he reminded himself. Overnight, Martin Lindgren had sent new images by encrypted email: Delkoff at the Riga airport, and in Paris, ID'd by facial-recognition programs. Exactly what Briggs needed. But then eight o'clock came and there was no call. 8:10. 8:15. 8:25. Briggs redialed the number from the night before, and got a Russian voice recording. He walked back to the beach, to the old fishing boats lined up by the water. Morning light glowed in the dew; the sea rippled, scuffing the sand, breeze tipping the masts of anchored boats. He breathed deeply the briny air and imagined coming back here with his family someday.

Briggs went for another run, down to the end of the pebbly beach. That's when, finally, his phone rang: 8:44. It wasn't Delkoff, as promised, but the gruff-sounding cousin again, Dmitri.

"He'll see you at 10:15," he said, speaking French.

Briggs sighed. "Where?"

"Be on the road driving north, we'll call with directions."

Briggs argued for earlier. But Delkoff had made up his mind. It was shortly after 10:00 when Briggs said goodbye to Celeste and set off in his rental car back up the coast into the bright morning.

At 10:18, Dmitri called with instructions. *Drive past the creek to the south of the village. There's an old fortified church—St. Mark—and an abandoned-looking farmhouse in a valley. There's a small wooden cottage behind it. We'll meet you there.*

Briggs followed the instructions, watching his mirrors. He found the cottage and parked behind it, surveying the hillsides. As meeting places go, it wasn't one he'd have chosen. Out of the way, but with wide-open sight lines. Good setting for an ambush. "Go inside," Dmitri told him on his cell phone. "Sit at the table, and wait for us. We'll be there in five minutes."

Jake Briggs walked into the little cottage holding the 9mm Glock that Martin Lindgren had arranged for him. The air inside felt stuffy. There was a fuzzy dust on the windowsills and counters. Briggs thought of his family in Virginia, the basket of apples in the laundry room, new schoolbooks, his children watching *The Croods.*

Fourteen minutes later, they arrived: a black SUV pulled up in front of the cottage and parked beside his car. Briggs watched: two big men came out. One the driver, a bodyguard in a leather jacket, the other Delkoff. Then a smaller man emerged from the passenger side. They looked like Russian gangsters to Briggs, all three of them, like Moscow hit men from the 1990s.

The bodyguard came in first with his gun raised. Briggs set his on the table and stood. He held out his arms for a frisk. The man took Briggs's gun and stepped back.

The screen door opened again, and Ivan Delkoff walked in, his cousin right behind: one man huge, the other small. Delkoff was dressed in military fatigues, old boots. Briggs immediately recognized the long, too-serious face.

"You remembered Antalya Kebab," Delkoff said in French, showing a thin smile, his mouth flattening and becoming lipless.

"I do." Briggs reached for his handshake. Delkoff clasped his hand with both of his. He pointed a pistol-finger at the table, and they sat, Delkoff swinging the chair out with two fingers. His face looked to Briggs as if it hadn't fully unfolded from sleep.

It was 10:38 now. Briggs wanted to do this quickly, and get Delkoff out of there. They'd lost three hours already, time enough to have driven to Paris. "Nous allons en parler et parvenir à un accord," he said. *We're going to talk and make an agreement.*

Little Dmitri stood in the doorway, his mouth open, rectangular like a slot. The other man went outside. He waited behind the SUV, smoking a cigarette.

Briggs passed his phone to Delkoff, showing him one of the images that Lindgren had sent via encrypted email from Belarus intelligence: Delkoff walking on the platform at the Minsk railway station.

Delkoff seemed momentarily stunned. "Turov has it too," Briggs said.

"How do you know?" He looked up. His eyes were watery and red-veined.

"They know you're here," Briggs said, taking back the phone. "They know what plane you took from Riga. They can figure the rest of it. We need to get you out. We'll offer immunity. But we need to go right away."

It was mostly bluff, but Delkoff didn't know that. Briggs showed him the other images on his phone, letting him slide through them. The psychological parameters were set by then. It was the same principle Briggs had honed in grade school, when kids would tease him about his height. As soon as you're able to assert yourself, size no longer matters.

"They followed you to Minsk," Briggs said. "Even with the false trail you left, they'll be here by afternoon."

Delkoff turned to his cousin, giving him a look Dmitri couldn't seem to read. *Delkoff is hung over*, Briggs suddenly realized. *Jesus Christ!*

"So what do you want?" he said.

"I want to get you out of here. In exchange for your story." Delkoff looked over his shoulder at Dmitri again. Dmitri's face registered nothing. "We drive to Paris, leave from there. Fly out this afternoon. We have a corporate plane set to go."

"To where?"

"Washington," Briggs said. "After that, it's not my business. You go to a safe house and work through all the details. Give them your terms. Whatever you want. Candidly? You can probably write your own ticket at this point."

Delkoff folded his hands. He squinted out the window. A faint aroma of alcohol rose to Briggs's nostrils. Delkoff was a weird guy with a lot of rough edges, he knew. A patriot, who was fighting a war in his head that no one else could see. But right now, he was also a worried man. "How do I know it isn't a trick?"

"Because I'm telling you it isn't," Briggs said. He put away the phone, acting impatient. "And because you don't have a choice. You need our help as much as we need yours."

Briggs reminded himself that Delkoff was carrying precious cargo in his head. If they got out of here, this guy's story was going to be on *60 Minutes,* the front page of the *New York Times,* the whole deal. "We know what you did, okay?" Briggs said, trying to nudge him. "We know about Turov. This is your chance to make up for it. You're hearing me?"

Delkoff looked over his shoulder at his cousin again. Something about him reminded Briggs of a dictator trying to keep his composure as his regime fell apart. Delkoff nodded. "All right. We can go this afternoon."

"No," Briggs said. "We go this morning—right now. You've been lucky so far. But luck is always a temporary condition. You hear me?"

Delkoff's thick chest rose and fell in the fatigues. He was silent.

"Someday," Briggs said, glancing out at the driver, "who knows, maybe you'll return to Russia a hero. But right now, we need to go." He was bluffing again, but Briggs could feel that he was connecting; Delkoff liked this sort of talk.

"Give us an hour, then," Delkoff said. He scooted back his chair.

"No. Not an hour," Briggs said.

Delkoff scowled as both men stood, facing across the table. "I need to get my things," he said. "Give us thirty minutes."

"I'll drive with you back to the house if you have to. But we leave from there." Delkoff wasn't going to fight it, he knew. He might have used his physical size to intimidate Briggs or to crowd his space, but he didn't. Briggs's authority had a sobering effect on him. Delkoff walked outside to discuss it with his cousin. Briggs could hear them speaking in Russian. The screen door squeaked as he came back in. Delkoff handed Briggs back his gun.

"All right," he said. "Follow right behind."

That was how they did it—Jake Briggs following the SUV back down the coast to the winding gravel roads that ended at the house. It was a lovely morning, turning warm and nearly clear, just a slight breeze; a nice day for a drive to Paris.

Except something about it didn't feel right to Briggs. He just had a feeling, a sense that there was going to be a problem.

THIRTY-TWO

B riggs went through a mental checklist as he followed Delkoff back to the house: the rental car was filled with gas; he had a micro-cassette recorder, four bottles of water, his cell phone, and a mobile Wi-Fi device; his personal belongings sat on the back seat in a carry-on. Briggs planned to record his conversation with Delkoff as he drove him to Paris. It was two-and-a-half hours to the airport. Plenty of time—more than enough—to get what Christopher needed.

The wild card, Briggs figured, was that Delkoff had been drinking. From his dossier, he knew that Ivan Delkoff had once had a debilitating drinking problem. Drinking made him unreliable, paranoid, self-destructive. It was the reason they'd lost three hours.

The vehicles spread out through the open expanse of country, tall wild grasses on either side of the road for a while. Briggs watched the sea and the red roofs of the little village to his left. He knew this road well, knew where it dipped and where it branched away. He'd driven it the night before with his lights out, several times, stopping to survey the house through his binoculars.

They turned due east again, toward the stone farmhouse. Two minutes later he saw the SUV slowing down. Brakes pumping. He thought at first they were just waiting for him to catch up. But then the brakes stayed lit and the SUV stopped.

Briggs pumped *his* brakes, reaching for the gun as he slowed. *Why the fuck are you stopping?* The house was still almost a quarter mile away.

As he eased to a stop behind the SUV he saw the security man talking with Dmitri in front. And Dmitri turning to Delkoff in back. Something was going on.

After a long interval, Delkoff came out of the passenger side. Then Dmitri. Both glanced toward the house, at something Briggs couldn't see. They walked around the vehicle and stood talking, the engine still running, Delkoff a foot and a half taller than his cousin.

Dmitri got back in the car and Delkoff began to walk down the road to Briggs, crunching in his heavy rhythm on the gravel. *What the fuck?* So maybe this *was* some kind of trick, after all.

He lowered his window as Delkoff approached.

"What's going on?" Briggs lifted his gun so Delkoff could see it. Delkoff held up the palm of his left hand as if to push it away. His other hand was a fist.

Delkoff leaned closer, his eyes moist. "I'm going to the house to try to work things out," he said, in a measured tone. "You need to drive back toward the village."

"What are you talking about?"

"We're going to meet you in the clearing at the end of the road."

"No, you're not."

But he saw something new in Delkoff's face, and suddenly understood. Delkoff pushed something into Briggs's shirt pocket, a small, rectangular object, and withdrew his hand. "I need to make sure everyone's been taken care of before we go," he said. "All right? I don't want you coming to the house. I don't want you coming any closer than this. You understand?"

Briggs studied his face. "What's this?" he said, touching his pocket.

"That's what I want you to have," he said. "It's my Declaration. All right? Go ahead, get out of here."

Delkoff stepped back. He began to walk to the SUV. Briggs's first thought was to go after him. But his instincts stopped him: do as

Delkoff instructed. There was a warning in his face and in his manner, the way an animal communicates an urgency. Briggs got that.

Delkoff looked back only once: he stopped and said something to Briggs in Russian. Smiling.

Briggs backed up his rental car and turned around; he drove to the rise in the road, where he stopped and parked, then pulled his binoculars from their case. Twice he scanned the hills, but saw nothing unusual. Then he focused on the SUV, continuing down the road to the house. Stopping by the front doors.

Briggs watched the security man step out from the driver's side with a Glock in his right hand. Then the cousin, Dmitri, getting out in front.

And finally Delkoff, his six-and-a-half-foot frame unfolding from the passenger side. Walking around the car with that now-familiar sense of purpose, following the other two men.

It was maybe thirteen steps from the car to the front of the house. Delkoff made it six. Briggs watched the dip in his stride, the look of confusion slackening his face.

The other two turned and saw Delkoff stagger briefly, then topple forward like a felled tree. And then both of their bodies began to jerk savagely from what Briggs knew was a barrage of gunfire. Moments later, the two killers emerged calmly from the side of the house, emptying their automatic weapons into the three men.

Briggs shifted gears. He felt the pump of adrenaline in his chest as he sped past the small private cemetery and cluster of cottages toward the coast, monitoring the undulating road behind him in the rearview mirror. Falling back on his training: he had to shut down his emotions now and think his way out of this. He couldn't fight it. Not here. Briggs was in a one-man op. And the op had just been compromised.

It wasn't until he'd tucked into the stream of traffic on the two-lane coast road past the village, headed south, that he allowed himself to consider what had happened. And it was then that he first realized Ivan Delkoff had just saved his life.

He drove through the coastal towns for twenty minutes before feeling comfortable enough to pull off at a rest stop. What Delkoff had left in his shirt pocket was a flash drive. Maybe it contained the information he would've given him on the drive to Paris. Maybe not. He parked beside a restroom and activated his mobile Wi-Fi device. Protocol was to contact Martin Lindgren first. Then Christopher. It was still the middle of the night in Washington, one hour later than France in Moscow.

Briggs typed an encrypted message to Lindgren. *Mission aborted,* he wrote. Then he plugged in the device, downloaded the files on the flash drive, and transmitted them.

He called Christopher later, from the outskirts of Paris, on his scrambled mobile device. "I've got good news and bad," he told him. "The bad news is that I fucked up."

But Christopher, as he should have expected, didn't want to hear about it.

"Come to Moscow," he said, before Briggs could explain. "ASAP."

THIRTY-THREE

Tuesday afternoon, August 17. Outskirts of Moscow.

"People give too little thought to the way things end," Andrei Turov said as Anton drove them through the midday birch shadows on Rublyovka highway, nearing the presidential dacha. "The Greeks understood that: regardless of what a man achieves in his life, the way it ends can cancel out everything that came before."

Anton hummed his acknowledgement, focused on the road. He knew that Turov was talking about Russia's president now, not the ancient Greeks. Anton played various roles for Turov—corporate manager, head of security, confidante. Listening was part of his job, and he was used to the peculiar turns of his boss's thought process. He preferred when they spoke of Russia's future or poked fun at people. But he could be a receptive audience, as well, when Turov turned philosopher.

The news that Anton's men had located Ivan Delkoff added a certain octane to Turov's thinking this afternoon. There was no confirmation yet that he was dead, but they would have it by the end of day. And he didn't need proof for his meeting with the president. Just knowing was enough. Turov was thinking of bigger things now. He was thinking of legacies. It was four days since the plane had been shot down over Ukraine. The news that the Americans had carried out the attack was spreading quicker than he dreamed, taking on a life of its own. Much of the world now believed the story that Russia was telling. Journalists were dutifully repeating the phrases that Turov had sent through the pipeline—"preemptive strike," "assassination committee." Even many respected American pundits now believed the United States had been involved. It presented Russia with a great opportunity.

An opportunity to change his legacy. Turov was offering Putin the elusive quality that his old friend could never achieve through force of will or political maneuvering: global respect.

He read Anton the draft of the speech as they drove, and Anton responded predictably. Turov shared nearly everything with Anton, although there was one aspect of "the children's game" he had decided to keep to himself—at least until after his meeting with the president.

Anton was curious, naturally, about his own future. Turov understood that. Anton had a girlfriend now, a German who spoke Russian and lived in Zurich, and he had moved his three children to Switzerland. But Anton also understood the requirements of loyalty.

"Your speech will give him the ending he deserves," he said, trying to sound encouraging. "No one else can do that."

"Thank you, Anton. Let's just hope he is receptive."

Anton glanced at his boss. "You think he won't be?"

"I think he should be," Turov said. "It will be a great opportunity for him. So long as he doesn't listen to the wrong people."

Seeing the twenty-foot brick walls around the president's property, Turov was struck—as he always was on this approach—by how far they had come: from the scrappy streets of Leningrad, where he and Volodya had grown up, to the heights of Russian power. Through it all, Putin had kept his earthy humor and his uncompromising values, which many of the intellectuals disliked but the common people loved. "He has the potential now to be a man for the ages," Turov said. "So long as he continues to look at the long view, rather than his day-to-day survival."

"Yes," Anton said. "He's a better tactician than strategist."

"That is correct." Turov smiled. Anton often repeated things Turov said, sometimes weeks or months later. He had an outstanding memory. And he was right: sometimes the president reminded Turov of Scheherazade, needing to invent a new story every day just to survive.

When Turov was alone with the president, the two of them came up with remarkable plans for their country; they sent idea balloons into the sky and marveled at how exquisitely they rose. But in between, the president consulted with his other advisers, men who tugged him in strange directions, and he was never quite as receptive to Turov the next time they met.

Turov's concern all along had been that Putin might be persuaded to turn the "fourth" move over to his military commanders, those unimaginative men who had been preparing for war in the Baltics for years. A war that Russia could win—but at enormous cost. He could move into Latvia and Estonia, if he wanted, or even annex eastern Ukraine, as he'd done with the Crimea. In the current environment, he might get away with it. But if he did, his chance to be great would be compromised. And so, Turov was thinking of endings—strategies instead of tactics. For Putin, and for himself.

Anton Konkin pulled the Mercedes sedan to a stop at the neoclassical gates. Turov and Konkin were searched, and then they continued down the fir- and birch-tree-lined road to the dacha grounds, past the residential buildings, the stables and greenhouse. Konkin stopped on the drive in front of Putin's country house, a two-story English Gothic columned mansion built in the 1950s.

Getting out of the car, Turov was met by a security man from the Federal Guard Service, who escorted him inside the grand doors of the mansion. He walked down the hallway to the parlor, a tall-ceilinged, paneled room dominated by an antique billiard table. Another guard brought him a bottle of water and made some small talk. It was a man Turov knew slightly, from past visits, a former security agent who'd broken his nose once playing ice hockey against the president. It had been his job to let Putin score several goals each game.

The president did most of his business here in the country now, which kept him away from the trappings of the Kremlin. But this mansion contained its own trappings, which concerned Turov a little. Volodya was still a young, energetic man, an athlete. Yet there was a feeling here of retreat and isolation, as there was at his palace on the Black Sea. What was the job really doing to him? The president was not a family man anymore. His ex-wife Lyudmila had suffered nervous problems for years—as Turov's own wife had, of course. He had a younger girlfriend now, although he didn't talk about her and was reluctant to speak of his two daughters. But there was something else that bothered Turov: his friend had become a little less disciplined out here. Turov noticed it each time he visited.

As he waited, Turov opened the binder and read through his draft of the president's speech, reciting how he would start: *In this time of great tragedy, we also have a great opportunity.* It was time to talk tough about terrorism. To set the foundation for Russia's next decade. During the four-year interval when Putin had given up the presidency to serve as prime minister, they had managed—cleverly, with little controversy— to extend the presidential term in Russia from four years to six, so that he could remain in office until 2024. It was a lot of time to work with, if they used it properly. American leaders did not have such luxury.

Last winter, the president had given his nod to the August 13 project in a meeting here at Novo-Ogaryovo. "This will be the catalyst," Turov had told him. "A new door to *Russia Mir,* to taking back lands that are rightfully ours . . . But also, a legacy project. For Russia, and for you."

The president had nodded periodically as Turov explained, making it clear that he was interested in outcomes and less so in details. Turov had built his plan to the president's idea of strategic relativism: we become stronger by weakening those powers that seek alliances against us. And by building counter-alliances, which circumvent the US dominance of global trade. In five to ten years, *voila*: the US-centric notion of the world has become obsolete.

The president had listened attentively as Turov explained the four moves of "the children's game," which would elevate Putin, and their country. The first move had been infiltration, creating an infrastructure through a network of deep-pocketed foundations, social media campaigns, and cyber-monitoring; by putting spies in the house. Second was the event itself, August 13, the catalyst. Third was the aftermath, engineering the shift in world opinion.

The president had seemed tired by the time Turov got to the "fourth move." Maybe it was just the timing. "These ideas show great initiative," he had said. "We'll talk about it again later."

Later was now.

Turov waited forty-six minutes this time for the president to summon him. Journalists sometimes sat for three hours in the parlor before their ten- or fifteen-minute audience with Vladimir Putin, so he counted himself fortunate.

The office was large and spartan. The president's desk was bare, as usual, except for a marble pen set, several folders stacked to his left, and a single document in front of him. On top of the folders was a leather-bound security service binder embossed with an eagle.

They shook hands, exchanging greetings and then regrets about the national tragedy of August 13. The president's handshake felt firmer than he remembered. The guards who had kidded with Turov in the parlor became meek choirboys in the presence of the president, lowering their heads and shuffling from the room as Turov sat.

Alone with Putin, Turov immediately began to feel the odd gravitational pull of his old friend's personality: there was always that temptation while in his presence to think as Putin did, to talk as he did, to chase the dreams he was chasing, rather than your own. Everyone felt it.

"I'm saddened, naturally," the president said, shifting in the chair, thrusting his left shoulder forward in that aggressive way he had. Turov, who had not seen Putin in several months, was struck by how his face seemed to have fleshed out a little. Putin no doubt noticed a change in him, as well. "But I am pleased by the support we have been getting," the president said. "I've seen the polls."

"Yes. It gives us a remarkable opening," Turov said. "For Russia and for you."

"There is more coming, I am told?"

"Yes." Turov explained to him what Anton had briefed him on that morning. "There will be a cache of leaked memos and emails confirming the 'no fingerprints' discussion and the transfer of funds to Kolchak, the Ukrainian, from a US-controlled account. In addition, I'm told there will be new photos from the meeting in Kiev."

"Evidence of direct CIA involvement?"

"That is correct. Clear attribution."

The president made a sour face, pretending to be upset. "It's a lucky thing I received warning not to board that plane. How could they do such a thing?" he said. "We must bring these people to justice."

"Yes."

"And is there any news yet on these secession movements you were talking about?"

"That is coming," Turov said. "Beginning in Texas. And California. It is being coordinated in Washington."

"By Ketchler."

"That's right. Once it catches on—" Turov opened his fingers in an explosion gesture. "It will be like their homosexual marriage, or legalized marijuana. No stopping it."

"Our friends with the goatee beards," the president said, which was how he often referred to liberals and intellectuals.

"Yes," Turov said. "But that will take more time."

The president pulled the document closer and leaned forward. "I am interested in this new poll I have just seen," he said, with a casual authority. He began to read the findings aloud, his lips glistening with enthusiasm. Turov felt his face flush, but otherwise hid his response. He had seen the poll, too, showing that a majority of Russians believed their country would be justified in retaliating against Estonia and

Ukraine for August 13. Turov had not expected it to be a topic of this meeting.

Putin finally pushed the document away and nodded at Turov. "So, what do you have?"

"You wanted to discuss your speech."

He nodded impatiently. Turov pulled out the draft from his binder and passed it to the president. "We need to talk about the fourth move," Turov said. "This shift in opinion is an opening for the country, but more importantly, for you. To be an example for the rest of the world, as we've discussed."

The president paged through the draft of Friday's speech as Turov talked about his legacy. "We can't risk going back to the kinds of protests and riots we've seen in the past," Turov said. "After all we've invested, we can't lose this chance . . ."

Turov saw the president glance at his expensive watch several minutes later and knew that he'd stopped paying attention. Finally, his old friend raised his index finger to stop him. "Okay," he said. "We're not ready for that discussion now. I will review this, and we will talk later."

Putin reached for the binder to his left. "I do have one other, more pressing concern," he said. He opened the leather folder. Turov recognized the insignia of the GRU, Russia's military intelligence service, on the top sheet. "My security services tell me that there was an unexpected development in the Donbas on Friday," the president said, leaning forward again. "Before Delkoff's men reached the border."

Turov felt a prickle on his scalp. "Yes. But that's now been taken care of."

"I don't want all the details," the president said, as if he hadn't heard. "But I am concerned, as you are. I did not want to involve security forces." Turov nodded. This he hadn't expected. There had been general parameters, not put in writing, and this was one: the less the president or Russia's secret branches know, the better. Turov was an outside contractor, an independent patriot. "How soon before it is resolved?"

"It has been. We have notification that all three of the men are dead."

"Including Delkoff."

"Yes. All three. Trust me." Turov took a deep breath. Putin continued to look at him with his hard blue eyes and Turov understood that this wasn't good enough. "I will have verification for you by the end of the day."

The president closed the folder. Turov had misjudged his friend. Volodya had little interest in talking about the televised speech, after all. Or even in the "fourth move." The president's concern was Ivan Delkoff, and what damage Delkoff might now cause for Russia. "Once this matter is taken care of satisfactorily," he said, "and I have your report, then we can talk about your other business. We will meet again in two days."

"All right."

The president stood. There was an abrupt, unfamiliar tension between them, and Turov was reminded of the toxic effect he'd seen the president have on other men: the power to cripple a man's confidence with just a few words. Putin could be very generous to those in his orbit; but if he stopped trusting you, he could ruin your life very quickly.

"I do want you to spend some time away, with your family, Andrei, in Switzerland, before we move on to other things," he said, speaking more softly as they walked through the hallway. "If anyone deserves it, you do. But we've got to make sure this is finished first, before you leave the country. Then we will help with your arrangements."

The president's tone carried an ominous undercurrent. And Turov knew, before they reached the front doors of the house, that he would have to change his game. The president was his friend, but he was not family. They walked down the stone steps side by side, like two diplomats emerging for the cameras. Anton sat waiting behind the wheel of the Mercedes. A large black dog, Putin's labrador, ran toward the car and stopped, as if knowing better than to get too close.

Putin leaned in to his old friend, speaking in a low voice at the bottom of the steps, his expression no longer synchronized with his words: "You should have had him hung by the balls, Andrei," he said. "And taken pictures of it for me."

Turov said nothing. He had heard these words before: the president had used them in speaking of Mikheil Saakashvili, the former governor of Odessa in Ukraine. Putin gave a quick, cordial nod to one of his FSO security men, the man who'd suffered a broken nose playing ice hockey.

Turov and the president smiled as they shook hands, firmly and impersonally. And then Turov got in the passenger side of the sedan. Anton could see that the meeting had not gone well. But he knew better than to say anything. They rode in silence through the long stretch of birch woods, past the giant brick wall, the sunlight dappling across the forest floor. *Sometimes things changed with the unexpectedness of an Arabian fairy tale,* Turov thought. It was a line from Dostoevsky, a line that got stuck in his head on occasion. He thought longingly of his daughters, and the twin grandchildren. He thought of the coming season—the beauty of the first frosts in the morning on the meadow outside his office, the rain of falling leaves on autumn afternoons. *He* was going to have to make his own move, then; without Putin. This meeting had been a warning call. Turov even began to feel a little sorry for his old friend as they rode on into the afternoon. Knowing that any move the president made at this point involving the military would ultimately be self-destructive. And destructive to Russia. *God help the president.*

First, though, Turov needed to take care of his new responsibility. He needed Anton to verify that Delkoff *had* been killed in France, and prepare a report on it. Once the report was filed, they could begin Turov's fallback, with a return call to the American. Christopher Niles. All along, there had been two possible fourth moves. Now there was one.

"Well?" Anton finally asked. "What did he say?"

Turov looked at his colleague. He wondered how much time had passed since they'd left the brick walls of the president's residence.

"We have some new business to discuss, Anton," he said. "And we're going to need to pack our suitcases. Things have just changed, I'm afraid."

THIRTY-FOUR

Capitol Hill, Washington.

I've been reading your column," Anna Carpenter said. "I just thought we might talk. It's sort of funny, actually, that we've only ever met in passing."

Jon Niles nodded and shrugged simultaneously. They were seated in Starbucks on Pennsylvania Avenue, three blocks from the Capitol. Jon had arrived first and ordered a Frappuccino. He was using the lid as a coaster.

"I agree with what you wrote in your blog," Anna said. "About noise at the expense of comprehension. And about who's causing that noise. But I also sense, reading between the lines, that you're not entirely sure we *didn't* do this."

"Well. 'We' is a pretty vague term," Jon said, allowing a smile. Anna nodded, studying him. Physically, the brothers were opposites—Christopher tall, blond, stylish; Jon average-size, darker, his shirt sleeves rolled up haphazardly, one of his collar points sticking out. They'd shared a privileged upbringing in the D.C. suburbs, and it showed in Chris on first look; with Jon, it was harder to see. "Although I think it's possible," he said, "that there was someone on our side who knew what was happening."

"And why do you think that?" she said, recalling what Christopher had said about "a spy in the house"—someone on our side helping the Russians.

"A hunch. Things I've been told." There was a slight flinch in his face when he began to speak, an odd sideways tilt of the head that was sort of appealing. "You don't think so?"

"I don't," Anna said. "I don't believe that we—our government— had anything to do with shooting down the plane."

"So this story about the CIA official—Gregory Dial—meeting with the Ukrainian arms dealer—?"

"I don't believe that story."

"You think this was the Ukrainian military, then. Or Russian secret services?"

Anna took her time. "Off the record?" she said. "I think there's another possibility that no one's mentioned yet. A story the media are all sort of missing."

"All right." One of the cashiers kept walking past, her head down, sneaking glances at Anna as if she were some celebrity. She'd be disappointed if she knew the truth. "So what is it the media's missing?" he said.

"The possibility that they did this themselves."

Jon seemed unsurprised. "A coup, you mean. A military coup. And, in the process, they managed to set up the United States—"

"No, not a coup," Anna said.

"Not a coup." His eyes stayed with her, curious. "You're saying, what—that Putin *knew* about it? That he was somehow involved?"

"I believe it's possible, yes." Anna's phone pinged once; she ignored it. "Russia thinks in ways that we don't. They were pioneers in the use of social media to spread false information, as you know, and to create false consensus. This idea of a post-truth culture that people keep talking about? Russia's been living in that culture for years."

"Okay," Jon said, with a note of skepticism. "So, I guess, all we'd need, then, would be proof, right? I mean, people have spun conspiracy theories about Putin for years. That he's had dissidents and journalists killed. But no one's been able to prove it."

"That may be true," Anna said. "And maybe this is our chance to change that." Jon narrowed his eyes. She could see the interest in his face. There was a muted sense of outrage in Jon's writing that Anna liked. He cared that a false story was being passed off as the truth. He understood—unlike many of her fellow politicians—that truth wasn't a point of view; that it was an edifice, carefully built, fact upon fact. And he cared that the White House wasn't responding to this "preemptive strike" story the way it should be.

The cashier walked by again, sneaking glances as she wiped off a table.

"Do you know about the Lisa Affair?" Anna asked.

"In Germany," he said. "Where Russia used a story about the gang rape of a Russian girl by immigrants to undermine Angela Merkel's party in regional elections."

"A rape that never happened."

"Right."

"The fact that the story was fabricated didn't matter," Anna said. "Russia ramped up its propaganda machine and tens of thousands of people poured into the streets to protest Merkel's immigration policy. The result was large losses for her party in the elections." She added, "Russia does that kind of thing often. And very well."

Jon watched her, one eye squinting more than the other. "Okay," he said. "So tell me this. If the story *isn't* true, why hasn't the administration come out and directly refuted it?"

"That I can't answer," Anna said. "Except to state the obvious: it's infected with politics."

"Okay." He glanced off for a moment. "And. An unrelated question: Does your meeting with me today have anything to do with my brother? Is that why we're here?"

Anna pretended not to be surprised. "No, I'm not on a mission for your brother. I called you on my own. Because—as I said—what you wrote in your column got my attention. And because I'm angry about what's happening, as you are. I think we've been caught flat-footed, as we were on 9/11, and if we don't respond properly, I'm afraid that the lie that's being perpetuated wins. Russia wins."

"9/11," Jon said. He gave her an inquisitive frown. "That's an interesting comparison."

"I think it's apt." She hesitated for a moment before explaining. "On 9/11, we were the victim of a kind of warfare that our intelligence community hadn't anticipated. Something similar is happening now. In a subtler way, of course. This time the target is bigger and less visible, but just as vulnerable, and not very well protected. And this time, the attack is harder to see."

His expression seemed to flatten. "You're talking about propaganda now," Jon said. "Information warfare."

"That's part of it. But a very sophisticated propaganda. Weaponized storytelling: telling a story so convincingly, with enough simulated corroboration, that people believe it. As we've become increasingly fragmented, there's a hunger for some big, unifying story. Russia understands that. And they're preparing to tell it, at our expense."

"What did I say in my column that interested you?" Jon said.

Anna smiled. "That someone in the administration was nervous about this preemptive strike talk getting out to the media. I won't ask who that was," she added. "But I'll just say: when I read it, I immediately thought of a colleague of mine. A man you probably know: Harland Strickland."

Jon Niles's jaw muscles clenched slightly; clearly, she'd caught him by surprise. "So," he said, "what are you suggesting?"

"I'm suggesting that maybe we could work together to counteract it," Anna said. "To tell a better story than they're telling."

Anna's phone pinged: a text reminder from Ming that she had appointments.

"You know what? I hate to do this, Jon, but—how about we continue with this later," Anna said, remembering her afternoon meeting in the Oval Office. Jon shrugged his mouth as if it didn't matter. But she could see that it did. Very much. "Let me get through the next few hours," she said, picking up her phone. "I think we may have a lot to talk about."

THIRTY-FIVE

Jon Niles always had a weakness for the offbeat—in music, film, books, and people. Until this morning, he never would've put Anna Carpenter in that category. On television she came across as pretty mainstream: self-assured, bright, a classic overachiever. Maybe a little too outspoken at times, but a politician, comfortable with the compromises that came with her job. This woman he'd met for coffee at Starbucks was a different story, bearing only the slightest resemblance to the Anna Carpenter he knew from television—headstrong, impatient, mischievous, and attractive in ways he'd never noticed before. It had even seemed—briefly, at least—that she might've been coming on to him a little, although Jon had an overactive imagination when it came to that.

Beyond his interest in Anna Carpenter's personality, he was intrigued by the prospect of working with her to figure out what really happened on August 13. And, in particular, by what she'd said about Harland Strickland. Jon had a strange feeling about Strickland, a persuasive, influential man who was interesting to talk with but hard to pin down.

Driving away from Capitol Hill, he decided that Strickland would be his next stop. With a little detective work, Jon was able to track him to the Wheel House, a dark, leather-boothed restaurant and pub in Tysons Corner, not far from the National Counterterrorism Center, where Strickland worked when he wasn't at the White House. Jon had made it his business to learn as much about his sources' personal lives as he could, and Strickland, he knew, had a handful of midday haunts where he liked to hold informal lunch meetings.

Jon stepped in and let his eyes adjust, scanning the restaurant booths. He finally found Strickland seated in a back booth with two other men in business suits and loosened ties. Strickland was talking as Jon approached, his arms animated, the other men laughing politely. With his exotic features and insistent eyes, Strickland seemed more like a character actor than a counterterrorism official, Jon had always thought. His newly added goatee enhanced the effect.

He turned his head as Jon approached, and his eyebrows jutted up theatrically.

"Mr. Strickland. Jon Niles. I'm sorry—I just wanted to ask you a question."

Strickland exaggerated a grimace, trading looks with the men across the table. Then he smiled in that accommodating way he had, casting sprays of wrinkles around his eyes, and stood, extending his hand.

"I'm sorry," Jon said again as they walked toward the bar. "I've been trying to reach you for several days. I don't know if you got my messages—"

"I didn't, no. What can I do for you?" he said good-naturedly, placing a guiding hand on Jon's back.

"Just needed to clarify something."

"All right." Strickland stopped in the corridor by the restrooms.

"When I talked with you last week, you confirmed to me that this Russia committee had discussed some sort of preemptive action by the US. But the last time we talked, you said that there *hadn't* been any discussion of it."

"That's correct."

"So I'm confused. Because I'm getting confirmation elsewhere now that the conversation *did* happen. I'm sure you've seen these latest reports—"

"Well, no, I think we're talking about two different things here." He stifled a smile, as if it were all a misunderstanding. "This is because of the paper, right? The editorials?"

"No," Jon said. "I'm talking about *our* conversations. You were very specific the first time we talked about it. You said this discussion happened—"

"No, no. Look." A wide grin creased his face. "Whether there ever was a conversation to that effect or not—and I think we're talking about two different conversations, but that isn't the point—the real question is, was there ever *serious* talk about regime change? And the answer is, unequivocally, no, there wasn't."

"So, in other words, you're not denying there *was* a meeting at which regime—"

"I'm not denying anything," he said. "I'm denying it matters. Okay?" Strickland had begun to breathe through his nose, Jon noticed, a sign he was becoming agitated. They moved sideways against the wall to let a man pass, coming out of the men's room. Strickland summoned a gentler tone and continued: "What I'm denying, and you can quote me on this if you'd like, although I'd prefer you didn't, is that there never was a plan—or knowledge of a plan—to take any sort of preemptive action on Russia. Okay?"

"Okay."

"And that's it, basically." He glanced at his watch. "But look. I need to get back to the office. You can walk with me to the parking garage if you'd like."

"All right."

He took his time paying the bill and saying goodbye to his friends, a cordial man whose graciousness made Jon feel like a predator. Strickland led the way out into the August heat, walking with his loose-limbed, self-assured stride, as if he didn't have a care in the world.

"We're off the record here, right?"

"If you want."

"So, look. Again. Just to clarify: there never was any discussion of a preemptive move against Russia. Okay? And that's it, basically."

"Never a *serious* discussion, you mean."

"Right. Or any discussion. But you see how these things get twisted?" He stopped and faced Jon in the shadows of the garage entrance. "As you know, there are people who think we're taking Russia too lightly. I understand that. Eighty-five percent of NSC meetings over the past twelve months have been on the Middle East. Okay? Unpredictability: that's the hallmark of Russian foreign policy. And frankly, we could take a lesson from them."

"And what about this 'no fingerprints' allegation?" Jon said, hearing a familiar echo in what Strickland had just said. "Where did that come from? Wasn't that discussed in one of these meetings?"

"I have no idea where that came from. None. All right?" He turned and began to walk the incline to his car. "Unless it was something one of the generals said," he added. "But it would've been in the context of war-gaming."

"Rickenbach?"

"I wouldn't know, I wasn't in the room. But I mean, even if someone said it, so what?" He smiled, shifting his tone again. "And, of course, if you report that, you're only drawing thunder from the real story."

"Which is what? What is the real story?" Jon said.

"The real story"—Strickland stopped walking again, surveying Jon—"is that Russia's *military* did this, okay, and I guess—from what I'm hearing—they're blaming us now? Which is how they do it. And a frightening prospect, considering the nuclear arsenal they're sitting on. Do you know, our two countries make up less than seven percent of the world's population but control ninety-three percent of its nuclear weapons?"

"Yes, I do," Jon said.

"And so that's where this is headed, frankly. And that's why the

White House has been careful. They're getting their ducks lined up. As they should."

"To say it was a coup attempt?"

"Coup attempt, right. *Their* generals, not ours." Strickland began walking again. "Look, don't make this more complicated than it is. What we have—will have—is incontrovertible evidence. As I say, they're in the process of dotting all the *i*'s right now."

"Evidence of—?"

"What you just called it: a coup. A plot that *did* involve this oligarch Hordiyenko. Hordiyenko, as you know, plays both sides. It would've been easy for the Russian generals to do business with him and set this up to look like a Ukrainian operation.

"Putin's security detail evidently caught on at the last minute and kept him off that plane, as you know. The man leads a charmed life, doesn't he? I'd hate to see what becomes of those generals," he added, smiling.

Strickland pointed his key fob at a Lexus sedan. The locks slid open. The story was beginning to feel confusing again and Jon wondered if that was the idea. *Noise at the expense of comprehension.* But whose idea?

"You're not getting any of this from me," Strickland said, seeming anxious to go, "but I can tell you a name. That might give you a little leg up on the competition. It's going to be out in a few hours anyway."

"Okay."

"The man in the Russian military who ordered the attack, I understand, is named Utkin. General Viktor Utkin. As I say, I wouldn't want to be in his shoes." He winked. "Now, do this country a favor and report that and stop trying to blame *us,* okay? Give America a break."

Jon nodded and tried to apologize again, but Harland Strickland was already pulling at the creases on his pants legs, getting into the car. He waved to Jon as he drove away.

As soon as Strickland was gone, Jon walked back into the sunlight and called his editor Roger Yorke.

"I've got a name," he said. "Supposedly the Russian general who ordered the attack."

"Mmm-hmm." Roger's voice had its familiar neutral tone.

"The name I was given was General Utkin, Viktor Utkin," he said. "Is that a name you've heard?"

There was a long silence, Roger making his odd purring sound, an indication there might be a problem with this information. "I've heard it, yes," Roger said. "But I don't know that it's the right one. Utkin. There's actually an old story about Viktor Utkin." Jon waited. "I'm getting a different name, actually," he said. "The name I'm getting is Ivan Delkoff. He's kind of a renegade colonel in Russia's military intelligence branch, the GRU. Important figure for Russia in eastern Ukraine, supporting the rebels. He was called back to Moscow in the spring, evidently, and may have hired the men who carried out the attack."

"Oh." Jon scribbled the name in his pad. "So why would the White House put out Utkin?"

"*Is* the White House putting it out?"

"Not yet. But I'm told they will be, soon."

Roger said nothing for a while. Jon recognized that he had just equated Strickland with the White House and wondered if he was being played: was Utkin a name the White House wanted to float in the media for some reason?

"Then you've posed a good question," Roger said, and Jon waited through another silence. "But it's Delkoff, I think, we need to go after, not Utkin. Delkoff."

As he drove away, replaying the conversation with Harland Strickland in his head, Jon felt a chill of recognition. A phrase Strickland had just said to him in passing: he suddenly remembered why it sounded familiar. Strickland might have just inadvertently given him the solution to a different puzzle: the identity and motivation of his 9:15 source.

THIRTY-SIX

Hotel National, Moscow.

When he heard Jake Briggs's voice, Christopher Niles was surprised but pleased. The lunch with Amira Niyzov had gone well, and Jake Briggs was the next step. But then Briggs's tone became unfamiliar. "Good news and bad news," he said.

The bad news was very bad. The good news, he didn't know yet. But he needed Briggs to not talk about it over the phone. He needed him to leave France right away and join him in Moscow.

Chris lay on his bed in the Hotel National that afternoon trying to put the change of plans into some kind of perspective. All Briggs's "bad news" meant was that they had gone off script a little. He'd expected that anyway. He exchanged encrypted emails with Martin Lindgren, Martin asking him to wait before he did anything. There was a document he would be sending, Martin wrote, something Christopher could use for his leg of the operation. Chris asked him to arrange for a rental car and handgun for Briggs through Moscow station, similar to the setup in France.

Martin complied, but ended their last exchange with, "May need to abort tomorrow, for your own safety."

Chris deliberately hadn't answered that one. He didn't know what pressures Martin Lindgren was under, but he knew he couldn't abort the mission. *Especially not now*, with Briggs en route to Moscow.

So Christopher waited, watching television, sometimes with the sound off. By then, Russia's coverage of August 13 had become so predictable he could provide much of the commentary himself: the foreign minister raised his fist, warning that America must face the consequences of what they'd done. "This is *provokatsiya!*" he declared. *Provocation!* "Any further escalation by the Americans will create a situation that no one desires."

Other world leaders expressed stunned sympathy, saying in carefully worded statements how they would wait for the investigation to run its course before making any comment about the United States.

When Lindgren's encrypted document at last arrived, translated from Russian to English, it became clear that Briggs's good news was better than good: during the final hours of his life, Ivan Delkoff had written an account of what actually happened on August 13, including the names of the planners and participants. He'd written it with the intention of giving—or, more likely, selling—his story to the United States.

Delkoff's document was the real thing, the first verification of what Christopher had traveled to Moscow to prove: that Andrei Turov had masterminded August 13. It also told them something more significant: that the operation couldn't have occurred without the blessing of Russia's president. Whether they'd be able to convince the world of it was still an open question.

Christopher read the file several times, sifting through the wording for hidden nuances. But it was all pretty straightforward, and pretty remarkable. Delkoff had written his "Declaration" to record a chapter of history that would otherwise never be known. The juxtaposition of these old-world furnishings, the view of the Kremlin and Red Square out his window, and this document alleging high-level crimes and deceit at the heart of Russia's government, was hardly lost on Christopher.

Briggs's op in France had in one sense been a failure. They'd intended to come away with a clean deal: Delkoff would be granted immunity and Christopher would gain the leverage he needed to negotiate with Turov. It didn't happen that way, but Briggs had given him what he needed anyway. It was some compensation knowing that Turov had a more pressing problem now than *he* did. And that Chris could help him solve it. Turov's mistake had been underestimating Delkoff. He'd gotten Delkoff in the end, just not quickly enough.

Still, Christopher knew that Russia was more accomplished than the United States was at the art of disinformation. If Delkoff's document went public, the Kremlin would claim the US had fabricated it in order to steer attention from their own involvement in August 13. And there would be no shortage of conspiracy theorists in the States—and supportive Russian bots—to help the story circulate.

But Chris didn't want Delkoff's document to go public. He had a much better use for it.

After a small dinner of salmon soup and crab salad in his room, Christopher shut his eyes and tried to catch a nap. He was deep in a dream about wandering through darkened corridors in the Kremlin, lost, hearing Anna's voice calling to him, when the room phone rang. The sound jolted him to an upright position. It wasn't late. Just past 8:20. He stared at the night sky for a moment, reorienting himself. Then he reached to answer it. "Hello."

"Mr. Christopher Niles."

"Yes."

"I'm calling on behalf of Andrei Turov." A male voice, with a heavy Russian accent. "Mr. Turov received your message. He would like to meet with you tomorrow afternoon. He will have a driver pick you up at 2:30. I'm going to give you the location." He did: a block Christopher knew, on the edge of Gorky Park near the river by the Metro stop.

Chris stood at the window, watching the domes of St. Basil's.

Tomorrow afternoon. Briggs would be here by then, so the timing was fine. Perfect. The caller, he knew, was Anton Konkin, Turov's security chief, who made all of Turov's arrangements.

"Come alone. Bring no recording equipment or tracking device. No weapons. Do not attempt to have anyone follow you." He added, "If you violate any of these instructions, the meeting will be terminated. And it won't be possible to reschedule."

"All right."

It was several hours later when Chris finally responded to Martin's email.

"Give me twenty-one hours," he wrote. "That's all I need to finish this."

THIRTY-SEVEN

Southwest of Moscow.

"The secret of wisdom is the systematic pruning away of excess," Andrei Turov told Anton as they walked back to the main house in the dark. Anton was gripping a bucket filled with ice and four bottles of Baltika #3, his favorite beer. "So when we travel tomorrow, there is no dishonor in each of us carrying a single suitcase."

Anton was silent. The security detail and house staff had been sent away the day before, and they were the only two on the property tonight. Together they had locked down the buildings not in use and shut off the water and electricity to all but the main house and Anton's cottage. Shostakovich's opera *The Nose* blared from the house as they worked, adding a surreal accent of whimsy to the darkening grounds.

Now, at last, they were going to relax. The irony of this day was that they'd received verification of Delkoff's death just an hour after leaving the president's dacha. Anton's men provided images of his bullet-riddled corpse, and an incident report, all of which Turov forwarded on to the president with a personal note. Delkoff's body would be shipped from France back to Moscow. His computer and communication devices would be turned over to Russia's foreign intelligence agency, SVR.

Turov had felt relieved seeing the proof of Delkoff's death. It would buy them some time. But for practical purposes, it didn't make a lot of difference. Turov had gone to the president's dacha expecting to sell him a plan that would earn Putin a new respect around the world, something he couldn't achieve on his own. And the president had been clear, as he often was: he did not trust Turov anymore. It was the sort of fissure that could not be repaired.

So Turov had explained to Anton the operation they would run instead. He instructed him to have two security men deliver the American to a meeting at one of his properties outside of Moscow Wednesday afternoon. And for Anton to prepare to depart Russia with him afterward.

Anton had phoned Christopher Niles at the Hotel National to arrange the meeting. Turov pictured his American counterpart as the men spoke, recalling their one meeting across a Gorky Park chess table four years ago: Niles watching with his shrewd gray-blue eyes, trying to figure Turov out. It had been an interesting game. It still was.

"Our president could have made himself a moral example," he told Anton as they reached the main house. Anton set down his bucket. "But instead he's chosen the more obvious path. To do what Caesar did when he made himself emperor for life."

"It's a sure way of shortening one's life, isn't it?"

"Yes, sadly, that's right."

Turov set up deck chairs on the lawn. They sat and each opened a beer, saying nothing at first. It was a comfortable silence, the shared silence of two friends. Turov hadn't tasted beer in weeks and the first sips intoxicated him. The air felt exciting as it cooled, stirring memories of Turov's childhood, and of his children's childhoods. Of long-ago expectations. The potent drug of nostalgia.

Anton displayed his usual reserve, not speaking until spoken to. Turov looked over at one point and saw him watching the sky, fighting a smile. "What is it?" he said.

Anton shook his head. He pointed with the neck of his beer bottle. "Do you think they ever really went there?"

Turov looked up. The moon was bright through the trees and drifting clouds. You could see shapes on the surface tonight like the earth's continents. "What—the Americans?" Turov said. "Well, it's history now, isn't it? The world believes they did, so it doesn't matter."

Turov knew what he was saying: the story Russians used to tell each other, that the Americans had never really gone to the moon, that they'd created the evidence of their moon walks in a Hollywood studio and fooled the world, using special effects to show how far they'd surpassed the Soviets. "It was a typical American project, though," Anton said.

Turov smiled. "Spectacular, but serving no purpose, you mean."

"Yes. Billions of dollars spent, and who did it benefit? Money that could have been used on medical research. Or feeding the poor. Or building infrastructure."

"But symbolically," Turov said. "Symbolically, it wasn't meaningless at all. It changed how the world thought about America. It ended the space race, which, of course, we'd been winning. In some ways, the Cold War ended that day, too. In July 1969, when they planted their flag on the moon. We started that race, by sending the first satellite into orbit."

"And then the first man," Anton said.

"Yes, that's right. But America ended it. And afterward, they became the country where you could imagine all sorts of crazy things and make them happen."

Anton took a swig of beer.

"It's funny," Turov added. "Several years ago, the Americans admitted that they'd lost the original film of that moon landing. There were some who thought we could take advantage of that, maybe knock a few dents in their armor. Putin even spoke to me about it. Not seriously. But he asked my opinion."

"What did you tell him?"

"That it was silly talk. In 1969, we were both very different countries. If we were going to tell that tale, we needed to do it then. Now, we have better stories to sell."

"The president's plane."

"Yes. That is one. The world believes that now, don't they?" Turov sipped his beer, feeling a muted pride and then a tingle of apprehension. Another long silence followed.

"Do you think he's going to try to stop us?" Anton said. He wiped the back of his hand over his mouth, watching Turov's eyes.

"He'd like to, yes." Turov looked up as clouds briefly darkened the moon. "I am his friend. But he thinks I am a threat to him now. He's not family, Anton. He's not to the end."

Anton held the bottle on his right leg, looking at Turov. "Is he going to try to kill us?"

"Probably, yes," Turov said. "That's why we've packed our suitcases and are leaving early. It's why we're meeting with the American. We'll be fine, Anton," he added. "We have something he doesn't have."

Turov felt good saying that, and not having to explain. The breeze was fresh in the trees and smelled faintly of coming rain. Turov didn't want to talk anymore. He just wanted to savor their last night here, the way he should have savored every day of his life.

THIRTY-EIGHT

The White House. Washington.

Anna Carpenter's meeting in the Oval Office was short by design. The president had wedged her in for five minutes, knowing that she was one of the public voices responding to the preemptive strike allegation—and, by implication, one of the voices speaking for the administration. It made sense for the president to have some face time with her.

Anna did not have a relationship with this president, although she had a deep-abiding respect for the presidency. Before her first visit to the Oval Office seven years ago, one of her political mentors had advised her, "Put it all out when you're in with the president. Waste nothing." It seemed particularly good advice today. As a first-term senator, she knew that she couldn't count on this kind of meeting again for some time.

The president gave her a warm but slightly awkward greeting, shaking her hand vigorously with both of his. This president was an accomplished businessman, with an ability to make people feel important—or part of something important. But he wasn't comfortable with the intricacies of international political conflict.

"I appreciate what you're doing," he said. "You've been a good ambassador for me and my administration. Even though they tell me you can be a troublemaker."

"Not really," Anna said. They shared a smile.

"I know you're going on television again this afternoon," he said. "I just want to make sure we're all saying the right things . . . reading from the same script."

"Okay," Anna said, not liking his choice of metaphor. But he'd given her an opening, and she decided to take it. "At the risk of adding to my troublemaker reputation, I guess I just wonder why the White House hasn't been helping more."

He nodded, expecting the question. "That's why I asked you here," he said. "It's a sensitive time right now, I don't have to tell you that. But I want you to know that we do have good intelligence tying this to the Russian military and to a general named Viktor Utkin."

"The coup story, you mean."

"Yes." The president lowered his eyes for a moment. "That's part of it," he added cryptically. "I'm sure you've seen the stories saying that this administration—or even me, personally—had some involvement in the attack. Obviously, it's a lie. But a lot of our own people aren't saying that. A lot of them aren't helping us out."

"What do you mean, that's *part* of it?" Anna asked, changing the subject. "What's the other part?"

"The other part, frankly, has to do with one of the copilots."

Anna frowned. This she hadn't heard.

"We don't have it all confirmed yet, and I can't comment publicly, obviously. But I can tell you there's going to be very strong evidence. You may even want to make some reference to it in your interviews."

"To the copilot?"

"Yes. One of the copilots on that plane suffered from—I won't say mental illness, but depression, severe depression. And may have attempted suicide on at least one occasion. As I say, we're still confirming all that."

Anna said nothing at first. She didn't know that she believed him, or what it meant even if it were true. "So, are you saying this may've been a suicide mission?"

"No. We don't know if it was or not. But we think it's possible he was recruited by the Russian military and convinced to redirect the plane into Ukrainian air space. That's all I can say at this point."

Anna noticed a momentary hesitation in his eyes. The president was a skilled persuader but also a man of surprising vulnerabilities. "If it *was* a coup attempt," she said, "wouldn't they have known Putin wasn't on board before they brought the plane down?"

"That's something we're going to have to answer," he said. "Obviously, the president was *supposed* to be on board. There were reports that he *did* board the plane. But remember, something caused that plane to change course. *We* couldn't have done that. How could we have done that? So that's one of the questions."

"But what about these other stories?" Anna said. "That there was an ongoing discussion within the IC about regime change? That funds were diverted from CIA-controlled accounts to this Ukrainian oligarch—Hordiyenko? The meeting in Kiev."

"It didn't happen. None of it," the president replied brusquely. "There *was* a meeting in July, I'm told. In Kiev. An *information-gathering* meeting. But there was never talk of assassination. Never. And, by the way, this man Hordiyenko? He wasn't there. Despite what the media's reported."

"Okay."

"People tend to think the worst of Russia, Anna. Often for the wrong reasons. But it's a very sensitive time right now, as you know." The president reached for the file folder in front of him and opened it. Then, to her surprise, he began to talk about Utkin and the copilot, sharing the man's name and details about his background.

"I can't tell you everything," he said. "But I will show you very quickly what we're dealing with, since you're here." He pulled a small map from the folder, which Anna recognized as the Baltic Sea region. "Just so you can see, in general terms: sixty Russian warships, support ships, and submarines left their bases yesterday to perform tactical exercises in here, all within range of Estonia. This is Estonia here. Full airborne divisions, marine units, naval strike forces. Hundreds of units. Thousands. All told, sixty thousand troops, mobilizing for war."

"And how is NATO responding?"

He sighed. "Frankly? NATO's not prepared for this. I hate to say that, but it's true. As you know, there's great support within Russia right now for retaliation. The Russian people actually want it. And the media there is reporting that more attacks may be coming."

"By us?"

"By us. By Ukraine." He closed the folder. "You know, people use the chess analogy to describe our relationship with Russia, Anna—if I can call you Anna. But chess is the wrong game. The game we should be talking about—and I'm told this by our generals, who know—is poker. A good poker player bluffs with a weak hand. And, sometimes, he can *win* with a weak hand. That's what Russia is doing. Trying to do."

He pushed the folder to the side and looked at her soberly, as if debating whether to say more. "There's one other consideration, frankly, that we have to weigh. I shouldn't be talking about it. But I'll just mention this so you know what we're dealing with, before you go on television. In fact, I'm going to give you kind of a scoop right now."

"All right." Anna forced a smile to meet his.

"We've also, frankly, been given warnings, privately," he said, "about how this might escalate if we aren't careful. We do have open channels with the Kremlin and are talking to them about a possible deal. But there's one threat on the table that—well, obviously no one wants to see, and, frankly, I'm working to make sure doesn't happen."

She could read in the flatness of his eyes what he was saying. "You're talking about the use of limited-range nuclear weapons," she said. "Is that the threat?"

He continued looking at her, and finally nodded slightly. "It would be the first-ever use of them in warfare, I'm told. And the only wartime use of nuclear weapons since 1945. I don't want that to happen. Nor does the Russian president. But, you understand, this is a war they have the public's approval to launch. The Russian public. And I'm frankly not so sure it's our business to get in the middle of that."

"It's the world's business, isn't it?" Anna said.

"It may be." He frowned at her tone. "Although, frankly, we have other enemies besides Russia, as you know."

"Sir?"

"I mean, Russia is not our only enemy."

"Okay," Anna said. "By other enemies—you mean, ISIS? North Korea?"

"North Korea, maybe, but I mean internally, too. Who's to say we don't have enemies right here at home? People don't like to talk about that, but it's true." His eyes seemed momentarily distracted. Anna recalled what Chris had said about a spy in the house helping the Russians; she wondered if it was possible the president himself was that person, or one of them. But her gut told her no. She wasn't even sure that the president really bought the coup story. It was possible that he was only backing it because his advisers had presented it to him convincingly. Anna wasn't going to work against the president, she decided. But she *was* going to work against this story.

"Anyway, it's a sensitive time right now," he said, closing down the conversation. They'd gone nearly twelve minutes. "And I hope we can count on you."

"I appreciate it, sir," she said, reaching to shake his hand as he grabbed at hers. "I'll do what I can to help."

Harland Strickland had called while Anna was with the president. The self-assured tone of his voice message touched a raw nerve in her. Strickland was the reason she had been summoned to the Oval Office, Anna suspected. He was among the most influential people in the intel community right now, and likely the driving force behind the coup story. There was a well-oiled rhythm of insincerity in his voice, which she knew well. But Anna had her own agenda now. She'd wait before calling him back.

First she contacted her son David, who was working from home today. "I need to ask you something in confidence, honey. Remember what you said about Russia doing unto others as they think others want to do unto them?"

"Okay."

"I wonder if you could put everything on hold for a couple of hours and check something for me—what Russia's doing right now. Is that possible?"

"Anything's possible, Mom. You told me that," he said.

Anna smiled. She gave David the names of the Russian pilot and General Victor Utkin and asked if he could run deep data searches on both, looking for any connections between them. Anna talked quickly, echoing the resolve she'd heard in Strickland's voice, wanting to get it done before she changed her mind. Wondering if she was crossing a line of loyalty by pursuing this. "I'll stop over tonight," she said. "We can talk then."

Finally, she called Harland Strickland. But, as often happened, she was sent to voice mail and left him a message. As she was signing off, Anna heard a familiar voice in her outer office. It took a moment to place it: Martin Lindgren.

Ming was laughing with uncharacteristic abandon, charmed by Martin's flattering manner. Martin seemed out of context here, though, almost as much as he had on the beach in Greece last Tuesday. In fact, it occurred to her that Martin had never been to her office on Capitol Hill before. Why now?

THIRTY-NINE

Martin Lindgren placed the new *Weekly American* magazine on Anna's desk and sat. "AUGUST 13" stretched across the bottom of the cover, below ominous clouds of dark smoke. The suggestion that August 13 was a date that would live in infamy, as December 7 had for her grandparents' generation or September 11 had for hers, was unsettling. And presumptuous.

"Have you seen that?" Martin said.

"No, I hadn't." She studied the cover momentarily and set it down. She could see from his expression that Martin hadn't come here to show her a magazine. "What is it?"

"Something happened in France last night," he said. "Big setback."

Anna felt her heart lift in her chest. "Christopher?"

"No. Briggs."

"What happened?"

"Ivan Delkoff," he said. "He was gunned down on the coast of France overnight."

"*Gunned down.*" Anna didn't know all the details of Christopher's operation, but she knew that Delkoff was at the heart of it.

"Broad daylight in France," Martin said. "He'd just met with Jake Briggs. Evidently, they were about to strike a deal. Two other men were also killed—a security guard and Delkoff's cousin Dmitri Porchak."

"What happened? Who was—?"

"Freelancers working with the SVR, probably," he said. "We don't know a lot. It's being handled by French secret services right now. The house where he was staying was ransacked, computers and phones taken. Russia wants the body back. Naturally, they're accusing us, saying we did it as a cover-up, although nothing's out publicly yet, thank God. Christopher knows. I communicated with him earlier."

Anna was speechless. She was also stunned that Martin would be telling *her* about it. "And Briggs—?"

"I spoke with Jacob Briggs, too," Martin said. "He's all right. Physically. Although he's stuck on the idea that his mission was somehow compromised. Or sabotaged."

"Well, obviously," Anna said.

"No. He means by us." Martin drew in a deep breath. "He thinks it was someone internally, in the intel community, who led him there and then set him up."

"Tell me he's wrong," she said.

"He's wrong. Of course, he's wrong. This was nothing more than what Chris said it was: an operation to find and talk with two Russians. Unfortunately, it's suddenly become much more complicated. Briggs is on a flight to Moscow now. At Chris's request. But there may be a saving grace in all this," he added. "That's why I came to see you."

He opened his case and took out a document. "Delkoff left something behind," he said. "It was on a flash drive that he gave to Briggs. It's been translated. There's another encrypted file we haven't been able to break. But this one's pretty telling. Have a look."

Anna reached for it. "August 13. A Declaration. By Ivan Delkoff." She began to read. The writing was slightly garbled in places because of the translation, but the message was clear. The document succinctly detailed the lead-up to August 13, beginning with a spring meeting in a residential neighborhood of Moscow, at which Turov hired GRU Colonel Ivan Delkoff to carry out the assassination. Over the summer, it went on, Delkoff trained a small team—men named Zelenko, Pletner,

Kolchak, Kravchenko, Tamm—and negotiated with an agent of businessman Dmitro Hordiyenko to purchase a Buk surface-to-air missile battalion. His "Declaration" gave specifics about when the missiles had been transferred and where they had been stored. It ended with a dramatic two-page first-person account of the attack itself. *I felt enormous pride that the mission to reclaim the Motherland had been achieved,* Delkoff wrote. *I did not know yet that I had been a victim of a grand deception. A deception not only by Andrei Turov. But also by our president. I am writing this so the World will know the crime this regime has perpetrated.*

Incredible, Anna thought. The document felt both selfless and self-serving, the parting shot of a patriot defending Russia with all he had left, hoping that his words could do what the missiles had failed to do. This verified Christopher's suspicions about Turov, then. Suspicions the IC had rejected years earlier. This would also blow Russia's story apart. *And the White House's version, as well,* Anna mused.

She looked up at Martin Lindgren. "This is our proof, then?"

"Well, yes," he said. "With one obvious problem."

"Delkoff's credibility."

"That's right. As I say, we're hoping there'll be more. But that's what we have to work with. Unfortunately, the idea that *we* did this is escalating faster than expected. There are protests planned for the weekend that are going to make the Occupy movement look like child's play."

"And make it easier for Russia to justify retaliation."

Martin nodded. "Obviously, they'll say we fabricated this. Our own credibility is becoming a problem now."

Anna read through the document again, imagining how it would play in the world media. How it might change the narrative about Friday's attack, the stories portraying the United States as a lawless kleptocracy. But would the public believe it? "Who else has seen this?" Anna asked.

"Right now, just Briggs and Chris. That's all. You, me, Briggs, Chris."

Anna stared at him in disbelief. "The president hasn't seen it?"

"Not yet, no." Martin's expression took on a detached indifference. "Christopher asked me to wait another twenty hours. I'm going to honor that. This is still Chris's op. I can't jeopardize that until I know he's safe."

"Okay."

"The other reason," he added, "is that the White House has its own theory about what happened. I don't think I could change their minds if I wanted to."

"The idea that this was internal, a coup attempt," Anna said, thinking of her Oval Office meeting.

"Yes," he said. "They're trying hard to inflate that. And there's a story about the plane's pilot now, too." Anna nodded. "You've heard it. So. I'm going to keep this dark until we hear back from Chris. Until we know he's out of harm's way. Then I'll take it to the president."

Anna felt her heart clutch. *Harm's way.*

But then she sensed what Martin was really telling her. "You're saying he's made contact with Turov, then?"

Martin's eyes closed affirmatively, the way other people would nod. "They're meeting tomorrow. For obvious reasons, he doesn't want any of this out before then. He's afraid that if the White House has it, the NSC will have it, and the press will have it. I'm honoring that."

"But I don't get it—why share this with *me*, then?"

"Because Chris asked me to. And he wants you to share it with his brother, too. Not for publication. Not until we hear back, anyway. But he wants his brother to know about this."

Anna reread the opening of Delkoff's statement, feeling touched that Christopher would want to share it with Jon. "Obviously, I can't go on television tonight, then, and talk about it."

"Not about *this*, no. But you can go on television. We need to keep a conversation going, Anna, to do everything we can to slow down this Russia story."

"All right." Anna felt a surge of apprehension, recalling what the president had shared with her, the "threat" of a nuclear strike in the Baltics. "I was tempted to ask the president about Turov," she said. "I'm glad now that I didn't."

"Let's wait and see what happens tomorrow." He stood then, not letting it get any more personal. But Anna felt the ties of their team tightening a little.

Once Martin left, she stared out the window at the atrium, sorting through what he'd told her. Still believing in the quaint idea that the truth counted for something, she swiveled around and pushed the number for Jonathan Niles's cell phone. He was at his office, he told her.

"I have something for you," she said. "Can I come over and drop it off?"

"I'm here."

"Anything new?" she asked. He sounded different, more abrupt, or maybe just distracted.

"A couple of things. I met Strickland and—I'm just thinking about numbers," Jon said.

"Oh?"

"Can't really talk about it . . . Have you read my blog, by any chance?"

"Not yet. Why?"

"You should read it."

"I will."

FORTY

Anna called up Jon Niles's blog on her phone and read it on the way to the CNN studios in northeast D.C.

The news today can be told in numbers. Over 75 percent of Russians now believe the US had a hand in shooting down the president's plane on August 13, according to a new poll by Levada-Center, Russia's largest independent polling organization. In Germany and France, it's just over 45 percent, with 20 percent of those surveyed saying they don't know. In the United States, 31 percent of respondents to a Gallup survey say they believe their country was either involved or had prior knowledge, with 30 percent saying they don't know.

And if that's not worrisome enough, consider this: 67 percent of Russians say that their country would be justified in taking military action against NATO over the attack.

But in Washington, the most troublesome number on Tuesday morning was three—as in, three more days. That's the number some military officials were giving for how long it will be before Russia takes retaliatory action against Estonia and/or Ukraine. Three days is also how long military analysts say it could take for Russia to capture Tallinn, the capital of Estonia, one of the countries the Kremlin has accused of conspiring to assassinate Russia's president. This isn't just Russian saber-rattling, but a very real possibility, warns one US military official.

But is it really? Other sources note that the Kremlin appears to be negotiating quietly with both Ukraine and Estonia, and even the United States, for what it really wants: a non-military solution to the standoff. What does that mean? The Kremlin is reportedly seeking a complicated agreement with the Estonian government that would include a "referendum clause." Some analysts see this as Russian hocus-pocus, a first step in turning Estonia (and perhaps eastern Ukraine) into a Russian satellite.

Could the future of Eastern Europe really be determined by what happens in the standoff over Estonia, a nation whose population is comparable to that of San Diego—and which most Americans couldn't find on a map? How did we get to this point?

By some accounts, it goes back to June, when a group of five US intelligence and military planners met to discuss strategies for dealing with Russia. The group was convened in response to intelligence showing that Russia was planning "a significant action" aimed at the United States, according to sources. In the course of the meeting, and several follow-ups, the possibility of a "preemptive" move against Russia was discussed. These talks were only "theoretical," said one source. But Russian intelligence services have apparently made them the basis for a successful disinformation campaign accusing the United States . . .

Anna looked up as they arrived at the CNN building on First Street. There were dozens of protestors outside, holding signs reading MURDERERS! and USA KILLS! which had become rallying cries of the August 13 "movement." *How did the protests escalate so quickly?*

She finished Jon's blog upstairs, waiting to go on air, pondering again what he had asked her earlier, at the Starbucks: *If the story isn't true, why hasn't the administration come out and directly refuted it?*

"Senator Carpenter, thank you for joining us," the interviewer, a youthful, intelligent-mannered blonde woman she'd never seen before, began. "This story about the August 13 attack continues to take some incredible new turns. There are reports now of a, quote, assassination committee and of a meeting in Kiev between a CIA official and a Ukrainian arms trader—"

"Actually, there are no credible reports of either one," Anna said. "I don't believe the meeting you refer to in Kiev actually happened."

"You're saying the meeting with this Ukrainian arms dealer never happened?"

"That's right. I think we have to be very careful what we call 'reports' and what's simply Russian propaganda magnified—"

"But with all due respect, Senator—you call this propaganda, but opinion polls around the world, including here in the United States, show that the public simply doesn't believe that."

"I think those polls are measuring response to media coverage more than what's actually happening," Anna said, feeling an old twinge of frustration. "I think it's up to us to pay close attention, and learn to differentiate between the stories Russia is spreading and the truth, which sometimes isn't known. Particularly considering what's at stake in the Baltic region right now."

"And who determines that?"

"Who determines what—the truth?"

"Yes." It was a surprisingly good question, Anna thought; but rather than let her answer, the interviewer fumbled: "I mean—what *is* the truth, then, would you say, regarding August 13?"

"Based on the intelligence we have? The truth is that this attack was planned in Russia and carried out by Russian and Ukrainian soldiers."

"With no US involvement or knowledge."

"That's right."

This seemed to momentarily derail her train of questions. "And so. But why isn't the president saying this directly?"

"I don't know. The president, as I understand it, is preparing to make a statement," Anna said. "I believe he *will* say it directly. But right now, *I'm* saying it."

"And are you aware of the comment from the Secretary of State earlier today? That this may've been a Russian military coup? Is that what you meant, that it was planned in Russia?"

"I can't really respond to that," she said, feeling a flicker of resentment toward Harland Strickland again and the president's advisers who were pushing this agenda. "Except to say this: personally, I don't believe it was a coup attempt."

"You don't." The interviewer's eyes clouded over with confusion. "And what does that mean, exactly?" she said. "You don't *believe* it was a military coup?"

"It means I believe the attack was planned in Russia, as I say, with the sole intention of damaging US credibility, of making us look like what *they* are: an autocracy with no respect for the rule of law. But that doesn't mean it was planned by the Russian military. I can't say anything more specific right now. But the key point is *we* didn't do this. End of story."

"And so, what can the United States do, Senator, as a member of NATO, to prevent this from escalating into war? And—a related question—wouldn't an attack on a NATO country be considered an attack on us, according to the NATO charter?"

"Yes." Anna took a breath. "Obviously," she said, "we're concerned about Russia's military ambitions in the region. But I think the evidence will clearly show that the governments of Ukraine and Estonia had nothing to do with the attack. And I would call on our partners in the world community to demand a truthful accounting. And to prevent any form of aggression there."

Anna wanted to say more. She wanted to say exactly what she now believed had happened: *that a man named Andrei Turov had planned the attack, with the knowledge of the president of Russia.* But she knew she couldn't go public with that. She had to wait on Christopher. Already, she'd said too much. "Let me add this," she said. "You ask about war.

I think Russia already *has* launched a war. An asymmetric war on the truth. And that's something we need to defend vigorously. All of us. The truth matters. And I think what we most need to do right now is mobilize an international army to defend it."

The interviewer seemed to like this and let it be her wrap-up before going to a commercial.

Anna monitored the response online as she rode back to her Capitol Hill office. Most of it was positive. People liked that someone was finally speaking up and defending the country. "We Didn't Do This—End of story!" read one headline. "The Truth Matters," read another; it struck Anna as sad that the US had come to a point where this argument had to be made.

But the people within the administration who mattered the most weren't so pleased. The president's chief of staff left a message asking her to call ASAP. The CIA director called himself several minutes later, sounding terse in his message: "Would like to hear from you." Anna understood: she'd been expected to repeat the administration's talking point that the attack was a Russian coup attempt. And she'd done the opposite. She'd said she didn't believe it.

When she reached her office, Anna was surprised to find that her mother was among those who'd left messages. Before dealing with the CIA director or the White House, she decided to check in with her mom.

"Honey, your father wants to talk with you," Anna's mother said, in her rich, reassuring voice. "He wants to congratulate you."

Anna didn't believe her at first. Alzheimer's disease had stolen her father's ability to express himself. Anna braced herself as she glanced at the faded photo of him on her mantel, dressed in his general's uniform twenty-some years earlier.

"Annie?"

"Hi, Daddy."

"You did a good job. We were watching you. Your mother and me. I'm proud of you." His voice sounded a little distant but his diction was surprisingly sharp. "You said it just right. About the truth. I was watching with your mother. You defended your country nicely."

"Oh. Well, thank you, I didn't expect you'd be watching."

"Of course, we were. Don't give up. Keep doing what you're doing, only more so."

"My gosh, thank you, Daddy." Moments later, Anna's father began to repeat himself and sound confused. She could hear her mother talking to him, trying to take the phone away. They'd spoken for less than three minutes, but the opening exchange had felt miraculous, like her father had reached back in time to pull out one of his old pep talks: *Keep doing what you're doing, only more so.* Anna stood in front of her office window after saying goodbye, her eyes full of tears, recalling how her dad could make her day with a compliment, or send her into a deep funk with a criticism. As an only child, Anna had sometimes been the buffer between her father, a lifelong military man who had little patience with popular culture, and her sociable, homemaker mother, who seemed to have patience with everything. That was how she had first learned the art of diplomacy.

Ming was standing in the doorway, her long face downcast, waiting for Anna to emerge from her thoughts. "You okay?"

"Sorry." She wiped at her eyes. "I was just talking with my father."

Ming pointed to her desk phone. Anna looked, and she saw the number of the next-to-last person that she ever expected to call, after her father: Gregory Dial. *Dial,* the old-school Cold Warrior, now accused of meeting with a Ukrainian missile supplier to discuss killing Russia's president.

"Hi Greg," she said, tentatively. Anna had called Gregory Dial three times over the past week; he hadn't called back until now.

"Anna. I thought you were quite good on television."

"Okay," she said cautiously. "Thank you."

"How about we meet for a few minutes," he said. "I think we ought to talk."

"If you'd like. When's convenient?"

"I'm in town," he said. "I could come to your office right now, if it isn't too late. Otherwise, tomorrow?"

"No. Come over now. I'll wait for you."

FORTY-ONE

The *Weekly American* offices. Foggy Bottom, Washington

After reading what Anna Carpenter had left with him, Jon Niles walked down the hall to Roger Yorke's corner office. It was an amazing document, which he knew could completely change the narrative about August 13. It was also amazing that Anna had a copy—and wanted to share it with him.

The problem would be proving Ivan Delkoff's version of events. As with all things Russian, there was a chance that the document wasn't what it appeared to be.

Roger was watching television as Jon walked in, his legs crossed on the desk: a press conference on the Texas secession movement, which had piggybacked onto the anti-Washington protests stirred up by August 13. Seeing Jon in the doorway, Roger muted the sound and nodded him to have a seat.

"I don't know the best way to preface this," Jon said. "But I just got hold of something I think is big. It's just—I can't do anything with it yet. We've got to wait twenty-four hours."

"All right. What've you got?"

"It's a document," he said, "explaining what happened last Friday in Ukraine. Written by one of the participants. Names, dates, money trail. It lays out the whole thing. I think it's the real deal."

Roger squinted and nodded soberly. Nothing seemed to surprise Jon's editor. He sometimes thought that if he were to remove his head, set it on his desk for several seconds then put it back on, Roger Yorke would simply watch with a slightly detached expression, pleased to observe something he'd never seen before. "'Written by one of the participants.' Not Utkin?"

"No. The man *you* told me about. Ivan Delkoff."

"Ah." Roger looked at him with new interest. "And what does it say?"

"It lays out exactly what happened. It details how Delkoff was hired in the spring to carry out the attack by a former FSB man named Andrei Turov. And that Turov was working with—for—the president of Russia. It's very specific. Names, dates, bank transfers."

Roger's eyes widened slightly, roughly the equivalent of anyone else exclaiming *Oh, my God!* "How'd you get it?"

"I can't go there at this point. But let's just say it's a good source."

"All right." Roger sighed. "The trouble is, as you wrote yesterday—this thing could blow up into war by the weekend. And I'm told another damaging story is about to drop. Today or tomorrow."

"Damaging to us?"

Roger made an affirmative sound. "What's being called a 'smoking gun.' Photos and emails, supposedly, about this meeting in Kiev. Confirming the deal between the Ukrainian missile dealer and our CIA man. Gregory Dial. There may also be video."

Jon sighed. He debated whether to share his suspicions about Harland Strickland or to wait. He decided to wait. "The Russians are good at this, aren't they?" he said.

"Better than we are, yes," Roger said. It was true, of course: while the US was still debating how to deal with cyber hacks and disinformation campaigns, Russia had fully integrated cyberwarfare into its military planning. Their 2008 war with Georgia marked the first time a nation had combined cyber attacks with military engagement. They'd since made cyber attacks a major component of their war with Ukraine.

"This will change it, though," he said, thinking of what Anna had told him: *If we don't respond properly, the lie wins.*

"Okay." Roger eyed Jon for a long time, as if reading answers on his face. "And you're sure this is legitimate?"

"That's what I'm going to find out. But yes, I believe it is."

"Then we wait," Roger said. "We wait twenty-four hours and hope that isn't too long."

Jake Briggs gazed out at the lights of Moscow as the plane came in to Sheremetyevo Airport, seeing, at certain angles, his own reflection in the window and turning his eyes away. The severe set of his face, the salt-and-pepper stubble, the rough, loose skin on his neck; the face looking back at him was someone he didn't recognize.

He was still numb, hours after witnessing Ivan Delkoff's murder, his thoughts recessed in the drone of the airplane engines. He'd called his wife Donna from Paris, to say that he was all right, to ask about Jamie and Jessie. But he couldn't tell her what had happened or where he was. He'd caught the last Aeroflot flight out of de Gaulle, arriving in Moscow at 3:20 a.m. Wondering all the while if he was journeying into another trap.

He kept thinking of Christopher Niles: his tough, steady temperament, his ability to suppress anger and subversive thoughts while he was working. Briggs didn't always do that so well. He had boarded the plane in Paris too angry to have a rational conversation with himself or anyone else, Delkoff's death still looping in his head: the way he'd taken an extra two steps before his body caught up with the fact that he'd been shot. Briggs had seen similar kills a dozen times in combat, but something about Delkoff's death felt more personal. Part of it was the last look he'd given him as he walked away from his car, as if he knew something Briggs didn't.

He tried counseling himself with the words of an old commanding officer, a gritty rear admiral named Ray Lacey: *Don't look for answers, look for better questions.* In service, in life: it was good advice. So Briggs came into Moscow telling himself to ask better questions. Not about what he might have done differently, which wasn't a good question, but about what he could do now. He arrived in the city with just a carry-on, pretending to be a tourist. Speaking to the cab driver with the few Russian sentences he could muster, the man all the while giving him uncomprehending looks.

Briggs stood on the narrow leafy Moscow street before entering his hotel, soaking in the pre-dawn silence, as a low mist rose from the ground. Upstairs, he went online to check messages and catch up on the news. There were fresh allegations about Washington's connection with the alleged August 13 planners and weapons supplier, he saw. The *New York Times* was reporting a meeting between the former Ukrainian intelligence officer Mikhail Kolchak, who allegedly operated the missile battery that brought down the president's plane, and "two American intelligence officials" in Kiev last month.

Briggs turned off his phone and watched the night trees for a while through the small window in his second-story room. He didn't think he could sleep, but finally he did; and sleep did its work, clearing away some of the flotsam in his head.

In the morning, Briggs did his hundred push-ups and hundred sit-ups. Then he called Christopher Niles on his cell to tell him he'd arrived.

"There's an anti-US rally today on Red Square," Chris told him.

"Okay." Briggs had forgotten how another human voice could shift his perspective so dramatically, particularly this one.

"Can you meet me at eleven?"

"All right."

Briggs walked down the street to a diner. He ate a big breakfast of scrambled eggs, smoked salmon, porridge, and hotcakes, still angry about losing Delkoff, but ready now to meet Christopher and whatever came next.

He saw that it was supposed to rain today, beginning by noon, and that seemed a good omen. Rain had been part of Briggs's training. It almost made him feel at home.

FORTY-TWO

Capitol Hill, Washington.

Gregory Dial's eyes were slits, as if he were looking at Anna from a distance, safe from scrutiny, his thin white hair combed up from the temples, his craggy features an affable shell. When Dial was younger, some said he resembled a clean-shaven Abe Lincoln, a blend of wise man and working man. Now, in what seemed an incredible turn of events, the press was accusing him of spearheading a US assassination plot against the president of Russia.

Anna hadn't seen Greg Dial in nine or ten months. He seemed thinner and a little frailer than she remembered, although his movements and his deep voice carried a familiar authority. He set a worn leather satchel on her desk, something Anna's grandfather might've carried.

"And how's your dad?"

It was always the first or second question he asked. This time, Anna had a good answer. "I just talked with him. He sounded great. He inspired me."

"Good, good," he said absently, beginning to open the satchel. There was something endearing about his bony fingers unwinding the leather strap. Dial was a former marine, who took issue with some of the administration's foreign policy. But he was by nature fiercely loyal.

"I commend you for what you did, Anna," he said. "Going on

television and speaking your mind like that. You did a nice job defending us. And me. Not that I needed it."

"I didn't think of it as defending anyone," she said. "I answered the questions I was asked."

"Yes, well. I came here to head off trouble. For all of us." He frowned as he reached in the satchel. Whatever he was about to do, he wasn't entirely comfortable with it, Anna could see. *You could have made this easier by just returning my calls,* she thought. "As you can imagine," he said, "the media's been calling me nonstop for the past few days. Legally, of course, I can't say anything. Not that I would, anyway—" He pulled printouts of four images and spread them on her desk. "These came to me this morning. From the Associated Press. I've been asked to comment. I'm not going to, but I wanted you to see. So you'll know what you're getting into."

Anna took a few moments to absorb what she was looking at: photographs of men seated at a small restaurant table, shoulder to shoulder. It resembled the blurry image that Russian blogs had sent out last Friday, purportedly showing "an American CIA officer" meeting with the Ukrainian missile dealer. These images were better focused and showed a wider view, revealing two additional men. This time, the "American CIA officer" was recognizable. In one of the photos he was looking right at the camera.

"That's you."

"It's me, yes. And this—" But he didn't have to tell her; she knew the big man sitting across from him, the man she'd seen in intelligence files: the serious face, flat mouth, crew cut. "—is Ivan Delkoff." He moved his index finger to the man beside Delkoff. "This," he said, "is Hordiyenko's agent, Petrofsky. And this man is Mikhail Kolchak, the Ukrainian who operated the missile battery that brought down the president's plane."

"My God," Anna said. "So you're saying this is real, then?"

"This is real, that's right." He scooted forward. "It's Kiev, July 12. This is the meeting that's been reported all over the Internet. I was there."

Anna stared at him, incredulous. So the reports were *right*? The US *was* behind the failed assassination attempt? Here was the evidence, the "smoking gun." They had them.

"The president told me today that this meeting didn't happen," Anna said. "I just went on national television saying it didn't."

"Well, it did. That's why I'm here. I understand these will go public tomorrow. Along with a story." They shared a look, Anna thinking about the damage ahead: this could instantly shatter US credibility around the world, maybe permanently.

"So, we *did* meet with Hordiyenko. The meeting in Kiev—?"

"The meeting in Kiev happened," he said. "As you can see."

"And the secret meetings in Washington—about regime change?"

"The Russia Strategic Planning Group, we called it. I was there for those, too, yes."

Anna dropped her gaze to the photos again, trying to imagine some benign explanation. "But it wasn't an assassination committee, as the media are calling it. You weren't meeting to discuss regime change in Russia?"

He exhaled audibly. "No. It was never called that. But we met. And we discussed regime change. Among other things. Many other things. The meeting in Kiev came out of those discussions. I was sent there, along with Maya Coles."

So was this *why the administration was pushing the coup story?* Anna wondered. Was it just to keep the real story out of the news? Did the president *know* all this? And was Greg Dial the spy in the house, who'd assisted the Russia plot?

"Help me understand, then," she said. "What happened at this meeting exactly? I was told it was exploratory, part of an information-gathering mission."

He shrugged. "'Information-gathering,' okay. We were looking at ways of dealing with the Russia threat in Ukraine. That was the information we were gathering. As you know, Russia is very threatened by what's going on there. If Ukraine succeeds as a sovereign nation, Russia's role in the region will be greatly diminished."

"So you went there and you met with Hordiyenko, Delkoff, and this Ukrainian military commander."

"No. We met with Hordiyenko's agent. Hordiyenko wasn't there." Anna felt a momentary relief. *The president was right about that, anyway.* "Hordiyenko is aligned with anti-Russian interests in Ukraine. He's someone we thought we might cultivate a relationship with. That's all it was. We met in a private room at a restaurant in Kiev. And discussed various things: politics, where the economy of the Donbas is headed, Russia's efforts to set up control there—replacing Ukrainian street signs with Russian street signs, for instance."

"But nothing was said about assassinating the president."

"Not in Kiev, no. Not a word." Anna sighed. "Of course," Greg said, "looking at it now, I see the whole thing must've been staged, to produce this." He tapped one of the images.

"You didn't know your picture was being taken?"

"No, of course not. Until this morning, I had no idea. Not until this showed up at my office and I received the call from Associated Press." Anna recalled something Christopher had told her once: how Russia was winning at games we didn't even know were being played. "Hordiyenko's man contacted us about a meeting," he said. "We went. Delkoff sat across from me for all of five minutes. He didn't say a word. Then he left. Kolchak, the missile captain, was with him. I asked at the time why they were there. No one had a good answer. Now I know."

"We can't just let this go out," Anna said. "We need to respond, to say what it really is."

"Perhaps," Dial said. "But that isn't my job." He began to gather the images. "I spoke earlier to the president's chief of staff. I spoke to the DNI. I'm now speaking with you. I'm not going to push it beyond that," he said. "I hear now that the White House wants to send out a different story," he added. "A counter story."

"Yes, apparently." *Counter story?* Was that what the coup allegation was? Anna thought about Turov: how he arranged simple but potent deceptions. If Ivan Delkoff was working for Turov, it would've been easy to put him in a meeting with an American intelligence officer long enough to have their photo taken together. A tactic from the Russian playbook.

"Tell me how this started," Anna said. "Tell me about the meetings of this secret committee. There were five people in the room, I was told." Dial lifted his chin, affirmatively. "Maya Coles. Edward Sears from the State Department. You. Two military?"

"One military."

"Rickenbach."

"Mmm."

"All right. And so who was the fifth?" She stared into his face, waiting, understanding why Gregory Dial would have been chosen: a loyal intelligence veteran with connections to Russia and the former Soviet states, an ability to work back channels, an aversion to publicity.

"The fifth man in the room was the head of our little committee," he said. "He was also the man who set up Kiev. Our contact point with Hordiyenko."

Anna's heart began to beat faster. Dial looked at her a long time. He was waiting for Anna to say it. "Not Harland Strickland?"

He moved his head just enough for her to see that his answer was yes. "I don't know how far you want to take that, Anna," he said. "I have issues with Harland, which pertain mostly to his personal life."

"*Personal* life?" But she could see that he wasn't going to explain that. "What role did Harland play in this? He *called* the meetings? Was he part of the setup?"

"Strickland called the meetings, yes. Candidly? It was his committee. And he was our liaison with Hordiyenko. The idea of regime change: it was his."

"So, *he* contacted Hordiyenko?"

"No. I said he was our *liaison*."

"In other words, *they* contacted him?"

"That's what I understand. But I can't tell you the rest of it. I don't know what was driving him, if he was acting on the president's direc-tive or someone else's. Or if he was working with Russia. And I don't know if he was part of the setup, to answer your question."

"But since Friday," Anna said, "he's denied—to me and others—that these conversations ever happened. Or that he was on this committee."

"Yes. I know." Gregory Dial smiled unevenly. "Once it got out in the media that maybe we *were* involved, he began telling people it wasn't true. I don't know why. But I guess it's reasonable to assume he's covering something up."

"And your guess would be—?"

"I honestly don't know, Anna. I think, candidly, it's possible that we *were* involved. That we did provide assistance, as the stories are say-ing. I hope that isn't true. But you asked me."

Either way, that's going to be the appearance, Anna thought. "Would you talk about any of this off the record?" she said, thinking of Jon Niles again.

Gregory Dial was shaking his head before she finished her ques-tion. "We used to have a saying, Anna. The more you stir something, the worse it smells. I came here as a courtesy, because I wanted you to know the score. I regret having been involved in this, frankly. But I'm not going to get into a shit-fight with Harland Strickland or anyone else. I don't think that would serve any useful purpose. And I know it wouldn't do anything for our country."

"But we can't let this go out just because we're afraid of getting into a fight, can we?" she said, feeling a surge of anger. Greg Dial showed no expression. That's how he did things. "Will you think about it?"

"If you'd like me to, Anna, of course I will," he said, sounding gen-tlemanly as he lifted his satchel. "But I'm not going to do it," he added. "Say hello to your father for me."

Anna felt betrayed and a little numb. She stared out the window for a long time after Gregory Dial said goodbye. Finally, she called Jon. "Where are you?" she said, as if it mattered.

FORTY-THREE

Jon Niles needed a drink. His girlfriend Carole Katz had left him another voice message during his meeting with Roger Yorke. That made three calls from her that he hadn't returned. Responding now felt more complicated than it would have if he'd just returned the first one.

"I'm sorry," he told her, walking to his car. "I've been kind of buried in this story."

"I can imagine. I was watching on television. How about we meet for a drink later?" she said. "Can you get away?"

"Oh. A drink? Sure. Why not?" *That* was easy, Jon thought. He let Carole pick the spot: a tapas bar downtown, near the Shakespeare Theatre, a place Jon had never been to and wouldn't have imagined she knew about. As he drove off, he thought of their early days together, after the improbable meeting at a checkout line in Safeway. It'd been sort of "cosmic," she used to say, how much they had in common back then, not just similar interests, but the same favorite lines in songs and films. The trouble was, mutual interests alone weren't the basis for a lasting relationship. Not that Jon was exactly a relationship expert. He'd gone through a series of girlfriends over the years, pursuing women—or letting them pursue him—mostly for the wrong reasons, following his curiosity often more than his common sense; sometimes

260 | MAX KARPOV

pursuing women who were completely wrong, or out of his league. Women like Anna Carpenter.

Speak of the devil. There she was, calling for him as Jon made the turn onto Pennsylvania Avenue.

"Hello?"

"Hi," Anna said. "Where are you?"

"Me? Driving. Downtown," Jon said. "Where are you?"

"I'm headed over to my son's for dinner. Listen. I need to tell you a few things."

"Okay. I do, too." Jon coughed, expecting that she wanted to talk about Delkoff's "Declaration." Or maybe there was news about his brother.

"I just met with Gregory Dial," she said.

"Oh," Jon said. "He called you back?"

"No, he came by my office. I can't talk about it over the phone, but there's going to be more coming out and—"

Processing that, Jon didn't notice a red light until he was into the intersection. Horns blared. Brakes slammed. He took a deep breath after reaching the other side. ". . . but he also mentioned Strickland," Anna was saying. "Something about his personal life that I can't—"

"*Strickland?*"

"So we need to talk in person, okay? Actually: what are you doing now?"

"Right now?"

"If you'd like, you could come over and join us for dinner. You could meet my son. He might even be able to help you on your story."

"Well, I'd like to," Jon said, catching what sounded like a flirtatious intonation in her voice again. He glanced at the dash clock, feeling his heart begin to race. He was just three blocks from the restaurant. "I do have another appointment this evening. Could we talk later? After your dinner, maybe?"

"Sure. Later's fine," she said in her poised, pleasant tone. Jon seriously thought for a moment about skipping Carole and calling Anna back as he came to the parking garage. He hit a button to get out of talk radio. Thinking of two roads diverging in a wood: how his life might be different if he chose to meet Anna Carpenter tonight instead of Carole Katz. He thought about what Roger had called the "smoking gun": evidence that the attack *was* supported, if not engineered, by the US government. Did that involve Gregory Dial?

He pulled into a space and parked, keeping his engine running. And then, incredibly, the guitar and harmonica opening of "Visions of Johanna" came on. It was Carole's favorite song—one of them, anyway. Jon turned it up, indulging himself for a few moments—*Ain't it just like the night to play tricks when you're tryin' to be so quiet? We sit here stranded, though we're all doin' our best to deny it* . . . before shutting it off.

Carole was already seated at a small window table by the entrance, watching for him. She looked good, a little dressed up in a thin black jacket and a royal blue dress shirt. She rose to give him a quick kiss and they sat. She'd already ordered Jon a beer, Budweiser in the bottle. Odd she wanted to meet here of all places, he thought, glancing around the restaurant. Jon decided that he was going to open up with Carole tonight; share some details of the story, let her into his life a little more.

"You look great," he said.

She smiled but kept on her serious face. Carole was thirty-nine, a graphic designer and illustrator. An earthy, intelligent woman, with thick dark hair, pale skin, fullish breasts, and a surprising laugh. But she was idiosyncratic: comfortable around men more than women; nervous in large chain stores; nearly always dressed in black. She straightened her napkin. Jon thought about her bowl of matchbooks.

"I know it's a busy day for you," she said. "I saw the news. A lot happening."

"There is. I'm really glad to see you, though," he said, making his tone a little more measured, to meet hers.

"I just thought it might be nice for us to talk," she said. "It's been so hard reaching you."

"I know. And I do apologize." Jon could see as he cleared his throat that he should have done the apology first.

"No biggie," she said. "I actually like that you're so involved in this. I think it's good for you. With the way this story's going and everything else—"

"Mmm hmm. So—Wait, you're not going to say you want to break up, are you? That's not what this is about?"

"No." She showed him a hard, unfamiliar expression. "But I think it wouldn't hurt if we allowed each other a little space for a while."

"Oh." Jon glanced at the television, saw the Breaking News banner. *What timing.* There was something new going on with the Ukrainian oligarch—Hordiyenko.

"You said the other day how you ought to be spending more time with this story," Carole said. "I just feel like I'm keeping you from it. From who you want to be."

"No. I didn't—I mean—"

"But you know what? Maybe it's keeping me from what *I* want to do, too," she said, nailing him with her eyes. "We do spend a lot of time sitting in the yard drinking beer and getting high. And a lot of nights I just sort of wait for you to show up. Which is strictly my own fault, I know—" This made her tear up and look away. Jon glanced again at the TV: there was a blurry shot of Ivan Delkoff now, a big, brutish man with a flat expression, large ears, and nonexistent lips. "It's like we've become each other's bad habits in a way."

She was right about that, Jon knew. He was actually impressed that she had the guts to call them out on it.

"I remember, you told me once that the one thing you do well is journalism, and you're not so good at anything else."

"I wish you hadn't remembered that," Jon said. "Because it's really more—"

"And I just don't want to stand in the way of what you love. Which I feel I'm doing."

"Mmm mmm." Jon felt a slow storm of anger forming, the natural reaction to rejection. But at the same time, he wondered if this Breaking News story was anything; he debated for a moment asking the bartender to turn it up. "Is this open at all for discussion?" he said, trying to sound steady. "I mean, is there any middle ground?"

"I'd just like to take some time apart," she said, gazing at the backs of her hands. "I'm not saying we can't stay in contact, or be friends."

"Okay." It felt like a high school breakup now, the part about staying friends.

"Let's just see how it goes," she said. "Nothing has to be etched in stone."

"Right." *What timing,* he thought again: we're potentially three days away from World War III and she wants to break up? "Why're you dressed up, anyway?"

"I'm meeting some people from work at the theater," she said. "No biggie."

She did this on occasion: went out to a show or dinner with "people" from work. She reached across the table for his hands. Her deep brown eyes glistened. Her fingers felt warm and fleshy around his.

"Let's talk again tomorrow or the next day. Okay?"

"All right."

"Good." She pulled her hands away and looked at her watch. "I better go. Call me if you want."

"Okay. Right." *Tomorrow or the next day.* Jon walked her out front. The Shakespeare Theatre was on the corner and she didn't seem to want him going all the way. He wondered if the "people" she was meeting was really one person. If so, it was strange asking to meet Jon here. But so was Carole.

"Enjoy the show," he said. She gave him a kiss on one cheek and turned. He watched her walk down the block with an independent hitch to her step, a very lovely stranger all of a sudden.

The waitress gave Jon a dejected clown-face look when he walked back in, as if she'd heard the whole conversation. Jon ordered another beer and his check, watching CNN. Missing Carole already. He sat for a long time, it seemed, waiting for the check, thinking about where he might stop on the way home to buy a pint of Old Grand-Dad for a nightcap. Then he saw Anderson Cooper talking about Texas secession and felt himself pulled back into the story.

He stepped up to the bar, turning sideways so he could hear the TV. "What do you think's going to happen?" he asked the bartender when it went to commercial. She'd been staring at the TV but seemed surprised by the question; he could see she hadn't been paying attention.

"Nuclear annihilation," a man at the bar said. "Texas will be the only state left standing."

Jon smiled. Something was playing on the edge of his consciousness, though, like a vaguely familiar song, tickling at his memory and fading before he could figure what it was. There: a raised voice, out of context, saying, "You *cannot* be serious." *Cannot* instead of *can't*.

Back at the table, Jon glanced discreetly around the restaurant, trying to stay cool as he waited for his check. The familiar voice seemed to be coming from a table of four across the room. But when he heard it again, it was behind him: "No, you don't even want to talk about this." Pronouncing "this" with a faint accent, so it almost sounded like "dis."

Where is my check? Jon stood and flapped his arms, but no one noticed. He walked around the bar looking for his waitress. But, also, listening. The familiar voice had faded out again like a late-night radio signal. Of course, it was possible Jon was imagining this. It might even be some kind of weird meltdown he was having, triggered by what Carole had just done.

But seated again, finishing his beer, Jon heard the voice more clearly. He looked at the doorway and saw the woman passing right by him, out into the street—young and slim, in a knee-length black dress, accompanied by a heavyset older man in a dark suit.

And that's when he felt certain: it was *her*. The voice belonged to Jon's mystery source. 9:15.

He left a twenty on the table and rushed out, pulling his cell phone as a prop. He began to follow, staying a dozen paces behind as they walked down the street past the theater. But it didn't matter: they were carrying on an animated conversation, too engaged to notice him. The woman was average height, but thin-hipped, well-dressed, with short dark hair and a slightly labored walk, as if her shoes were too tight. Not at all how he'd pictured her.

They stopped in the next block, and their argument suddenly flared up: the woman gesturing emphatically, her right hand poofing open in front of the man's face at one point, as if she were casting a spell on him, or maybe a curse.

Jon gazed at his cell phone as he strained to hear what they were saying. The woman was young—not much more than twenty, he guessed. The man was at least twenty-five years older, heavy-jowled, gray, wearing a slightly oversized suit, no tie. Maybe her father.

They went two more blocks, saying nothing. Then the woman stopped beside an old model Jaguar parked at the curb. The man rounded the back of the car and opened the door for her. The woman glanced quickly Jon's way, and he saw the unusual cast of her face—tall cheekbones and a wide mouth; smooth skin, like the face of a child.

Jon began to memorize the license plate number, watching as the car jerked away from the curb. Then he made his first phone call.

The DMV registration on the Jaguar came back to a man named Michael Ketchler. Forty-nine years old, home address a residence in Fairfax, Virginia. It took just a few minutes of online sleuthing for Jon to learn that Ketchler was a Washington attorney, a partner in the firm of Carrick & Carson Associates. There was a Russian connection, too: Ketchler had lived in Moscow during the mid-2000s, according to one bio, and worked for a year or so as a company attorney for Sputnik, the Russian news organization based in Washington.

Jon remembered what Anna Carpenter had said earlier about her son. David Carpenter was, among other things, a "penetration tester," who sought out vulnerabilities in computer networks. But he could also negotiate his way around the dark web and access databases that Jon couldn't. His next call was to Anna.

"Sorry to bother you so late," he said.

"It isn't late. What's up?"

"Remember when you asked me about my sources on this story?" Jon said.

"Kind of."

"I have an anonymous one," Jon said. "She was the first person who told me about the preemptive strike discussion. 9:15, I call her."

"9:15?"

"Yeah. Each time we've talked, that's when she's called. 9:15 in the evening. She's the one who told me about the 'no fingerprints' thing," he said.

"All right."

"My editor, Roger Yorke, thinks that finding 9:15's motivation might be the real story here."

"Hard to do when she's anonymous."

"I know. Except that kind of just changed. I think I just saw her."

"Oh?"

"I don't have a name yet, but I just got an ID for the man she was with. I was wondering if maybe your son could help me dig a little deeper. I know he has access to databases. I don't know, I just thought, if he could run some searches, the magazine will cover whatever—"

"Oh." Anna laughed, her good nature immediately contagious. "Of course, he'll help. He'd be glad to."

"Good." Jon took a breath. "So. I was wondering: how could I reach him?"

"David? I'm sitting next to him. He'd be delighted to help you. But call on his phone," she said, and she gave him the number.

Jon looked out at the street, the night shadows, the pieces of sky among the buildings. David Carpenter answered on the first ring.

"Hey," he said, receptive in a gruff, low-energy sort of way. Not exactly "delighted."

He listened silently as Jon explained what he now knew about Michael Ketchler.

"Anything you can add to the picture would help," Jon said. "Especially if he's married or has a girlfriend. Or a daughter." He described the woman he had seen earlier with Ketchler: early twenties, thin, short dark hair, five foot five or six. "Any images you can find of him with women matching that description would be helpful."

"All right. I'll have something for you by six, then," David said, his tone surprisingly matter of fact.

"Six—?"

"A.m. I work at night," David explained. "It's quieter. I'll send you a file in the morning."

FORTY-FOUR

Wednesday, August 18. Moscow.

Jake Briggs walked across the Bolshoy Moskvoretsky Bridge toward Red Square, stopping at the spot where Boris Nemtsov had been murdered in February 2015. He looked out at the river and the crazy-colored onion domes of St. Basil's, the famous cathedral built by Ivan the Terrible in the sixteenth century, now Moscow's most recognizable tourist site.

Briggs knew the story about Nemtsov's murder: the former deputy prime minister turned opposition leader was shot here on a Friday night while walking home from dinner with his girlfriend. Two weeks before the killing, Nemtsov had written on a Russian blog, "I'm afraid Putin will kill me." They were crossing the bridge at 11:40 when a car stopped behind him; a gunman got out and shot Nemtsov four times in the back. Nemtsov had been planning to lead an anti-Putin rally in Red Square that Sunday; he'd also been finalizing a report on Russia's clandestine military role in Ukraine. The killing turned Sunday's rally into a memorial and sent the opposition movement into retreat.

After the shootings, the sidewalk had overflowed with flowers. There were half a dozen bouquets marking the spot today, along with several homemade posters. A lot had changed in Moscow since Briggs had last been here. In 2011 and 2012, ahead of the presidential election, there'd been huge anti-Putin demonstrations in the city. Pundits had predicted for months that the Arab Spring fever then sweeping the Middle East would soon reach Moscow and might cost Putin reelection. But the pro-Putin forces managed that election well, busing in their own demonstrators, some of them paid in rubles or vodka to chant support. And Putin had prevailed. The laws on public demonstrations had tightened since then, making it more difficult to march and organize against the government. In December 2015, the Kremlin had passed a law authorizing the Russian security services to open fire in crowds "if necessary."

Putin took it as an article of faith that the United States had been behind the 2011–12 demonstrations, much as he believed the CIA had engineered Ukraine's Euromaidan revolution of 2014. Putin's greatest fear, Briggs knew, was still that a populist Arab Spring–style uprising would rock the streets of Moscow, bringing chaos to Russia and toppling his rule.

The demonstration in Red Square today was a different kind of rally: a protest against the United States for the August 13 assassination attempt. It was the sort of demonstration Putin welcomed.

Briggs walked across the bridge to Red Square, which was filled with thousands of protestors, and he was awed all over again by the architecture: the cathedrals and statues, the elegant pyramid of Lenin's tomb, Resurrection Gate, the Kremlin walls. Most of the people here were oblivious to the history, though, waving the Russian tri-color flag or holding up cheesy anti-America signs. Some of the signs were in Cyrillic but most were in English for the international cameras. Lots of "USA KILLS." To Briggs, the protests felt cheap and inappropriate for this magnificent setting. But then, Moscow had always seemed a schizophrenic city to him. He watched a group of four inebriated young men stomping on an American flag and fought the impulse to grab one of them and knock his head into the pavement. *You could ruin your life acting on impulses like that,* he counseled himself.

It was the same everywhere, demonstrators carrying on like

overexcited children. There were cardboard cutouts of the US president with his face X-ed out; protestors trying to set oversized fake US currency on fire, becoming like passionate monkeys every time a camera went on to record them. *Don't waste it. Don't let them do it to you,* Briggs thought.

He began to feel a kind of morbid curiosity, though, as he walked among the protestors. This didn't even feel real to him; it felt like a kind of manufactured anger, stirred up by fake stories portraying the West—the United States—as Russia's dire enemy. He tried to keep his eyes on the ground, picturing himself in a tunnel with Christopher Niles at the other end. *Just keep going. What happened in France had nothing to do with this.* He felt sprinkles of drizzle on his arms as he crossed the cobblestones, and smiled as some of the demonstrators pulled out umbrellas. He recalled an old saying he liked: Americans never carry umbrellas.

"Jake." He looked to his right and there was Chris, walking into step beside him. Dressed in old loose-fitting slacks and work shirt, a gym bag slung over one shoulder. Slapping him on the back instead of shaking hands. Christopher'd always had a skill for blending in. Somehow he'd found Briggs among all these people.

"Performance art," Briggs said. "All for the cameras."

"Yeah, I know." They kept walking through the crowd, Briggs feeling the moisture gathering on his face, the cobbestones waxy with falling drizzle. "You didn't fuck up," Chris said. "Your good news was very good. Okay?"

"And the bad news very bad."

"No. You got us what we need."

"Except they're going to say that what he gave me isn't real. They're going to say the US made it up."

"Probably," Christopher said. "If it comes to that. But I don't think it will."

Okay, Briggs thought. *So tell me about that.* A wet gust of wind cut across the square, and for a few fleeting seconds it felt to Briggs as if they were two soldiers walking toward a battlefield.

"I'm meeting Turov at 2:30 this afternoon," Christopher said, speaking just above a whisper. "The document gives me what I need for that."

"Okay." Briggs waited through another silence, Chris Niles seeming almost too calm. "Do you want me involved?" Briggs finally said.

"I'd like you to be, yes." *Good,* Briggs thought. "I'd like you to follow and cover me. Martin has arranged a car for you. I need you to be a witness to where we go. And provide a way out, *if* I need it." Christopher stopped among a loose crowd of demonstrators and spectators. The incongruity of their conversation and the anti-American hysteria all around struck Briggs as funny. "So. Tell me what happened," Chris said, meaning France.

Briggs gave him a ten-minute version as they milled among the protestors: how he'd arrived in Paris late Sunday and made his initial contact Monday night; the phone calls with Delkoff's cousin Dmitri; the meeting Tuesday morning at an abandoned caretaker's cottage; the final drive back to the house; Delkoff pushing the flash drive into his shirt pocket, saying he needed to "try to work things out" at the house. And then he told him the last part: how Ivan Delkoff had turned and looked back with that strange half-smile and said something to him in Russian, probably knowing that he was about to die. "It was very weird. It was a kind of bravery. Like he was ready to sacrifice his life for this."

Chris Niles said nothing until Briggs finished. Then he told him, succinctly, about the mission they would be working together. "However this turns out," he said, "it's just us. No one's coming in to rescue us. It's a two-man op. But that's a good thing."

"Does Martin Lindgren know what you're doing?" Briggs asked.

"He knows general terms. What he needs to. They're providing a G-5 to get us out. It's up to us to make it to the airport. I asked Marty to wait on releasing Delkoff's statement for twenty-one hours. Or until he hears from us. Or doesn't hear."

"Twenty-one?"

"Yeah." He smiled. "I picked a number." Christopher gave him the rest as they walked away from Red Square: Briggs would find a Lada parked at a residential address three subway stops from his hotel. "There's a 9mm in the car," he said. "Let's hope you won't need it."

The rain made a steady beat now through the leaves, raising a dusty scent off the pavement as they came to the river. "Do you think Turov's already seen the document?"

"I assume he has," Chris said. "They raided the house in France where Delkoff was staying. That'll give him a head start."

"And couldn't this just be some kind of trap?"

"Sure, of course." They kept walking, Briggs thinking about ambushes, because that's what this felt like, a classic reversal ambush: you think you're pursuing your prey right up until the moment you catch him; then the prey turns and takes you.

"But I don't think so," Chris said, and Briggs saw from the long-view clarity in his eyes that he'd already considered this and rejected it. "What's he going to accomplish killing me? I'm out of the business now. And anything I know is also known by others."

"Unless it's personal."

"Unless it's personal." Chris made a face. Briggs regretted putting that thought in his head; but then he saw that it didn't matter: Chris had thought of that, too. When he was working, Chris Niles carried the qualities that all thinking people aspired to but most couldn't maintain—staying focused, avoiding distractions, making right choices. If he could bottle that stuff, he'd be a billionaire many times over.

"If anything happens, we put Delkoff's statement out immediately," Christopher said. "I told Martin the same thing."

"Okay."

By the time they reached the street, they had run out of things to say. Talking too much loosened the focus; Briggs understood that. In a bus shelter, he saw a poster reading US KILLS INNOCENT PEOPLE. Briggs watched the rain dimpling the river as they went, a slow gust of wind tugging the leaves in one direction. He looked at Christopher, surprised how much his hair had grayed, and thought about the reflection of his own face in the airplane window, nearly unrecognizable. He thought of his boy on his knee last Friday in Virginia, watching the news about the "tear-riss" on TV. That seemed a long time ago now.

"What's this rain going to do?"

"Supposed to rain all day." Christopher glanced at him. "I thought you liked rain."

"Yeah, I know. I do. You taking the bag with you?"

"No. You are." Under a canopy of leaves, Christopher removed the gym bag from his shoulder and handed it to Briggs. "That's for you. It's got my phone and personal effects that I can't carry to the meeting. Bring it with you."

"Okay."

Minutes later, Christopher slapped Briggs on the back, the same way he'd greeted him. Physically Briggs liked how this day was turning: the prematurely dark sky, the sopping hiss of car tires, the shiny reflections on the pavement, the white-blue-red lights strung across Moskvoretsky Bridge, the textures of the world sparkling with mysterious clarity all of a sudden.

He didn't notice when exactly it was that Christopher Niles began to move away from him. But he looked over at one point and saw that he wasn't there anymore. Briggs stopped and turned, looking all directions among the dripping trees. But Christopher was gone.

FORTY-FIVE

Washington.

Jon's cell phone woke him at 5:58. Reaching for it, he knocked the water bottle from the nightstand and it splatted on the floor.

"Hello?"

"I've got your information, I just emailed it to you."

"Okay." The voice sounded unfamiliar, although he knew it had to be David Carpenter.

"Look at your email."

"Did you have any luck?"

"Look at your email. I'm here if you want to call. If it's her, and you want more, let me know."

David clicked off. All business again, intense, unsociable, the opposite of his mother. Jon got up and fixed a cup of coffee. He sat at his kitchen table and skimmed through the notes that David had sent. It became apparent very quickly that he had found more than Jon expected, including a name and bio for his 9:15 caller: Sonya Natalie Larsen. She worked as a legal secretary for the high-end D.C. law firm of Carrick & Carson, which represented charitable foundations and nonprofits. Her boss was Michael Ketchler, the man Jon had seen her arguing with the night before.

David had sent eight images along with the text file. Only one identified her by name, and the photo was grainy. Of the others, which he'd ID'd through facial recognition, the first three were marked "probable," the other four "possible." It was one of the "possibles" that clinched it.

He called David back six minutes later. "Yeah. It's her," he said. "Great work." David said nothing. "How soon can you get me more?"

"Now, if you want. The senator asked me to drop everything else. Which I can do."

Jon smiled. *The senator.* "I really appreciate this," he said.

He began to read through David's preliminary report more carefully. Sonya Natalie Larsen was twenty-five years old; at work, she apparently went by the name Natalie, according to a company website. She had moved to the United States last summer from London, where she'd worked for Linklaters LLP. "Married, and separated. To attorney Edward Larsen," according to David's report. For eleven months, she'd been renting a two-bedroom apartment in Alexandria.

It was all pretty weird, Jon thought. He'd assumed before last night that 9:15 would be someone older, and better connected. A political operative, or someone in the IC. Maybe the wife or girlfriend of a high-level operative at Defense or CIA. Someone with a clear political agenda on US-Russia relations.

So who was Natalie Larsen? And how would she have been privy to classified intelligence conversations about Russia? Jon spent half an hour running his own data searches on her, but they turned up nothing. And that was sort of weird, too.

Then he got a different idea. Recalling his conversation with Harland Strickland, and his last phone call with 9:15; and the place they had intersected.

He read through the Delkoff document again, considering the scenario it detailed about what had led up to August 13. Remembering what Roger Yorke had said Thursday, after 9:15's third call: *"I wonder if her agenda may be the real story rather than what she told you."*

He called David Carpenter back. "I need you to try something for me, if you can. I need you to run a search on somebody else."

"Go ahead."

Jon told him what he was thinking. Afterward, he walked to the window, sipping coffee. Letting this new idea spool out in his head for a while longer. He watched the news as he ate a bowl of Raisin Bran. There was breaking news—real breaking news—on all the networks, just as Roger had said: photos from the meeting last month in Kiev, with "senior CIA operative" Gregory Dial and two of the August 13 "co-conspirators," Mikhail Kolchak and Ivan Delkoff.

Delkoff was now being called the attack's "ringleader."

The photos had been released through a WikiLeaks-style website called InternationalEthicsWatch. There was also a rough audio from the meeting, on which Dial purportedly said, "We want this to happen, but can't be connected in any way." Jon listened to it several times and couldn't make out anything except the word "connected."

"Is this the smoking gun proving that the United States *was* involved in the assassination attempt?" asked the CNN newscaster. "So far, there has been no formal response from the White House, although one senior official is questioning the authenticity of the tape, calling the story a 'diversion.'"

On Fox, he saw that Russia was running snap drills with twenty thousand troops on the Ukrainian border right now; meanwhile, the Russian foreign minister had announced plans to meet with the president of Ukraine. "Sources say a resolution may be under discussion which could eventually result in a partition of Ukraine," said the Fox newsreader. "But the State Department calls the story 'completely unfounded.'"

Jon took a shower, anxious about the fragmented, confusing way the news was playing out, but energized by his new idea. *If we don't respond properly, the lie wins. Russia wins.* He was in the kitchen running his own searches again when David Carpenter called back. "Okay," he said. "You were right."

THE PLOT TO KILL PUTIN | 277

"You confirmed it?"

"Yeah. How did you know?"

"Can you email me what you found?"

"I just did. How did you know?"

Jon listened to David's breathing. "I don't know how much your mother told you—"

"I know what's going on," he interjected, a slight tremor in his tone. "But as I told her last night: we need to prove the real story, not just disprove the false one. Especially with this threat of war. Everything else is just a sideshow."

"Okay. I agree."

"I found more on Ketchler, too," David said. "His businesses *do* have a presence on the dark web. No question. Some of these foundations are using an overlay network—which is an anonymous network within a network, basically—"

"Okay," Jon said, no longer following. "I want to hear more about that. But I need to check on something else first."

David went silent for a moment. "I'll be here if you need anything else," he said.

As soon as he hung up, Jon called David's mother.

"I think I just figured something out," he said. "Can we meet?"

"Okay. But it'll have to wait a couple hours. I'm about to go into a meeting."

Jon said nothing at first, feeling a surge of impatience. He had to remind himself that he was talking to a US Senator. "Okay. A couple of hours would be fine. Sure."

Anna asked, "What did you figure out?"

"I think, maybe, everything?" Jon said.

FORTY-SIX

Northwest of Moscow.

It was still raining heavily as Anton drove into the gated neighborhood, the Mercedes's wipers whipping furiously side to side. Rain felt like the wrong accompaniment to this afternoon, Andrei Turov thought, although it fit nicely with the music inside their sedan, which was Tchaikovsky's Fourth Symphony: the stormy, emotional melodies his mother used to listen to when he was a boy. Turov had hoped to say goodbye to his country home in the sunlight. But many things were beyond his control now.

Much of the world believed that the US government had been the invisible hand behind August 13, a perception that earned Russia enormous empathy capital. The latest revelations were being characterized internationally as "the smoking gun." Which was good. Just that phrase, repeated by Turov's bot armies and political operatives on social media, would cause enormous damage, much as the phrase "assassination committee" had done. Soon, Washington would revert to full panic mode, and eventually make some rash overcompensation, only worsening their position.

Yes, Russia would surely benefit from this. But Turov's old friend, he feared, was only going to squander it, thinking that he could outplay history somehow. Going back to their schooldays in Leningrad,

Putin had been a gambler: if he took a risk and won, then his next move was to take a bigger risk. It had worked for him so far. But it was not the way to build a legacy. In truth, his old friend was not really a nationalist as he pretended to be; he was a gambler and a kleptocrat, as his critics charged. Turov did not want to be around him when he finally lost.

In Switzerland, Turov would have a spectacular view from his office window, of enormous white mountaintops. There—and wherever he traveled next—he would nurture new dreams, surrounded by his family, by Olga, Konkin, and a few associates.

They parked in the two-car garage at the house Anton had rented. Turov had never been to this one before, and it was a little larger and more modern than he liked. But otherwise it felt like the dozens of other dwellings he'd used for his client meetings, designer-furnished properties rented or purchased for him by Konkin. Even though Russia as a whole was losing population every year, Moscow itself was growing and decentralizing, expanding into hundreds of gated villages and residential developments such as this one.

In the plush corner office, replete with dark woods, leather, and brass, Turov unpacked his briefcase: a cell phone, a laptop, a writing tablet and gold pen, three classical CDs, and a Makarov 9mm handgun, which he set in the upper middle drawer of the desk. He was going to keep this meeting with the American as simple as possible.

Anton put on Tchaikovsky's Fourth Symphony in the house, too, and Turov sat and listened for a while, to the music and the rain, the melodrama of his mother's beloved melodies—the first and second movements, in particular, music that had seemed to make up for the lack of drama in her own life.

Turov needed just one more thing now: his collaborator. And the collaborator was coming right here to this room. He was scheduled to arrive by 3:30 p.m. The American, Christopher Niles. Then Turov could finish this game on his own terms.

FORTY-SEVEN

Capitol Hill, Washington.

Anna Carpenter was supposed to meet Jon Niles at eleven, in Starbucks again. But it was a hectic morning and she was running late. She'd attended a 9:30 intelligence briefing on Russia's military buildup, learning that a series of cyber attacks had just crippled parts of Ukraine and Estonia, crashing military, police, and government computer systems. But this news would be overshadowed now by the so-called "smoking gun" allegations against the US.

It's still moving too fast, Anna thought. *Much too fast.* This time, though, she was going to do something about it. Anna set goals for herself each morning during her workouts. Today's was ambitious: to disprove the story the president planned to sell to the American people.

She was eleven minutes late to Starbucks, where she found Jon standing just inside the doors, waiting anxiously, a ten-by-twelve envelope in one hand. "Sorry," she said. "Meeting ran long."

"It's okay. Lot going on." He flinched in that affecting way he had, then led her to a table.

"Did David help much?"

"David helped a *lot.* David's kind of amazing, really."

"Yes, I've thought that. He's helping me, too," she said. They sat. Anna told him first about her conversation with Gregory Dial, and the revelation that Harland Strickland had been the fifth person on the so-called "assassination committee." Surprisingly, Jon seemed unsurprised.

"I'll try to make this brief," he said when she finished, "because I know you're in a hurry. I think I understand now what's going on. The document you gave me is accurate, I believe. You were right, we *didn't* have anything to do with this."

"Okay, good," Anna said. "That makes two of us now who know it. All we have to do is convince the rest of the world."

"Which we're going to do," Jon said. The smile she expected didn't appear. Anna liked his intensity this morning. He scrolled through a file on his phone and began to explain what he'd found: beginning with the car registration he'd traced to Michael Ketchler, a nonprofit attorney with the high-end D.C. firm of Carrick & Carson. Then he showed her the images David had sent of Ketchler. "This is the man I saw last night."

"With your 9:15 source."

"Yes. 9:15's name is Natalie Larsen," he said. "*Sonya* Natalie Larsen." Jon slid through several images of her, showing Anna. It wasn't anyone she recognized, or a name she knew. "David did a face recog search. It was this image, from a Russian embassy party, in 2015, that did it."

Anna looked. "And that's her—the woman who called you anonymously? Who gave you this information about Russia."

"Yes," Jon said. "She works for Ketchler. But David found something else, too," he continued. "An interesting coincidence. I thought you might like to see. This is from the same embassy party. Do you recognize this man?"

The man he'd enlarged in the next image resembled Harland Strickland. Anna looked again. "That's Harland."

"Yes."

"So Harland Strickland was at the same party as your source? Does that mean anything?"

"Probably, yes," Jon said. "Didn't you mention that Gregory Dial said something about Strickland's personal life?"

"Yes." Her phone pinged and she looked quickly: Ming Hsu, calling her back to the office. "Harland's what used to be called a ladies' man," Anna said. "'Womanizer' is probably a better word, considering he's married. There were a few incidents in his past, where he went out for drinks with women a lot younger than he was. One a newspaper editor, I think. I don't know that it's anything more mysterious than that." Jon was nodding, as if this confirmed something. "Why? Why does that matter?"

"I think 9:15 may've been one of those younger women," he said. "And I think it's possible that she had something on him."

"*Kompromat*?"

"Possible."

This made sense to Anna. Harland would be easy prey for an alluring Russian girl in her mid-twenties. Was *he* the spy in the house, then, if not Dial?

"So tell me about this thing you figured out," she said.

"Well. First of all, I'm starting to see that it was Strickland who leaked the story to the media," he said.

"Strickland did?" Christopher's little brother was as focused as a monk now. But he wasn't making a lot of sense. "Wouldn't Harland be the last person to leak that information?" Anna said. "Considering he's been leading the cover story—about the coup?"

"Unless he didn't *know* he was leaking it." Jon opened the ten-by-twelve envelope and pulled out several sheets of paper. "I asked David to dig into Natalie Larsen's background. *Sonya* Natalie," he said again. "Larsen is her married name. She came to D.C. a little over a year ago, we think, from England, where she also worked for a law firm. She apparently separated from her husband sometime before that, but they're still legally married, or at least she kept his name. Her husband was an environmental attorney. The interesting thing—and this is where I began to make a little leap—is that David found out her maiden name was Fedorov. She's Russian, not English."

"Interesting because—?"

"Fedorov also happened to be the maiden name of Andrei Turov's wife. Ex-wife."

"So—you're saying she's related to Turov."

"Yes. I think it's his daughter, in fact," he said. "That's what David and I figured out. Turov has two daughters. One lives with him in Moscow. Her name's Svetlana. Sonya is the older daughter. She's more of a free spirit, kind of a thorn in her father's side for years. After the divorce, she went to live with her mother in England, took her mother's last name, and became a citizen of the U.K. After that, she seems to have dropped off the map."

Anna was amazed by this turn and that he'd come to it so quickly. But she wondered how it pertained to what was going on in Russia. "What happened to the mother?"

"She died in 2014. An alcohol-related traffic accident in England. There are some accounts online saying that both mother and daughter died. But David thinks she may have planted those herself."

Anna nodded for him to continue. She'd seen this same keenness in other journalists, once they'd gotten the scent of a story. But Jon seemed to have more than just the scent. He seemed to know exactly where this was leading. "And how does Harland figure?"

"So I called David back," he said. "Asked him to run searches on Sonya Turov. And we hit a few bingos. Including Harland Strickland. It doesn't mean she's some kind of high-level spy or anything. She might just be a smart, self-sufficient woman who was able to get Strickland to talk—"

"But you're thinking Strickland told Turov's daughter—your 9:15 source—about the preemptive strike, and the 'no fingerprints' talk, in the course of a fling? Pillow talk? That he inadvertently leaked details about those meetings through her?"

"Or that she managed to pry it out of him," Jon said.

"And now Strickland's pushing this story about the Russian coup because he's trying to cover, to change the subject? To divert attention from the fact that he may've been talking about classified information? Or that there may be some sort of tape or other compromising evidence against him."

Jon nodded. "With a woman who happens to be the daughter of the organizer of the attack."

"Do you think he knew that?"

"He probably didn't at first. But I suspect he's figured it out by now. Obviously, the truth could be very personally damaging to Strickland. He's in damage control mode and he's pulling a lot of people—maybe the country—down with him."

It was sort of stunning, Anna thought, and said a lot about our times: that a sexual imbroglio could lead to war or threaten the fall of a great nation. "How'd you get all this? How did you figure the connection between Strickland and this woman?"

"After we got 9:15's maiden name, I made the Turov connection. I'd always thought 9:15 was someone older, who had some link, however tangentially, with the administration. But when I saw her on the street, and I saw how young she was, I realized I needed to rethink that."

"How did you connect her with Strickland, though? Just through the photo?"

"No. There was one other thing," Jon said. "A number. Something Strickland told me about national security meetings: he said eighty-five percent of national security meetings in the past year have been about the Middle East, not Russia."

"So?"

"So, those were the exact same words that my 9:15 source used when we talked last Thursday. And it's not a number anyone else seems to be using. So when Strickland told me the same thing—almost word for word—I realized she had been talking with him."

Anna remembered something, then: Martin Lindgren mentioning

to Christopher that he had a Russian "asset." Was it possible this Natalie Larsen could be the asset?

"And why was she calling *you*, in the first place?"

"I'm not sure yet," Jon said. "I don't think I was the only journalist getting calls. Maybe she *was* doing this for her father, or more likely for this Michael Ketchler. That's still to be determined," he added. "I think we have to go full-court press now. We can't let what is essentially a sideshow derail our country."

"Sideshow."

"David's word. I think he's right. Our country has become good at turning sideshows into main events. Sacrificing big things that matter for little ones that don't." Jon clicked his pen anxiously.

"So what are you going to do with this?" she said. "What's your plan?"

Jon shrugged. "Talk with Sonya. I have a call in to her. I think I'm going to just go find her if I don't hear back. But I wanted to know what you think," he said. "Since we're working on this together."

Anna sighed. "What I think," she said, "is that you *should* talk with her. But I also think you should wait."

"Why wait?" Jon said.

"You asked me the first time we spoke if this had anything to do with your brother," she said. "It does. Christopher has put together a very small team of people who are looking at Russia in a slightly unorthodox fashion. Without going into all of the specifics, I sort of recruited you for that team." Jon's face went blank, as if this didn't surprise him. "I took it upon myself to do that. I just never got around to telling you." She smiled. "But, as your brother sometimes says, the weakest point in the intelligence community is information-sharing. Or lack of it. I wonder if you could share what you just told me with someone else."

"I could. I guess," Jon said.

Anna called Ming as they walked out together. "Will you cancel all my appointments this afternoon?" she said.

FORTY-EIGHT

CIA headquarters. Langley, Virginia.

On the thirty-five-minute drive from Capitol Hill to Langley, they filled gaps in each other's understandings about what had happened on August 13. Jon explained to Anna the rest of his theory about Sonya Turov and Harland Strickland. Anna told him more of what she'd learned from Gregory Dial; and they traded what they knew about General Utkin and the supposed "coup" plot.

By the time they checked in and were issued orange *V* visitor badges, it felt as if they were operating in sync. Which was what Anna wanted. In a sense, Christopher had accepted Jon as a member of the team, too, when he'd asked her to share Delkoff's "Declaration" with him. Now she just needed to put him together with Martin.

Lindgren met them in the lobby, coming out with his clipped walk, wearing a slightly rumpled gray suit and fashionably loosened tie. His face lit up as they made eye contact.

"So good to see you, Anna," he said, taking her hands and kissing her on each cheek.

"This is Jon Niles. Christopher's brother."

"Oh, yes. Pleased to meet you," he said, surprisingly formal with Jon.

Jon had been to CIA headquarters only once before, he'd told her, and just to the "new" building. He'd always wanted to see the Memorial Wall in the lobby of the Original Headquarters. So once they passed through the white marbled lobby with its iconic CIA seal, Martin took him to the north lobby wall and let him look. Unlike most memorials in D.C., this one was not open to the public.

Anna felt a sense of reverence standing before the wall, which honored members of the Central Intelligence Agency who had died serving their country. There were 125 stars on the wall right now: eighty-eight named CIA employees, and thirty-seven others, whose identities remained a secret even in death. This was also where every CIA officer swore the oath to serve his or her country their first Monday on the job. The wall was flanked by a US flag on one side, a CIA flag on the other. Jon's father, Anna knew, was one of the anonymous stars.

While Jon read though the names in the Book of Honor, she wandered with Martin to the main lobby, stopping in front of the engraved quote that had become CIA's unofficial motto: "And ye shall know the truth and the truth shall make you free," from John 8:32. It always struck Anna a little peculiar that CIA had adopted this quote—of Jesus speaking to his disciples—and engraved it in the lobby, along with the citation of chapter and verse.

"The quote was Allen Dulles's idea," Martin explained to Jon, as they walked to the visitors' cafeteria, his unruly eyebrows lifting. "His father was a Presbyterian minister."

"The fourth director of the CIA?" Jon said.

"Fifth, uh-huh."

"But of course, the quote was taken out of context," Anna said. "When Jesus said it, he was asking the disciples to follow his word. 'I am the way, the truth, and the life.'"

"And here?" Jon said.

"Here, in the context of the CIA, truth means information," she said. "The CIA pursues information in the service of liberty. Liberty being one of our rights."

"God-given rights. Doesn't it say?" Jon said.

288 | MAX KARPOV

"More or less, it does." Anna smiled. "It's hard to get far from God in this country, isn't it?"

They bought coffees in the cafeteria. Anna chose a table in a corner. She had explained only vaguely to Martin why they were coming, just that Jon had something to share with him. Martin still seemed slightly perplexed.

"Well, we're up against it, aren't we?" he said, stirring cream into his coffee. "You've seen the smoking gun stories, no doubt."

"Unfortunately."

"And the latest polls. Sixty-seven percent of Russians support military action now against Ukraine or Estonia." Anna grimaced a nod. "Which is roughly the same percentage that favored Russia going to war with Chechnya after the apartment bombings. Did you know that?"

"I didn't," she said. "And it didn't take long for them to take advantage of that, as I recall."

"No, that's right," Martin said. "The day after the explosives were found in Ryazan, Putin ordered the bombing." It wasn't hard to draw parallels, Anna knew: The four Russian apartment bombings in 1999, blamed on Chechen rebels, killed 293 people and created a wave of fear in Moscow and other Russian cities. Several days after the fourth bombing, a fifth attack was thwarted when an unexploded device was found in the city of Ryazan. Putin, who was then prime minister, praised the vigilance of the Ryazan people; the next day Russia ordered the bombing of Chechnya, launching the Second Chechen War. This was also the event that established Putin's reputation as a leader with the Russian people. But the Ryazan device was later traced to Russia's own intelligence services, and some Russia observers still believed the apartment bombings were a false flag carried out by the FSB at Putin's direction.

"I talked with the president," Martin said. "The NSC is putting its full weight behind this coup story. Saying the copilot supposedly has a connection with one of the generals. The CIA is being asked to support it."

"Colonel General Utkin," Anna said.

"Utkin, yes."

"That story worries me a little," she said.

"It worries me a lot," Martin replied. "The public is starting to believe Russia's version of events now, particularly with these new revelations about the Kiev meeting. If we come out backing this coup story, and the media tears it apart—which they will—we're going to have a tough time recovering. Our country, I mean. I don't know that we will. And I have to think that Russia knows that. They're counting on it. Which is particularly worrisome now, as Russia prepares for war."

"That's why we're here," Anna said, surprised at Martin's pessimistic tone. "I think the war's already started. But Jon has a theory you need to hear." His eyes swung to Jon, then back. "If nothing else, we need to make sure we're not crossing signals."

He briefly showed Jon a gracious face, part of Martin's charm. "All right. Please."

"Jon has learned something about Andrei Turov's daughter," Anna said, "and I'm curious how much of it you know."

"His *daughter?*"

"Yes. Christopher mentioned something the other day about a Russian asset. I know you can't discuss that, but I just want to make sure we're not talking about the same person."

"I don't follow," Martin said. Comfortable talking with her, not him.

"Jon thinks Andrei Turov's daughter is the person who leaked this story about the so-called assassination committee to the media. Maybe working for the Russian government."

Martin frowned. "And how would that be?"

"We think she's living here in D.C." Anna said. "And that, for whatever reason, she may have become friendly with someone in the intel community. Who inadvertently gave her some classified information. As pillow talk."

Martin's smile was careful. "I don't think Svetlana Turov's ever even been to the States, actually," he said. "She's been living with her father in the country outside of Moscow. Or staying at their vacation home in Switzerland."

"Not Svetlana," she said, glancing at Jon. "Sonya. The older daughter."

"Sonya." The vertical lines deepened between his brows. *Sonya's not his asset,* Anna could see. "Sonya Turov's been estranged from her father for years," he said. "Living in London under a different name."

"We don't think she's in London anymore," Anna said. She realized that he hadn't denied that *Svetlana* was his asset. "We think she's in D.C."

Jon summarized for Martin what he and David had discovered, as they'd discussed on the drive over. "I wanted to make sure she wasn't your source first," she said once he finished. "I didn't want to—" Anna stopped, so as not to say the rest out loud.

"No," Martin said, picking up on it. "Have you made any contact with Sonya Turov?" he asked Jon, taking on his more formal tone again.

"Not directly, no. But I plan to."

Martin looked at Anna. "So even if this is true, we have to be prudent. We can't do anything, of course, until we hear back," he said.

"I agree." They couldn't risk this story going out while Christopher was still in Moscow pursuing Turov.

Jon lowered his eyes. He seemed to be tuning them out as they spoke in coded language about Christopher and his mission in Russia, without using names. But Anna had a sense that in his faraway silence, in his look of detached disinterest, Jon was absorbing every bit of it, every word and nuance. It was funny, catching a glimpse of Christopher's personality in someone else's face. It was the first time she really saw them as brothers.

FORTY-NINE

MOSCOW.

Christopher Niles walked through the rain alongside the river after meeting Briggs, enjoying how the sky had turned dark like evening, headlights skimming off the wet asphalt and apartment facades.

At the hotel, he changed into a dry shirt and pants and lay on the bed, focusing, the way he used to focus before Friday night football games. Thinking about the trajectory of events that had brought him here—not Turov's four-move chess game, but the game Turov was playing with *him*. And returning to the same question: How much of this had been a setup? *The urgent summons to London for the meeting with Petrenko. The revelation of "the children's game." The toss-away detail that maybe the first move had already been played. And now this meeting. Could all of that have been Turov, tugging on the same string?*

Before going out again, Chris said a prayer, because he had promised Anna he would do so each day, and it felt like a way of connecting with her. Having given his travel bag to Briggs, he walked into the rain carrying only an umbrella and a binder with Delkoff's "Declaration," which he'd printed out in the business center at the hotel.

He walked to the Metro stop and caught a train to the Park Kultury station at Gorky Park. There he waited for several minutes out of the rain, watching traffic, stepping to the curb just before 2:30 p.m.

as a white cargo van stopped, its emergency lights flashing. The van's rear doors opened and a thuggish-looking man in jeans and a leather jacket waved him in. The man frisked him for a weapon and asked to see his passport. Then he stepped out and closed the doors, leaving Christopher inside, seated in an old armchair.

He heard the front passenger door open and close. Then the van lurched from the curb, speeding into the thundering rain. Music played through a single speaker, a Russian symphony he half-recognized: Tchaikovsky, maybe. He tried to picture their route for a while, recognizing when they came to the MKAD, Moscow's ten-lane beltway that circled the city. Wondering if Briggs was with them, although he wasn't especially worried about that. Jake Briggs was good, relentless, and a little crazy. He'd find them.

Chris eventually closed his eyes and tried to rest his thoughts in preparation for what was coming. There was a story he'd heard once about meeting Andrei Turov: when he summoned you to his home—which wasn't really *his* home, but a residential front in one of Moscow's new gated "villages"—Turov sometimes gave his guest what was known as the Turov Option. Visitors had the choice of accepting or declining. If you accepted, your life entered a new, more prosperous phase; if you declined, you didn't leave the house alive. It wasn't much of an option.

The drive went on for nearly an hour, although Chris suspected from the turns and reversals that they hadn't gone far, entering and exiting the MKAD several times. Finally, the van slowed to a stop and he heard the faint whirr of a gate through the rain and over the Russian music. Minutes later, they stopped again for another gate; he felt them turning around and backing into a garage. Then suddenly the rain was muted.

The man who greeted him when the doors sprang open was Anton Konkin, Turov's lieutenant and chief of security. Chris recognized him right away, although they had never met. Konkin had been Turov's liaison to the main office of Turov Security for eight or nine years. It was Konkin who oversaw the large "hackers-for-hire" operation that

Turov ran out of Moscow. Supposedly he had earned his stripes carrying out several high-profile political killings during the late 1990s. A small, heavily muscled man with a shaved head, he led Christopher down a polished wooden hallway in what seemed a brand-new two-story house, with lots of modern touches, to a corner office. Konkin stood outside and motioned Chris in, closing the door behind him.

Briggs watched the van's turn signal begin to flash and he immediately pulled to the side of the road. He had followed the van for nearly an hour, never losing sight of it for more than a few minutes as Turov's driver doubled back on the MKAD and finally took a highway northwest of Moscow to this two-lane country road. Now he'd have to go the rest of the way on foot.

He parked the Lada in a gully off the shoulder, stuffed his 9mm Glock inside the waist of his pants, and jumped out. He began to run toward the fenced development, where the van was now queued up to enter. On the other side was a mishmash of nouveau mansions: English country estates, Italian villas, neo-modern monstrosities. Most of them, Briggs suspected, were owned by Moscow's young capitalists and robber barons. Some were still under construction. The gated community was set off from the road by a wrought-iron fence, which Briggs was able to climb easily.

Once inside, it took him a few moments to spot the van, which was now moving down the main road of the development through the rain. Briggs ran full tilt across an empty lot. He stopped on the road to catch his breath and to get his bearings, having lost sight of the van again among the houses. But then he found it: the familiar pattern of the taillights braking in the distance, seeming to blur and disappear and then reappear in the open spaces.

Briggs began to run again, cutting through another empty lot. Seeing the lights brighten and blur and then disappear behind a brick wall.

Briggs stopped, figuring his options. He was maybe a third of a mile away now. He saw the house lights go on. Christopher had asked him to provide cover, to be a "witness." To do that, Briggs needed to stay close. Ready if Chris gave a signal, and even if he didn't. Christopher's words played like dark music in his head as he walked across the field in the rain: *However this turns out, it's just us. No one's coming in to rescue us. It's a two-man op. But that's a good thing.*

Briggs didn't know how the op was going to end, but he knew this: it wasn't going to end the way France had ended.

FIFTY

The office was furnished with expensive leather and brass, dark
cabinets and shelves, a plank floor with oval throw rugs. It took
Christopher a few seconds to find Turov, seated at a desk in the far
corner, his face in shadows behind a desk lamp. "Welcome," he said,
rising to extend his hand as if they were old acquaintances. "It's been
a few years."

Chris recognized Turov's understated confidence immediately,
as he did the reasonable set of his mouth and the strange, pale blue
eyes. *The great Turov.* There was the reputation—which even Chris had
allowed to become inflated in his mind—and there was the man, who
always struck people as smaller and more ordinary than they expected.

"You're a teacher now," Andrei Turov said, speaking Russian in
a soft, pleasing voice. "You're in Moscow researching the Orthodox
Church."

"Yes."

"A worthy subject. The church has become an integral part of
Russia's vision for the future. As you know."

"I see that," Christopher said.

Turov motioned for him to sit in the leather chair in front of the
desk.

"Shall we talk in English?" Turov said.

"Please."

Turov nodded to the laptop screen on his desk: a Russian television newscast. "It's not going so well for your country. I'm sorry to see that," he said, grimacing as if the news troubled him personally. As with many people who were despicable from a distance, it was surprising again to find Turov so likeable up close. But then, Turov was in the illusion business, Chris reminded himself. "The world's opinion has turned," he said. "They don't believe you anymore. They've found the 'smoking gun' now, they're saying."

"That's the story, anyway," Chris said.

Turov moved a folder to the center of his desk. Christopher noticed the dirt crescents under two of Turov's fingernails as he opened it. "I have a copy here of the report you wrote about me, several years ago." This surprised him, that Turov had this, and he wondered for a moment if Briggs had been right, if this meeting might be a trap. "We've met only once. But you write here as if you know me. You did a very thorough job. I was impressed," Turov said, speaking English with just a trace of accent, his "r"s rolling slightly. "But your conclusions made me seem like a very bad man." He flipped several pages, past sections highlighted in yellow. "For instance, you claim here, on Page 8, that I was quote 'potentially the most dangerous man in Russia.'" He looked up. "I guess I should be flattered."

Christopher shook his head. "I didn't say that. I quoted someone who did. Is that why you contacted me? To discuss my report?"

"No." Turov closed the file, serious again. "Actually, you contacted me first, I believe." His eyes turned to Chris's binder. "You've brought some business with you?"

"Yes. I thought you'd like to see what Ivan Delkoff left behind for the world to read. If you haven't seen it already." He handed Turov a copy of Delkoff's "Declaration." "They have copies of this in Washington," he said. "The media will have it, too. It's his account of August 13. Not what we've been hearing so far on television."

Turov's face retained a mask-like expression as he skimmed the document. By the time he set it down, and smiled, Christopher knew that he'd already seen it. "No one's going to believe this, of course," Turov said. "We both know that. There's too much evidence now against your country. And there's more coming, I hear. Much worse."

"Maybe true," Chris said. "And from what I'm reading, it may only be two or three days before Russia takes retaliatory action in Ukraine or Estonia."

"Yes." For a surprising moment, the bulb of Turov's confidence seemed to dim. "Obviously, we'd all like to avoid that. Publicly, of course, your country has been locked out of a serious negotiating role, for obvious reasons." Christopher said nothing. "But privately, it's a different business, isn't it? Privately, there's no reason we couldn't try to work something out on behalf of our countries. As two outside agents."

"Sort of like a Track II negotiation, you're saying," he said.

"Something like that, yes."

"Which you could sell to the Kremlin. And I could sell to Washington?" *As you sold them the attack of August 13,* he wanted to add. He watched the steadiness of Turov's expression. Only his eyes did not seem ordinary; his blue eyes were so unusual that looking at them for long felt almost voyeuristic.

"Yes, why not?" Turov said. "So much is done now by third parties, anyway, isn't it?"

"Forgetting for a moment the twenty-six people who died in that attack," Chris said, in a tone that he expected would prod Turov.

But Turov just smiled. "What happened on August 13 was a terror attack," he said. "Right now, your country has its own theories about who was behind it, we have ours. There is some common ground in those ideas, and maybe that's where we could start to work together. We could agree, for instance, that the attack was carried out by a rogue GRU colonel named Ivan Delkoff. And that a Ukrainian financier named Dmitro Hordiyenko—who operates a private militia and has funded campaigns against President Putin—procured the equipment.

"We could also agree on who carried out the mission: Zelenko, Pletner, Kolchak."

"I won't argue with any of that," Chris said.

"And so, the real question becomes: What could be accomplished if we were to align our narratives? If you were able to put aside your prejudices and conspiracy theories about Russia, to step back from your notions of American exceptionalism—or triumphalism, as we call it—so we could tell a story that benefited both of us."

"Is that what you're proposing?"

"It was, yes." Turov smiled privately. "I have two proposals, actually. But we could begin with that: What if our countries were to agree—after a proper investigation, of course—on a public accounting of what happened on August 13? To say, for example, that the attack was planned not by the Kremlin, and not in Washington. Sparing our governments that humiliation."

Chris was silent. A sustained rumble of low thunder shook the house. Humiliation, he knew, was a sensitive subject in Russia; 1991 and the lost Soviet empire still sat uneasily in the psyches of many Russians.

"Instead, we present evidence, at the conclusion of an international inquiry—and after negotiating certain concessions—showing that the operation was planned and carried out by Delkoff, working with extremist, right-wing forces in Ukraine."

"So that both the United States and Russia come out as winners, you're saying."

A tiny smile tugged the corners of Turov's mouth.

"Your proposal would benefit Russia far more than us, though, wouldn't it?" Chris said.

Turov frowned, as if not comprehending. "Really? Most of the world now thinks that August 13 was planned and funded by your CIA. What I'm saying is, imagine what we could do if we were able to move past that story. And work together, on matters of substance: terrorism. ISIS. North Korea. Israel-Palestine. We could do some remarkable things together. We might even give the world a better example. One that would make war less likely in the future. Sometimes," he

THE PLOT TO KILL PUTIN | 299

added, "it's up to people like us to make the moves that our governments aren't able to make. I think you probably feel the same."

"Probably," Chris said, knowing now what Turov was doing. "Although that sounds more like an American sentiment than a Russian one."

Turov smiled and turned to look at the rain. Christopher didn't disagree with him. But he also sensed that this was a trick. For whatever reason, this conversation felt like a prelude to something else.

"You mentioned concessions. What would they be?"

"Both countries would remove sanctions," Turov said. "You would consider repealing your so-called Magnitsky legislation. NATO would back away from our borders. And back away from this European Reassurance Initiative. Which gives you the right to put troops on our borders in violation of past agreements. It would be like us putting our troops along the borders of Mexico and Canada." Chris smiled. "Instead, we'd resolve to work together. You'd come to respect Russia's history and traditions, our role in the Middle East, our partnerships in Asia, and we'd respect America's interests. Within reason."

A sudden burst of thunder shook the house, rattling the windows. Christopher felt Turov's blue eyes watching him. "It's a nice idea, anyway," he said. "But none of that's going to happen, is it? That isn't why you called me here."

"It was." Turov's smile was like a twitch this time. "I wanted to give you the optimistic, more American version first, as you say. An idea we might come back to."

"All right."

Turov looked away, as though hearing something unsettling outside in the pounding rain, and Christopher caught a glimpse of his darker calculations. And understood: there was one more Turov illusion coming.

"So tell me about the second proposal," Chris said. "Tell me the reason I'm here."

FIFTY-ONE

Jake Briggs stood behind the wall, staring up at the bricks and mortar as rain fell in hard slants though the trees. He'd scaled walls like this hundreds of times in training. That wasn't the issue. The issue was whether he should. Christopher had said nothing about following him onto the property. Only that he wanted him to know where he was, to "be a witness." Briggs knew that he might jeopardize the mission now if he made a wrong move. He reminded himself that this was Chris's operation, not his. He was here as backup.

At the same time, Briggs didn't care for Christopher's vulnerabilities. There was something reckless about him going alone into the lion's den this way. Niles was an analyst and a retired intel officer; he wasn't a soldier. And Briggs wasn't convinced Turov hadn't laid an elaborate trap for him.

It's just us. No one's coming in to rescue us.

He debated it for several minutes as gusts of rain shook the treetops. Finally, Briggs stepped back, visualized what he was going to do, and did it—running up to the wall, planting his foot waist-high, swinging his arms for leverage, grabbing the top of the wall, and pulling himself up and over. He dropped down on the other side and lay flat on the edge of the lawn, knowing the rain had given him some camouflage. But was it enough?

He raised his head and studied the setup: the house they'd taken Chris to was a modern-looking job, with geometric designs, tall ceilings, giant windows. Between him and the house was a long, manicured yard with topiary hedges, a narrow decorative pool, and four modern-looking sculptures of giant figures. Briggs skittered crablike to the cover of the closest sculpture, what seemed to be a large bronze of a kneeling nude woman. The sculpture would serve as his observation post. Briggs lay down behind it and waited, surveying the back of the house, looking for cameras, for the ways in and out.

What he thought at first was a bush or a statue on the back porch, he began to see, was in fact a person: a security guard was standing outside the door under a metal awning. The tiny red glow against his face was a cigarette.

Briggs knew that Turov depended on a handful of security men, and suspected there were just two or three with him here today. Like Christopher, he preferred small numbers. Anton Konkin, Turov's security chief, was inside, probably monitoring the property on video cameras. Whether Konkin had already spotted him he didn't know. But it was best to assume he had.

Briggs saw moving shapes through the window of a corner room—smudges of shadow and light. *Christopher's in there.* Briggs wasn't going to make any move now unless he had to, he decided. Unless he was confronted. He wasn't going to do anything that would jeopardize Chris's mission . . . As he lay in the grass, Briggs thought of his respite at the French harbor—how the early morning scent of the sea had drawn him to the pebbly beach while he waited for Delkoff. And he thought of what had happened later that morning—the surprise ambush of Delkoff and his men. Other images filtered through his thoughts as the wind blew sheets of rain across the pool: the young Russian men dragging American flags over the cobblestones in Red Square, their faces strained with manufactured hate. *This isn't about what you saw in Red Square,* he told himself, *or about Delkoff.* It wasn't about anger, or revenge, or chasing phantoms. This was Chris's mission, not his.

But how will I know when enough time has passed? Or too much time?
He'd have to trust his instincts.

He saw movement again on the back porch: the guard was stepping out into the rain now, finished with his cigarette. Briggs lowered
his head, flattening himself on the ground. He lifted his eyes and saw
the man walking parallel to the house, beginning a surveillance round,
maybe. Briggs recognized him now from the leather jacket and jeans:
it was the man who'd opened the van doors for Chris near Gorky Park.

Halfway across the back of the house, the man stopped. He turned,
looking his way. Then lifted something to his face. A phone. Briggs
reached for his gun. He rose to a crouch, shielded still behind the
sculpture. The guard stepped away from the house and walked toward
him for several paces. Then he stopped, and stood still.

Briggs lost sight of him for a few seconds in the rain. Then he
noticed something else—there was motion to his right now: another
man was coming from around the front of the pool.

So they'd seen him. Or seen something.

The second man stopped. Briggs heard voices, the men talking
above the beat of the rain. They began to move again, their paths con-
verging as they walked toward the back of the yard. Briggs took a deep
breath. He peered around the sculpture. One of the guards shouted
something in Russian. He fired a shot that was wide to his left, maybe
intentionally so. Briggs stepped to the side, returned fire and scrambled back to cover. Three more shots rang out immediately, two of
them clanging off the head of the sculpture. Briggs waited. Briefly he
had a clear view of the second guard, who seemed suddenly disori-
ented. Briggs stepped out from the sculpture again and fired, hitting
the man three times as he tried to aim his gun. Briggs watched him go
down, both legs tucked underneath him.

That's when he saw that the first man was down, too.

The rain seemed to turn deafening after that, as if someone had
turned up a volume knob. Briggs looked at the men he'd shot, both

lying in the grass beside the pool, like modern sculpture. He scurried to the cover of a side hedge, and waited for the other one. Anton Konkin.

Lit up with adrenaline, Briggs began to step along the perimeter of the yard toward the house. Knowing that Konkin must've seen, or heard, what had just happened. Briggs's advantage was the storm. And momentum. And desire.

He stood, flush against the house, out of range of the cameras.

Waiting for the back door to open.

When it did, Briggs didn't hesitate. He knew that he had no choice anymore. There could be no half measures now. He had to keep moving forward, until this was finished.

FIFTY-TWO

"The second proposal you'll prefer," Andrei Turov said, lowering his eyes in a way that suggested humility. Chris was still thinking about the first: the utopian idea of using the August 13 attack to create an alliance between their countries, a partnership dedicated to higher aims, such as "eliminating" terrorism. The grandiosity of Turov's ambitions always seemed to blossom in the presence of other people, Chris knew; he'd written that in his report, a copy of which sat now on Turov's desk. "If—let's say—the Kremlin was unreceptive to what we just discussed. We might then bypass them altogether and negotiate a different arrangement."

"Okay."

"Your country's loss of credibility and internal divisions will only worsen, as I'm sure you know," Turov added solemnly. "Analysts are predicting that your country is on course to break into pieces, much as the Soviet Union did in 1991."

"You're underestimating the United States, Andrei, but go ahead."

Turov smiled slightly. Then his expression stiffened, as if correcting itself. Chris could see he didn't like that. "If," Turov said, "some documents existed—not here—but say some documents existed, the kind of evidence you'd need to tell a different story about August 13."

"Evidence—?"

"Digital recordings of phone conversations. Records of trans-actions between Colonel Delkoff, Anton Konkin, my head of secu-rity, and the Kremlin. More significantly: a transfer of funds from a Kremlin-run RFM account—the president's personal financial intelli-gence unit—that ended up with Delkoff. Real evidence. Not these ram-blings of the 'crazy colonel.'"

"Tying the events of that day to the Kremlin, in other words," Christopher said.

Turov nodded once. "Evidence that would allow your journalists and political leaders to tell the story you've been trying to tell about Russia for years now."

"Okay," Chris said. They'd come, at last, to Turov's real trick, he sensed: for years, Putin's critics had portrayed the Russian president as a high-level "thug," the silent force behind the murders of jour-nalists and dissidents. But there'd never been good evidence linking him directly to those crimes. Here was someone offering that. Putin Kryptonite. Turov was taking this in a direction he hadn't expected: offering to betray his country, to sell out the president. Cassius schem-ing against Caesar.

"Okay," Chris said. "And in exchange—?"

"We would need to work out terms." He looked away for a moment. Perhaps Turov saw this as his only way out now; maybe he felt that Putin had hijacked his original plan and he needed the US to bail him out. Or maybe this was something else. Chris reminded himself that Turov was an illusionist.

"I'd want some personal assurances, obviously," Turov said. "Information for immunity."

"For you."

"For my family. I'd want an assurance that neither of my daughters would be prosecuted or harmed in the event that details ever came out. I'd want immunity for my daughter Svetlana, in particular, and her children. And for my closest staff, Olga Sheversky and Anton Konkin, and their families. And lastly, for myself, yes. That's all I would ask."

Chris waited on a boom of thunder. "Immunity beginning—?"

"Tonight. Now."

The diplomat in Christopher wanted to agree; the pragmatist wanted more details. He recalled what Amira had told him on Tuesday, about Turov's concerns for his family. "I don't know that I could do anything that quickly," he said.

"Unless you had to." His eyes went calmly to Christopher's report. "You have a private plane at the airport, don't you? You are planning to fly to Washington tonight, correct?" Chris tilted his head to acknowledge it was possible. "I think you understand how we can help each other. And our countries."

Chris glanced at the blur of rain out the window, almost believing Turov. Here was a man who had devised a project to destroy the United States's credibility in four moves, while creating the conditions for a regional conflict in the Baltics that could easily escalate into a war against the West. Now he was trying to play ambassador? It meant that on some level he must feel that *he* was being betrayed by his own country.

"You're not afraid that you're under FSB surveillance now?" Chris asked.

"Not here, no. We are safe in this building. We've been very careful."

Chris knew that he was nowhere right now, in a neighborhood he'd probably never find again. "What are you proposing, then? Specifically?"

"I can provide a set of nine documents, including bank transfer records, phone transcripts, and emails, which will confirm the Kremlin's role. They will include a document I generated summarizing the entire plan, a copy of which was handed to the president."

"Where are they now?"

"I've given them all to a personal carrier. They're not in this country," he said. "Once we complete the deal, however, the information is yours."

"Once you're out of the country, in other words."

"Yes."

"And this information will prove conclusively that the president was directly involved in August 13?" Turov nodded in that almost imperceptible way he had. Chris held his gaze. He had come to Turov hoping to strike a deal; he didn't expect Turov would make it so easy. "And explain to me exactly why you want to do this."

"Because." He looked at Chris as if he already knew the answer. "We all have an expiration date. I have no reason to think mine isn't coming soon. I can't just go into exile in London like some of the president's other former friends. But even if I could, it's my family I care about. My grandchildren, and their children. My lineage. At the same time," he added, "I care what happens to our countries. The big war that is coming will not involve nuclear weapons, you know that. It will be a game that is played in rooms that most people will never see."

"The children's game."

Turov said nothing. But there was a twinkle now in his eyes. "And I could help you with that. I could help your side."

"Why me?"

"Because." His smile this time was unexpected. "You know me. You know who I am. And no one else in your government seems to, as this shows." He tapped an index finger on Chris's report. "We might even make a good team. Certainly an interesting one."

"And if I say no?"

"Then we'd drive you back. Or to the airport. And you'd leave. And I'd make other arrangements. But you won't say no," Turov said. "You didn't come this far to say no."

Christopher gazed again at the rain, beginning to play out the moves he'd need to make for this to work. "All right," he said. "Tell me what you need, then, and let's do it."

He saw something give in Turov's face; a distant relief seemed to flood his strange blue eyes. It was a vulnerable and very human look, as if Christopher had just agreed to save his life.

Turov's cell phone rang on the desk in front of him. He lifted it and placed the phone to his ear.

"Yes?" His eyes shifted to Christopher's as he listened. "Oh . . . Yes, you're sure who it is? All right. Take care of that, then," he said, speaking in Russian. "No, I'll stay here. Yes. No, come to see us when you're finished."

He set the phone back on his desk without averting his eyes. Then Turov slid open his desk drawer again. He pulled it back farther so Chris could see what was in the center: a handgun, a 9mm Makarov pistol.

He lifted the gun from the drawer and pointed it at Christopher Niles. Four quick booms sounded outside, then two more. This time, it wasn't thunder. "So," he said, "it turns out you're no more honest than your country is, after all."

FIFTY-THREE

Turov kept the Makarov aimed at Christopher's head. There was a starkness to Andrei Turov's face all of a sudden, like an actor who'd slipped out of character.

Seconds passed and the phone on his desk rang again. Turov put it to his ear.

"All right," he said.

He set it down, his eyes still on Christopher. "You made an agreement, didn't you?" Turov finally said. "That you would come here alone. I'm disappointed you chose not to honor that." The pupils in Turov's eyes seemed to darken. "This is why your country has lost so much trust around the world, you know. You pretend to be a moral leader. You think you are somehow entitled to play the world's police and prosecutor. But you always fall back on your American arrogance and petulance: as soon as your own interests are threatened, you think you no longer have to follow any rules. You think you can break your own agreements."

Chris, watching him, was silent. This was ironic, coming from Turov.

"Tell me, what was your real intention?" Turov said, raising the gun slightly for emphasis, his face still showing no emotion. "You brought your man out here to kill me?"

"No. Not at all," he said. "I wanted cover. A witness. I took precautions, in case anything went wrong. This doesn't have to change our arrangement, Andrei. I can stop this."

"It's late for that," Turov said. "You have put me in a difficult spot, I'm afraid. Once trust is lost, what do we have?"

Christopher said nothing. He recognized Turov's cycle of paranoia: a man whose business is deceiving others always thinks others are trying to deceive him. He ascribes his own motives to adversaries whose real motives may be benign. It was one of the fatal flaws of men like Turov. It was also the case that Turov, despite his peculiar genius, could become stubbornly unforgiving if he felt that someone had wronged him. They were getting into that territory now. "We can still do this," Chris said, trying again.

"Possibly," he said. "But it will be difficult." Turov continued to point the gun, a faint flush reddening his face. He seemed to be trying to decide whether to end this right now. Chris thought of Anna Carpenter, at her office in the Capitol. He thought of his father.

Turov reached again for the phone, looked at the readout, and set it down. There was another boom of thunder. Then something closer: this time within the house. A door closing. The squeaking of footsteps. *Someone was in the house.* Someone was walking down the hallway toward Turov's corner office.

Turov extended the gun, pointed at Christopher's face.

"*Anton?*" he called.

There was no answer.

"Stand up," Turov said, motioning Christopher to the door. Then he stood himself. "Go ahead. Go to the door and open it."

Chris took several steps across the room. He stopped. Both men listened. Someone was right outside. In the next instant, the door burst open. Turov fired two quick shots from the Makarov.

"No! Don't!" Christopher shouted.

Simultaneously, Briggs fired once and Turov staggered back. Then Briggs fired again, twice, hitting Turov in the leg and arm.

But Briggs's first shot had gone through his chest. Turov's gun fell to the floor and he dropped back into the chair, no longer moving. His otherworldly pale blue eyes remained open, facing the doorway, his expression still alert, as if waiting for someone to come and explain what had happened. But there was no light in his eyes. There was no one home anymore.

FIFTY-FOUR

There were, Christopher would later explain, three witnesses to the killing. Because no known video existed and because one of the witnesses also happened to be the victim, that left just two men to explain what happened. And two, he thought, was a pretty manageable number.

The human memory, of course, was famously unreliable in cases like this. Christopher had once participated in an Agency class in which twenty-five students witnessed the same mock crime and gave twenty-five different versions of the event, diverging even on such details as the skin color of the participants.

Two, though, was a good number, and Chris and Briggs would give markedly similar accounts of what had happened. That there had been, for instance, five gunshots in total: the first two from Turov, the next three from Briggs.

After the fifth, Briggs had dropped to a crouch, they would recall, his gun still raised in both hands. A long silence followed. They both remembered it like that.

Andrei Turov had come to his final rest in the desk chair, eyes open, lips pressed together in that firm, reasonable-looking expression. One of his arms was on the armrest, the other on his upper thigh. Chris felt for his pulse and didn't find one. He had never before seen a dead man who looked so alive.

It seemed to spook Briggs more than it did Christopher. A shadow of rain flicked on the desk from the window and Briggs raised his gun to Turov's head.

"Don't!" Chris said, stopping him.

Briggs lowered his arm.

"Are you all right? Were you hit?"

"I'm all right," Briggs said, still out of breath and dripping rain. "I'm going to clear the house."

Briggs looked carefully at Turov before turning away, as if expecting him to leap back to life. Christopher walked with him down the hallway, covering Briggs as he went room to room and into the garage. Calling out, "Clear . . . clear . . ."

They walked outside to the three security men, confiscating phones, checking pockets. Christopher used his own cell to take photos of the dead men, which Headquarters would run through face recog software after they were out.

"The guards ambushed me, I had no choice," Briggs explained as they came back inside. "There was no way of dialing it back."

"We're fine," Chris said. "Let's just focus on getting out of here. Do something for me."

"Name it."

"See if there are any suitcases or bags in the car and the van, or anything personal. Then we're gone. Stay clean, no fingerprints."

Christopher went back to the corner office and the unsettling sight of Andrei Turov seated in the leather desk chair, his eyes open, lips together. He felt again for a pulse. Nothing. He was tempted to tip him over, to make him look more like a dead man should look. But he didn't. For some reason, he didn't want to spoil Turov's final impression.

He stood by the window and looked at the scultpture pieces in the rain, surprised that he was becoming emotional, thinking about Anna again. It wasn't just the normal feeling that accompanies sudden death, the reminder of how fleeting life is. And it wasn't just Turov, a man he'd obsessed over for years. Mixed in was the loss of Turov's proposal, the chance of connecting with his "carrier," if such a person really existed; the idea of two major countries forming an alliance, using their strengths to benefit the rest of the world. *Wouldn't it be nice?*

Chris had never explained Turov properly to Jake Briggs, and maybe he should have. But it didn't matter now. This mission had ended in an elemental game of self-defense. As Briggs had said, there was no way of dialing back now. Maybe it was for the best. There would be no more Turov deceptions.

"Two suitcases in the trunk," Briggs said, standing in the doorway, his eyes turning to Turov.

"Okay, let's get out of here."

Christopher's silence seemed to make Briggs uneasy again. He raised the garage door and climbed in the passenger seat. "I had no choice," Briggs said as he drove toward the entrance gate. "I wish I did."

"Don't worry about it." Chris *was* angry with Jake Briggs, in a superficial sort of way. But anger didn't travel well. He'd weigh all that later: costs versus outcome. Briggs was an honorable man, unpredictable, wound a little tight. An old-school operative in some ways, the kind of man the CIA used to prize when Chris's father was coming up, before the shift from human intel to electronic SIGINT. Had Briggs intended all along to kill Andrei Turov? He'd worry about that after they were back home. Chris's thoughts had to be tactical now, not analytical. Briggs had changed the op, but he hadn't ended it.

Briggs took them through the gate and back to the Lada. They shifted bags to the back seat and then he drove to the M10 motorway and the airport. Chris sorted through Turov and Konkin's suitcases as they went: mostly clothes, and a few personal items, but he also found three flash drives in a small cotton tote bag in Turov's case.

At Sheremetyevo International Airport, they bought casual business clothes at a Paul & Shark store and changed in the dressing room. Briggs came out with his hair slicked back, walking in his stiff-legged wrestler's strut.

Martin had arranged for a concierge business-traveler package at Sheremetyevo, which allowed them to pass through security and passport control in a private VIP lounge, avoiding the queues and the scrutiny in the main concourse. When the flight was ready for takeoff, an English-speaking agent accompanied them to a private SUV, which delivered Chris and Briggs through the rain to their waiting Gulfstream V. The plane was registered to a CIA-owned NGO called Holstake Industries, which did millions of dollars of business in Moscow. It was one of about thirty charter planes owned by the CIA. The plane would deliver them to a private airfield north of Williamsburg, Virginia.

"Have a wonderful trip," the personal agent said, with her pleasant Russian accent, standing in the rain beneath a giant umbrella.

Chris called Martin on the plane's encrypted satellite phone once they were airborne and out of Russian air space. "The op's over. I'm sending data," he said. "I'll need to call you back."

"Are you all right?"

"We're fine. I'll call in thirty minutes."

He made his two business calls, then. First, to the FSB agent whose office he believed had run surveillance on him in Moscow. "You will be interested to know," he said, speaking Russian. "There has been a shooting, a robbery. Andrei Turov. I think one of his political enemies may have been responsible." He gave the location and hung up.

Then he called Amira Niyzov on the number she'd written for him over lunch on Tuesday. Amira sounded pleased to hear his voice, but also cautious, a reminder of how delicate this op was. "Thank you again for talking with me for my story," he said, "about the Russian Orthodox Church. I have a copy of what we spoke about, and am sending it to you." Amira would be the first to receive the Delkoff document, other than Chris's brother. "You know what we said Tuesday about returning to the cornfields?"

"Our philosophical discussion? Yes, of course," Amira said.

"I'm told a crow died tonight, northwest of the city."

"*What?*"

"Someone said the FSB may be there, or on its way now."

"What are you talking about?"

"There's a story that's about to go public, about him. Obviously, some people won't be pleased. You'll be hearing about it."

Amira was silent.

"Can you do what we said?" he asked. He felt an anxious twinge, worried for Amira. "Without putting yourself in jeopardy."

She sighed and made a faint "mmm-hmm" sound. Chris knew that if she wanted to, Amira could spread this story to a handful of influential opposition leaders who could open up the network again. But she'd have to decide if doing so was worth the risk. "Where are you?" she said.

"I'm already out," Chris said. "Probably you should leave too." Amira didn't respond. "I'm sorry. Be careful. I'll be in contact," he said. "Godspeed."

His next call was to Anna, although he didn't expect to reach her. It was midafternoon in D.C., and she was probably in a meeting.

"Christopher?" For a moment, he didn't say anything. It was wonderful just hearing the timbre of her voice again.

"We're done," he said. "I'm coming home." He listened to Anna's silence, savoring the connection. "I just wanted to say: I've missed you. And us." He added, "You can tell my brother to go ahead and publish now. Say he got it from a government source."

"None too soon," Anna said. "Have you talked with Martin?"

"Briefly. Why?"

Chris glanced up at Briggs, who averted his eyes. "Call Martin," she said. "He's got something to tell you. I love you."

"I love you, too." He gazed out the window after hanging up, as the plane rattled through a mild turbulence. He tried for a while to imagine what Martin had to tell him. Maybe they'd discovered that Turov had arranged the meeting in London. Or maybe something had happened to Petrenko. That had been worrying Chris, for some reason.

He closed his eyes and felt the presence of Turov, felt his ghost traveling with him back across the Atlantic. *We might even make a good team.* He considered Turov's proposal, a plan for two countries to think against their prejudices. Or maybe that had all been illusion. Maybe Langley would find Turov's true intentions on his phone or on the computer drives in his suitcase. Or maybe they'd never be known.

Finally, Christopher called Martin back. "Turov's gone," he said. "We've got photos, flash drives, digital evidence. It wasn't planned that way, but that's how it went down." Martin drew in a breath. "I think it's possible the media's going to report that he was killed by Russian intelligence services. By the FSB," Christopher added.

"Because—?"

"Retribution. Because Turov let Delkoff get away. And because of what he knows. Knew. Delkoff's story's going to go viral by morning. The story will name Turov as the organizer of the August 13 attack."

"The Delkoff document, you mean."

"Yes, the Delkoff document." Christopher smiled at his lapse. Martin already knew about the document; Briggs had sent it to him first. "I understand the FSB may still be on the scene."

He heard a crackle of static before Martin spoke again. "You were there first, though."

"Yeah." Martin waited. "We were there first. Turov's guards tried to stop Briggs. He responded." Chris gave a sketchy picture of what had happened, leaving out details that he hadn't worked through yet. "It's not a perfect outcome," he said.

"Well, no. Obviously not."

But they were talking about two different things, he knew. "I just gave my brother the go-ahead to run this story. The Russian opposition has it too. Just so you know. That's our alternate scenario now."

"Better late than not at all," Martin said.

"Anna said you had something to tell me."

"Yes. I do. It's about your brother. He's tracked down the story of CIA involvement in August 13. He thinks some of it's coming from Turov's older daughter, of all things."

"*What?*"

"It caught us off guard, too. She's an NOC for Russia, evidently, that we, and the FBI, missed somehow. Living here under a different name. Your brother's trying to track her down. They wanted to know that you were safe before they took it further."

Christopher said nothing. As far as he knew, Turov's oldest daughter had made a clean break with her past—and her father—and was living in England.

"What did you mean, then, not a perfect outcome?" Martin said.

Chris sighed. "I'd thought Turov might be returning with us. That didn't work out." And then he explained, in abbreviated form, the deal that might've been, the connection with the "carrier" they had lost. "I don't know where the line is between real negotiation and Turov's deceptions. Or delusions. I just regret that we may have lost an opportunity."

"I guess we'll have to wait and see," Martin said.

His response was odd; the lack of explanation made it odder. "What do you mean?"

"Just—I don't know that we've lost the carrier," Martin said. "The carrier may be fine."

"What are you talking about?"

"I may have spoken with the carrier this afternoon," he said. "She may be fine. I'll explain when you get here."

And then, in vintage Martin Lindgren style, he hung up, leaving Chris with a puzzle. He sat back and closed his eyes again, knowing that he had the rest of the flight to figure it out. It was still ten hours back to Virginia.

To kill a man like Andrei Turov was not difficult; it was no more difficult than killing any other human being, Jake Briggs thought, watching Christopher as he talked on the satellite phone. But for a *country* to kill someone, and claim a legitimate *reason* for it—a legal one, anyway—could be more problematic. There were multiple legal structures for that sort of thing; the laws of armed conflict being different from the laws of criminal justice. Certain enemies of the United States could be deemed legitimate kill targets by White House legal counsel. But killing a businessman, in his own country, in his own home, was a little trickier. A businessman who hadn't even made the Russian sanctions list.

He still needed to talk with Christopher about that. Briggs understood by then who Turov was, and what he represented; he knew that, in killing him, they'd also eliminated a threat against the United States. To Briggs's thinking, that was good enough. The only thing that worried him was that, technically, he'd been on assignment for the Central Intelligence Agency when it happened. If some ambitious journalist or elected official were somehow tipped off to that, it could become a problem for Briggs; it could even become a politically-driven investigation resulting in criminal charges.

He watched Christopher Niles finish his phone call and close his eyes. He took a seat across from him and cleared his throat.

"Talk?" he said.

FIFTY-FIVE

The *Weekly American* offices. Foggy Bottom, Washington.

I t's one thing knowing the truth," Roger Yorke said. "Now all we have to do is convince the rest of the world." Jon Niles smiled to himself: it was almost what Anna Carpenter had said, during their second meeting at Starbucks.

Liz Foster and KC Walls nodded in agreement. They were all watching the television across the room, waiting for news about Andrei Turov.

The *Weekly American* had been the first US media organization to post Delkoff's "Declaration" online, after reports appeared on German and Ukrainian websites. But so far, the news was playing to a skeptical mainstream audience.

On ABC, it followed reports of the tornadoes that had ripped through Oklahoma, and the latest "smoking gun" revelations about the CIA: "Meanwhile, there are explosive but unsubstantiated new charges out of Germany about the August 13 attack," David Muir began. "The newspaper *Bild* is reporting that a six-page document sent to a journalist by alleged August 13 mastermind Ivan Delkoff claims the assassination attempt on Vladimir Putin last week was a so-called false flag operation planned by a Russian oligarch with the possible cooperation of Putin himself.

"The Kremlin was quick to refute the report, calling it a 'laughable fabrication' and 'further signs of America's desperation to cover their crimes at our expense. Russia remains indivisible.' There has been no official response from the White House. And some in the intelligence community have privately expressed doubts about the veracity of the document . . .'"

"And so," Roger said, lowering the volume when the segment ended, "if we can't count on it to prevent a war, then maybe the truth *doesn't* matter anymore."

Jon glanced at his boss to make sure he was kidding. It was after midnight in Russia and Europe. Jon expected the story would take on a new life with the light of day.

"You're joking, I hope," Liz said.

"I should be, I guess. Although I am concerned about the public reaching a saturation point. Particularly now, with the White House preparing to come out with its own official version of events."

"The coup story," KC said.

"Yes." Roger glanced out the window. "Part of what we're dealing with now are the limits of the human attention span. Which Russia, no doubt, has factored in. Many people have already made up their minds. Or else they're so confused—or fed up—that they're starting to tune out the whole thing. There's no good reason for them to accept Ivan Delkoff's version."

"Even if his version is the truth," Liz said.

"Even if it's the truth. At this point, I'm not convinced the truth will have much bearing on what Russia does in Ukraine or Estonia," Roger said. "It's a little like saying one sports team is better than another because it's more virtuous. That may be the case, but will it affect the outcome of the game? Russia appears to understand that better than we do."

Liz frowned. She glanced at Jon, not getting it. But Jon could see she understood the gravity of what he was saying.

"I hope I'm wrong on that," Roger said, his eyes returning to Jon.

"Although I'm hearing from Pentagon sources that this is still on the fast track. Russia's military is positioning for a 'retaliatory' strike by end of the week. This story may actually give them a new urgency."

Jon recalled what Martin Lindgren had said about the Moscow apartment bombings, how they'd created a sense of outrage and urgency that had led to the Second Chechen War in 1999 and established Putin's credibility. Jon wasn't sure if journalism was up to the job of telling a story that revealed "the truth" anymore—or if people were interested. Even the Western media were letting the story of US involvement play out episodically.

"Going to war on false pretenses wouldn't be unprecedented," Liz said, looking at Jon. "It wouldn't be something *we* haven't done."

"Which may be part of the calculation," Roger said.

"This word indivisible," KC said. Her face looked strange this afternoon, flushed or sunburned. "Are they pulling that from our pledge of allegiance?"

"Indivisible." Roger smiled. "No, it's sort of interesting. It's actually an old tsarist slogan that goes back to the start of the twentieth century. It was the rallying cry of Anton Denikin, the leader of the White Army in the Russian Civil War. 'Great Russia, one and indivisible.' Russia's current president—Mr. Putin—has made no secret of his admiration for Denikin."

Jon waited for KC and Elizabeth to file out once Roger clicked off the television, KC again showing a little attitude. Jon closed the door after them.

"I know what you're saying about our national attention span," he said. "But I don't think I agree with the rest of it." His editor raised his eyebrows and nodded, inviting an explanation. "The part about the truth not having any bearing on winning and losing. I don't agree. I think this story's right. And I think it's going to prevail for that reason. I want to make sure it does."

"Okay." Roger nodded. "So how do you intend to do that? Where do you want to go with this?"

"I'd like to pursue Turov's daughter right now," Jon said. "I don't know if she'll talk with me. But I don't think anyone else in the media knows about her yet. So I'd like to try."

"Do you know how to find her?"

"I do." David had found Sonya's home address; Jon planned to go there if he couldn't reach her through the law offices.

"All right, then." Roger showed the edges of a smile. "Just keep in touch."

"I will." It was all Jon needed to hear. Whatever he didn't know about this story—and there was still a lot, including Chris's role and what Anna Carpenter wasn't saying—Sonya Turov Larsen was a part of it that no one else knew. Walking down the corridor to the elevator, he glanced over at Liz Foster's cubicle, and decided to keep going.

"Hey!" she called. Jon stopped. She looked sort of radiant, smiling as she turned from her computer. Maybe it was the break with Carole, but seeing Liz Foster melted all his resolve to keep his distance. "You're doing great on this," she said.

"Well. Trying, anyway." For a long moment they just traded a stare. It was sort of nice. "Maybe go out for a drink sometime?" Jon said. She lowered her eyes and glanced back at her screen. "Or not," he said. "It's all right, bad timing—"

She began to blink. "I guess I ought to tell you," she said. "I've kind of been seeing someone. I'm sorry, I should've said something before. Nothing super-serious or anything. But I just probably should let you know."

"Oh, okay." Jon laughed. So it really *was* bad timing, then. "No. I mean. Congratulations. And. We'll catch up later," he said and turned to go.

The evening air revived him a little as he walked down G Street to the parking garage. With all that was happening, it was easy to pretend the exchange with Elizabeth Foster didn't hurt. But as he drove away, Jon felt a little like Bogart on the platform in *Casablanca,* after having his "insides" kicked out.

"It's better this way," he said aloud to console himself. "It really is." Ten minutes later, he wasn't even thinking about her.

Anna Carpenter finally lost her patience with Harland Strickland several minutes after Ming Tsu shut down the outer office. She had been studying the file she found on General Viktor Utkin, from the Senate Select Intelligence Committee archives: sixteen months earlier, a Russian souce had passed the CIA details of "subversive" conversations between two top-ranking officers in the Russian military, one of them Utkin. But the CIA's counterintelligence chief at the time had written a follow-up assessment calling the source "unreliable." Had something changed since then?

Strickland—the man who could answer that—was still avoiding her calls. But Anna knew things now that might force his hand. She decided it was time to be more direct.

"I'd like to see you tonight, Harland," she said to his voice mail. "We need to talk about this Delkoff document." She paused for a moment, adding, "And Sonya Natalie Larsen. ASAP?"

Six minutes later, he called back. "What's this about Natalie Larsen?" he said, using a pseudo-comical tone.

"I was hoping you'd tell me. Can you meet?"

"Tonight."

"Now."

"Give me an hour?"

FIFTY-SIX

The address David found for Sonya Natalie Larsen was an apartment complex in Alexandria. Jon swung by his own apartment in D.C. first to pick up a tape recorder. The parking spots along his street were all taken, so he ended up driving around the neighborhood for fifteen minutes before giving up and parking seven blocks away.

He used the walk to formulate the questions that he would ask Sonya once he found her. It was a pleasant night, the breeze cooling, stirring the trees that were thick with summer leaves. Why had she chosen Jon to call? Who was she really working for?

After six blocks, Jon noticed an SUV inching along beside him in the shadows. He glanced over several times, but couldn't see through the tinted glass. All sorts of ideas began to churn in his thoughts. Russia's security forces were known to chase down threats or perceived threats in other countries now, he knew; journalists and opposition figures had died mysteriously, and some not so mysteriously, in London, Washington, Los Angeles, and the Middle East, not to mention in Russia and Ukraine. In 2006, Russia had passed a law permitting the killing of "enemies of the regime" abroad.

When the tinted window began to whir, Jon stopped, half-expecting to see a gun barrel poke out over the glass.

But there was no gun. Instead, a woman's arm emerged and her hand dangled to get his attention. Her fingernails were painted black.

"Hey. Why'd you call my office this afternoon?" she said.

Jon, speechless, scanned the street both ways, then took several steps toward her.

"Are you planning to write about me?" she said.

"No," he said. "Do you want me to?" It was *her:* Sonya Larsen. 9:15. Thin face, wide mouth, serious eyes, short dark hair, a faint shadow of down on her upper lip.

"No. I want you *not* to," she said. "How did you find out who I was?"

"Long story."

"Do you want to talk and tell me?" she said.

"Sure."

"Get in, then. I'm not going to talk here." Jon hesitated for just a moment. He was half a block from his apartment, but sensed that if he didn't get in now, she might drive off. As soon as he closed the passenger door, Sonya Larsen sped away through the narrow residential street in the direction of downtown. It wasn't until they came to the traffic light at Wisconsin Avenue that Jon realized he'd left his cell phone in his car.

"How did you know who I was? How did you know where to find me?"

"Research?"

"What does it mean, research?"

"I found your picture online," he said. "A party at the Russian embassy. We used facial recognition software to ID you."

"Well, you shouldn't have," she said. "You've got me in trouble now."

"How are you in trouble?" Jon asked.

She didn't answer. She kept glancing at him as she drove, edgy and hopped up, maybe a little high on something, Jon thought, weaving wildly through the traffic on Wisconsin Avenue; running yellow lights, checking her mirrors compulsively.

"You've seen the news, right?" Jon said, when she finally slowed down. "About your father?"

"I've seen the news," she said. "Of course, I've seen it." She punched her horn at a slow driver in front of them, but not hard enough to make a sound. Then swung her car wildly around him. Several blocks later she made a sharp turn onto a residential street in Georgetown. "I know what happened to my father, yes," she said, inching down a hill of brick townhouses. "Okay? I know he's dead. I know who killed him. I know all about that."

"I'm sorry."

She made a scoffing sound—"pshh. Don't be sorry," she said. "It doesn't even surprise me. I always knew this would happen: when the time was right, they'd send FSB after him. But the story they're reporting in the news is all wrong. You know that, right? The media always gets it wrong. Especially about Putin. Always. I could tell you the real story, you wouldn't believe it."

"All right."

"But I need you to help me. I'm afraid they're going to be after me now, too."

"Okay," Jon said. "What do you want me to do?"

They'd come to Connecticut Avenue, where she pulled to the curb outside the Hilton Hotel. "I don't want to be seen out right now, okay? How about if we get a room here. I'll talk with you upstairs. Go in first and get the room. I'll park."

FIFTY-SEVEN

Capitol Hill, Washington

Anna met Harland Strickland at a bar four and a half blocks from the Capitol. A tiny place with a lot of framed black-and-white photos and eccentric taxidermy on the walls, including a deer's hind-quarters and the front end of an anteater. It was one of Strickland's favorite downtown haunts. A Nationals game was on television behind the bar.

He gave her the once-over as Anna slid into the leather booth, even though she was dressed conservatively in a dark suit. Anna ordered club soda, Strickland a bourbon on ice. He wore a navy pin-stripe suit but had loosened the tie and undone the top buttons.

They talked superficially about their children at first. But she could see that beneath his well-put-together façade of confidence, Strickland was worried.

"So what's this about?" he finally said. "What about Natalie Larsen?"

"I'll get to that. Tell me about the Delkoff document first. Tell me what you think about it."

"What I think about it." Strickland shook his head dismissively. "Not a lot. I think it's a fabrication."

"Go on."

"I think it's a little too obvious. And not supported by our intelligence. Frankly, I'm surprised the Russian opposition's getting behind it."

"Are you? I'm not."

Strickland flashed her an accusatory look. "What I'm afraid of," he said, his hands encircling the drink glass, "is that someone in the Russian opposition movement invented this thing out of whole cloth— seeing it as a chance to regain some of their lost glory. Russia's going to have an easy time debunking it, you know. That's not just me talking; that's what our Russia experts think. They don't buy this at all—"

"You mean because it doesn't fit with what you want the president to tell the world tomorrow." His eyes narrowed. "That this was a coup engineered by the Russian military."

"That's not me, Anna, that's the IC. Between us? We have solid HUMINT that it *was* a coup attempt. We had implants on their computer networks, bank transfer records, intel traffic. And—on top of that, we know that this copilot who flew over Ukraine had a history of mental issues. Bottom line, Anna: we can't afford another half-baked story going out. Like this Delkoff thing. You know that. That's exactly what they want." Anna sighed, disappointed at how convinced he sounded. He had a point, she thought. But it wasn't the right one.

"We need to change the conversation," Strickland went on, buoyed a little by her lack of challenge. "I mean—why *wouldn't* the administration go out with this tomorrow? If we have solid intel behind it. Which we do. What do we lose?"

"In the short term, not much," she said. "In the long term, maybe a lot." His eyes narrowed again. "I've researched this coup allegation a little. Most of the intel on it is old. It came to us from a less-than-reliable Russian asset more than a year ago. A former military intelligence officer. There are some national security reporters who are going to recognize that."

Anna turned on her phone and called up the document she'd found in the intelligence committee files. She rotated the phone and showed him. "I haven't seen all the intel you have, Harland. But this is where the story about General Utkin originates, isn't it?"

He scanned it quickly and pushed her phone back to her. "I don't know what that is," he said. "But even if he came on the radar before, so what?"

"No, you're right," Anna said. "Although I was told the date may have been removed or changed on one of the internal memos to enhance what the president saw, which could be a problem. You know how the media is when they get information like that."

He grinned, probably suspecting that she was bluffing, which she was. Anna watched him as he took another sip of bourbon. "What *about* Natalie Larsen?" he said.

"I'm getting to that. Where did you first hear about this coup plot, Harland? Where did it come from?" He started to speak, but seemed to change his mind. "Don't you think it's possible this is the story the Russians *want* us to put out? So that the media can then prove us wrong?"

Strickland lowered his eyes, shaking his head, but with less conviction, it seemed.

"I agree with you in principle," she said. "We need to change the subject, and turn the blame away from us. But not at the expense of the truth."

"There's that word." He looked up, forcing a smile. "Okay. And so what *is* the truth, then, Anna? Tell me about that."

"Ivan Delkoff's version is the truth," she said.

"Ivan Delkoff was a crazy warmonger. Have you seen him? The man looks like a reject from the World Wrestling Federation—"

"He was a key figure in the Donbas war," Anna said. "And a man people underestimated. He had a whole network of fighters in eastern Ukraine who could have made August 13 happen."

"Not without Utkin and the generals," Strickland said.

"That's where we disagree. This wasn't a coup attempt, Harland. It was something more sinister. It was an attack on us. I think on some level you know that."

Strickland sighed, holding up his hands in a deflective posture. "Look, I hate to state the obvious here, Anna. But the world doesn't believe this Delkoff story. You know that. We can't just wave a magic wand and change that."

Yes, we can, she thought. "You have influence with the president I don't have," she said, feeling a stir of emotion. "And with the DNI and DCI. You could talk to the president before he goes on television tomorrow. Tell him you have doubts about this intelligence. Tell him we need to do more than just 'change the story.'"

"Come on," Strickland said. Which seemed to Anna a good cue to show what her son had found. She scrolled through the images on her phone, coming to the one of Sonya Natalie Larsen at the Russian embassy party. She pushed it in front of him.

Strickland lifted the phone and studied Sonya's picture. He exaggerated a frown, looked again, and replaced it on the table.

"How long did it take, Harland, before you realized she was getting information from you and slipping it to the media?" Strickland said nothing, and Anna knew for certain then that Jon was right: it was Strickland helping the Russians; he was the spy in the house. "When you brought me that story about preemptive action last week, you must've been sweating this. You did a good job of not letting on. Is this whole coup story an attempt to cover up now for Sonya? To keep the press from finding out that this story really came from you? Through her?"

Strickland's eyes seemed to be searching for somewhere to look now. Anna sensed the hurt and confusion behind them. Sonya Turov had used him, preying on Strickland's weaknesses, much as Russia had done with the United States.

"I mean, I would hope we're not putting the country's reputation on pins and needles because of Harland Strickland's love life," she said. "Or is there more to it than that?"

"*Love* life?" He tossed back his head in a mock laugh. "Please," he said. His response struck her as false this time. In a funny way, he'd just shown his hand. And they both knew it.

"That's what it sounds like," she said. "It sounds like you were see-ing this woman for several months, and along the way, she got you to talk about things that you shouldn't have—in some cases involving these meetings on Russia. Maybe not a lot, but enough for her to know that there'd been this discussion of preemptive action."

"*Hypothetical* discussion," Strickland said. "It was discussed hypothetically."

"And then, when some of these stories began to leak to the media," Anna said, "you became worried that it might come back to bite you. Because this was classified information and only a few people knew about the meetings." She paused for effect. "I can see how it evolved. Russia takes a tiny thread of truth—that there *was* talk about a preemp-tive strike—and spins it into an elaborate fiction, using all the resources of social media. Then fits it to their larger plan, which included the meeting in Kiev. Which I understand *they* set up, not you."

"Of course."

"Meanwhile, as you say, the infighting in Washington has pre-vented us from responding properly. So a small group in the admin-istration decides to push an alternate story. Thinking that if the pres-ident takes it to the nation, giving it his stamp, the preemptive strike story may go away. But that's just what Russia wants us to do. You're doing their work for them. Sometimes consensus is more dangerous than dissension, Harland.

"They'll say the story is a cover-up, and they'll be right. But you're not covering up a plot to assassinate Russia's president, as they'll charge. You're covering up your own personal indiscretion. It's a Washington sideshow." Anna felt a momenatary tingle of pride, quot-ing her son. "You could save us a lot of trouble by simply ending it."

"Come on." He exhaled a lengthy sigh. "It's not that simple. You know that."

"We could *make* it that simple. I'll help."

Strickland gazed toward the street. She knew what he was think-ing. This was his life now. He understood that Anna was sitting on a story that could damage him personally, irreparably. A story that could wind up as a sentence or two in his obituary. Maybe the lead sentence. But it was also a story that could be made to disappear. That's what she was offering him. "How long have you known this?"

"Not long. I'm sorry, Harland, I didn't want to do it like this. But you kind of brought it on. You insisted to journalists—and me—that those meetings never happened. You denied having had contact with Hordiyenko."

"You know I couldn't talk about any of that. Legally, I couldn't say a word."

"But you *did* talk about it. You told us those conversations didn't happen. When in fact you called this committee together and *you* discussed preemptive action."

"*Hypothetically.* It was discussed hypo*thet*ically."

"Yes, I know," Anna said. "But you said it was never discussed."

He drew out a sigh. "You know what the media does with this stuff, Anna. Sometimes it's okay to cover your ass. And also, I thought—frankly—that it was possible I was being set up."

Anna didn't know if he really believed that or was saying it to draw empathy. Or shut her up. At this point, it didn't matter.

"What do you want me to do?" he said.

"Talk to the president. Tell him the truth. Tell the DNI. Call them tonight. You'll also be helping yourself. We need you on board."

"We?"

"Me. I need you on board." He frowned, the skin wrinkling around his eyes and cheeks. "The intel on this Russian general isn't going to check out," she said. "The media will tear it apart if it goes out. Let's cut it off now before it becomes a national humiliation."

Harland seemed more interested in his drink again, his hands cradling the glass. But Anna knew she'd reached him. She took back her phone and put it in her purse.

"Okay," he said at last, looking up as if admitting to a minor error. Then he reached out and put his hand on hers. Anna waited a moment and pulled her hand away. She knew from experience that when Strickland got like this he was liable to do something embarrassing.

Strickland finished his drink. He set a twenty on the table. They both stood.

"Need a ride?"

"I'm fine," she said.

They walked outdoors and stood on the sidewalk, breathing the warm night air. Anna was going the way he wasn't. Saying goodbye, he pulled her against him and he kissed her hard on the lips, a misplaced act that felt violent and sad. Anna put a hand on his chest and pushed away.

"Let me see what I can do," he said, as if nothing strange had just happened.

FIFTY-EIGHT

Hilton Hotel. Washington.

To tell you the truth, I think I'm in trouble," Sonya Larsen said, absently swirling a glass of merlot in her right hand. "I'm worried about Michael. But I'm more worried about myself. Especially after today, after you called me. I'm afraid someone's going to be hurt."

"Michael's your boss."

"Yeah." Her black eyes studied him, roaming his face from his lips to his eyes and back as if he were some species she hadn't seen before. He wondered how much she really knew about him. They were seated four feet apart on the ninth floor of the Washington Hilton, Sonya on the bed, Jon on the desk chair. She was willing to talk, she said, to tell him "the real story," but she didn't want to be quoted. Jon was hoping the ground rules might change slightly after a glass or two of wine.

"Where do you want me to start?" she said.

"How about with Michael. Who is he?"

"I don't know how much of *that* I really want to go into—" Her eyes turned to Jon again, roving his features like a slow camera. "I work for Michael. He works for my father, indirectly. But I'm not supposed to know that. Michael represents nonprofits, basically, throughout the country. My father helped me get the job," she said, speaking with a slight accent—shortening her vowels, a faint v sound at the start of "work."

"Whose idea was it for you to contact the media, to spread this story?" he said.

"Michael's. I only did it because I thought the story I told you was true. Both of our countries have conspiracies," she said. "The difference is, yours become known, ours don't." She smiled at that, lamplight glinting on her white teeth as she turned her head. It was a line she'd heard someone else say, Jon could tell.

"So what happened last week? Did you have any idea this was coming?" he said. "I got the sense from your call on Thursday that you did."

"You mean the *plane?* No, of course not. I mean, I knew *something* was coming. I'd heard the government was planning something against Russia. And Putin."

"That's why you called me."

"That's why I called anyone. Of course."

"And you knew this how? Because of what Harland Strickland told you?"

"In part." She glanced out at the city and took another drink of wine. They'd bought a bottle at the bar downstairs and Sonya had just poured her second glass. Jon was still nursing his first. "There were others. But I took pieces of the story from him and put it out there, yeah. It was sort of fun for a while."

"How did you *choose* Harland Strickland? Or anyone? Who put you on to these people?"

"Michael did." She looked at him, her face very young all of a sudden. "They had a list of people, at various levels of government, CIA or Defense or wherever, that they believed could be accessed. That's part of the business. They compile lists of people and their weaknesses. People who drink too much, or have a gambling problem. Or the honeypot, as they call it. People vulnerable to *kompromat*. And sometimes I was hired to help exploit that. Get people to talk."

"Like Strickland."

"Yeah." She turned her eyes to him, her lips darkened with wine. "His weakness is that he likes to feel important. He likes people to talk to him like he's important. And he also likes young girls." She looked down and smiled quickly.

"And what did Strickland tell you, exactly?"

"Not much. No more than a few sentences that were worth anything."

"Tell me."

She shrugged. "Just—we'd be talking about Russia, or Putin, and he would say something like, 'And what if it was possible for us to *eliminate* that problem?' And I'd make a stupid face and ask a couple of questions and store it all away. I think I may've eventually freaked him out a little with my questions. In the end, he cut me off cold turkey."

"When was this?"

"A week ago? Ten days."

"And then the plane happened," Jon said. "You say you had no idea ahead of time?"

"Of course not." He noticed the shadow of hair across her upper lip as she turned her head. "But then when I saw what happened, and I saw your country was being blamed, my first thought was, 'So, they were right. The US really *did this*.' And at the same time, I felt guilty."

"Why guilty?" Jon said.

"Because. I knew *something* was coming and I hadn't been able to stop it. Of course, it took another few hours before I found out the truth. And then I realized I'd been duped."

"How?"

She looked at her wine, formulating a reply. "Until then I believed that the United States, or some group in the government, or the military, really *was* planning to eliminate Putin. Michael was egging me on a little with that, making me believe it. So when I found out he was alive, I freaked out. Because there were a couple of remarks Michael made that were very suspicious in hindsight. And then eventually it all came together. And I thought: of *course* they knew about it. They knew about it because they had *planned* it."

"'They' being your father? And Michael?"

She nodded, keeping her eyes down.

"You need to talk to someone," Jon said, feeling responsible for her all of a sudden. "You need to make a request for immunity."

"I know I do." She held her wine glass in both hands. "Why do you think I'm talking with you? Are you going to help me?"

"I will, yes."

Jon tried to remember Roger Yorke's phone number. But he wanted to hear the rest of her story first.

"So you believe now that your father was involved? That he may've planned the attack, as these reports are saying—"

"*Helped* plan it. Yeah, I do."

"And you believe the Russian president was also involved?"

She made a face. "If not, there's no reason my father would've done it," she said, a catch in her voice. "But I'll tell you the thing I'm afraid of. It's that my father gets blamed for all this and the little monster gets away again. My father, he used to say, 'little thieves are hanged, the great ones escape.' I used to think that maybe he was a great one. He acted like it. But he wasn't; he just *worked* for one." She took a long drink. The glass made a louder-than-expected thunk on the wooden table. "You know, my mother used to say, 'Why does your father make things so difficult for himself?' We never knew. I think it goes back to his own family. *His* father left when he was three or four years old and he was always looking for authority figures. And Putin became kind of a father figure to him. The biggest authority figure in the world, right?"

"So tell me the real story," Jon said, pivoting to what she'd told him on the drive downtown. "You said there was a 'real' story you could share."

"Yeah. There is." She gave him a lingering look. "There was this thing my father used to say, going back, about the 'catalyst.' That's what he called it. 'All it takes is a catalyst.' A match to light a fuse and the United States will go up in flames, same as the Soviet Union did in 1991. The US is just as vulnerable, even if they don't know it yet. They talk about that a lot in Russia now, you know, the so-called political theorists. They talk about the breakup of the United States and the resurgence of Russia as if they're the same thing."

"Strategic relativism," Jon said.

"Yeah, right." A flicker of recognition crossed her face. "Anyway, the catalyst sets off a chain reaction. But first you have to create a pathway. That's Michael's business, basically. That's what his mission is here: creating the pathway. I'm not supposed to know that, of course," she said. "But you spend enough time around someone, you figure things out."

"Michael works with nonprofits, you said."

"He helps coordinate a whole network, yeah, that's what he came here for. Nonprofits, think tanks, media companies, charities, political action groups. Influence operations, basically. My father used to say, 'America is sleeping. Anyone can walk in the house now and take whatever they want. Even the ownership deed.' It's the weakness of an open society."

"The ultimate purpose of this infiltration being what, then?" Jon said. "To break the country apart?"

"I guess. I don't really know the ultimate purpose." She lifted her glass and pointed it at the blank television screen; the color of her fingernails was slightly darker than the wine. "Secession is in the news now in Texas, right? But it's set up to go in other states, too. If you want to break up the United States, do it from within. Disrupt their culture; create racial, social, and political unrest. But let their *own people* do it. Make them *think* things are bad and soon they will be. That was one of my father's big ideas.

"And in some cases, of course, there are organizations already doing it," she went on. "Ready-made fringe groups, Michael calls them. Like some of these so-called patriot groups that want to destabilize the government. They've done the same thing in Europe."

"So August 13 was a catalyst for that. That's what you're saying?"

"I think so." She took a sip of wine and set her glass down. "You know, when I was little, my father taught me a certain kind of chess that you could win in four moves. But he warned me: it only works with players who don't know the game."

"And the United States doesn't know this game. Is that what you're saying?"

Sonya shrug-nodded.

"How much of this can I write?" he said.

"It doesn't really matter. I don't care that much about your story, to be honest. I care about what's going to happen to me."

"All right. Let's make the call."

Jon had left his cell phone in his car, he remembered. So he used the room phone instead, as Sonya stood and walked to the window, taking in the view of the city. He reached Roger Yorke at his home, hoping no one was listening in on them. *Stay with Sonya,* Roger instructed him, and he would contact the federal marshals program. Ten minutes later he called back to say that a federal agent was on his way to the Hilton. Roger, too, would be down, to give Jon a ride home.

He wondered for a while if Sonya might change her mind in the interim. If she'd be tempted to return to the familiarity of her life in Washington with Michael Ketchler. But he could see she was already past that. Whatever secrets and self-consciousness she had carried into this hotel room fell away and she talked with an expanding energy and confidence, telling Jon about her upbringing, her parents, her younger sister Svetlana, her mother's death in England, her brief, troubled marriage to Edward Larsen, and the odyssey that had brought her to Washington. Her resolve only seemed to harden as they talked, and he understood why she had brought him here: this room was her escape hatch to a new life. Jon listened, prodding her slightly with questions while becoming lost several times in the dark intensity of her eyes— imagining the places they'd been, the people they'd seen.

When the conversation ended with a knock on the door, it felt to Jon like coming awake from an interesting dream and knowing he could never enter it again. Talking with Roger in the elevator, he was already struggling to remember some of what Sonya had said. But he walked out of the hotel that night with something he didn't have going in.

FIFTY-NINE

Thursday, August 19. Bethesda, Maryland.

The call from the president woke Anna Carpenter just after sunrise. It was the first time he had ever called her. The president's chief of staff actually placed the call, but in two minutes Anna was on with the president.

"I just met with Harland," he told her. "I wanted to tell you, we're getting behind this Turov story. I wish you'd mentioned it to me on Tuesday."

"I guess I should have." Anna stood in the living room in pajamas and a kimono robe, looking at the backyard, as her dachshunds nudged competitively against her ankles.

"No. You shouldn't." He chuckled. "I wouldn't have listened to you if you had. As we both know." Anna slid open the glass doors. She breathed the damp air, blinking at sunrise gleaming on the porch wood. "I'm going on television at 10:00 to talk about this Delkoff document," the president said. "I'd appreciate it if you could carry the torch for us this afternoon."

"Sure. I'd be honored to." *Although I'm supposed to pick up Christopher first, in Virginia,* she thought. "How's Harland?"

"He told me about your conversation last night," the president said. "I don't know how you persuaded him. But obviously, you did."

"I'm a politician," she said. "It's what I do."

"Yes, you are. Frankly, I'm disappointed in Harland. He's been blocking us on this for several days. Even if he meant well."

Anna was silent, imagining what Strickland had told POTUS. Pleased that the "spy in the house" wasn't the president himself.

"He offered his resignation," the president continued.

"You didn't accept."

"No, of course I didn't. We don't need any more distractions at the moment. But also, I can use his help. He's assured me he'll be on the phone all day working this story for us. And he might help us on Turov going forward. I mean, what's his resignation going to accomplish?"

"Not a lot."

"I like what I'm hearing from Russia, by the way, that the opposition groups may be getting behind this," he said. "We're going to win, Anna. In a big way. But the next two days are critical. I'm having a copy of my talk sent to you. I'd like you to follow up on the afternoon shows. And do some interviews with the print media if you could."

"All right." Anna stood barefoot on the edge of the wooden porch. So Harland Strickland *had* done the right thing. It was sort of hard to believe. But at the same time, Anna had a funny feeling about him again. Wondering if they'd given Harland a pass in some way.

Just before hanging up with the president she looked at the mantel clock and realized that Christopher had already landed back on American soil.

It was still dark as the Gulfstream V commuter plane began its descent to the small airport north of Williamsburg, Virginia. Christopher gazed down at the scattered clusters of lights and felt far from the human folly of Washington, much as astronauts viewed mankind's problems as inconsequential from the vantage point of space.

But as the rural highways and the patches of scrub pines and soybean fields began to regain their authority, he thought about Anna, knowing that she was down there, waiting for him, and Washington became increasingly appealing again, follies and all.

The Delkoff document had been online now for several hours, but it wasn't gaining the traction Christopher had expected. The prevailing opinion still seemed to be that the United States was complicit in the assassination attempt on Russia's president, that the CIA had worked a deal with a Ukrainian arms trader and Ukrainian intelligence officers to bring down the plane.

There were several stories online about Turov's death, some calling him "a prominent Russian businessman with ties to the Kremlin." One Russian news site reported that he'd been killed at a home in the Moscow suburbs, the victim of a "burglary gone bad." But many opposition blogs and tweets were spreading the story that it was the FSB who had assassinated Turov, possibly as payback for leaking details about the Delkoff op. Amira had come through.

Chris Niles and Jake Briggs were shuttled from the airport to a mirror-sided government building eighty minutes to the north. A debriefer from AS Division got them first, separately, although the stories they told about Moscow were nearly identical, accurate if incomplete. Chris said nothing about the deal that he had almost struck with Andrei Turov. He described Turov's killing as self-defense. The official accounts of their mission would be filed away in the guts of the CIA, he knew, with thousands of other "black" operations carried out over the past sixty years. It was unlikely anyone would ever read them.

He met Martin Lindgren in a little conference room down the hall. Even here, Martin had an English tea set, like a man transported from an earlier time. They shared a heartfelt handshake. "Welcome home," Martin said. "You know, I'm not sure I ever apologized for spoiling your vacation in Greece."

"Next time we're not leaving a forwarding address."

Martin showed his uneven smile as they sat. The sun was up,

shining through the trees. On the table was a single file folder and a stack of paper that resembled a book manuscript.

"Coffee?"

"I'm fine."

Chris waited. "I spoke with the president," Martin said. "The administration's getting behind Delkoff's account. The opposition in Russia is on board, too. I suppose you had something to do with that?" Chris didn't respond. "It's beginning to cause a slightly awkward situation for the Kremlin, as you can imagine. More than they'd care to let on."

"I'm a little surprised it's not getting more play here, though," Chris said.

"It will. Unfortunately, as you may have seen, some influential people on our side have been pushing a different story over the past few days. That set us back a little."

"The story that the attack was a coup attempt, you mean?" Chris said. Martin nodded subtly. "I've caught pieces of it. It's mostly an old story, isn't it?"

"It is. One of our top counterterrorism men, Harland Strickland, had been standing in the way of Delkoff's story. I'm not sure why. Mostly for personal reasons, evidently. Anna sort of called him out."

This surprised Chris, but only a little. He knew Strickland, a national security veteran of several administrations. He was a smart man, charismatic on first impression, but with a tendency toward self-aggrandizement and a weakness for young women. "Does the president know about me?"

"Not yet. How do you feel about that?"

Chris shrugged. "I don't want to be any more a part of this story than I have to be."

"I figured." Martin opened the file folder. "You were right, by the way, about Turov. He evidently pulled this off with fewer than a dozen people—"

"*Almost* pulled it off," Chris corrected him. "I counted ten, not including those already working in the States."

Martin nodded. He named them, reading from the list in his folder: Delkoff, Zelenko, Pletner, Kolchak, Kravchenko, Tamm, Hordiyenko, Hordiyenko's agent Petrofsky, Turov, Anton Konkin. "Ten men: they thought that's all it would take to bring us down."

"They were expecting we'd do most of the heavy lifting."

"Yes."

Christopher watched Martin's squarely cut nails on the cup handle, the coffee still steaming. "You gave me a puzzle on the airplane," he said. "About the 'carrier.' I have an idea what the answer might be."

"Go ahead."

"When you came to see us in Greece last week, you mentioned that you had an asset in Moscow. You said she'd confirmed some of what Turov said, including the use of this phrase 'the children's game' in a telephone call."

Martin winced slightly. "I didn't mean to say she."

"I know you didn't." Chris smiled. "Turov told me that the carrier wasn't in Russia anymore. Because his daughter Svetlana had recently left the country, I thought of her. But Turov also has a girlfriend, who cares for the daughter. Her name is Olga Sheversky, I believe."

Martin was silent.

"I'm speculating a little now, but here goes: because your asset had gotten close enough to hear Turov's phone conversation, I'm thinking the carrier and your asset might be the same person. And I'm thinking that person might be Olga Sheversky."

"Okay." Martin reached for his coffee. "You always bring me back to the same question, Christopher," he said, showing his reluctant smile. "Why do I ever underestimate you?"

"Where are Olga and the daughter now?"

"I wish I could tell you."

Chris nodded, understanding what Martin was doing: they'd come to the border where their business relationship ended. There were things Martin couldn't share. That was fine.

"Before you leave," Martin said, "I wanted to show you what we got from the flash drive Turov gave her. Supposedly containing the confidential documents he told you about. It was concealed inside a Swiss clock he had shipped to Switzerland, she said." He pushed the stack of paper on the desk toward Christopher.

"All this?"

"All that." Chris began to read, from the top of the first page: "*Well, Prince, Genoa and Lucca are now just family estates of the Bonaparte family. But I warn you that if you do not admit we are at war, if you still defend all the infamies and atrocities of this Antichrist . . .*"

He stopped and looked at Martin. "This sounds like the opening of *War and Peace*."

"Yes. Actually, it *is* the opening of *War and Peace*. That's Turov's 'Data,' as the files were labeled. The whole novel, in nine separate files. There was nothing else on the drive."

"Nothing about the August 13 operation."

Martin shook his head, his face betraying disappointment.

"So Turov *was* a loyal man," Chris said.

"More likely, his girlfriend remains a loyal woman. Loyal to President Putin and to Russia, anyway, despite everything. Loyalty goes a long way in Russia."

"Olga substituted this flash drive for the one he gave her about August 13 to protect him, you're saying?" Chris said. "To protect Putin?"

"It's a theory. To quote you: I'm speculating. We don't have the full picture yet."

Chris pushed the pile of paper toward Martin and sat back. "Which would mean the trail ends with Turov, then. Or with Ivan Delkoff's version of events, anyway."

"For now, yes," Martin said. "I'm not convinced Turov ever really intended to undermine the president. But there may be more coming. There are still several files that we haven't broken the encryption on. The ones you brought back. The important thing is that world opinion *is* starting to turn a little. Not quickly enough—and some of that's our own fault—but we're hoping the president's speech to the country this morning will change that.

"Thanks to your brother, by the way," Martin added, "Turov's older daughter—Sonya—is in a safe house this morning. With some stories to tell about her father. And this shady character she worked for in Washington, Ketchler. I think she's going to wind up in witness protection."

Christopher smiled inwardly, wondering if Anna had played a role in getting to Sonya Turov. He looked out at the sun-bleached morning, the traffic five stories below, soundless motion beyond the glass. He felt ready to go.

"So, what else can I do?" he said.

"Nothing. You can go home," Martin said. "Watch the president's speech. Get some sleep. You've done your part."

Christopher felt like a man emerging from prison as he strode into the first-floor lobby and saw Anna Carpenter across the room, waiting with his travel bag. They held each other and shared a long, gentle kiss. Then walked into the parking lot holding hands. There was something about the air and the light that signaled he was home, back to his life as a university lecturer. But more importantly, to his life with Anna. This time, he knew, he'd be here for a while.

Jake Briggs caught up on the news as his wife Donna drove them toward the mountains of western Virginia. Briggs was more than ready to disappear again, knowing he'd helped eliminate a terrorist threat named Andrei Turov. Whether the world ever found out about it didn't matter to him.

"Thanks for your service," Martin Lindgren had said, as they shook hands in his CIA satellite office. The words were a cliché, so routine they didn't mean much. But they'd meant something to Briggs. No one had said that to him in a while. He was grateful to have served, grateful that Chris Niles had chosen him, and grateful now to be going home.

As Briggs saw it, he had been recruited to fight a small war; and small wars were sometimes the way you prevented bigger ones, the kind that Russia was preparing to fight. Russia wanted to fight bigger wars because it wanted to be a bigger nation; because it had become a second-rate country, burdened with unsolvable economic problems and historic expectations it could never realize. Russia was busy inventing new weapons systems for those wars: the weapons of disinformation and mass deception. Briggs expected the international community would get wise and outlaw those weapons, as they had banned biological and chemical warfare. He just hoped they didn't wait too long. Already, he'd seen Russia's political influence spread to places it shouldn't be: throughout Europe, the Middle East, and the United States.

To Briggs, the wars Russia was preparing for were nothing more than a sophisticated form of terrorism. Terrorism came in many guises. A terrorist could be a poor Middle Eastern kid who lived in a one-room apartment or he could be the wealthy leader of a giant country who lived in palaces. Both operated out of the same need. The kind of wars that Russia was planning for always came to the same end, Briggs knew: in the long run, civilization won. That was the natural order. Not everyone bought into that notion; the idea had faced some formidable opponents over time, dictators who'd tried to replace the natural order with an artificial one.

Briggs believed in his country the way some people believed in God, even if he had little use for government institutions. Still, for right now, he was okay leaving the wars to other people. Right now, more than anything else, he just wanted to see his children again.

SIXTY

"Good morning," the president said, standing behind a podium in the hallway by the East Room. "Today we can report with certainty to the American people—and the world—that last week's tragic attack on the Russian president's plane was carried out by forces from within Russia.

"Our intelligence agencies, working with the governments of several nations in the region, have now conclusively identified the planner of the attack and the men who carried it out.

"We have also determined that, despite news accounts to the contrary, the United States did not play a role in or have any prior knowledge of the August 13 attack. Nor were the governments of Ukraine or Estonia involved in any way."

Christopher glanced at Anna and felt a tiny stir of redemption. This was the work their team had done. The evidence that Jake Briggs had brought home from northern France. And it was exactly the story the United States needed to be telling. He liked the optics, too, the president's steady, unapologetic tone, giving Americans what they'd wanted to hear since August 13: their president resetting the national agenda, reassuring the electorate, giving hope to the people who'd hired him—and to some of those who hadn't.

"We have irrefutable evidence this morning that the August 13 operation was planned by a Russian businessman and former FSB officer named Andrei Turov and commandeered by Ivan Delkoff, a Russian military intelligence colonel. Both men have now been killed, apparently by agents of their own country."

Chris was reminded of Turov's eerie final impression: seated in the desk chair, his strange blue eyes open, as if watching the man who had killed him. But he wondered where the president got that line about Turov and Delkoff being killed "by agents of their own country."

". . . and while there is no longer any question about who planned and carried out the August 13 attack, there are still unanswered questions about why it occurred and whether or not the Kremlin had any direct involvement. I expect these questions will be answered by our intelligence agencies in the coming days and weeks.

"In the meantime, we will continue to work diligently to make sure the people of the United States, and the world, are kept fully informed. Because the tragedy in Ukraine last Friday was not only an attack on twenty-six innocent people. It was also an attack on democracy, and on the freedom we enjoy as Americans. Which is something that we will continue to defend with all of our resources. This morning I call on every citizen of our country, and everyone who loves freedom throughout the world, to stand with us in this fight. Thank you."

"Nice," Anna said.

"Wonder how Russia's responding."

Minutes later, they saw: Moscow quickly issued an outraged rebuttal to the president's speech, calling the Delkoff document "an obvious fabrication." *The United States is desperate to cover its crimes,* said the Kremlin's official statement, *and further attack the Russian Federation.*

"It's a reversal of roles," Chris said. "Russia's suddenly in the position of having to defend itself. Which we'd been doing since Friday. We've just changed the game. That's the only way we win."

"Meaning, advantage USA?"

"Maybe," he said. "Although it's dangerous to think that. Particularly with Russia."

"I know." Anna reached for Christopher's hand. She stood and led him to the bedroom. There were still a couple of hours before she had to leave for downtown. They lay on the bed for a while and held each other, enjoying the silence and the slow, late-morning breeze rustling through the woods and through the open windows. Together, for a few minutes, they managed to shut out the story and enjoy some intimate time. It was a nice interlude.

"Good luck," he said when she went out, headed downtown for her interviews. "I'll be watching."

But Christopher had his own plans for that evening.

SIXTY-ONE

Jon Niles felt slightly hungover as he watched the president from his apartment in Northwest Washington. It was a strong, well-delivered speech, one of the best he'd seen this president give. But would it change anything? Would it counteract Russia's version of events, or just be seen as a self-serving cover-up? And—either way—would it have any effect on what Russia was planning in the Baltics?

Jon didn't know. His thoughts were still with Sonya Larsen. He had stayed up late, talking with Roger Yorke and then trying to reconstruct his long, strange conversation with her, drinking beer, slightly dazzled by the spell she had cast over him. The whole experience seemed even more dream-like in the morning.

One comment Sonya had made nagged at Jon, though. And the president's speech had just accentuated it.

Had Andrei Turov really been killed by "agents" of his own country?

Jon thought several times about calling Anna Carpenter to ask for clarification, but then he wasn't sure. He didn't know how Anna would respond, because his question involved Christopher.

He finally left her a text message and drove downtown to the *Weekly American* offices to ask Roger. When Jon arrived, Roger was on the phone, his long legs propped on a corner of the desk, one arm crooked behind his neck, patting the top of his head as he talked. It was hard to imagine him looking any more comfortable. He waved at Jon and pointed at the guest chair.

"Anything new?" he asked when Roger hung up.

"We're still on alert, evidently," he said, his eyes turning to Jon. "Russia's doubling down. Of course, they don't really *want* to attack. They'd rather negotiate. But they see the president's speech as provocation."

Roger's brow furrowed. He looked at Jon in that perceptive way he had. "What's wrong?"

"I need to talk with you."

Roger sighed, pointing to something on his desk. "Is it about that?"

Jon reached for it. It was a printout of a brief news story. Something he'd missed. Jon felt his chest seize up as he read the headline. "Russian Attorney Found Dead in Motel Room."

He read the lede paragraph: "Prominent Russian attorney Michael Ketchler was reportedly found dead in a motel room in the Virginia suburbs this morning. Police are investigating. A police source said Ketchler may have died of a heart attack."

"You hadn't seen it?"

"No. I haven't." He remembered watching Michael Ketchler on the street, arguing with Sonya, and heard the echo of Sonya's words to him: *To tell you the truth, I think I'm in trouble . . . I'm afraid someone's going to be hurt.*

"KC made a few inquiries with the police," Roger said. "The motel room was rented by a woman believed to be a prostitute. Ketchler's physician and his family attorney say it appears to be a heart attack. But according to the responding police officer, he had several broken bones, including two broken fingers, and severe bruising on the back of his neck."

"A Russian heart attack, in other words," Jon said.

"Yes."

Jon read through the brief news item again.

"What was it you wanted to talk about?"

Jon leaned forward, feeling deflated. "It was something the president said in his speech this morning. Something Sonya told me last night, too. About how her father died."

"That he was killed by 'agents of his own country.'"

"Yeah. Sonya Larsen called it a betrayal. Putin sending the FSB to kill her father after all his years of loyalty. The White House seems comfortable putting that story out there. That he was killed by agents of his own country."

"You don't think it's true."

"I don't." He glanced at the glare of afternoon light on the windows across the street and took a deep breath. And then he explained why: Jon didn't believe it was true because he knew that Christopher had been in Moscow on Wednesday when Andrei Turov died. He'd gone there to find him, probably as a CIA black op. Whatever happened to Turov, Chris had been part of it; not the FSB. Jon wasn't supposed to know that. But he did. He'd picked it up on his visit to Langley with Anna Carpenter. He couldn't unknow it.

"And if the US *was* involved in killing Turov," he told Roger, "then the story isn't quite as clean as it appears. We'd have an obligation to report that, right?"

"Possibly."

Possibly. "I keep thinking about what you told us the other day," Jon said, "about fighting disinformation with disinformation. I'm sure other reporters will figure it out eventually."

"Mmm-hmm." Roger continued to frown. "It's a good question," he said. "Although I think it's also important to weigh proportions."

"Okay," Jon said. "And what does that mean?"

"In other words, I'm not sure that how Turov died is the most important part of his story, is it?" Jon tilted his head to one side, conceding the point. "Or—to take it another way: you told me you went out to Langley the other day, right? You saw the memorial stars on the wall there."

"Okay."

"Some of the stars on the wall are anonymous. One of them, I believe, is your father, correct?" Jon felt his face color briefly. He'd never talked about this with Roger. "My point," he went on, "is that there are some stories that shouldn't be publicized. It wouldn't serve any purpose, and might even compromise future intelligence operations. That's why the stars are anonymous."

"And you're saying how Andrei Turov died is one of those stories that shouldn't be told."

Roger shrugged. "I'm saying it's not as important as a dozen other stories you could tell about Turov. I'm saying what he did with his life, and who he did it for, is the bigger story. I just think we need to weigh all of that carefully."

"Okay."

Roger went on, but Jon only heard pieces of it. He was thinking about Michael Ketchler. And about Andrei Turov's unusual daughter: her dark, probing eyes and animated hand gestures. Wondering if he would ever see her again.

Afterward, he walked down the corridor to his tiny office and closed the door, wanting to avoid Liz Foster. At 5:15, he turned up the sound on CNN to watch Anna Carpenter's live interview. She looked nice, in a dark suit and light blue shirt, her blond hair pulled back; for a moment Jon felt a flash of envy that she was his brother's girlfriend.

"There is now undeniable evidence," she told the interviewer, Wolf Blitzer, "that last Friday's attack originated from within Russia, and that the governments of Ukraine and Estonia were not involved in any way. We have also authenticated what is being called the 'Delkoff document,' which anyone can now access online."

Wolf Blitzer interjected: "One of the allegations in that document, Senator, is that Russia's president knew of the attack beforehand and may have even been involved in its planning. Is that something you can verify for us here today?"

"We're not commenting on that specific allegation yet, Wolf, other than to say that we believe in the veracity of the document."

"It's a remarkable development," Wolf said. "Although we should point out that Russia is claiming this document is a fabrication, a fake."

"It's not. And I think that will become increasingly clear as more is known about it."

"The other question people are asking tonight is, of course, will any of this be enough to prevent a war in the Baltics? There are new reports coming in this afternoon of troops mobilizing on the borders with Ukraine and Estonia—"

"That's true," she said. "And obviously of great concern. We're doing all we can diplomatically to prevent military action. The UN ambassador, as we've seen, has brought the matter before the General Assembly. And NATO is meeting tomorrow in special session in Brussels."

Wolf was nodding. "Senator, this entire standoff has been characterized by some as a new kind of warfare. A war of information, if you will—or disinformation. Is the United States underestimating the power of disinformation in the world these days?"

"I think it's possible we are," Anna said. "Disinformation is a weapons system the Russians are more invested in than we are. Frankly, I don't think it's an arms race we want to escalate, if we can help it—but at the same time, it's not something we can ignore. We need to look at ways of policing it, for instance." She seemed to shift seamlessly into another gear, then, running on the same fuel that had powered the president this morning: "You know, my office on Capitol Hill is just a couple of blocks from the National Mall. When you go out on the Mall, what you see is a collection of stories, which, together, tell our national story. It's not just a story of triumph or liberty or sacrifice or individual greatness, although those are the things we most often hear about. It's also a story of deep and prolonged suffering, profound error and painful growth.

"We are an imperfect nation, as other countries sometimes enjoy telling us. But one of the remarkable things about this country is that we have a Constitution that allows us, and expects us, to correct ourselves. And it is in that desire to improve that we find our greatness. Real greatness, as the Russian writer Leo Tolstoy said, comes from humility and generosity more than from power. I think we need to summon some of that greatness right now to fight this disinformation war that you mention. Our best weapon is the truth. And it's our responsibility, all of us, not just as a country but as individuals, to be aware of that and become guardians and defenders of the truth."

Jon sensed right away that the reaction to Anna Carpenter's interview was going to be off the charts. He could hear it in the awed voices of the pundits who tried to follow the interview with commentary. It wasn't only the words she'd used, but the inspired cadence of her tone, which, like the president's, seemed to carry the timbre of a country waking up. Two days ago, Anna had told him that the US was culturally fragmented, hungry for a big story to draw people together. August 13, he sensed, could become that story.

Jon clicked off the television. He powered on his computer and began to draft a column about Anna Carpenter's interview. He titled it "On the Meaning of Greatness."

SIXTY-TWO

Bethesda, Maryland.

Christopher had been planning this evening since before he left Moscow. He'd visualized himself walking into the food market on River Road and picking out the ingredients for his Maryland gumbo—onions, green peppers, tomatoes, hot pepper sauce, scallops, crab meat, shrimp. Then driving to the florist to buy Anna a bouquet of roses. And making one more stop before returning home.

He was stirring the gumbo on a low heat, watching Anna's CNN interview for the second time, when car headlights turned up the drive. He cued up one of her favorite pieces of music—the Intermezzo from Mascagni's *Cavalleria rusticana*—and went to greet her at the door.

Anna smiled, hearing the Intermezzo, smelling his gumbo and the French bread, as the dachshunds scampered at her feet for attention. "Mmm mmm," she said.

They kissed and hugged hello and then she kneeled down to greet Zoey and Mr. Smith.

"You were great," he said. "I've just watched it again."

"We still have a ways to go," she said, standing. "Although I hear there's been a little shift of opinion since the president's speech . . ."

"A little, yes." Chris had felt it all afternoon, watching the reaction to the president's speech on television. The change in the winds of opinion could become a problem for Russia, maybe even a big one. In a war of stories, you lost when the public stopped believing you.

"Let me change," Anna said.

Chris finished preparing dinner as she did, taking salads and bread onto the porch, along with the bottle of 2007 Sauvignon Blanc that Martin Lindgren had shipped to them during a vacation in France. He'd set the table with a linen cloth, dinner candles, her good china and silverware. The air had freshened with evening, the woods behind the house growing dark.

Anna slid open the door to the deck and came out. She was dressed in slacks, a light sweater, and sandals. "What's all this?" she said, displaying her lovely smile, seeing the flowers and the tablecloth. She wasn't really surprised, but the emotion in her eyes was real. Anna could be touched by simple kindnesses. It was one her gifts.

"I just thought it might be a nice evening to have that conversation we started last week."

Anna walked to him and they kissed, then stood by the rail, breathing the night air, watching fireflies blinking in the woods. "It *is* funny," she said, "we went all the way to Greece to have it—"

"And then never did."

"Thanks to Martin Lindgren."

"No, thanks to Andrei Turov."

"Okay," she said, studying his face. "So. Shall we have it now?"

"Yes. Let me start," Christopher said. He reached into his pocket and brought out the small square box he had picked up that afternoon. He opened it to show her the engagement ring. "Will you marry me, Anna?"

"Oh my." This time, her surprise was genuine. "Yes," she said. "Yes, Chris, of course."

His phone rang moments later. Chris ignored it, and they kissed again. Then Anna's phone rang. It was Jon.

They sat at the table and Christopher poured them each a glass of chilled wine. Anna held out her hand again to admire the engagement ring. She was beautiful, her green eyes rising to meet his across the table in the candlelight. "Your brother contacted me today," she said as Chris spooned a helping of Maryland gumbo. "Twice."

"Really."

"The first time he texted me to say that he had a question. About Andrei Turov. What really happened to him. That's how he put it."

"I see."

"But then he called back and told me he realized that he was asking the wrong question. Many of the world's problems begin with someone asking the wrong question, he said. Something like that. He said he'd call you later."

Chris was smiling. "All right," he said. He didn't really want to talk about his brother, though. Not now. Not for another day or two.

Anna sipped her wine, watching him, the breeze swishing through the leaves high above. "I wasn't supposed to tell you any of that, of course."

"Of course," Chris said. He tried—just for a moment—to figure out his brother again. "Don't worry," he said. "I'm pretty good, actually, at keeping secrets."

EPILOGUE

In the weeks after Andrei Turov died, Christopher Niles would sometimes catch glimpses of his face in the expressions of men on the
street, and feel his presence in class as he spoke to his students about
Russian espionage in the twenty-first century. It was the ordinariness
of Turov that haunted him, the idea that he could be anyone, anywhere, living anonymously. The deceptions that played out unnoticed,
that we failed to imagine, that we accepted without questioning: those
were the real enemies, not the ones we spent billions of dollars arming
ourselves against.

The Russian state buried Andrei Turov at his country property
southwest of Moscow on August 23. The burial was arranged through
the Kremlin by Olga Sheversky and Turov's daughter Svetlana.
Svetlana wanted her father to rest in the meadow beside the dacha
where he'd found peace in the final months of his life, and Russia's
president granted her that.

Moscow continued to blame the United States for the attack on
the president's plane. But the tenor of its accusations grew more tem-
pered as world opinion began to shift against Russia. Turov's role in
the August 13 conspiracy dominated the news that fall, and the public
found his personal story almost as intriguing as what he'd done. Turov
became the symbol for a Russia that most Americans didn't know, a

charmingly deceptive businessman who had operated successfully for many years outside the traditional bounds of law, ethics, and morality.

If there was a hero to the August 13 story, it was Ivan Delkoff, despite his role as the attack's ringleader. Delkoff's "Declaration" provided the only reliable account of what actually happened that day, and became the basis for a US counter-strategy. Courage was one of the human qualities Christopher most admired, and Delkoff certainly had that.

Some of the best reporting in those weeks came from Jonathan Niles, the only journalist granted an interview with Turov's older daughter Sonya. Most of Jon's stories were not about Sonya Turov, though, or her father, but about a network of Russian influence operations monitored by an elusive, Moscow-born attorney named Michael Ketchler. Jon's stories traced a series of phony loans, donations, and debt agreements that had steered hundreds of millions of dollars out of Russia through banks in Cyprus and Latvia to organizations in the United States overseen by Ketchler. Jon shone as a journalist reporting those stories, becoming a minor Washington celebrity in the process, with his sometimes offbeat interviews on cable news shows. But to his older half brother, Jon remained a mysterious and remote presence.

Among the other news stories to play out that fall was the sudden death in early October of Harland Strickland. The veteran intelligence official was found dead in the bedroom of his Falls Church home, apparently of a self-inflicted gunshot wound. But some in Washington suspected that Strickland, who had been leading an investigation of Turov and Ketchler's US network, might have died from something else. A few called his death a case of "Russian suicide."

The leaves changed early that year in Washington. Chris and Anna spent most evenings on the back deck of their house in the suburbs, watching the flames of color in the woods as the air cooled and the sun went down. In mid-October, Anna organized a small dinner party for the members of their "team." Chris was skeptical at first if Jon or Anna's son David would accept the invitation, but both of them did, along with Marty Lindgren and his wife Heidi. Only Jake Briggs declined. Jon brought his new girlfriend Liz Foster, a personable fellow journalist he had dated years before, who ended up talking with Chris and Martin for much of the evening.

It was after the others had left, and Chris was ready to turn in, that Martin tugged on his sleeve and pulled him outside, a glass of scotch in his left hand. It was after eleven by then.

"I thought I should tell you, before I go," Martin said, his tone deceptively casual. "We did find something else. From Turov. It was on one of the USB drives that you retrieved in Moscow. It took us several weeks to break the encryption."

For a moment, Christopher wondered if Martin was going to try to recruit him again. He had hoped he'd be safe now at least for a couple of semesters.

"It contains what you described when you returned," he said. "The timeline, Turov's layout of the operation. It's what he must've given the Kremlin. The proposal for an alliance between our countries. Much of it's as you said."

"So. His intentions were good, then."

"No. Bad," Martin said. "From the way it's laid out, the alliance would've just been a further step in Russia's infiltration. The objective, according to this, appears something akin to a total infiltration, with Turov running—and here I quote—the 'US liaison operation' from within our borders. It's possible the US was going to be Turov's final retirement destination."

"Oh," Christopher said.

"For all Turov told you, he never did give up Putin, did he?"

"So maybe that was the real fourth move. Is that what you're saying?"

"That's what I'm saying," Martin said. "*War and Peace* being his idea of a little joke."

Christopher listened to the leaves blowing. "Any chance I could get a copy of that file?"

Martin, as often happened, was already ahead of him, pulling a copy from his jacket. Chris skimmed the document in the light through the back windows. Had this been Turov's real objective, then, with "the children's game"? Operating undetected from inside the States, influencing its politics and policies, monitoring electronic communications, turning the generous but gullible United States into a giant, unwitting satellite of Russia? If so, did the game really end with Turov's death? Could there still be a spy—or spies—in the house?

He slipped the document back into the envelope, thinking he would pass it on to his little brother. "I guess it's a good thing we cut things off when we did," he said.

Martin closed and opened his eyes, acknowledging only that he had spoken. "Who knows what other monsters are going to crawl out of the sea," he said, "while we're busy with our political jousts and televised distractions . . ." He paused to finish his drink.

Forget about crawling from the sea, Christopher thought. *What about the ones already here?*

Just then the back door slid open and they both turned to look: it was Martin's wife Heidi, saying it was time to go. They had a forty-five-minute drive back home to northern Virginia, she reminded him.

Anna and Christopher walked them outside for a long goodbye in the driveway. They waved from the street as the Lindgrens finally pulled away, watching their taillights disappear over the rise in the road. Chris felt Anna's hand close around his as they began to walk back through the mist.

"So. Here we are," she said. Chris felt a tug of gratitude. A gust of cold wind shuffled through the dead leaves in the side yard.

By the time they reached the house, though, he was thinking again about Russia. He looked up at the clouds sliding past the moon and thought of his country's enemies, those real and those imagined. And he thought about stories, the kind that people tell, with beginnings, middles, and ends. And the real kind, which were never so tidy.

ACKNOWLEDGMENTS

Special thank you to Laura Gross and her staff for all of their good work on this book. And to Cal Barksdale, executive editor at Skyhorse/Arcade, for taking on the project. I'm also grateful to Alexandra Hess, for her editorial suggestions and guidance along the way, and to the talented and creative staff at Arcade Publishing.

And thank you to the many experts who shared their thoughts about disinformation warfare and Russia-US relations.